The Black Pyramid

J. FitzGerald McCurdy

The Black Pyramid

The Mole Wars, Book Two

■ HarperCollins*PublishersLtd*

Published by HarperCollins Publishers Ltd

First edition: 2006

HarperCollins books may be purchased
for educational, business, or sales promo-
tional use through our Special Markets
Department.

HarperCollins Publishers Ltd
2 Bloor Street East, 20th Floor
Toronto, Ontario, Canada
M4W 1A8

www.harpercollins.ca

Library and Archives Canada Cataloguing
in Publication

McCurdy, J. FitzGerald (Joan FitzGerald),
1943–

The black pyramid / J. FitzGerald
McCurdy.—1st ed.

(The mole wars trilogy ; bk. 2)

ISBN-13: 978-0-00-200574-6
ISBN-10: 0-00-200574-3

I. Title. II. Series.

PS8575.C87B53 2006   JC813'.6
C2005-905578-2

HC 9 8 7 6 5 4 3 2 1

Printed and bound in the United States
Set in Sabon

For Melissa, a sparkle in the night sky over Libertyville

Towering Rage

Driving the magma before them, the Tsilihin, whom we named Death, exploded from the mountain creating a catastrophic eruption column that loomed fifteen miles into the sky. The sun disappeared. Darkness fell. In the cool upper air, melted rock solidified, magma formed pumice stones and rained death on the city below. Massive, dense boulders shot into the air and plummeted to earth like rockets. Volcanic lightning and pumice bombarded the city. In three brief hours the mountain dumped a hundred million tons of ash and rock on the city and its unsuspecting population.

Panic and terror gripped the people. Many had already fled, but twenty thousand remained. Now they, too, fled their homes as roofs collapsed from the weight of the pumice. The stone and ash sucked the moisture from the air. Those who made it outside could neither breathe not swallow; the very air was on fire. Death continued to rain from the sky.

But the worst was still to come.

—**Excerpt from** *The Wardens' Logs*

Chapter One

The Windy City

The bitter north wind screamed across the bridge where Steele Miller and his friends stood frozen outside the long black limousine. It buffeted the street lights and sucked up dirt and grit from the ground in whirling devils, flinging them at Steele's face. They stung his flesh like splinters of glass. Squinting to protect his eyes from the flying debris, Steele peered at the tall buildings, his gaze lingering on a particular white structure dominating the opposite side of the street at the end of the bridge. Floodlit, it presented a ghostly appearance. Steele tilted his head back and looked up. Even the sky in this unfamiliar city looked cold and forbidding. The fat, silver moon wrapped the tops of the tall buildings in its frosty embrace, making them appear as if they had been sculpted from ice.

Nothing moved on the bridge or the narrow river or the broad street stretching ahead. It was as if the city had been abandoned. And, except for the wind whining about the girders, it was as silent as death.

"Where are we?" Riley Puddle shouted in Steele's ear.

Steele didn't have a clue.

A minute ago, he and Riley and Mac Moran were huddled with Maddie Fey and the old Mage, Fidus, in Maddie Fey's dining room in a netherworld somewhere, plotting a course of action in their search for the missing kids and their war against the deadly Fire Demons. Then Riley had asked if they could call their parents, and Nilats the rat had shown them the way outside to find a phone. Now, here they were, standing in the middle of a bridge in a strange city, turning blue from the cold.

"Let's ask Nilats," said Riley.

They looked over at Maddie Fey's black limousine, at the dark, secretive windows. Steele shuddered involuntarily. The vehicle looked like a huge cat, crouching, the way cats behave just before they pounce. There was no sign of the rat.

He turned to Riley and shouted, "You and Mac knock on the windows. I've got to do something about Pyrus."

Inside Steele's backpack, the salamander was scratching at the fabric, desperate to claw its way out and into the warmth under Steele's jacket. Worried that Pyrus might cut himself on the sharp blade of the sword sheathed in a long outer pocket, Steele turned his back to the wind and shrugged the pack from his shoulders. Dropping to his knees, he carefully removed his sword and placed it on the ground. Then he pulled off his gloves, opened the top flap, and wrapped his hands about the salamander, gently scolding until Pyrus stopped shivering.

"Stupid salamander. You wouldn't be in this mess if you'd stayed home. Did I invite you to come with us? Did I? No. It was your idea to hide out in my backpack."

Pyrus cocked his head and stared at Steele as intently as if he understood every word, then answered by turning invisible and flicking his tongue at Steele's nose.

Smiling indulgently, but keeping a firm grip on the salamander, Steele opened the top of his jacket just enough to drop Pyrus inside. Then he zipped the jacket up and buried his chin deep into the collar. He picked up the sword, amazed as he always was by the feel of it in his hand, as if it belonged there.

Forged from an opaque black metal, the actual blade was no more than a foot and a half long. A scab forming on Steele's thumb was a testimony of its sharpness. The handle was also black; Steele thought it was probably made from the horn of an animal. He rotated his wrist, turning the blade over. Here he was, carrying a real sword around in his backpack as if it were the most natural thing in the world. A short time ago, he'd have laughed if someone had predicted that his life was about to change and that he'd need a good, sharp sword if he hoped to survive. But he wasn't laughing now. His life *had* changed, drastically, and he *had* needed the sword. If he stared long and hard at the blade, he could still see faint dark patches on the metal, bloodstains from worms he had slain with this very sword two and a half days ago. Oblivious to the world around him and to the chill seeping through his jeans, Steele's mind raced over the events that had led him to this windy place far from home.

Toronto had been Steele's world, and Wychwood Park his private realm. If asked, Steele would have said that, except for two problems, his life wasn't all that different from the lives of other kids his age. One problem was Dirk the Jerk—the school bully. Steele couldn't count the number of times over the past two years that Dirk had chased him home, or beat him up, or extorted his allowance. On more than one occasion, Steele had wished that Dirk would disappear for good.

The other problem was GM, Steele's maternal grandmother. Eight years ago, shortly after the death of Steele's mother, GM had stopped speaking entirely and had begun knitting a scarf—a never-ending scarf. As the scarf grew alarmingly enormous, Steele worried that GM was shrinking, growing smaller with each stitch, almost as if she were knitting herself into the scarf. But no one, not even his father, believed him.

That was Steele's life before the afternoon of November first, when he heard a voice coming from the edge of Taddle Pond at the bottom of the ravine near his house. The voice said, "I am Darkness. Come to me. I'm waiting." That was the defining moment—the moment Steele's world began to spin crazily out of control. When a neighbourhood kid, Ryan Massey, went missing, Steele couldn't shake the feeling that something evil had been let loose, and that it was coming closer.

And then a long black limousine appeared outside Steele's school. Maddie Fey alighted from one of its many doors and looked at Steele, singling him out from the other kids, her cold, unfriendly blue eyes flashing silver, and things seemed to go from bad to worse. Steele's wish came true. Dirk the Jerk disappeared the same night a sinister homeless man appeared in Wychwood Park, limping behind an old shopping cart. On November twenty-fifth, three nights after Dirk went missing, Steele found an unsigned note hinting that unpleasant things might happen if he failed to show up at a meeting downtown in the dead of night.

Steele had gone to keep the assignation, unaware that Mac and Riley had followed him. There he'd found Maddie Fey's limo, and his last glimpse of Toronto had been of a shadowy figure limping toward him from the far end of a darkened alley, seconds before sharp claws grabbed him and dragged him into the blackness of the vehicle.

Before he knew it, he and his companions were fleeing through the streets of New York, chased by Fire Demons, and fighting for their lives against monstrous worms in the sewers and tunnels deep beneath the city. They battled with anything they could get their hands on—pitchforks, knives, spears, and the sword now in Steele's hand.

The moment he had spied the sword in the Moles' underground armory, Steele had to have it. Looking at it now, he was reminded of the Moles—the homeless men, women, and children who lived in New York's abandoned rail and subway tunnels, playing out their short tragic lives amidst daily skirmishes with worms, gigantic mutated insects that stole children, fed their memories to the Fire Demons, and then feasted on human flesh.

For several heartbeats, Steele was transported back and down into that subterranean nightmare. It seemed so real— the stink clinging to his throat, the dampness chilling him to the bone, the screams of wounded and dying Moles deafening him—that his grasp on the sword tightened until his hand was as white as the frost forming on the windows of the black limousine barely visible out of the corner of his eye.

"Get up," said Riley, touching his shoulder, jarring him back to the present. "We've been pounding on the windows, but we can't get into the limo."

Mac shoved his hands into his jacket pockets and hunched his shoulders. "I don't like this," he muttered. "No people. No traffic. It's creepy, man."

Steele replaced the sword in its outer pocket, shrugging into his backpack as he stood and looked about. Mac was right. Where was everyone? Where were the automobiles, the buses? The river on either side of them, the lights on the bridge and along the empty street, the stars in the silver sky above, all hung in the emptiness as if nothing else existed at all.

What had happened here? Had the people run away? Were they dead? Had the Fire Demons already come and gone? Steele shook his head. No. There'd be signs—ashes and burning, and a really horrible smell. Gazing up at the pale, glowing tops of the buildings, Steele experienced a crawly feeling on his skin. It was as if he were standing before a vast one-way glass window and something or someone he couldn't see was watching him from the other side of the glass—its intent dark and hostile.

Riley said, "It's like a bad dream. I keep hoping I'll wake up and everything will be the way it was before Maddie Fey came."

"The trouble we're in has got nothing to do with Maddie Fey coming to Earth," said Steele. "She came to stop things that were already happening."

"I'm not blaming her," Riley said. "All I'm saying is that if she hadn't showed up, we wouldn't be here now." She looked about. "Wherever here is."

"Maybe things would have been even worse."

Riley wrapped her arms about her chest and shifted her weight from foot to foot. "What could possibly be worse than being kidnapped by aliens, and chased by Fire Demons?"

"Yeah," agreed Mac. "What could be worse than fighting those worms under Grand Central Terminal?"

"*You* didn't fight the worms," Steele reminded him.

Mac bristled. "That wasn't my fault. Riley and I would have stayed and fought them if Fidus hadn't forcibly dragged us away."

Steele remembered how outraged Mac had been, or claimed he had been, when Fidus the Mage, Maddie Fey's mentor, had whisked him and Riley away from the battle and sealed them up behind a stone wall. Steele believed that the old Mage had probably saved their lives, but he knew Mac would disagree.

Riley stamped her feet. "Come on! We're supposed to be phoning our parents." When the others didn't move, she tugged on Steele's sleeve impatiently. "Come *on*, Steele! My feet are so frozen, I can't feel them anymore."

But Steele hung back. He had no idea where they were, and that made him jumpy.

"What is it now?" said Riley. "Since we're already here, let's just find a phone and get it over with." She pointed at the brilliantly flood-lit building that Steele had noticed earlier. "There! There's sure to be phones in the lobby."

"Stop whining," shouted Mac. "You're driving me insane."

"Shut up!" Riley exploded, placing her hands on Mac's chest and pushing him backwards. "Sometimes I really hate you!" She marched toward the building.

The anger in his friends' voices shocked Steele. Their constant bickering and baiting used to get on his nerves, but they had always been quick to laugh and make up. But that was before Maddie Fey had come looking for Steele, before they'd ever heard of Fire Demons. It seemed like ages ago, but in reality only five days had passed since he had found the note and had set out for the meeting place.

Mac rolled his eyes skyward. "What's eating her?" When Steele didn't answer, he shrugged and took off after Riley.

Steele followed slowly, glancing about. A flash of blue

caught his eye. It was a sign on a low building attached to and situated at the back of a massive office tower ahead. He read the sign aloud. "'The Chicago Tribune.' Hey!" he shouted, quickening his pace. "I know where we are."

But Mac and Riley were too far ahead; the wind snatched Steele's words and scattered them like paper. He broke into a run, squinting up at the building Mac and Riley were approaching. As he drew closer, he realized that there were actually two connected buildings. On the front of the nearest structure, a tower jutted into the sky. Halfway up was an enormous clock, the hands pointing to a quarter past eight. The building looked as if it were made of electrified icing sugar.

It also looked familiar.

Steele frowned, puzzled. He had never visited Chicago, but he was positive that he had seen that building before. Even now, its stark whiteness triggered an image of a wedding cake with the building perched on top. Perhaps he had seen it on TV or in a book. Then, like a light illuminating the darkness, he knew. He ran faster, suddenly uneasy.

"Stop!" he shouted through the wind. "Don't go in there!"

A.D. 79

The four-thousand-foot mountain known as Vesuvius belched lava. The pyroclastic flow surged down its slopes. Steam as hot as molten rock rose from the flow and rolled over the city, killing everyone and everything. Frail human children were scalded alive, birds melted on the wing, and dogs and other animals boiled on the streets. The steam cloud then passed over the water to the boathouses of nearby Herculaneum and other towns and obliterated all those within. The once-prosperous resort towns along the coast were now buried tombs, places of death.

On that inauspicious day, the Tsilihin escaped from their prison at Earth's core in violent, simultaneous eruptions in hundreds of densely populated locations on Earth. We could not stop them. Nothing could stop them.

While we streaked across the burning lands, fighting them with fiery claws and teeth, Pompeii burned.

—Excerpt from *The Wardens' Logs*

Chapter Two

Distracted

Mac and Riley heard Steele's shouted warning. They stopped abruptly and spun toward him as one, their eyes bright and watchful.

"I saw this building when I looked in Ees," said Steele breathlessly as he reached them.

"Yeah?" said Mac. "So?"

"Did you see something happen?" asked Riley, glancing at the building over her shoulder.

"No!" answered Steele, and then, "I'm not sure." As he spoke, he instinctively pressed his hand against his chest, past the lump that was Pyrus, avoiding the salamander's playful nips at his fingers, seeking through the thickness of his jacket the outline of the flat, blood-red medallion hanging from a chain about his neck, and now tingling against his flesh.

Ees had belonged to Steele's mother and was now Steele's. When Maddie Fey had given the medallion to him, she had said, "It will show you the things you need to know."

If he lived to be a hundred, Steele would never forget the first time he had stared into the disk. The thought of it still left him weak and trembling. Ees had swallowed him alive and burned the flesh from his bones. Convinced that he was dead, Steele had wandered in a silent, monochromatic world where nothing existed. And then a familiar sound intruded upon that silent world—the distinctive *click! clack!* of his grandmother's knitting needles. Steele found GM rocking gently back and forth in her rocking chair, which was perched precariously on the edge of the steep downward slope of a hill. She took no notice of Steele; her eyes were fixed on the distance. As her delicate fingers danced on the knitting needles, she seemed oblivious to the fact that she was knitting nothing. There was no yarn to feed the needles.

What happened next was so extraordinary that it had left Steele reeling. A magical scarf began to grow from the tips of the needles. Stars and planets, rivers and oceans, mountains and forests burst into being. Sound, colour, and light exploded in a rush. Birds flew, snakes slithered, animals bounded from GM's needles as if they had suddenly been set free from iron chains that had bound them for a billion years.

And as the magic scarf had grown, Steele remembered seeing images of a city with many bridges spanning the river that flowed through it, and the tall, dazzling white building that stood at one end of a bridge.

Now, his hand tightened on Ees as he explained to Mac and Riley why they shouldn't enter the white building. "Look, maybe nothing'll happen if we go in there. All I know is that this city was in the scarf GM knitted in Ees. I remember it, and I remember this building and some sort of castle with a tall tower."

Mac whistled. "Are you saying that . . . what exactly are you saying?"

"We're in Chicago, Mac. I saw the name on a sign from the bridge."

"Chicago!" exclaimed Riley. "What are we doing in Chicago?"

Steele and Mac shrugged.

"Why didn't Maddie Fey tell us before we left the limo?" Riley persisted.

"Maybe she wasn't paying attention when we left," said Steele. "Maybe she doesn't know where we are."

"How could she not know?" pressed Riley. "It's her limo, her doors."

"I don't know," Steele admitted.

"Ah!" said Mac knowingly. "But it wasn't Maddie Fey who walked us to the door. It was—"

"The rat!" cried Steele, as if that explained everything. He turned quickly back toward the bridge, relieved to see that the limo was still parked in the same spot. He wondered why Nilats hadn't appeared when Riley and Mac had knocked on the windows. "The nasty rodent is probably hoping we'll get lost."

"Never mind the rat," said Mac. "What I'm trying to say is that we're not exactly dealing with normal people here. Maddie Fey and Fidus are Mages. They're *aliens!* They're not like our parents, always worrying about us and wanting to know where we are and what we're doing every second. In fact, they're sort of dangerous."

"What's your point?" asked Steele.

"My point is we shouldn't assume anything when it comes to Maddie Fey. Even if it turns out that she knew we were going to be in Chicago when we left the limo, so what? She probably wouldn't think anything of it."

"I don't care," said Riley. "I'm still going to ask her why it happened and why they wouldn't let us in when we knocked."

"That can wait," said Mac. "Right now, we've got to decide whether to go into this building or not." He shifted his gaze from Riley to Steele. "Just because you saw it in GM's scarf doesn't mean we're doomed if we go inside. Does it?"

"No," admitted Steele.

"Maybe GM knitted the building because she wanted us to go inside."

"Maybe," Steele said doubtfully. "Oh, I don't know what to think. All I know is that it was part of the vision. And yes, GM must have knitted it for a reason. But what? Maybe I'm being paranoid, but I'd feel a lot better if we stayed away from it."

The others nodded and looked about for an alternative. Across the street, a bit farther along, the tower Steele had seen from the bridge seemed to point at the sky. Steele looked up. The top quarter of the building was floodlit, revealing striking Gothic ornamentation. It reminded Steele of Canada's Parliament buildings.

He pointed at the tower. "Let's try over there."

As they hurried across the street, Steele was relieved to see Riley sling her arm about Mac's shoulder as if they had never quarreled in their lives. Steele let them go ahead. He still felt tense, but he couldn't say why. Mac and Riley waited for him outside the entrance. When he joined them, they crowded into the same compartment of the revolving door and burst into the lobby, shutting out the force and sound of the wind.

The lobby was surprisingly small and cozy for such a huge building. Like the streets outside, though, it was deserted, and unnaturally quiet. Spotting a bank of telephones against a wall behind the information desk, Riley rushed over to the last phone in the row, shrugged out of her backpack, and rooted through the contents.

"Aha!" she cried triumphantly, waving a phone card for the others to see.

Steele followed. "Remember, Riley, don't say too much. Just tell your mom that we're OK, that we haven't been abducted. Tell her you'll try to call again, and then hang up."

Mac nodded. "Yeah, Riley, think you can manage not to blab your head off or be a crybaby?" He moved quickly out of range of Riley's backpack.

When Riley didn't respond to Mac's jibes, Steele realized that she hadn't even heard him. "Leave her alone," he hissed at Mac.

A determined look appeared on Riley's face. She snatched the phone off its hook, inserted the calling card into the appropriate slot, and punched in her home phone number. Abruptly, she reached out and pressed the disconnect button, her expression now panicky.

"I can't," she cried.

"What's wrong?" asked Mac. "You've been desperate to call home ever since we left Toronto."

Riley's eyes glistened with tears. "I know," she said miserably. "But I can't. As soon as she hears my voice, Mom's going to start crying and screaming, and I'm not going to know what to say. Oh God. She's going to be totally mad."

"What's the worst thing she can do?" reasoned Mac. "She can't do anything over the phone."

"Then *you* do it," snapped Riley, throwing the phone at Mac and stomping a few paces away.

Mac stared at the phone in his hand as if he had never seen one before. Then he sighed and looked from Riley's back to

Steele's face imploringly. "We've been gone for almost a week. They probably think I'm dead. I know someone's got to tell them I'm alive. But I can't do it." His eyes brightened. "Here! Your dad's cool. You do it." He thrust the phone at Steele.

Steele sighed in frustration. The fact that his friends liked his dad and said so pleased him enormously, but he wouldn't exactly call his dad cool. Maybe . . . different. Because of his police training, he really listened when Steele talked to him and, as Steele had learned early on, remembered every word. He was also cautious, and more protective of Steele than Mac's and Riley's dads were of them. Toronto was probably the safest city in the world at the moment because every policeman would be out searching for him. Perhaps the search had been called off by now. Perhaps his father believed Steele was dead. The thought made Steele sad. Like the others, he knew he had to let his parent know that he was alive. But the thought of hearing his father's voice made his heart ache.

"Go on, Steele," urged Mac. "Your dad won't yell at you. He listens to you."

"Just do exactly what you told me to do," added Riley. "Tell him we're OK, and to tell our parents not to worry."

Steele looked at his friends, guilt flooding through him at the realization that when he had told them about the images he had seen in Ees, he had purposely kept back two things. One was an image of him summoning his Mage power and drawing the fire from hundreds of Fire Demons into himself, while his friends huddled in terror behind him. Even as he had watched the action unfolding from GM's knitting needles, he had known that he could not absorb all of the fire from all of the Fire Demons. There were too many of them.

He had seen fire licking at his clothes as his body glowed brighter and brighter. Then GM's knitting had burst into flames and everything had been consumed in a great ball of fire. Steele hadn't told anyone about this.

Because the second image had hurt a thousand times worse than the fire from the Fire Demons, he had shared the secret with Maddie Fey and no one else. In that image, a spacecraft had shot from GM's needles and soared into the sky. Through its windows, Steele had seen a woman. She had raised her head as if she had seen him, too. It was his mother—who had died when Steele was only three years old. As Steele stared at her, he thought he could actually hear her heartbeat. And then, odder still, he had heard the barely perceptible murmur of a second heart. Two hearts! His mother had been pregnant in the image, which came from before she'd met his dad. Discovering that his father wasn't his biological father had shattered Steele's world.

Before Steele had looked into Ees, being afraid to call home was unthinkable. But now that he knew the truth about his father, he felt knots tightening in his stomach.

As if he feared that Steele might wimp out, Mac quickly punched in the Millers' phone number. Steele drew the phone to his ear and held his breath, listening to the ringing at the other end. It was the loneliest sound he had ever heard. He was conscious of the receiver, slippery in his sweaty palms. When the answering machine cut in, he let out his breath in a sigh of relief and listened to the greeting, going over in his mind what to say.

"Dad . . . It's me . . . Steele," he said finally, feeling tears spring to his eyes. But he didn't try to hide his crying from his friends; one look at their faces and he saw that their eyes were misty too. "I'm OK," he continued. "I'm with Mac and Riley . . . uh, please let their parents know that we haven't been abducted . . . nothing like that. . . . Oh, if you're wondering about Pyrus, he stowed away in my pack. . . . I really miss you and GM. . . . I couldn't call before because—"

Mac jabbed him in the ribs. "What are you doing? You're supposed to tell him we're OK and then hang up," he hissed.

Steele pushed Mac away, turning his back. His words came in a rush. "Dad, I can't tell you where we are or what we're doing. I can only tell you that it's got something to do with the missing kids. They were kept underground, in tunnels. And, Dad, this is going to sound crazy, but remember when Megan Traft turned up in New York? How nasty she was, how she tried to bite her fingers off, and how her parents kept saying that she wasn't their daughter? We know what's wrong with her. Her memories were gone. Some really bad creatures erased all of the kids' memories so they don't know who they are. We haven't found Ryan Massey or Dirk yet, but check out the subway . . . old tunnels . . . underground storage rooms—"

The line went dead.

Steele turned and saw Mac's hand on the disconnect button. "What did you do that for?"

"Why do you think?" Mac snapped back, pale eyes narrowing. "You're the one who told us to say as little as possible, and then you go and blab everything—"

"I wasn't blabbing—"

"You were," accused Mac. "Who knows what else you would have said if I hadn't hung up."

Riley jumped in. "Stop it! What's done is done. At least they know we're OK now, so let's get back to the limo."

Steele thumped Mac's shoulder. "I'm sorry. You were right to hang up. I think I would have told Dad everything. I don't know what came over me. I just wanted to keep talking."

He realized that he was still holding the phone to his ear, unwilling to break the connection and sever the link to the only family he had ever known—his father and grandmother.

Finally he let it drop.

Outside, the wind was waiting for them. It attacked with renewed fury, stealing their breath, and screaming like a wounded beast. Steele broke into a jog, heading back to the bridge and the waiting limousine. He held his hands over his abdomen, partly because he felt sick and partly to cushion Pyrus against jostling. A sudden flash of light caught his eye and he glanced across the street at a ground-level window. A TV inside had just been turned on. At he stared, puzzled, a dozen TVs flashed into life.

"Look." He pointed. "Let's check it out."

Without waiting for his friends, Steele darted across the street and stopped before the shop window. He gasped at the familiar images on the TV screens.

"Oh my God," cried Riley, coming up beside him. "It's New York."

The graphic images of New York after the Fire Demons had rampaged along Park Avenue and through Grand Central Terminal played like a nightmare, but Steele couldn't tear his eyes off the screens. Park Avenue was a pile of rubble, and Grand Central Terminal looked as if a cyclone had raged through it. But it was the images of sheet-covered dead bodies lined up on the sidewalks and in straight neat rows in Grand Central Terminal that brought home to him the horror of the attack. He couldn't hear what the news anchor was saying, but from her puzzled expression, he realized that the cause of the devastation remained a mystery, except to him and his friends.

Suddenly the TV screens blinked and a new image flashed on the screen. Steele heard Riley suck in her breath.

"It's you," she cried. "Steele, you're on TV."

They stared in disbelief at the dozen identical images of Steele.

"What's that in your hand?" Riley let out a delighted cry. "I can't believe it. It's a snowglobe. I love those things."

"When did they take those photos?" Steele wondered. "Riley, I've never seen those photos before. And that's definitely not my snowglobe."

Inside the transparent globe was a miniature castle with towers and crenellated battlements. It was the same tower Steele had seen when he had looked into Ees. He read the words printed on the base of the globe: *The Water Tower, Chicago.*

"Riley, that's the other building from GM's scarf, the castle with the tower."

"Don't you think it's strange that we suddenly find ourselves in Chicago, where those other kids disappeared?" said Riley.

"I don't know what to think," admitted Steele. "I don't know who that person on TV is, but it's not me."

And as they stared in wonder at the snow whirling about inside the snowglobe, the tiny flakes suddenly turned to sparks. Only when he saw the miniature water tower burst into flames did Steele realize that something was wrong. But by then it was too late.

Even before he turned from the window, the wind ripping the shout from his throat, he knew Mac was gone.

Remembering

Before we departed from Arjella, our home planet, the Mages charged us with the task of guarding the Tsilihin prisoners until the end of time. Neither the Mages nor we could have known that the fire that was to be the creatures' grave caused a chromosomal change in them. Instead of dying, they mutated, evolving from creatures armoured with bone and scale to fiery beings of burning fang and claw.

Born of fire, they were driven by an insatiable hunger to destroy by burning everything that existed beyond the bounds of their molten prison.

And we named them Death.

They numbered in the thousands; our number was twelve.

—Excerpt from *The Wardens' Logs*

Chapter Three

A Cry in the Wind

Frantic, Steele spun in a circle and scanned the deserted street and sidewalks for Mac. But nothing moved on the street as far as he could see in both directions. He tore across the broad street like a deranged thing, not giving any thought to where he was going or what he was doing. He ran instinctively, aimlessly, shouting Mac's name until his voice cracked. Not that it mattered; the wind snatched the words from his mouth, scattered them into the Chicago night like silent snowflakes, and then gathered them up and flung them back in his face with a howl that sounded suspiciously like laughter.

This can't be happening! Steele tried to think, to reason, but his brain was racing faster than his legs, over which he seemed to have lost control. At last, sheer exhaustion slowed him. But his heart continued to pound hard and fast, and his lungs felt as if they were on fire. He stopped, braced his hands on a low concrete wall separating pedestrian traffic from the open space outside an office tower, and slumped forward, gasping for air.

Come on! You're supposed to be a Mage. Do something!

Beneath his shirt, Ees felt hot against his chest, as if it were trying to tell him something. He pulled the medallion free.

"What?" he asked, blinking repeatedly to stop his eyes from staring into its core, afraid that Ees might pull him inside as it had that first time, or suddenly speak to him, or show him Mac dead. But nothing happened. No sudden burning sensation swept over him; no voice came from the magic red disk; no image of Mac appeared out of its fiery centre. Except for a noticeable drop in the disk's temperature, nothing happened at all.

Steele clutched Ees tightly and closed his eyes, recalling the strange heightened sense of hearing he had experienced after the battle between the Moles and the worms. Then, he had been able to distinguish the negligible scratching of a tiny insect as it burrowed inside the concrete wall of a long-abandoned railway terminal deep beneath New York City from the grieving shouts of the Moles as they gathered their dead and laid them out on the ancient platform. Perhaps if he concentrated hard enough, he could hear Mac or even the sounds of those who had taken him—and there was no doubt in Steele's mind that Mac had been taken. Steele strained to hear other sounds in the wind. He listened for human voices, Mac's in particular. He listened for fleeing footsteps, the sound of something being dragged along the street, but he heard nothing except the wind, howling. Trembling and sobbing, he shoved the now ice-cold disk inside his jacket.

"How could I have been so stupid?" he sobbed, bringing his gloved fist down hard on the wall. "All those TVs coming on at once . . . and the burning snowglobes. I should have known it was a trick to distract me and Riley."

Now Mac was gone. If he had been alert, as he should have been, the abductors would have failed and Mac would still be here. Steele raised his head.

He looked about for Riley, but she wasn't anywhere on the sidewalk. He tried to recall if he had seen her after he had run off searching for Mac. Yes. He was positive she had been with him the whole time. But where was she now? Panicked, he dashed into the deserted street and turned his back to the wind.

"Riley! Riley!" he screamed. And then, "Not Riley! Oh please, not Riley!"

The possibility of a double trap had never entered his mind. While he had been blindly searching for Mac, somehow the abductors had snatched Riley!

Steele's shoulders slumped in despair. Both of his friends were gone, and he had been powerless to prevent their disappearance. He had to get help. The wind was beating against his back; he let it push him toward the bridge and the black limousine waiting there like a punishment.

He kept his eyes on the windshield. After showing them to the door, where had the rat gone? Why hadn't it appeared when Mac and Riley had knocked on the window? Had it seen the abductors snatch Mac and Riley? Had it watched, and done nothing? Steele had no trouble convincing himself that Nilats had seen everything from the bridge and hadn't lifted a claw to help Mac and Riley. It felt good to blame someone aside from himself. He hated that rat, had hated it from the moment it grabbed him and dragged him into Maddie Fey's limousine.

Ignoring a small voice in his mind that said he wasn't being fair to Nilats, Steele broke into a run, anxious to reach the limo. He was half a block from the bridge when he caught a blur of movement out of the corner of his eye. Before he could turn his head, something slammed into his side, almost knocking him off his feet. Instinctively, he clenched his fists and swung at his attacker.

"Cut it out!"

"Riley!" Steele was so relieved to discover that he hadn't lost her, too, that he grabbed her shoulders and shook her until she yelled at him again.

"Stop! You're hurting me."

Steele loosened his grip. "Sorry!" He still couldn't believe that she was OK. "I thought they got you, too."

"Well, they didn't," Riley replied indignantly. She pointed to a sheltered doorway in a building off to the side. "I was looking for Mac."

"Nothing?" asked Steele.

Riley shook her head. "I get sick just thinking of that snow-globe stunt. I can't believe we fell for it."

"It's my fault," said Steele. "I felt that something was wrong, but I just let it go."

"We better head back. The sooner we tell Maddie Fey what happened, the sooner we'll find Mac." Riley touched Steele's arm. "We *will* find him."

Steele nodded but said nothing. As they silently made their way back toward the bridge, he felt a deep, sad weariness wash over him. When he glanced at Riley and saw her expression, he guessed that she was feeling the same. He wanted to make her feel better, or at least give her hope.

"I know we'll find him," he said. "I promise I won't stop looking until we get him back."

Riley's lips tightened into a thin line. Steele thought she might start crying, but she merely nodded glumly.

They picked up the pace. Ahead, Maddie Fey's black limousine shone silver in the white moonlight. The thought of having to tell the Mages that they had lost Mac filled Steele with dread. Blaming himself and the rat for his friend's disappearance was one thing; being blamed by the Mages was quite another.

"They better let us in this time, or I'll break–" Riley stopped and spun about, staring back along the street.

"What?" asked Steele, heart jumping.

"Listen!" hissed Riley. "Do you hear that?"

Steele listened. Except for the wind and the sound of his heart, he heard nothing. "What?" he asked again.

Riley didn't answer for several long seconds. Finally, she shook her head. "I thought I heard someone moaning."

"It's just the wind," said Steele. "It sounds so human sometimes that it's freaky."

They stood together, listening intently. Then they shrugged at each other and prepared to set out once more.

"Listen! There it is again! Don't you hear it?" She turned around again and looked toward a shadowy alley they had passed a minute earlier. "It's coming from over there."

Steele heard it now. It was a high keening sound, like someone was hurt or dying. But he couldn't tell if it was the wind or an actual human voice.

"We better check it out," he said. "Let's stick together; it could be another distraction."

"It's Mac. I just know it," said Riley.

They retraced their steps and stopped at the mouth of a narrow covered passageway and peered along its length to where it ended at a flight of broad stairs going up.

"Look!" cried Riley, pointing. "There. By the steps."

There was something there, a dark lumpy shape; Steele thought it looked like a large, stuffed garbage bag, but it could be a person, it could be Mac. The passage was cobblestoned and dimly lit, filled with shadows; the shape was too far away to identify. They cautiously approached the lump. Protected from the wind's unrelenting screaming, the passageway seemed unnaturally quiet. The crunch of their boots on the cobblestones grated on Steele's nerves.

"I don't like this," he said.

"Me neither," said Riley. "The quiet is even creepier than the sound of the wind, if you know what I mean."

They were near enough now to the shapeless form to see that it was indeed a person. The figure was lying on its side, its back against the bottom step. Steele and Riley exchanged glances when they heard a groan escape from a dirty cloth bag covering the person's head and face. Hearing them coming, the figure frantically drew its knees up to its chest and pressed its back against the steps as if trying to hide. Then it went still.

"It's all right," said Riley gently. "We're not going to hurt you."

Steele noticed that the figure's arms were behind its back, bound with the same duct tape that was wound about its middle. He knew at once that it wasn't Mac. This figure was bigger and stockier than four Macs. He and Riley dropped onto their knees and carefully removed the bag from the figure's head. The boy's face was a mess. It was coated with blood and dirt, but Steele recognized him immediately.

It was Dirk the Jerk.

A.D. 79

As we circled high above the ruined city and the smoke, we shivered in the cold night air and opened our minds to one another, pondering a question that burned in our thoughts like lava snaking down Vesuvius' distant slopes.

The Tsilihin were incapable of planning the multiple attacks that had kept us preoccupied while Pompeii burned and thousands of people died. They were not sentient beings. But the attacks had been planned.

Who or what had directed the attacks?

—Excerpt from *The Wardens' Logs*

Chapter Four

An Old Enemy

"Dirk?" Steele spat out the name as if he were getting rid of a bad taste in his mouth. He recoiled from the bully involuntarily, as he had always done. A long moment passed before he realized that this time their positions were reversed.

Dirk opened his swollen eyelids and peered at Steele from reddened slits. His lips were split and puffy, and blood bubbled from the side of his mouth and dribbled across his face, forming a small slimy pool on the ground.

"Steele?" he grunted, his mouth open in shock. His eyes darted to Riley. "Puddlescum . . . er, Riley? What . . . ? How . . . ?"

Steele noticed Riley flinch at the hated nickname and he felt her hurt as if it were his own. Riley stepped over Dirk and ran up the stairs, disappearing around the corner. In that instant, Steele was transported back to Toronto, to the days when the mere thought of the school bully turned his insides to mush. He felt the old fear clawing at his chest. All the times he'd gone to school, the thought of staying out of Dirk's line of sight uppermost in his mind. Two years of being a different person whenever Dirk and the Jerks were around. A voice in his mind urged him to lash out, to kick Dirk until he begged for mercy. *It's payback time! Go on. Do it now. You'll never get a better chance than this.*

But as he stared into the frightened eyes in the bruised and puffy face, his fear and anger drained away. He still hated Dirk passionately, but he also felt compassion. Whoever had abducted his old enemy had not treated him kindly.

"Who did this to you?" he asked quietly.

Dirk squeezed his eyes shut. "I'll tell you," he murmured, as tears leaked from the corners of his eyes. "Help me get this tape off."

Steele looked up the stairs and called for Riley, then gripped Dirk's arm and tried to help him sit up. Riley appeared on the landing and ran down the stairs toward them.

"Here, take one of his arms," said Steele.

She did as he asked, none too gently, Steele thought, but he couldn't blame her. Together, they helped Dirk to a sitting position. Steele had removed his gloves and was leaning over to get at the duct tape binding his wrists together, when he noticed something sparkling in one of Dirk's pudgy hands.

"What's that?" Before Dirk could answer, Steele pried open his frozen fingers and took the familiar object. He stared down at the red, yellow, and blue gemstones studding the casing of the dragon knife resting in his palm. Mac's knife. Steele would have recognized it anywhere. He and Riley had knives just like it, gifts from Maddie Fey; his was tucked inside his sock. He waved the knife in Dirk's face. "Where did you get this?"

"Give it back. It's mine," said Dirk petulantly.

"Liar," growled Steele. "Where did you get it? Tell me or I'll . . ."

For a moment, Steele thought that Dirk was going to morph into the bully again. The moment passed, but Dirk continued to bristle like a cornered rat. "OK! OK! The other boy dropped it when they grabbed him. It's a good knife. I was going to use it to cut the tape."

Riley suddenly lost it. "That's Mac's knife!" she cried, catching hold of the front of Dirk's jacket and shaking him until his head lolled and his teeth rattled. "Where is he? Who grabbed him?"

Dirk groaned. "Back off! That kills, man!"

Riley suddenly seemed to realize that Dirk was injured, perhaps seriously. She snatched her hands away in horror. "Mac's disappeared," she said by way of an apology. "When I saw you with his knife—"

"Yeah! Right!" Dirk interrupted. "You saw the knife and thought I stole it. Well, you're wrong. I didn't. In fact I didn't even know the other boy was Mac until you told me."

"Just shut up and tell us where they've taken him," demanded Riley, clenching her fists.

"I can't tell you," Dirk began, then, seeing a murderous look appear on Riley's face, he added quickly, "But I can take you there."

Riley glared at him. "You know where they've taken him?"

Dirk nodded. "The same place they took me after Toronto. I escaped yesterday . . . and you've got to believe me, I swear I didn't know it was Mac."

Riley pushed him roughly against the bottom step and muttered to Steele in disgust. "I don't believe him. He's involved somehow."

Steele didn't know what to make of Dirk's story. "How did you get from Toronto to Chicago?"

"Chicago?" Dirk looked surprised. "That's news. If we're in Chicago, I must have been out of it, because all I remember is being home in bed and the next thing I know I'm waking up in some filthy dungeon."

"Chicago doesn't exactly look like Toronto," said Riley. "Surely when you escaped you must have known you were in another city."

Dirk's tongue flicked over his split lips. "I wasn't thinking. I just wanted to get away from *them*."

"Who is 'them'?" asked Steele, slowly opening Mac's knife.

Dirk watched, his eyes widening in terror. "What are you doing? I'll tell you everything, man. Hey, be careful with that." He spat another mouthful of blood and saliva onto the ground. "I'll tell you." He shot Steele a guilty look. "Listen! I'm sorry for . . . you know . . . the things I've done. I'm sorry about the money . . . and beating you up. But, please, you've got to believe me. I had nothing to do with them taking Mac. I'm not like that anymore, man. I'll take you to Mac. I'll talk. I'll do anything. Just don't hurt me."

"I'm not going to hurt you," said Steele angrily, thinking about Dirk's confession and wondering if he could trust him. "I'm going to cut through the tape."

The look of relief that suddenly replaced the fear on Dirk's face clinched the debate going on in Steele's head. *It's not an act,* he realized. *He's scared out of his mind.* Working carefully, he sliced through a layer of tape and began to unwind it from Dirk's wrists. Catching sight of a curious gold band on the middle finger of Dirk's right hand, he bent closer to examine it. He had seen Dirk's fists frequently in the past but had never noticed a ring on any of his fingers.

As he squinted in the dim light, he realized that while the object looked like a ring and even gleamed like gold, it was actually a tattooed band. Steele pulled at the duct tape, at the same time twisting Dirk's hand around to see the tattoo from the front. Set in the centre of the band was a round black mark roughly the size of a peppercorn. It looked like a hole in Dirk's finger. Steele touched it, anticipating the feel of the depression. Then he snatched his finger away, surprised that the dot was a black gem or stone of some sort.

That's odd, he though. *What's holding it in place?*

Dirk twisted his hands, stretching and straining at the tape.

"Keep still," said Steele, quickly pulling off the last of the duct tape. He felt the other's eyes focus greedily on Mac's knife as he shoved it into his jacket pocket, but when he looked at him, Dirk was staring down the passageway, his face shiny like wax, his eyes guarded.

Steele watched him for a second, then he and Riley helped Dirk stand.

Riley crossed her arms and tapped her foot impatiently. "Now, show us where they've taken Mac. And don't even think about running away."

Dirk rubbed his wrists and arms vigorously to bring back the circulation. Steele could see the black gem more clearly now, but he was too far away to see how it was anchored. Wanting Riley to take a look at it, Steele tried to catch her eye. But she wasn't facing his way, and by the time he glanced back himself, Dirk's hands were jammed into his jacket pockets, the ring hidden.

He said to Dirk, "Before you show us where Mac's being held, tell us who abducted you, and what you know about them."

"Some really weird stuff has been going on around me, man," said Dirk. "I'll tell you, but not here. It's not safe.

Come on, I'll take you to Mac first. It's not far. But we got to get there before they . . . I mean . . . we got to get out of here before they come back for me."

"You were going to say something else," said Steele. "Was it about Mac? Do you know what they're going to do to him?"

Dirk turned away and coughed, but Steele thought he was faking.

"You better be telling the truth—"

"Why would I lie?" Dirk shouted, and wiped his mouth on his arm. "Look at me! Do you think I bashed my own face in and tied myself up on the off chance I'd run into you? Jeez! If that's what you think, why are you hanging around? Go. Good luck finding the Mor—Mac on your own."

Steele ignored Dirk's slip in almost calling Mac by the insulting nickname Moron. Dirk's suggestion that he had hurt himself sounded ridiculous, but still Steele wondered. He had a strong feeling that there was something wrong with the entire scenario, but he couldn't quite put his finger on the problem. Dirk was selfish and hateful, and habitually cruel to others weaker than himself. Steele knew from bitter experience how much the bully enjoyed inflicting pain. Dirk preyed on others, used them to do his bidding, and if they had something he wanted, he snatched it. In the past, Steele would have said that the only thing Dirk might respect was someone bigger, stronger, and meaner than him. Could someone who fit that profile change, become a different person, in less than two weeks?

Steele didn't think so. Besides, there were too many coincidences. What were the odds of Mac disappearing and Dirk showing up? And in Chicago of all places! Still, someone had beaten Dirk badly. The thought that it might have been Mac brought a ghost of a smile to Steele's lips. But even though Mac had a big mouth, he wasn't stupid. He often called Dirk names, but always under his breath so the bully couldn't hear. No, Steele decided. It definitely wasn't Mac.

"Steele?" Riley got up and signalled him to join her.

As soon as they were out of earshot of Dirk, she pulled Steele close until their faces were almost touching. "Do you believe him?" she whispered.

Steele frowned. "I don't know."

"There's something wrong," insisted Riley, keeping her voice low and watching Dirk over Steele's shoulder. "I don't trust him. We can't go off with him just like that, not without telling Maddie Fey."

"What if he's telling the truth?" asked Steele. "After all, he *did* have Mac's knife."

Riley shook her head. "Yeah, well, knowing Dirk, he probably beat Mac up and stole the knife."

"I don't think so," protested Steele. "It doesn't make sense. Do you seriously think he smashed his own face like that and then duct-taped his hands together?"

"I don't know what to think," admitted Riley. "All I know is I don't like him and I don't trust him."

"I don't like him either, and I wouldn't normally trust him," said Steele. "But even if he did those things to himself, where's Mac? Don't you see? He was taped up; he couldn't have taken Mac."

She said, "He could if someone helped him."

Steele had to admit that Riley could be right. Dirk might have engineered the whole thing. What didn't make sense was the timing. Dirk had had no way of knowing that Steele,

Riley, and Mac would conveniently end up in Chicago just steps away from here, at the exact moment Dirk was getting the stuffing beat out of him. No one could have known. Steele and his friends didn't even know until they stepped out of Maddie Fey's limousine and discovered that they were no longer in Manhattan.

"I'm not saying you're wrong, Riley, but I don't see that we've got a choice," Steele continued. "Look, we know he saw Mac because he had Mac's knife. We've got to trust him this once. If there's the slimmest chance he can lead us to—"

"Mac's my friend, too," Riley interrupted. "I want to find him as much as you do. But I don't think going off with Dirk the Jerk is the way to find him. I think we should take him back to the limo. Let Maddie Fey decide what to do with him."

"You think it's a good idea, letting him know about the limo?"

"It's the only *sensible* thing to do," said Riley. "I don't trust him and there's no way I'm going off with him without telling someone."

Steele couldn't think of anything that might convince Riley to change her mind. Besides, she was making more sense than he was. It would be insane to follow Dirk blindly. He nodded grudgingly. "OK! Let's take him back to the limo."

They rejoined Dirk, whose eyes were switching nervously from the mouth of the passageway to the stairs. As he rubbed his hands together, Steele caught another glimpse of the strange black stone and made a mental note to tell Riley about it the first chance he got.

"Come on. Let's get out of here," urged Dirk. He jabbed his thumb toward the stairs. "That way's faster."

"No," said Steele, taking a firm hold on one of his arms. "We're going to meet some friends."

"What friends?"

Steele looked at the scowl twisting Dirk's face and knew he wasn't happy with the change in plans, or the news that Steele and Riley weren't alone. *He says he's changed,* thought Steele, *but the old Dirk's still there inside him, very close to the surface, and it wouldn't take much to bring him out.* Supporting Dirk's weight between them, Steele and Riley staggered out of the passageway onto the street and turned left toward the bridge and the waiting limousine. The wind had mysteriously died and a heavy stillness had fallen over the city. It was as if the air were eavesdropping on them.

"What happened to everybody?" he asked Dirk.

Dirk doubled over, coughing and spitting bloody phlegm onto the street. When the spasm subsided, he stared into the distance for such a long time that Steele wondered if he had heard the question. But when Dirk spoke, he couldn't hide the awe in his voice or the greedy glitter in his eyes.

"I'll tell you this much for now. You don't want to mess with the people who captured me and Mac. They're more powerful than you could ever imagine. If you think governments and banks rule the world, you're so wrong, man. They're nothing. All this"—he waved an arm at the great, silent city—"They did it. They cleared the city."

"How?" asked Riley.

Dirk glanced from one to the other disdainfully. "It doesn't matter *how* they did it. Don't you get it? It's enough that they *did* it."

"Well, excuse me for not knowing who *they* are," snapped Riley sarcastically.

But Steele's mind was racing. Dirk's non-answer bothered him. "Why did they clear the city?" he repeated. "What are they looking for?"

But Dirk looked about furtively and wouldn't answer. The harder Steele pressed him for information, the deeper he retreated inside himself. Fighting down the urge to kick Dirk's butt, Steele finally gave up.

They were just abreast of the huge block-like towers standing like obese guardians on either side of the bridge when a tall, dark shape split off from the shadows of the tower to their left and moved almost leisurely into the middle of the bridge between them and the limousine. Another shape followed, and then another, and another, until Steele counted six dark figures. He and his companions stopped, watching the figures shuffle slowly toward them, arms reaching. Steele felt Dirk's body slump forward, as if defeated.

It was impossible to tell if the creatures were human. They could have been men. Steele judged that they were close to seven feet tall. Except for their shuffling gait, they walked upright like men. But their long garments, the colour of the night, disguised their forms. And nothing was visible in the darkness beneath their deep hoods. Even though they were downwind, Steele gagged at the stink of them. They smelled nauseatingly sweet, like a dead squirrel he'd found in Taddle Pond one spring.

"What are we going to do?" cried Riley, her voice quivering. "We can't get to the limo."

"It's OK, Riley," Steele said, keeping his voice calm. "Look at them. They're slow. We can dodge them." He hoped he was right.

"What are they? What do they want?"

Steele glanced at Riley. Her face was deathly white and he knew that she was on the brink of panic. He guessed that she was thinking of New York and their desperate flight from the Fire Demons. "Don't let them see that you're afraid," he said, adding meaningfully, "Our *friends* will know what to do."

Between them, Dirk groaned. "Me. They want me. You guys go. Leave me. They won't follow you. Go on. Get out of here."

"What are they? Fire Demons?" hissed Steele, aware that he too was close to panic.

"Fire *what?*" Dirk shot him a puzzled look.

"Never mind," said Steele. "What are they?"

"Maladroids," said Dirk, his eyes darting from one creature to another.

"Maladroids?" repeated Steele, glancing at Riley. "What's that?"

Riley shook her head. "It doesn't sound good."

"They smell dead," said Steele, trying to breathe through his mouth.

"They're not exactly alive," offered Dirk, swallowing nervously. "Believe me. You don't want to know any more than that. They're the ones who grabbed me and the Moron."

Steele wanted to jab his elbow into Dirk's ribs, but he kept his anger in check. Since Mac wasn't here, it couldn't hurt him. "Where do they come from?"

Dirk shrugged. "I don't know. I heard stuff . . ." He clammed up.

Steele wanted to press him, but it would have to wait until they found a way out of their present predicament. As the Maladroids shuffled toward them, Dirk inched closer to Steele. "I'll tell you this much. There are more where these came from . . . hundreds of them. I thought I could get away before they came back for me. But there's a chance for you and Riley. So do it. Take off. Now."

"Shut up. We're not leaving you," Steele said through his teeth. "We're in this together."

Behind the Maladroids, Maddie Fey's sleek black limousine shone like a ghostly apparition in the cold moonlight. Steele thought it strange that the Maladroids hadn't even glanced at it, as if they couldn't see it, or it wasn't there. He also thought it strange that Dirk hadn't said anything about the vehicle.

"We just have to make it to the limo," he said to Riley, his voice low. "We'll be safe then."

Maddie Fey and Wish, and the other aliens, Fidus and the rat, were their only hope against the creatures facing them on the bridge. Despite his fear, Steele almost laughed aloud at the thought of what lay in store for the attackers. He couldn't wait to see their reaction when Maddie Fey burst through one of the doors and raised her arms toward them. *And just wait until you meet Nilats,* Steele thought. He had witnessed the rat's ferocity in an alley in New York. The memory of Nilats tearing the worm creatures apart piece by piece, never mind the sounds of screaming and then crunching and smacking, sickened him. He looked over at Riley.

"They're in for a surprise," he said, ignoring Dirk's curious glance.

"Serve them right," muttered Riley.

Steele turned back but as he did so, to his horror, the limousine rippled and blurred, and then it simply vanished like smoke in the wind. Except there was no wind and Steele and his companions were alone and helpless. He stood frozen in shocked disbelief, all hope having vanished with the limo. He didn't have to ask Riley if she, too, had seen the limousine disappear. He heard her soft, sad whimper.

"Maddie Fey left us here all alone."

Seated at his long, silent table somewhere in the city, the Prince of Darkness bent his head and peered into the lustreless black globe and watched the boy and his two companions staring in wide-eyed terror at the black-clad figures approaching.

Past Times

On a summer night in the human year AD 64, something momentous occurred. Death changed. Death became more cunning. On that night, for the first time in the billions of years that we had been guarding our prisoners, groups of three or four Tsilihin broke through the Earth's crust and hurled their deadly fire at innumerable cities across the globe. We did not rest. We tore from place to place, our powerful wings creating tunnels in the air. Our blazing claws snatched Death and bore it back and down into its prison. And Death shrieked and bit and spat to no avail. We brought prisoners back, only to learn that others had escaped. There was no end to our labours.

But while we toiled, a thousand creatures exploded into the great Imperial City of Rome.

—Excerpt from *The Wardens' Logs*

Chapter Five

Friend or Foe?

Riley looked at Steele, her eyes desperate in her pinched, white face.

"What happened, Steele? Why did they leave us?"

Steele searched his mind for an explanation, but he couldn't find one that kindled even the tiniest spark of hope. He shook his head, felt his mouth form a thin angry line. He wished that he could offer more than "I don't know, Riley. I don't know." But that was all he had.

Ahead, the menacing figures shuffled closer. They moved slowly, purposefully, not bothering to hurry, as if they shared a secret. Steele noticed that one of them carried a sack slung over its shoulder. Something was in the sack, and from the way it was thrashing about it seemed alive. The Maladroid hoisted the sack off its shoulder and thumped it down hard on the surface of the bridge. Steele cringed at the anguished cry of pain that came from inside. Again and again, the creature hoisted the sack as high as his shoulder and smashed it on the concrete. As if they were the ones caught inside the sack, Steele and Riley flinched each time. After a while, the cries and struggles ceased. Then, as if the sack were filled with air, the creature effortlessly swung it over its shoulder and breathed a long, low, satisfied sigh.

Steele wondered who or what was trapped inside, and if it had been knocked unconscious, or killed.

What if it was Mac?

According to Dirk, these were the same creatures that had grabbed him and Mac. Anger boiled inside, blinding Steele. He fought the urge to fly at the monster holding the sack and attack him. Instead, he reached for the powers that lurked within, intending to blast the Maladroids off the bridge so fast they'd be halfway to the bottom of the river before they knew what had hit them.

He could feel the power, had almost grasped it, when the Maladroids suddenly went as still as boulders. An expectant hush fell over the bridge. Steele felt his magic slip away. The creatures' heads snapped to the left, toward the square tower at the end of the bridge on the opposite side of the street. There, shadows seemed to be swirling, forming into something even darker. A chill mist rose from the darkness and drifted over the bridge. The Maladroids waited, motionless.

Steele shivered. What now? He focused on the shadows, also waiting, afraid to blink in case something horrific happened. They didn't have to wait very long.

A lone creature appeared out of the darkness of the tower and moved toward Steele and his companions. Beside Steele, Dirk gasped.

"What?" asked Steele.

"It's bad for us," Dirk said. "It's the Disciplinarian. He controls the Maladroids. I heard stories about the way he disciplines them. And man, he's one sick dude."

"Is he human?" asked Riley.

Dirk gulped. "Probably not."

Steele stared at the creature known as the Disciplinarian. It was taller than the others and wore a similar black cloak, but without a hood. In the light from the bridge lamps, its head gleamed white like polished bone. It was a hideous, skull-like head, misshapen and hairless. One side seemed to be crushed. Steele could see that its bottom jaw hung open at an angle that made it appear broken, and its eyes were sunk so far into its head they weren't visible. Unlike the slow, shuffling gait of the others, this one's movements were confident, fast. Steele and his companions stumbled backwards.

A prickling sensation on the back of Steele's neck prompted him to look over his shoulder, back the way he and Riley had come. He saw them at once. Four Maladroids. As they slunk along the side of the building Steele had seen in GM's knitting, they stood out like black stains against the dazzling white tiles. Soon they'd be on the bridge, sandwiching Steele and his companions between them and the creatures in front.

"More trouble," he said. "Four of them behind us."

Riley and Dirk looked.

"Where?" said Riley.

Dirk pointed. "There, by the Wrigley Building."

Steele glanced at Dirk sharply. How would he possibly know the name of the white building if he hadn't known where he was until Steele told him? Something was wrong. Since Dirk didn't seem to realize his little slip, Steele decided to keep the knowledge to himself for the time being. But he intended to keep a sharp eye on his old enemy.

He focused on the hoodless creature Dirk had called the Disciplinarian, wondering if the creature carried a weapon. It was impossible to tell what was beneath its long cloak.

Even its hands were lost in the loose sleeves. Steele reached over his shoulder and slowly removed his sword.

"Get your knife ready," he said to Riley.

"What about me?" said Dirk, holding out his hand.

"Don't give him a knife," hissed Riley.

Steele had no intention of putting a weapon in Dirk's hands. With his sword and Riley's knife, they might be able to take out two or three creatures, but not eleven. They didn't stand a chance. Unless . . .

"Listen," he said. "Even with our weapons, we can't fight them. Our only chance is to run. If we can make it back to the alley where we found Dirk, we might be able to lose them." He gripped Dirk's arm. "Those stairs in the passageway, where do they go?"

Dirk flashed him a sheepish look. "I don't know." He shrugged.

"What do you mean you don't know?" snapped Steele. "You were going to take us that way. You said the stairs were faster."

Dirk flushed and looked away. "I just wanted to get out of there, man. I was scared."

"Never mind him," said Riley. "I know where they go. I checked them out. The stairs turn left and go up about the same distance. At the top there are glass doors into a restaurant. The doors aren't locked."

"Excellent," said Steele, squeezing Riley's arm. "On my word, we make a run for it, back to the passageway and up the stairs, through the restaurant and, hopefully, out the other side. Then we duck into the next building and take one of the exits onto another street and disappear. We lose them in the buildings."

"There's one big flaw in your plan," said Riley. "If there's no exit at the other end of the restaurant, we'll be trapped."

She frowned, and Steele saw her eyes mist up with tears. He knew that she was thinking about the limo and wondering why Maddie Fey had abandoned them.

"There has to be a good explanation," he said, as much to reassure Riley as himself. "They wouldn't run away, Riley. They wouldn't leave us here."

Riley sniffled. "Where *are* they, then?"

Steele wished he knew. "We'll be OK," he said. And then he said it again as if he had to make himself believe it.

"Uh, guys," broke in Dirk. "I don't know what you're talking about, but if you're done, I suggest we get out of here."

"OK," said Steele. "RUN!"

Before the words left his mouth, Riley and Dirk were already bolting back along the street like stampeding buffalo. Then Steele was running too, skidding on the pavement as he rounded the sharp right turn into the passageway, the sounds of the Maladroids' unhurried pursuit muted by the pounding of his heart. He stopped abruptly and looked around the corner toward the bridge. The four Maladroids that had been slinking along the side of the Wrigley Building were halfway across the street, about to join the six from the bridge. Steele looked past them, scanning the bridge until his eyes distinguished the glowing white head from the haloes of the street lights. The Disciplinarian stood motionless in the shadows of the western tower. Steele couldn't see the creature's eyes, but he felt them boring into him, filling him with ice.

He turned and ran after his companions. When he reached the end of the passage, he raced up the stairs, taking the steps two at a time, silently thanking Riley for having checked them out. Halfway up, he caught up with Dirk, who was slumped forward, holding his sides and gasping for air. Steele stopped.

"Get up!" he urged, listening for their pursuers' steadily advancing footsteps. For a second, he wondered again why the creatures weren't racing after them. They were certainly bigger and probably faster than they appeared.

"Move!" Steele couldn't help but feel like the bully now as he yelled at Dirk, but it worked.

They made it to the top of the stairs and pushed through the glass doors. Dirk made a beeline for a similar pair of doors ahead in the distance. Steele paused and looked about. They were in a long, narrow restaurant. It reminded him of a dining car on a train, except that the walls and ceiling were constructed of glass. Along either side were round, white, heavy-looking tables, each with four white chairs. *But they can't be heavy*, thought Steele. *Otherwise they'd be hard to move around.* Down the middle of the restaurant was an aisle, the monotony broken by several tall Corinthian pillars painted dark like eggplant. Lush green plants spilled from wicker baskets suspended from hooks fastened to the narrow metal beams supporting the glass ceiling. It was a lovely place—a virtual greenhouse.

Dad would like this, Steele said to himself. Thinking of his father evoked a pang of loneliness in his chest and an overwhelming yearning to give up the search for Mac and the other missing kids and go straight home. Had his father played Steele's message? Steele could almost picture him sitting on the gilt settee in the living room, telling GM that Steele was alive.

A sound from the stairwell below drove thoughts of home from Steele's mind. He spun about and peered through the thick glass doors down the stairwell into the dim light. A shadow appeared on the floor, where the stairs turned left toward the restaurant, and spread onto the pale concrete wall, looming larger and larger until it bumped the ceiling. It spread over the concrete, soaking into it and darkening the grey stone like black ink on a blotter.

Horrified and fascinated at the same time, Steele couldn't pry his eyes off the slowing spreading blot. He knew that the first pursuer was only seconds behind its shadow, but he couldn't make himself move. His legs felt like blocks of lead. It was Riley who broke the spell by gently tugging on his arm and urging him to look away.

"I felt it too, on the bridge," she said. "It was horrible, like a bird mesmerized by a snake."

"Yeah." Steele could barely get the word out. His mouth and throat felt dry. For a moment, he felt he'd die if he didn't get a drink of water.

"Hurry," said Riley. "Dirk's gone ahead."

Steele nodded and followed Riley down the centre aisle. He thought about toppling the pillars into the path of the Maladroids, but as he dodged the first one he realized that their pursuers would have to dodge the pillars too. If he pushed them over, he'd only be making it easier for them to catch up. He didn't look back, but he sensed that the first creature had reached the top of the stairs and was just outside the glass doors, its eyes raking his back from the blackness beneath its loose hood. Fear spurred Steele to move faster. He looked for Dirk, but the bully was nowhere in sight. A horrible thought flashed into his mind. *It's a trap. Dirk's led us into a trap*. Realizing that it was too late to turn back now, he quickly chased the thought away, but he couldn't do anything about the bitter taste it left in his mouth.

Just before he reached the opposite end of the narrow restaurant, Steele grabbed one of the dining chairs and raised it over his head. It was heavier than he had thought and he almost dropped it. The wounds the worms had inflicted on his shoulders and upper arms reopened. He felt blood sticking to his shirt, but ignored it.

"Check the door. If it's locked, move aside and cover your face," he cautioned Riley.

"Put the chair down," protested Riley. "Dirk just went through these doors. They're not locked."

Unless Dirk locked them behind him, Steele said to himself, keeping a firm grip on the chair.

Riley reached for the bar across one of the doors and pushed. It opened with a sharp *click*. She pushed it open all the way and held it for Steele. Just before he stepped through, Steele turned and let the heavy chair drop from his arms. It landed on its side at the end of the aisle, creating a hurdle, albeit a minor one, for the creatures pursuing them. Then he was through the door and running alongside Riley down a darkened hallway in brooding silence, wondering how this night would end for them. At the end of the hallway, they turned left and scrambled up two flights of stairs, through another doorway into a narrow corridor. Steele kept his eyes peeled for Dirk. The feeling that his old enemy had run out on them continued to gnaw at his mind.

"Wait till I get my hands on him," he muttered.

No sooner had the words left his mouth than Dirk poked his head around a corner ahead and waved frantically. Steele felt a twinge of guilt over his suspicions. By the time they reached Dirk, he and Riley had to stop and catch their breaths.

But Dirk seemed anxious to be away. "If we go down there," he said, indicating more stairs, "we'll end up back outside. If all's clear, we'll cut through Tribune Tower and out one of the other exits."

Another slip, thought Steele.

Since Steele didn't know their final destination, he could only nod and follow Dirk's lead. They hadn't run far before they found themselves outside once again, dashing across a broad open space to the building next door. Steele recognized the building at once. So did Riley. It was the building they had entered to call Toronto.

"We're back where we started," she exclaimed, looking about, frustrated. "We've been running and running. We should be miles away from here by now." She flew at Dirk, her fists raised, pounding the air. "Where are you taking us? Around in circles, so your creepy friends can catch us?"

"Back off!" warned Dirk, raising his arms to ward off Riley's furious onslaught. He appealed to Steele. "Get her off me. I'm not trying to trick you, man. I'm trying to get us away from the Maladroids."

Steele pushed his way between Riley and Dirk and turned to Riley. She looked so different from the Riley he had known most of his life back home that his heart ached. Her once-sparkling green eyes were now like the eyes of the Moles in the tunnels under New York. Her face was thin and pale and, like GM, she seemed to have shrunk, for Steele noticed that her clothes looked two sizes too big.

Steele blinked to clear his stinging eyes. "Let him go, Riley," he said, wrapping his arms about her and speaking to her soothingly, the way he spoke to Pyrus. "It's OK. We'll be OK."

Riley broke down and sobbed uncontrollably against Steele's jacket. Dirk, who had moved off to the side, muttered under his breath and viciously assaulted a metal railing, kicking it again and again while glaring at Riley with such hatred in his eyes that it made Steele sick.

"Yuck!" Riley chose that moment to shriek and put some distance between herself and Steele. Flushing, she glowered at him, wiping her cheek furiously.

"What?" he asked innocently, throwing up his hands.

Riley continued to glower. And then to his surprise, she broke out laughing.

"What?" Steele repeated, and he found himself grinning and then he was laughing with her. It felt good.

"I thought you licked my face," she said, her eyes sparkling.

"Don't be disgusting," said Steele indignantly.

Riley giggled. "Exactly," she said. "But it wasn't you. It was Pyrus."

As if the sound of its name was the signal it had been waiting for, Pyrus emerged, almost guiltily, from the neck of Steele's jacket.

"What is that thing?" asked Dirk, hearing the laughter and catching sight of the salamander.

"His name's Pyrus," answered Steele.

"God, talk about ugly," said Dirk, his lips curling down in distaste. "Put it down on the ground and I'll put it out of its misery."

"Why don't you shut up!" shouted Riley, the sparkle in her eyes dimming and the laughter dying. "I wish someone would step on *you*."

"Jeez," muttered Dirk, assuming a pained expression. "Can't you take a joke?"

"Come on. We'd better keep moving," said Steele, wary once again. "If those Maladroids are still around, we probably just told them where we are." He turned to Dirk. "Where now?"

"There," said Dirk, pointing to the Tribune Tower. "Follow me. We'll take the stairs down and leave through one of the lower exits."

They ducked into the lobby and ran past the deserted information desk. Off to the right, Steele noticed that the telephone receiver he had used to call his father was dangling from its cord. He must have forgotten to replace it. They hurried along a narrow passage flanked on either side by a wall of elevators, the slap-slapping of their feet on the stone floor echoing loudly in the cavernous lobby. Stopping at the first elevator, Dirk reached for the down button. But before his finger connected, a clear *ping* shattered the quiet. They reacted instantly, their heads whipping toward the green light above one of the elevators on the wall just ahead.

Someone or something was inside the elevator, and it was about to come out.

A.D. 64

Fanned by the summer breezes, the fire roared as it leaped from one wooden structure to the next, consuming everything in its path. The conflagration grew. It climbed the seven hills and when there was nothing left, it turned and swept back down upon the city.

When we became aware of the larger fire in Rome, it was already too late. The fire had taken on a life of its own. It raged for nineteen day and twenty nights, and when it finally devoured itself, all that remained of Rome were ashes and bones.

—Excerpt from *The Wardens' Logs*

Chapter Six

Confusion

Steele and his companions stood transfixed, not daring to breathe. Their unblinking eyes were riveted on the elevator doors. The pungent smell of their own fear soured the air about them. Steele knew with absolute certainty that something terrible, something not human, was lurking inside the elevator, and that he and Riley and Dirk should flee at once, for their very lives depended upon it. He had to act now.

But then to his horror, he heard another elevator signal its arrival at the lobby level with its distinctive *ping*. He looked about for the lit-up indicator.

And *ping!* Another light flashed on. *Oh, no! Oh, no! Whoosh!*

With a sound like that of a brush rubbing over a rough wall, the doors of the first elevator parted in the middle and slid open. Too many things were happening simultaneously and Steele's mind reeled. He was vaguely conscious of pain in his right hand, but he wasn't aware that he was clutching Ees that tightly. He focused on the pitch-black interior of the elevator, momentarily reminded of the inside of Maddie Fey's limousine. Nothing happened. Nothing appeared.

Perhaps it's deserted like the rest of the building, Steele reasoned. Or perhaps all of the elevators were on a timer system, programmed to return to the lobby after a certain time had elapsed. . . . Then, from behind, he heard the patter of running footsteps and wheeled about just in time to see a figure break from one of the elevators and dash toward the revolving doors.

A boy.

Steele acted quickly. The boy might have seen what happened to Mac; he might even have been involved in the abduction. They mustn't let him get away. "Stop him!" he shouted, bounding after the kid.

The boy almost made it to the revolving doors before Steele tackled him and brought him down. Then Riley and Dirk fell on him, pinning him to the marble floor.

"If it's money you're after, you're wasting your time," said the boy, his voice muffled as he struggled to slide his head out from under Dirk's stomach. "I don't have any."

"We don't want your money," barked Steele indignantly, offended by the boy's assumption that they were thieves. "Who are you? What are you doing here?"

"Get off," demanded the boy.

The boy didn't seem to be the least bit intimidated by them. Steele and his companions slowly got up, but they watched the boy warily. Steele motioned to Dirk to station himself between them and the revolving doorway in case the boy bolted again. Dirk obeyed reluctantly, but Steele caught the angry look the bully flashed him before he turned away.

The boy pushed himself to his feet, brushed himself off, and slowly gave his attackers the once-over, his eyes finally resting on Steele. "Who are you?" he asked, studying Steele as if he were a specimen under a microscope.

Steele guessed that the boy was close to his own age, perhaps a year older. He was taller by a good inch, and his long, serious face was framed by straight, ear-length, rust-coloured hair. His blue eyes were clear and unwavering as they met Steele's. For some strange reason, Steele found himself liking the boy immediately. Besides, he couldn't argue with the boy's demand. Since they had attacked him, it was only fair to answer his question.

"I'm Steele," he said, and then introduced Riley and Dirk. "We're from Toronto." He thought for a second, working out how to tell the boy that they were being hunted by half-dead creatures and that he'd better get out of here before the Maladroids found them, without making him think they were mentally deranged. But no matter how he worded it in his mind he knew how *he'd* react to such a story.

"We're sorry for jumping on you," said Riley, coming to Steele's rescue. "We're trying to find our friend, Mac. He disappeared just outside. When we saw you running away, we thought you had something to do with it."

The boy shook his head. "It's too bad about your friend, but don't look at me. I haven't seen him. In fact, I haven't seen anyone since I got here . . . which is weird." He looked from Riley to Steele. "I'm Travis Culver. My dad works here."

"What is this place?" asked Steele, remembering that Dirk had let its name slip.

The boy's disdainful expression implied that Steele should know the answer, but then he seemed to remember that they were from Canada, for his expression changed.

"Trib Tower," he explained. "The newspaper. *The Chicago Tribune!* My dad's a reporter. So am I, sort of . . . well . . . not really. But I'm going to be . . . someday." He paused and looked thoughtful. "You say your friend went missing right outside this building?"

Steele nodded.

"About an hour ago," added Riley.

"There's something very strange going on," said Travis. "I usually walk here after school and wait for my Dad to finish work. But today, the streets were totally deserted. There was no traffic, no people, no kids, nothing. When I got here, everyone was gone. I waited and waited, thinking they were going to come back any minute, but when no one showed up I started to get really scared. I thought maybe something seriously catastrophic was going to happen—an asteroid or an attack—and they forgot to tell my school. Thinking of that totally freaked me out. I just wanted to get out of here as fast as I could. That's why I ran." He looked from Riley to Steele. "I'm real sorry about your friend, though." Suddenly his eyes lit up and he smacked his forehead with the palm of his hand. "Of course! Dad's research! The missing kids!"

Steele and Riley shared an incredulous glance.

Riley asked, "What do you know about the missing kids?"

Travis held up his hand. "Listen! This is going to sound weird, and I hope your friend's disappearance isn't connected, but in September, kids started to disappear in Chicago . . . a lot of kids—"

"Like Lara Mahoney and Kathy Lee O'Shea," cried Riley.

"And that boy, David something," said Steele. "Riley, you know. He went missing outside his school. The one whose sister said she wished he'd disappear."

"David Draken," said Riley.

Now Travis stared at Steele and Riley, his expression changing from astonished to suspicious. "What do you know about David and the girls in Libertyville? And you better tell the truth or I'll—"

"You don't have to threaten us," said Steele, keeping his voice calm. "We're trying to find the missing kids, too. I heard about the Libertyville girls on the news. Riley told me about David."

"Did you know them?" asked Riley.

Travis nodded. "David's a friend from school."

"Kids are missing in Toronto too, in case you haven't heard, and New York," continued Riley. "We had a theory that there was a connection between the missing kids in our city and those in other cities. Our research proved that we were right."

Travis whistled. Then he rummaged through his jacket pockets and pulled out a notebook that looked as if he had nibbled at all of the edges. "This is so freaky. My dad's working on a feature story about the Chicago missing kids. I've been doing research for *him*." Producing a pen from another pocket, he opened the notebook to a blank page, bent his head, and scribbled furiously.

"What are you doing?" asked Riley.

Travis grinned. "Making notes." He looked up, pen poised over the page. "Tell me more about this theory of yours. How did you come up with it in the first place?" Out of the corner of his eye Steele noticed Dirk inching closer. *To spy on us,* he thought. He desperately wanted to hear more about Travis's research, and talk about Mac and the missing Chicago kids, but he didn't want to do it within earshot of Dirk.

"Listen, Travis. We've got to talk . . . in private," he said quietly, rolling his eyes meaningfully toward Dirk. "Right now, though, we've got to get out of here. You better get away, too. There are some bad creatures after us. We managed to lose them in the building next door, but they'll find us if we hang about here much longer. We're going with Dirk; he said he knows where they've taken Mac. Write down your phone number, and we'll try to call you."

"I've got a better idea," said Travis. "Why don't I come with you? I know this area. I can help you . . . at least I'll make sure you don't end up getting lost."

"I've got an even better idea," snarled Dirk, coming up behind Travis. "Why don't *you* get lost before I break your skull?"

Travis looked at the bully scornfully. "What's your problem?" he countered. "I'd have thought you'd be happy to have your own personal guide."

"Yeah, Dirk," said Riley. "What's wrong with you? Travis can help us."

"Good," said Travis, smiling amicably at Dirk. "That settles it. I'm coming with you."

For a moment, Steele thought Dirk was going to explode with rage. The bully was shaking uncontrollably; his face turned a violent shade of red, his eyes narrowed, and his lips curled up in a snarl. Steele and Riley moved swiftly between Dirk and Travis.

"Back off, Dirk," warned Steele. "We need all the help we can get. What's wrong with you? Why don't you want Travis to come with us?"

Steele could see that Dirk was making an incredible effort to contain his anger. He breathed a sigh of relief when the other boy's body began to relax and the darkness slowly drained from his face, restoring his complexion to its natural tones. Steele wondered what was behind Dirk's aggressive behaviour toward Travis. Was he jealous? Did he feel that Steele and Riley had slighted him for the Chicago boy?

"Nothing's changed, Dirk," he said. "We're still in this together. We need you, too. You're the only one who can take us to Mac."

Dirk didn't answer, but he looked as if he wanted to spit in Steele's face. Instead, he turned on his heel and limped along the passageway, past the elevators, deeper into the building. Steele and the others raised their eyebrows at one another, shrugged, and followed.

As they hurried after Dirk, Travis asked, "What's with your friend?"

"He's not our friend," said Riley.

When Travis looked at her quizzically, she proceeded to tell him how Dirk had terrorized the students at Hillcrest Community School in general and Steele in particular from the moment he set foot on the school grounds over two years ago. "Until he disappeared over a week ago," she finished.

Steele took up the story. "Tonight when we were looking for Mac, we found Dirk instead. He was in an alley nearby, all bound with duct tape. He was pretty badly hurt. He said that the people who beat him up took Mac."

"Who are these people?" asked Travis.

"You don't want to know," said Riley.

"I'm serious," said Travis. "Who are they?"

Here goes, thought Steele. "We don't know who they are, but we were trying to get away from them when we ran into you. Actually they're not people and they're, uh, not exactly human."

He waited for Travis to burst out laughing, but the other boy surprised him.

"What do you mean they're not exactly human?"

"We don't know," Riley told him. "Dirk called them

Maladroids. They wear these long black cloaks with big floppy hoods. We couldn't see their faces."

"And you're saying these things nabbed your friend and are now after you?" The notebook reappeared in Travis's hand.

Steele and Riley nodded.

"I know it sounds incredible . . ." Steele began, but Travis cut him off.

"Chill, Steele," he said. "I believe you." He opened the notebook and wrote MALA-DEES in capital letters.

"It's Maladroids," Riley corrected him.

"I know." Travis grinned. "That's just a sort of shorthand. I do it a lot."

"But it's almost as long as the actual word," said Riley.

Steele was having second thoughts about bringing Travis with them. He liked him a lot, and he could tell that Riley liked him also. What if something happened to him? "What about your parents?" asked Steele. "Aren't they going to worry if you don't go home?"

Travis thought for a second. "I've been waiting in my dad's office since school got out. I don't know what's happened, but it's clear that something is terribly wrong in Chicago. My cell phone doesn't work, and when I tried calling home from Dad's office, all I heard were busy sounds and static. I can't go home. You probably noticed that the buses aren't running. And I'll bet it's the same for the subway. The way I see it, I have two choices. I can wait for my father to show up, or I can go with you and maybe we'll discover what happened to everyone. Maybe we'll find my dad."

"Why don't you leave him a note?" suggested Riley.

"Good idea," said Travis, tearing a page out of the middle of his notebook. Then he placed the page against the wall, and began writing. When he finished, he folded the sheet of paper in half. "Wait here. I'll leave it at the information desk. All of the reporters check there for their messages." He sped down the corridor toward the elevators.

Steele took advantage of Travis's absence to share his concerns with Riley.

"I don't think he'd listen if we told him he couldn't come with us," said Riley. "He'd probably follow us."

"Yeah," Steele agreed. "I just hope we're doing the right thing."

Travis returned shortly, red faced and short of breath. "It's done, so let's go before Dirk gets suspicious."

As they moved forward, Travis asked where Mac was being held.

Riley shook her head. "Dirk doesn't know the name of the place, but he said he could take us there."

Travis looked sceptical. "Do you trust him?"

"NO!" said Riley and Steele together.

"But we've got no choice," added Steele. "If he's telling the truth, it might be the only chance we have of finding Mac."

"And if he's lying . . . ?"

"I don't know," said Steele.

"If he's lying, I'll kill him," said Riley vehemently.

"Are you guys coming or what?" Dirk shouted from somewhere ahead.

"We've got a lot to talk about," said Travis, quickening his pace to keep up with Steele. "There's this girl in New York whose brother disappeared—" He stopped abruptly and stared from Steele to Riley. "What?"

"Sydney," Riley burst out. "You're talking about Sydney Ravenhurst."

Travis's mouth dropped. "How do you—?"

"We know her," Steele explained. "We were in New York before we came here. We helped her find her brother."

"No way! You've got to tell me everything."

"We will," promised Steele, "as soon as we get somewhere safe."

"I hope you have lots of paper in that notebook," said Riley. "You're going to need it."

Dirk was waiting near an exit, the scowl on his broad face a clear indication of his dark mood. "Keep up, or I'm out of here."

Steele and the others remained silent, but they rolled their eyes at one another the instant Dirk's back was turned. They followed close behind as Dirk pushed through the door and paused to glance both ways on the street. Realizing that they were no longer on the street that led to the bridge, Steele looked about for a street sign, but they were in the middle of the block.

Travis leaned close and spoke in Steele's ear. "We're on Illinois Avenue. It runs perpendicular to North Michigan where Trib Tower's main entrance is. We're heading east. I'd really like to know where he's taking us."

Dirk continued to scan the street and buildings on the opposite side carefully.

"Are we lost?" asked Riley.

But then Dirk took off again without answering. As the bully strode across the street confidently, Steele noticed that he was no longer limping. The others followed like well-trained soldiers. Moving quickly, they covered several blocks before Dirk stopped abruptly at the mouth of a narrow alley.

"Aha!" he announced triumphantly. "I remember now. This is the way we came." He pointed at a Dumpster parked against a brick and concrete building on the left, about half-way down the alley. "See that? There's a stupid drawing of an alien on the front and over it there's some writing. Check it out if you don't believe me." While his words were an invitation, the scowl on his face dared anyone to accept it.

"I'll check it out," said Travis, undaunted by the bully's threatening manner, and Steele found himself liking the Chicago boy more by the minute.

A moment later, Travis returned. "He's right about the Dumpster." Then he spoke to Dirk. "But you couldn't have come through the alley. It's a dead end. There's no way out."

"Are you calling me a liar?" said Dirk, his voice deadly quiet.

"No," said Travis quickly. "What I'm saying is you couldn't have come through the alley. It's impossible."

Steele waited for Dirk to speak, his eyes glued on the bully's face. *If he's lying, I'll know it.*

"There's a narrow opening just past the building at the far end," said Dirk. "You wouldn't know it was there unless you knew what to look for." He sneered. "You want to check that out too?"

How can he remember so much about an alley he saw only once? thought Steele.

Travis turned to Steele and Riley, grinning sheepishly. "I could be wrong. I've been to the end of the alley and back before. I go past it on my way from school. I don't remember any opening. But then, I've never looked for one."

"What do you think, Riley?" asked Steele.

"I don't like it," she answered promptly. "One of us should go and find the opening. The rest of us should wait here." She looked from Steele to Travis, but Travis was staring intently into the alley.

"There's someone there!" he said. "Look!"

The others peered into the alley, to the far end where a flashlight or some sort of lamp was weaving and swaying, drawing eerie patterns on the ground.

Riley gripped Steele's arm. "What if it's one of the Maladroids?" she said.

Steele placed his hand over hers. "Look how low the light is to the ground, Riley. It can't be a Maladroid, it's too small."

Without a word to the others, Dirk stepped into the alley and moved into the shadows against a wall. Then he crept cautiously toward the waving light. Steele and the others followed. It was so dark in the shadows that Steele could barely make out the person in front of him. They moved carefully to avoid stepping on broken bits of glass or accidentally kicking a can and announcing their presence to whatever was behind the light.

As they passed the Dumpster, a creature with a huge, round head and wide, bulbous eyes attached to the end of double pairs of antennae smiled at him. It was a goofy rendering of the artist's notion of an alien, and above it someone had printed in block letters: We Are Not Alone! Steele grimaced at the irony of it.

The air here was still; it reeked of garbage and the sharp smell of urine and vomit. With each step deeper into the narrow, confined space, Steele grew increasingly uneasy. He noticed that Pyrus, who had been squirming restlessly under his shirt, was also still, but tense. Steele kept glancing nervously over his shoulder, back to where the street lights brightened the broad avenue they had left behind. Once, he thought he saw a shadow drift into the mouth of the alley, but when he blinked it was gone.

"Stop imagining things," he scolded himself. "Stay alert."

They stopped about ten feet from the end of the alley and huddled against the wall, watching in silence as the light danced before their eyes. When Steele couldn't stand the suspense any longer, he said to the others, "I need to get closer. Wait here. And be quiet."

"Be careful," cautioned Riley, as he slipped ahead and inched along the wall.

He had taken only a few steps when the figure, who Steele now realized was sitting on some steps leading up to a barred door, abruptly directed the light beam in his direction and began playing it slowly at the shadows along the wall just ahead. Steele froze, pressing his body flat against the bricks. He sucked in his breath and threw an arm across his face.

Don't let it spot me, he pleaded silently.

"Wh-Who's th-there?" asked the figure, trying but failing to sound fearless.

The voice was as familiar to Steele as the sound of his own name.

Behind Steele, Riley gasped. "Mac!"

The sound of Mac's voice brought tears to Steele's eyes. He roughly brushed them away on his sleeve. When Mac had disappeared, he had felt as if a part of himself had gone missing. He remembered how afraid he'd been for his friend, how desperately he had raced about trying to find him. And he remembered the promise he'd made. He said it now, under his breath: "I'll never stop looking until I find you." He had meant every word. He welcomed the numbness that flowed through him now as he stared at the forlorn figure on the steps, his eyes settling on the mop of dazzling white hair.

Riley brushed against him as she rushed past, sobbing and

laughing at the same time. Steele reached out and caught hold of her arm, stopping her in her tracks.

"It's Mac, Steele. I can't believe we found him," Riley cried. Then she laughed again and tried to free her arm from Steele's strong grasp. "Let me go. I'm going to murder him for getting lost and scaring us like that."

"That *thing*," Steele said quietly, "is not Mac."

Questions

During their long evolution in the fires that form the core of this planet, the Tsilihin remained creatures of instinct. They were incapable of tactical planning. As purely instinctual creatures, they attacked wantonly. The planned strikes on Rome and other cities puzzled us.

We asked ourselves the same question again and again. Who or what was organizing our prisoners?

Because Pompeii and other cities lay buried under millions of tons of rock and ash, we would find no answers there. That left Rome. But fifteen years had passed since the great fire. Would Rome speak to us?

—Excerpt from *The Wardens' Logs*

Chapter Seven

Into the Fire

Despite the darkness, Steele watched Riley's face turn grey, like slush.

"You're wrong." Her eyes kept shifting from Steele to Mac. "Steele, it's Mac." Then she went as still as the air in the alley. "Oh God! You think it's like Wood all over again, don't you!"

Steele nodded unhappily.

"Are you saying that kid on the steps is wood?" Travis sounded as if he wasn't sure he wanted to know the answer.

"Not that sort of wood," said Riley shortly.

Steele explained. "There's some weird stuff you don't know yet. We were going to tell you later, but some of it you need to know now. Sydney Ravenhurst had this friend named Wood who was helping her find her brother. Wood was killed by a . . . by something even worse than the Maladroids. But we never suspected anything because the thing that killed Wood . . . well . . . it sort of took over his body." He studied Travis's face, but his expression was hard to read. He wanted Travis to believe him.

Travis backed away. "Are you telling me that the boy over there isn't your friend but some sort of creature that has taken over his body?"

"I know it sounds crazy, but it's true," said Steele. "It looks like Mac, but it's not him. It's nothing like him. It's evil and dangerous."

"You're not serious. . . ." Travis sounded more amused than alarmed, but he took another step backwards. "It doesn't *look* very dangerous."

"You're right," Steele agreed. "But we've fought others like it. Trust me, Travis. It's dangerous."

"But . . . what exactly is it? Some sort of . . . but no, you said it was worse than a Mala-dee—"

"Be quiet!" Steele cut him off and raised his hand for silence. He had heard a sound coming from the creature on the steps—a sound like a rising wind. He stared at the thing that looked like Mac, but wasn't. Before, if anyone had suggested that the very sight of Mac would cause him to break out in a cold sweat, Steele would have died laughing. *But this isn't Mac,* he reminded himself. *This creature wants me dead.*

Ssssteeeellll! No longer bothering to sound like Mac, the thing breathed in Steele's mind. *Ssssteeeellll!*

Pain exploded in Steele's right temple, driving him to his knees on the glass-strewn ground. Beneath his shirt, as if he were also in pain, Pyrus went berserk, racing up Steele's back, over his shoulders, and across his chest, his sharp claws digging into Steele's flesh.

"Steele! What is it?" cried Riley, coming to help him.

"It's calling me," groaned Steele.

Riley grabbed an arm and helped him stand, glowering at Travis, who was keeping a safe distance from them.

"Go and hide," Steele warned, pressing his hand against his right temple to ease the sharp pain.

"What about you?" asked Travis, who seemed to be withering under Riley's stern gaze. "What are you going to do?"

Steele looked at him, but it was Mac's face swimming before his eyes.

Travis appealed to Riley. "Why isn't he coming with us? What's he going to do?"

"Come *on*," said Riley, taking his arm. "We've got to hide."

She and Travis ran back to the Dumpster and squeezed into the tight space between it and the wall. Steele watched until they disappeared from sight. Feeling terribly alone, he turned back, just as the Mac-thing began to rise slowly from the steps. The creature opened its mouth, like a furnace door, and the roaring of the fire within grew in volume until Steele feared that his eardrums would burst. As if to moisten parched lips, a thin orange tongue darted from the thing's open mouth and licked from side to side, melting the flesh away from its lips and turning its white teeth to blackened stumps.

When Mac's pale eyes exploded with a *pop-pop,* Steele yelled, even as he gagged. The sight of his friend's familiar face cracking and peeling away was more than he could bear. Frantic, he ripped off his gloves, threw them on the ground, and fumbled at the open neck of his jacket where Pyrus crouched in the hollow of his collarbone.

"I'm sorry, Pyrus," he said, gently extracting the salamander and wishing he had thought to give him to Riley. "I've got to let you go." He dropped onto his heels and set Pyrus on the ground. "Go to Riley," he said, knowing that Pyrus, though staring at Steele with bright intelligent eyes, didn't understand. Instead of darting to freedom, Pyrus raced up Steele's leg and clung to the top of his boot. Steele lifted his foot and tried to shake him loose, but Pyrus held on as if glued in place.

"Go, you stupid salamander," sobbed Steele. "Go!"

The Fire Demon laughed—a horrible cracking, shattering sound. Steele forgot about Pyrus. He forgot about Riley and Travis. He forgot about Mac. He forgot everything as he reached over his shoulder and slid his sword free. Then he pulled Ees from about his neck and focused all of his attention on trying to repeat what he had done in the abandoned railway station under New York. Then, he had drawn the oxygen fuelling the Fire Demon from the air and suffocated it. Could he do it now?

Ees felt cool in his hot, sweaty palm. Clutching both the sword and the medallion tightly, he moved closer to the Fire Demon, breathing deeply, filling his lungs with the smoke-saturated air about him. The heat from the creature was almost unbearable, but he had to get close enough to use his magic to construct an airtight dome over himself and the Fire Demon. His body was soaked with sweat, but at least he wasn't burning.

No! said a voice in his mind impatiently. *You must go into the fire!*

Steele's entire being rebelled at what the voice was telling him to do. "I can't!" he screamed aloud.

Go into the fire!

"No! I can't! I'll burn up. I won't."

Steele didn't know if it was his own voice in his head or another's. All he knew was that if he took one step closer to the fiery monster he'd be burned alive.

Steele!

The voice hurt like a bullet penetrating his brain. "Stop! Stop! I have to do it my way!"

Your way won't work. You must go into the fire.

And then he lost all control over his physical body. As if they had a mind of their own, his legs moved toward the Mac that no longer resembled Mac. The clothes the Mac-thing had worn moments ago were gone, burned to ashes. The last bits of flesh that had concealed its hideous form were flaking from its mass and drifting in the night air like black snowflakes. As Steele's legs took him ever closer, the dazzling white hair that distinguished Mac more than any other feature ignited and vanished in a puff of flames and smoke.

Do not be afraid!

But Steele barely heard the words. He raised his arm, pointing the tip of the sword at the Fire Demon. Tightening his hold on Ees, he squeezed his eyes shut and, with a wild yell, charged straight into the living inferno, his body tensed to absorb the flesh-melting heat. The last thing he saw before he closed his eyes was Pyrus clinging to the toe of his boot like a hood ornament.

Then the screaming started.

"Is he dead?" The girl sounded sad and scared and angry at the same time.

Steele opened his eyes and blinked up into the frightened eyes of Riley and Travis. Their faces were so pale, the thought crossed his mind that they, not he, were dead.

"I'm alive." His voice was raspy in his dry throat.

Steele felt faint touches on his face and realized they were snowflakes, fat, lazy flakes that melted almost the instant they landed. He rolled onto his side and coughed, choking on the black guck he had inhaled in the fire. When the fit left him, his friends helped him up. He knew he was too weak or too exhausted, or both, to stand on his own. As he wiped his face with his hands, he was amazed that he felt no physical pain at all. He looked down at his soot-caked clothes and the blackened flesh on the backs of his bare hands. His sword lay on the ground at his feet. Holding onto Riley, he bent and retrieved it.

Riley took it from him, turned him around, and slid the sword into the backpack he was wearing.

"I can't believe you're still alive," she said, echoing the thought that was uppermost in Steele's mind.

Steele nodded, afraid to speak for fear of inducing another coughing fit. With a start, he remembered Pyrus. The salamander was no longer clinging to his boot. He turned away from the others and covered his face with his hands, his eyes swimming with tears.

"Is this what you're looking for?" said Riley, freeing Pyrus from the folds of her scarf and holding him out to Steele in trembling hands. "He's OK. He must have run away, and returned when you destroyed the Fire Demon. We found him on your stomach, trying to wriggle under your jacket. He was a bit stunned and very sooty, but he's fine now." She looked at her filthy scarf doubtfully. "I think I got most of the soot off."

Steele gently took Pyrus and held him up to his face. "Stupid salamander!"

Pyrus licked a snowflake from the tip of Steele's nose.

Travis was staring at Steele as if he were a ghost. He hadn't uttered a word since Steele regained consciousness, but now he swallowed loudly and opened his mouth. "Would someone please tell me that I didn't see what I just saw."

Blinking the tears from his eyes, Steele dropped Pyrus down his neck and looked at Travis. "What *did* happen? I don't remember anything after I charged at that creature."

Riley thrust her shaking hands into the pockets of her jacket, but she couldn't hide her trembling lips. "What were you thinking? I almost had a heart attack when you disappeared into that thing."

Steele shook his head sadly. "I'm sorry you were scared, Riley. But it wasn't me. I heard a voice telling me to go into the fire. I didn't want to. In fact, I tried to fight it, but it was too strong."

"No one could live through that," breathed Travis. "You should be fried."

"Travis, Steele's a Mage," explained Riley patiently. "That's why he—"

"A what?" Travis asked incredulously.

"A Mage," Riley repeated. "He's got magic, and . . . uh, well, he's the only person on Earth who can destroy the Fire Demons."

"I don't believe you, Riley. You're just making that up."

"I can't destroy all of the Fire Demons, but the Mage part is true," said Steele, flushing. "I'm just not a very good Mage yet." He examined his hands and then held them up. "Look! They're not even blistered."

Travis seized one of Steele's hands and examined it from back to palm. "That's impossible," he said in awe.

"You might not have any blisters, but you could sure use a bath," said Riley, wrinkling her nose. "You stink."

"I'm so confused," admitted Travis. "If I hadn't seen your friend turn into that horrible fiery thing, I would never have believed such a thing, not in a million years."

"It's a Fire Demon," said Riley.

Travis waved his hand in front of his face as if to shoo away mosquitoes. "Steele, when you ran at that Fire Demon thing, you disappeared, and it started to grow. It got really huge—didn't it, Riley?"

Riley nodded and jumped in. "It grew into this humongous fireball, and the alley got as hot as a furnace. The Dumpster and the wall were so hot we had to get out of there and find someplace else to hide."

"Right," said Travis, bright-eyed. "And then the Fire Demon started exploding. Whoa, man! You should have seen it. It was like a volcano. Great gobs of magma stuff were flying all over the place." He stopped and let Riley continue.

"And you should have heard it screaming. It screamed and screamed. I thought it would never stop. But it did, finally. It sizzled and bubbled and made these awful choking, gurgling noises and then its fire sputtered and died. When the smoke started to clear away, there was nothing left except you and Pyrus."

"You were awesome," Travis said, staring as if he had discovered hidden depths to Steele. "I wouldn't have walked into that fire for all the money in the world. But I still don't understand how you knew it wouldn't burn you."

"I didn't, not really," said Steele. "I destroyed one of the Fire Demons in New York and it didn't burn me then. But with this one, I wasn't sure what it would do. Besides, I already told you something was pushing me into the fire. When I realized I couldn't make myself stop, I just hurried it along."

"Didn't you feel anything?"

Steele nodded slowly. "I felt the heat, Travis. I felt that my skin was melting." He wrapped his arms about his chest. "It didn't burn me, but it hurt worse than anything."

"Please tell me everything now," said Travis. "The suspense is driving me crazy."

"There's a lot to tell," said Steele. "But it'll have to wait." He glanced about, peering into the shadows, feeling uneasy again. Had he overlooked something important? "Where's Dirk?" he asked suddenly.

They walked about searching for Dirk, but there was no sign of him.

"I don't remember seeing him after we entered the alley," said Riley. "Knowing him, he probably slithered under a rock."

Travis shook his head. "I saw him just before Riley and I ran to hide behind the Dumpster. He was over there." He pointed in the direction of the narrow opening Dirk had described so graphically.

"Come on," said Steele, so exhausted that he couldn't hold back a yawn. "I've had quite enough of this place. Let's find Dirk and get out of here. Travis, do you know a safe place where we can get some food and spend the rest of the night? I'm beat and starving, in that order."

"Oh, Travis, please make it a place with a bath," pleaded Riley.

Travis nodded sympathetically. Then he added mischievously, "I think I can find us something. There are several five-star hotels in the area."

"We haven't even got enough money for a *no-star* hotel," cried Riley.

Steele laughed. "Riley, the whole of downtown is deserted. The hotels are empty."

"Oh," exclaimed Riley, her eyes lighting up. "I get it. We're going to stay but we're not going to pay." She giggled and gripped Travis's arm. "You're a genius."

"I don't know about that," said Travis, "But I sure hope

my parents are in a hotel somewhere. I don't like not knowing where they are."

They stood together for a moment longer, staring at the
smouldering ashes—all that remained of the Fire Demon and
the wooden steps. Despite the darkness, Steele could see that
the outsides of the buildings flanking the alley were charred
and black. The smell was overpowering. It found its way into
their eyes and throats, making them cough violently, and all
the while, tears trickled from their stinging eyes and streaked
their blackened faces.

Anxious to find soft beds, warm baths, and food to fill
their empty stomachs, they turned away and walked quickly
toward the last building on the right. Riley sprinted ahead
and reached the end of the building first.

"Go back!" she cried out in disgust. "Dirk lied. There's no
way out."

Steele's mind raced as he frantically tried to fit the pieces of
the puzzle together. So Dirk had lied about the opening. No
surprise there. Why? *That's easy*, he thought. *To get us in here,
that's why.* But if that was true, Dirk had to have known that
the Fire Demon would be waiting for them. That could mean
only one thing: Dirk was involved with the Fire Demons. The
notion seemed ridiculous, but it was the only thing that made
sense. What didn't make sense was what Dirk had hoped
to achieve by leading them into the alley. They could easily
escape. All they had to do was turn around and race back
to the street, as they were doing now. Once there, they could
duck into one of the deserted buildings and get away.

A horrible thought popped into his head. He stopped suddenly, aware that Riley and Travis were staring at him, their
expressions a strange mixture of surprise and fear.

"It's a trap," he said, reaching for their arms and looking from one to the other. "Dirk went back for the others."

"No!" Riley cried out.

"We've got to reach the street," cried Travis. "It's our only hope."

"No!" said Steele quietly. "It's too late."

As one, they looked toward the light at the mouth of the alley. They spotted Dirk at once, pressed flat against the wall, out of the path of the black-clad figures pouring slowly into the alley from the street beyond. Steele and his friends stood there by the Dumpster, frozen.

"Mala-dees?" Travis's whisper went unanswered.

"There must be another way out of here," said Steele a moment later. "Look for a fire escape."

He studied the Dumpster, seeking a way up. Ignoring the graffiti of the alien grinning stupidly at him, he scanned the wall above and behind the Dumpster. But there were no doors or windows or ledges. There was no way out of the lane except through the creatures blocking the entrance.

Suddenly aware of a shift in the dynamic among the Maladroids, Steele turned toward the mouth of the alley just as the dark figures shuffled to either side and went as still as if they had been petrified. A deep and oppressive silence spread over the gathering. A lone hoodless figure appeared at the entrance, sending a blast of cold air before it that swept through the passage and chilled Steele and his companions to the bone. It was the lone creature that had appeared on the bridge, the one Dirk called the Disciplinarian!

From where Steele was standing, the leader of the Maladroids was so much larger than the others that it blotted out the light from the street behind. It paused in the entrance, its stark white head rotating slowly from side to side and then stopping abruptly to stare straight ahead to where Steele and his friends stood rooted in terror, their hearts ticking like bombs in their chests.

Steele gulped. The ten Maladroids didn't scare him a fraction as much as the lone figure. He sensed intuitively that, while the other creatures were undeniably dangerous, their combined strength fell far short of that of their leader.

"What are we going to do?" wailed Riley.

"I'm not giving up without a fight," said Travis.

Steele touched his shoulder. "There are too many of them, Travis. We can't fight them all."

"What, then?" cried Riley. "We can't just give up."

"No, Riley," said Steele. "Remember what I said on the bridge? They're big and awkward."

"And slow," added Riley.

"And slow," agreed Steele. "We can outrun them. If we wait until they're almost on us and then split up and charge between them, we should be able to get past them." He looked from Riley to Travis. "The Disciplinarian's the one we have to watch out for, so steer clear of it."

Travis's face took on a determined expression. "Let's do it."

It was a good plan, but they never got the chance to execute it. At that moment, they heard thumping sounds behind them and on either side. They wheeled about to see giant black shapes closing in from behind, and others leaping from somewhere high above them and landing heavily on the ground.

And then the creatures were upon them and Steele's world went as black as the soot on his hands.

A.D. 79

A grand city of stone and marble had risen from the ashes. All that remained of the Great Fire were memories. But memories helped us. From memories, we learned that the Emperor of the new Imperial City had blamed the fire on a certain sector of the population and had publicly fed them to the lions or had dressed them in tunica molesta, the naptha-impregnated shirt of death.

But the Emperor was dead now, by his own hand.

And the people believed that their Emperor had summoned a shadow from the depths of Hell to rain death and destruction down upon his enemies.

—Excerpt from *The Wardens' Logs*

Chapter Eight

Caught

Steele wrapped his legs about the thick limb and inched forward until he had an unobstructed view of the Wytch. Perched motionless on her stone bench in the darkening evening, she was a hulking presence. Steele could hear the familiar sound of water trickling from the open mouth of the serpent coiled about the Wytch's raised arm. Steele had climbed the old maple tree over an hour ago after spotting one of the Maladroids slipping furtively through the gate into the park. He had spied on the creature as it tore away the metal grate at the edge of the worn footpath skirting Taddle Pond, and had watched in horror as others of its kind crawled out of the drain and melted into the shadows.

A twig snapping near the base of the tree warned Steele of the presence of at least one of the creatures below. Slowly parting the thick leaves with his hand, he peered down, but saw nothing. He was just about to exhale the breath he had been holding when he detected a slight movement. Something was there, its body pressed against the trunk of the tree directly beneath him. The nearness of the thing left a cold hollow place in the pit of Steele's stomach. What if it looked up? Steele forced himself to remain still, to become one with the tree. Above, a bird stirred on its branch. A door slammed. Steele recognized the distinctive sound of his own back door, and a moment later he heard footsteps thudding along the road.

"Steele!" His father's deep voice resounded through the park. "Time to come in!"

Heart sinking, Steele listened to the footsteps growing louder as his father came nearer. Then they slowed and stopped. *He's at the top of the ravine.*

Go home! Steele pleaded silently. *Please, Dad! Turn back!*

The suspense was unbearable. Would his father turn back to the house as he usually did after calling Steele or would he, this one time, take the footpath to search for Steele down by Taddle Pond?

For the first time in his life, Steele was afraid for his father. His father was big and calm and strong, afraid of nothing; his solid, sensible presence was a constant in Steele's life— as fixed as the moon's orbit around Earth. But he was no match for the Maladroids. They could snap him in half as easily as if he were a dry twig. The sudden realization of his father's mortality hit Steele hard, like a jab in the gut from Dirk's baseball bat, leaving him nauseated. In an instant, the safe haven he had taken for granted burst like a bubble, and another little part of his adolescent world was gone, never to be recaptured.

Steele felt the tension mounting in the air as he, and the Maladroid below, waited for his father's next move. Then he heard his father's shoes slipping down the path.

I've got to warn him.

Eyes glued to a small stretch of path visible through the leaves, Steele watched for his father's familiar figure to come into view. He almost fell out of the tree when a larger figure appeared on the path. As he stared at the figure's hoodless white head, it seemed vaguely familiar.

Where's Dad?

Within seconds, Steele heard the rustle of the creature's cloak brushing over dead leaves as it approached the tree. He stopped breathing, and watched it coming closer. With a mixture of fear and horror, he remembered where he had seen the creature before—in Chicago, on the bridge and again in the darkened lane. Dirk had given it a name.

The Disciplinarian.

The Disciplinarian moved directly to the foot of the tree, and without hesitating, began to climb. Steele felt cold sweat trickling down the back of his neck.

Quick! Do something! But Steele couldn't move; he could only stare at the dome of the glowing white head growing bigger as the Disciplinarian climbed steadily closer. Even now, if the Disciplinarian stretched its arms up, it could touch Steele's legs. As if it felt Steele's eyes burning into it, the creature tilted its head back and looked up.

Steele screamed as he stared into a pair of red eyes burning in the scarred face of the Prince of Darkness. He tried to slither backwards, but the tree and the leaves were out of focus. He lost his hold on the limb and fell, and the ground rushing up to meet him was spinning like a top.

"Dad! Dad! Help me!"

Steele sat up with a start, his heart racing. "Uhhh!" he groaned, slumping forward and covering his face with his hands. The dream had seemed so real that he was actually trembling. He couldn't erase the image of the Prince of Darkness from his mind.

Dropping his hands, he took in the surroundings, carefully surveying his situation. He was in the middle of the floor, in a narrow room . . . *or cell,* he corrected, noticing the thick bars across one wall. There were no light switches or fixtures that he could see, but weak light from somewhere deep along the outer passageway reached several feet into the chamber, casting pale barred shadows on the concrete floor. The air was stale and reeked of a mix of sweat, mildew, and urine. The dark walls were smeared with something darker. Steele put his hand on the floor and found that it was sticky.

He looked toward the back of the cell and saw Riley, propped up against the wall, her head lolling forward on her chest. In the corner, Travis was rocking back and forth holding his head between his hands and moaning softly. His notebook lay open on the floor beside him, but Steele noticed that the page was blank.

Steele crawled over to Riley, gently saying her name as he lifted her head and brushed her straggly hair from her face. She was out cold, but the strong pulse on the side of her neck told Steele that she was alive. Should he awaken her? She looked so peaceful that he didn't have the heart to disturb her. But if the Maladroids had hit her on the head, if she were concussed, he shouldn't let her sleep too long. Determined to keep an eye on her, he moved on to Travis.

"What happened?" moaned Travis, opening his eyes and squinting at Steele. "Oh, man. I feel rotten."

"You look it, too," said Steele.

"So do you," countered Travis. "What were you shouting at?"

"Someone might be listening, so keep your voice down," warned Steele, tilting his head toward the corridor. Then, after he told Travis about the Prince of Darkness and the

Disciplinarian, he described the dream. "It's so weird the way things unfold in dreams, like the way the Disciplinarian turned into the Prince of Darkness."

After a while Travis said, "It could be true."

"What?"

"Your dream. Maybe the Disciplinarian *is* the Prince of Darkness."

Steele rejected the notion immediately. "Don't ask me how . . . it's sort of complicated . . . but I'd have known if it was the Prince of Darkness the moment he showed up on the bridge. No. It was just a crazy dream. They don't share the same body, but I've got a feeling they're connected somehow."

Travis groaned and looked about. "What is this place?" He rested his head against the wall, closed his eyes, and took a long breath. "From the smell, it's definitely not the five-star hotel I promised you."

"It could be an old prison," said Steele. "There are no windows, so we must be underground."

"I wish my dad was here. He'd know what to do." Travis swallowed audibly. "What do you think they're going to do to us?"

Despite the fact that Travis had invited himself into the group, Steele felt responsible for what had happened to him. "Did I mention that being around me could be dangerous? I shouldn't have let you come with us, Travis. I mean, you've known me for only a few hours and you've already been captured by creatures that aren't exactly human, and thrown in prison. And you're probably still weirding out over the Maladroids, and especially that Fire Demon."

"It's not your fault," said Travis, opening one eye. Then he grinned crookedly. "Besides, you warned me about those

Mala-dees that were after you. And you tried to warn me about the Fire Demon, but I sort of didn't believe you."

Steele grinned at Travis's name for the Maladroids. "Sometimes I'm not sure I believe myself."

He got up and prowled restlessly about the cell, examining the walls for weaknesses and gripping the bars in both hands, shaking them back and forth and up and down to test for loose ones. Once he looked back to check on his companions, but Riley was still out of it and Travis's head was bowed over his tattered notebook, so he turned away and resumed his inspection of their prison.

He scrutinized every square inch of the floor, walls, and ceiling. Then he moved back to the front of the cell and retested the bars one by one, only to confirm what he had already suspected. There was no escape. Weary and disappointed, he sank to the floor, his back against the bars, and stared at his companions without really seeing them. His fears for Mac, which he had driven into a dark corner of his mind, broke through his defences and consumed him.

What had happened to Mac? Was he locked away in a cell in this very building? Had the Fire Demon used its shape-changing magic to morph into a Mac look-alike? Or . . . Steele braced himself for the unspeakable question.

"Mac's dead, isn't he?"

Steele blinked, momentarily confused. Then he realized that the flat, unemotional voice that had uttered the dreaded words belonged to Riley. He got up and hurried to her side.

"Are you OK?" he asked, dropping beside her.

"No," Riley answered at once, avoiding his eyes. Then she shrugged. "I guess. Tell me the truth, Steele. Do you think Mac's dead?"

"I don't know. I guess I don't want to go there . . . yet. I can't."

Riley's face was even more ashen than it had been back in the alley. Her skin seemed almost translucent.

"Are you sure you're OK?" asked Steele again. "You were asleep for such a long time, I was worried about you."

"I wish I could stay asleep forever." Riley curled up on her side on the floor, her knees against her chest, and closed her eyes.

Steele bent over until his lips brushed her ear. "Don't say anything important unless you whisper. Someone might be listening."

When she didn't respond, Steele sighed and sat back against the wall. Riley was suffering and he didn't know what to do for her. But as he watched her, a frightening thing began to happen. Riley disappeared, and in the spot where she had been lying, there was complete and utter blackness. Steele recoiled, shaken, his heart thumping. At first, he was certain he had gone blind, but then he saw a ring of hideous, fanged creatures writhing about a small figure cowering in the centre of the ring. The creatures opened their mouths and spat fire at the figure, whose screams made Steele's hair stand on end.

He knew then that somehow, unintentionally, he had done something so unforgivable that he wouldn't blame Riley if she never spoke to him again.

He had opened a window into her mind.

Riley must have sensed the intrusion because in an instant she was up and on her feet. "What was that? Was it you?" She glared down at Steele, her face reflecting her outrage.

Steele pushed himself up. "Shh!" He didn't want her

saying anything about magic in case someone was listening. "Sorry," he said.

Riley opened her mouth. At first, Steele thought she was going to yell at him, but he breathed a sigh of relief when she spoke quietly, even though he could see the anger still etched in deep lines on her face.

"What happened?"

The expression on Steele's face must have told her that he was as distressed as she, because when she opened her mouth again, she no longer looked angry.

"I don't understand. You were there . . . in my head. How did you do that?"

Steele shook his head and leaned close to her. "I don't know," he said, so softly he could barely hear his own words. "It just happened. I was looking at you, and I felt so sad I couldn't stand it. Then everything went black and I could hear your thoughts . . . or see them . . ." His voice trailed off.

Riley stared at him in silence for a long time, then she shuddered. "I never want to feel like that again. Someone coming into my head like that . . . I felt it at once . . . it was horrible."

"I don't understand what's happening to me, Riley," said Steele. "I didn't ask to be a Mage. I'm supposed to have powers, but I don't know how to use them. So far, they seem to be using me. I hated seeing you so sad. I think I was so desperate to make things right . . . you know . . . about Mac and everything . . ." He stopped, unable to explain what he meant. "I just want you to know that I didn't do it on purpose. I'd never try to read anyone's mind."

"I know," said Riley. "Just promise that it won't happen again."

"I can't," said Steele miserably. "Until I learn more about the magic and how to control it, I can't promise anything. But you've got to believe me. I didn't want to go there."

It seemed like hours before Riley said, "I believe you."

"It's scary to think that the magic might obey my unconscious mind. What if it misinterprets everything I'm thinking, and does the wrong thing?"

"Like?"

"Like what just happened. What if it happens again? What if whenever I'm worried about someone or thinking about them, I end up in their mind?"

"You'd soon have no friends left," Riley said, but not unkindly. Then her eyes lit up with an idea. "Listen! What if you could get into Mac's mind? Think of it, Steele. Maybe that's how we can find him."

"Excuse me," said Travis, startling his companions. "I can't hear you when you're whispering. So now that we're all awake, tell me what's going on."

Steele motioned Travis over and said, "We know for sure that Dirk is involved with the Maladroids. We know that the Disciplinarian is their leader. We also know that they have a connection to the Fire Demons. I mean, that Fire Demon in the alley couldn't have been a coincidence. Could it? No. Dirk led us right to it. I think he thought it would destroy us. When I destroyed it, he went and got the others. Before we—"

Travis interrupted. "If the Fire Demon was supposed to destroy us, why didn't the Mala-dees kill us instead of taking us here?"

"Good point," said Steele. "I haven't got a clue. But something must have happened. Maybe their orders got changed."

He gripped Travis's shoulder. "Before we tell you what we've been doing, I want you to understand how everything is linked—the empty streets, Mac's abduction, the missing kids, the Fire Demons, the Maladroids, Dirk—everything." He paused and looked through the bars. "I don't know if anyone is listening to us, but I think we're dealing with magic, and we've got to be careful and not say anything out loud about some of the stuff we're going to tell you."

They huddled in a circle on the floor, heads bowed and almost touching, while Steele and Riley, speaking in hushed voices, shared their adventures with Travis. They scraped their boots on the floor to make it difficult for anyone who might be listening in on their conversation to eavesdrop. Steele did most of the telling, with Riley filling in the gaps and keeping him focused on events as they had happened.

Steele began with that November evening when he heard the voice of the Prince of Darkness coming from the grate at the edge of Taddle Pond. He told about Ryan Massey's disappearance and how he, Riley, and Mac set out to find a connection between kids who had gone missing in Canada and in the United States.

"Don't forget the horrible face we saw in the grate near Taddle Pond the day after Dirk disappeared," Riley reminded him.

Like Steele's father, Travis was a good listener. He didn't interrupt once as Steele and Riley shared their adventures with him, but his eyes grew wider when Steele got to the mysterious letter in his smashed guitar and the midnight assignation with Maddie Fey and her alien companions, Wish, the Arjellan Great Hound with its spooky eyes, and Nilats, the nasty red rat. And they grew wider still when Riley told how Maddie Fey had come to Earth to search for the lost wardens, and to find Steele because she believed he possessed magic that would destroy the Fire Demons.

He didn't interrupt when Riley described the missing wardens.

"Maddie Fey said they're like dragons, only much grander. Their scales are gold like the sun or silver like the moon. And they have powerful wings and sharp, sharp claws."

And Travis remained silent when Steele revealed that the many doors in Maddie Fey's long black limousine were portals into other cities and, perhaps, even worlds. By the time Steele finished telling about the Fire Demons exploding out of the earth on Park Avenue, and the great battle between the Moles and the worms in the tunnels under New York City, Travis's eyes had grown so enormous, Steele was afraid that they might fall out of his head.

With Riley's prompting, Steele shared everything with Travis. He told him where they had found the missing kids, and how Fidus had rescued them.

"Just in time, too," said Riley, the words tumbling from her mouth in a rush. "The worms were coming to eat them. And Sydney's brother was there, but it was sad because he didn't know who she was. All of their memories were gone. We think the Fire Demons stole them."

When they finally reached the end, no one spoke. The only sound was the scratching of Travis's pen racing over the pages of his notebook. Steele watched, mesmerized, wondering how Travis could remember everything they had talked about. He felt that he had left out something important. He tried to jog his memory, but then Travis whistled, breaking his train of thought.

"If I hadn't been there tonight, I'd think that you guys were seriously warped telling a story like that," said Travis. "But I was there. I saw impossible things happen. No one, maybe not even my father, is going to believe us."

Riley said, "People would laugh at us."

"It's not just that people will laugh," reasoned Steele. "We'll lose credibility, and it'll stick to us forever. No one will believe anything we say."

Travis sighed. "I so want to tell my dad. He's a reporter. He believes lots of impossible things, though probably not this story."

"It's your turn," Riley prompted Travis. "How do you know about Sydney Ravenhurst?"

Travis cleared his throat and told them how, after David Draken went missing, Travis's father began work on a story about the Chicago kids who had mysteriously disappeared. "After school, he gave me lists of things to research for him. One day I found an article in *The New York Times* about Syd's brother. I don't know why, but I just had to speak to Sydney. I phoned all the Ravenhursts in New York until I reached her." He grinned sheepishly. "Not that there were that many. Anyway, she told me how she had organized homeless people in New York to search for William. We started e-mailing each other and she was great, always encouraging us to keep going, to keep hoping. But then everything fell apart. All of the homeless people in Chicago disappeared."

"Like the kids," said Riley.

Travis nodded. "My dad and I looked everywhere, but they're not here."

"Maybe they went underground like the Moles in New York," suggested Steele.

Travis shook his head sadly. "I wish I knew." Then he reached for their arms. "I'm not a Mage. I'm just a kid, but I know my way around Chicago better than most adults. I want to stay and help you find your friend and David and all the other missing kids . . . and the wardens. I don't know about finding the kids' stolen memories, but I want to help with that too." He climbed to his feet and shook his fist at the ceiling. "But most of all," he shouted, "I want to be there when those creatures get what's coming to them."

"Wrong!" sneered a voice from the passageway. "That's not going to happen."

Three heads whipped toward the sound. In the corridor on the other side of the bars stood Dirk the Jerk, calmly studying them. His lips were curled in a smug, knowing smile, but his eyes shone with a wild, fanatical light. Coiled about his left hand was one end of a length of chain; the other end was out of sight.

"*You're* the ones who are going to get what you deserve." He clutched his windpipe and made choking noises. "A pity, really! I enjoyed our little game for a while." Dirk's expression underwent an abrupt change; his face twisted in fear and pain and his voice took on the wheedling tone of the beaten boy in the alley. "Please don't hurt me. Waaah!" He smiled.

Steele ached to plant his fist in Dirk's smile.

"I fooled you," Dirk gloated. "I thought it would be fun, but it was too easy. I pretended I was you, Squeal. Remember all those times you whined and begged me not to hurt you?" Dirk turned to Travis. "Didn't he tell you about me?"

Travis slowly approached the bars. "It must have slipped his mind." He pointed at Dirk's bruises. "Did you really smash yourself in the face?"

Unfazed, Dirk continued to grin wickedly.

At first glance, Steele was astonished at the change in Dirk. Gone was the boorish schoolyard bully. Gone was the frightened boy he and Riley had found just hours ago, despite the cuts and bruises on his face. Standing before him was a colder, more calculating Dirk. Steele decided to push Dirk, to discover if it was an act. If they were lucky he might let something slip that would help them escape and find Mac.

"Admit it, Puddlescum. I fooled you."

"Actually, we fooled *you*," said Riley, her fists clenched at her side. "We fooled you into thinking that you were fooling us."

Dirk frowned and studied her as if she were a new species. Then he sighed with exaggerated tolerance. "The problem with people like you, little girl, is that you think small. You've got no vision. You can't see the big picture."

"What *is* the big picture?" asked Travis.

When Dirk didn't respond at once, Steele was afraid that he had said all that he intended to say. He leaned close to Riley and said, "Keep him talking."

Riley nodded ever so slightly. Then she marched up to the bars and stopped just outside the reach of Dirk's fists. "He's not going to answer, Travis." She looked into Dirk's face without flinching and boldly challenged him, all the while insulting him by speaking to Travis. "He can't answer, because he wouldn't recognize the big picture if it fell on his head."

Steele turned away to hide his proud grin. *Good old Riley! If anyone can push Dirk's buttons, she can.*

Dirk's head fell forward until his chin rested on his chest. Then he shook it back and forth as if the burden of having to explain his world vision to these inferior beings was too much to bear.

Steele watched him closely. *It's an act,* he decided. *He's trying not to lose his temper.*

"Fool!" Dirk hissed at Riley. "Stupid little fool." He pointed toward the ceiling. "Toronto. Chicago. Up there. It's finished. There's a war coming and only the strong are going to survive. *I'm* going to survive. Feeble-minded weaklings like you are going to die. There's no place for you in the new order."

Riley laughed harshly. "If you believe that, then you must still believe in the Easter Bunny."

Dirk took a swift step toward the bars, his right fist aimed at Riley's face. Just before his hand shot between the bars, he suddenly stopped and moved back, dropping his arm to his side. Steele noticed the black stone on his right middle finger and realized he still hadn't mentioned it to Riley and Travis. He put the ring away in his mind and thought that Dirk hadn't really changed at all. As much as he hated Dirk, he was disappointed. It was all so predictable. The big surprise would have been if Dirk *had* changed for the better. But he hadn't. He had taken the inevitable next step toward evil.

"Doesn't he realize he's just a kid, and kids get hurt?" Steele said under his breath.

There's always a bigger bully. Steele thought it strange that something his father had said years ago should suddenly pop into his mind. He remembered all the times he had complained to Mac and Riley that his father didn't understand about Dirk. Had he been wrong?

Travis jumped in. "She's right. This new world you're talking about is all in your head."

Dirk laughed contemptuously. "You know nothing. What I'm into is so big, you . . ." He turned away. "What's the use? You wouldn't understand. Besides, you'll be joining your little Moron friend down there soon." He looked down at the floor.

"What have you done to Mac?" demanded Riley.

"You'll find out soon enough," answered Dirk without turning around, "because they're going to do the same thing to you."

"You're going to be sorry," warned Riley.

Dirk laughed again as he turned and stared at Riley. "I hate to disappoint you, Puddlescum, but I think you're the ones who are going to be sorry. Before it's over, you'll beg them to kill you. But me, be sorry?" He thumped his chest with his fist for emphasis. "Oh yeah, I'm going to be real sorry when I get my reward for catching Squeal." He spat through the bars at Steele. "I don't know why they're so interested in you, but I know what they're going to do to you." He sliced his hand across his throat. "I'd like to hang around to see it, but in a couple of days I'll be heading off to my kingdom, being sorry." He laughed, his eyes glinting shrewdly as they moved from Steele to Riley. "That's right. They gave me a kingdom for trapping Squeal. You're looking at a *king*, Puddlescum."

"Yeah, right!" said Riley. "King of the Jerks."

"Who gave you this reward?" asked Steele quietly.

"None of your business, loser," snapped Dirk.

"Come on. You said they're going to kill us anyway. It can't hurt to tell us where your kingdom is," said Travis.

"In case we want to come to your coronation," said Riley sarcastically.

Dirk leaned closer to the bars. "While they're cutting out your tongue, Riley, think of me. I'll be plucking gold off the streets of Neverland."

Steele and Riley exchanged horrified glances. Riley said something, but all Steele could hear were Sydney Ravenhurst's words replaying in his mind. *Neverland. That's where the cannibals live. Neverland! Cannibals!*

"Dirk," Steele said urgently, "listen to me. Riley and I know about Neverland. You can't go there. Whoever made you king of that place lied to you. They used you. It's not a reward. It's a death sentence."

Dirk's face twisted in rage. "Squealing liar," he hissed. "Jealous little squeal. You know nothing."

Steele ignored the insults. He had to do everything he could to stop Dirk. "Please listen to me. They're *not* your friends. If you go to Neverland, you'll never be seen again. There's no gold, Dirk—only cannibals."

Dirk opened his mouth to respond, then closed it abruptly.

Steele and Riley nodded vigorously. "It's true."

"That's so totally lame." Dirk laughed so hard that his face turned red and he staggered about, acting as if he were trying not to fall down. His jacket popped opened and Steele saw the outline of something round and flat under his shirt.

Steele gasped and reached for his mother's medallion, already knowing that Ees was hanging from the bully's neck. At the same time, he realized that neither he nor Riley had mentioned Ees when they described their adventures to Travis. He also had a feeling that there was something else they had forgotten, but he couldn't think of that now.

Dirk smiled knowingly. "Do you like it?" he said, pulling out the disk and letting it dangle, hypnotically, before their eyes. "It's mine. I found it in the alley."

Riley called him a liar and accused him of stealing the

medallion before a quick look from Steele warned her to say nothing more about it

"It's wicked, man—way too wicked for the likes of you." Steele watched, disgusted, as Dirk spat on the medallion and polished it on his sleeve. "Finders keepers."

"Look!" cried Riley. "He's got Mac's knife."

Sure enough, Mac's knife hung from a ring on Dirk's studded, black leather belt. The sight of it and the medallion made Steele seethe with anger.

"Thief!" hissed Riley.

"It's mine, all mine," Dirk sang. Then he turned to Steele and held up one pudgy fist gripping a chain. "Want to see my new belt?" He pulled on the chain.

Steele heard scratching, as whatever was attached to the other end tried to resist. But Dirk was stronger than the little salamander that was soon dragged into view. Steele's heart wept. Pyrus! How could he have forgotten about Pyrus!

He lunged at the prison bars, gripping them in both hands as if to rip them apart. Then he was crying out in pain, his body jerking spasmodically as shock after shock tore into him. Out of the corner of his eye he was barely aware of Riley and Travis rushing to his side. He had to keep them away.

"Don't touch me," he yelled, and then fell to the floor.

More Questions

From the ashes and bones buried deep beneath Rome came whispers of a massive shadow that had passed between Earth and its moon three nights before the Great Fire. And on the night of the fire, black wraith-like strangers had been seen slipping through the streets of Rome, killing those who tried to douse the flames. It was even said that the fire itself had possessed life, that it had stalked the streets, hurling gobs of its flaming flesh into unburned buildings.

What was the shadow? Who were the wraith-like strangers? On those questions, the ashes and bones were silent.

—Excerpt from *The Wardens' Logs*

Chapter Nine

Company

Steele crawled into a corner at the front of the cell near the bars and forced himself to vomit until he was heaving up air.

He went over in his mind what had happened when he gripped the bars and felt the current surging through him. He knew at once, without knowing how, that the current was not electrical; it had been created by magic. Still, in that instant he had been convinced that he had less than a heartbeat to live. But nothing happened. The deadly current flowed into his hands, along his arms, and into his body, and then seemed to be drawn away. Steele's hands seemed to fuse with the bars, and the iron began transforming into something thick and malleable—sort of like Silly Putty. Aware of Dirk staring at him, waiting, fleshy lips screwed into a cruel smile, Steele had acted instinctively, screaming and pretending that he was being electrocuted.

Sticking his finger down his throat until he gagged and vomited disgusted him, but it was necessary to convince Dirk that he wasn't faking, that he actually had been shocked senseless. He kept it up until he heard the bully mutter under his breath and shuffle away along the corridor. The sound of Pyrus's claws scraping on the stone floor was heart-wrenching.

Feigning weakness, Steele crawled to the back of the cell,

where Riley and Travis were sitting on the floor watching him anxiously, their backs against the wall. Noticing his companions' worried expressions, he felt a twinge of guilt, but quickly pushed it away. He desperately wanted to tell them that it was all an act, that he hadn't been electrocuted, and that he had found a way out of their prison.

But I can't tell them, he reasoned silently, *not even if I whisper. Someone might be listening.* He managed the ghost of a smile, avoiding Riley's eyes.

"I'm OK," he reassured them. "Sorry about that."

"We'll just breathe through our mouths," said Travis stoically, looking at the vomit. He drove his fist into the palm of his hand. "God, I hate that Dirk the Jerk. He knew the power was on, and he was just waiting for one of us to get fried. Steele, you could have been killed."

"Dirk knew the power was on," said Steele. "I noticed how careful he was not to touch the bars. I just didn't make the connection." Steele knew he should tell them that the power in the bars hadn't been electrical, but he held back.

"Mala-jerk!" muttered Travis.

"I've got a bad feeling about Dirk," answered Steele. "He doesn't know what he's got himself into. I can't explain it, but even though I hate his guts, a part of me feels sorry for him."

"Don't ask me to feel sorry for him," said Riley, her voice low and angry. "Travis is right. He hurt you, Steele. I hope he does go to Neverland. I hope the cannibals catch him and eat him alive. He deserves it for what he did to you and Mac and Pyrus."

Steele put his hand on her shoulder. "I'm OK, Riley. We're going to find Mac, and I'll get Pyrus back if it's the last thing I do."

Riley sighed. "Poor Pyrus. I can't believe we didn't notice he was missing."

"It's not that surprising, considering everything that's happened," said Travis. "We would have noticed sooner or later."

"What about Mac's knife?" continued Riley. "And Ees? Oh, Steele, your sword. They took everything, even our backpacks."

Steele shook his head miserably. "We'll get out of here. We'll get our stuff back."

"What's Ees?" asked Travis.

Riley opened her mouth to answer, but Steele caught her arm and squeezed it meaningfully. *No!* He mouthed the word, shaking his head. He didn't know how much Riley intended to tell Travis, but he wasn't about to let her say anything aloud about the medallion's magic. Unless they told him, Dirk had no way of knowing that the prize he had stolen from Steele had come from another planet. He didn't know about its magic. As far as he was concerned, it was just what it appeared, a cool disk. *And that's the way we've got to keep it,* Steele told himself. *The less Dirk knows the better.*

He led Riley and Travis into the darkest corner of the cell, and in a barely audible voice told Travis about Ees and about his journey inside the medallion. He did not mention his mother's pregnancy or how he was supposed to destroy the Fire Demons.

"I would have told you before," he said to Travis, "but I totally forgot about Ees until I saw it around Dirk's neck. I'm telling you now because if I don't, you might say something that will draw their attention to it. We can't let that happen."

"Steele, is it true? Is the disk really magic?"

"Yes, but it's no good to Dirk. He can't use it." He laughed. "Ees belongs to me, and I don't even know what it can do."

"Then what do you care if Dirk finds out about the magic? If we're lucky, he'll go insane trying to figure out how to use it."

"It's not Dirk I'm worried about. It's the one who brought him here—the one who commands the Disciplinarian and the Maladroids."

"I know what you're thinking," said Riley. "You think it's the Prince of Darkness, but you're wrong. We're not in New York anymore."

Steele shook his head. "Why can't he be in Chicago, Riley? I heard him in Toronto . . . and I'm sure that it was his face we saw through the grate in Wychwood Park. I saw him in New York in that underground corridor."

"But how does he get from city to city?" pressed Riley.

Steele couldn't tell her, because he didn't know.

"I think his magic is very powerful, Riley. Who knows what he can do?"

"The alien you told me about . . . Maddie—" Travis began.

"Maddie Fey!" Riley supplied.

"Maddie Fey," Travis repeated. "If Maddie Fey can have a limo with magic portals for doors, what's to stop the Prince of Darkness from having his own portal? From what you and Riley told me, you don't know anything about him. You don't even know where he came from, or whether he's human or anything."

Steele had to admit that Travis was right. What did they know about the Prince of Darkness? Nothing. And he obviously used magic to cover distances quickly. Did he use his mind to transport himself, or did he have access to a portal between Chicago, New York, Toronto, and perhaps other cities?

Steele sighed, frustrated—always more questions, but never any answers.

They settled down then, trying to ignore the hungry growls erupting from their stomachs. Before long they drifted into sleep.

Sometime during the night, Steele was awakened by the pounding of his heart. He sat upright, instantly alert. It was dark inside the chamber, an eerie blue-black darkness; someone had extinguished the weak light in the corridor and replaced it with something that emitted a blue, pulsing glow. As Steele's eyes adjusted to the darkness, he found that he could pick out objects and shapes without any difficulty. Forcing himself to relax, he got up and moved quickly across the cell. He cocked his head to the side, listening at the bars, and identified the muffled patter of footsteps approaching along the corridor. Accompanying the footsteps was another sound, the continuous rasp of something being dragged along the floor.

They're coming for us! Hide! Hide! Panic gushed up inside him—raw panic that drove him back against the far wall and down on his knees, desperately digging and scratching at the stone floor until his fingertips were bloody. But there was no place to hide. As the footsteps sounded nearer, Steele thought of waking Riley and Travis, but he realized that whoever was coming would reach the cell before he could act. Steele fell onto his side facing the bars, and stared at the wavering light cast from a flashlight or lantern in the hands of whoever was approaching. He held his breath and waited, desperately praying that his friends wouldn't wake up and start yelling.

It wasn't long before two tall hooded figures stopped outside the cell. *Maladroids!* They were identical in size and appearance, and their movements were slow and awkward. One set its lantern on the floor, searched its dark clothing, and removed something from an inner pocket. In the light from its companion's lantern, the figure waved its hand at the bars. Steele thought it was probably releasing the magic current that warded the cell.

With a distinctive clanging sound, a section of the iron bars slid back, leaving an opening the size of a standard doorway.

It took all of Steele's willpower to remain motionless and not make a wild dash for freedom. Beside him, Riley mumbled in her sleep and stirred. He tensed, willing her to stay sleeping. He didn't look at her, but he could tell from the sudden silence that she was now awake and very much aware of the two figures silhouetted in the opening between the bars, going about their murky business.

The object the Maladroids had dragged along the corridor was a dark mound on the floor behind them. The figure that had opened the cell door picked up its lantern and stepped into the cell, holding the light out before it. Steele heard it hiss as it peered at Travis and Riley, studying them intently. When the light fell on him, Steele snapped his eyes shut and forced himself to breathe evenly. The figure stared at him for such a long time that Steele felt sweat beading on his face. At last, the creature uttered a long, slow, satisfied hiss and lowered the lantern to the floor. Turning, it picked up one end of the mound and dragged it into the cell. Moving quickly, it backed into the corridor and the bars clanged back in place. Steele didn't stir until the sound of their footfalls died away.

Riley let out her breath in a rush. "What is that?" She scuttled over to Steele.

"I think it's the sack one of those Maladroids had on the bridge." He said no more. He knew that Riley was remembering the monster smashing the sack on the concrete ground and hearing again the blood-curdling screams coming from inside.

They moved closer together and stared at the sack.

Riley whimpered, "I'm scared."

"Me too," admitted Steele. "But we've got to look inside. We can't do nothing."

Riley took a deep breath, as if to steel herself against what they had to do. "I know. But I don't want whoever's in there to be dead, Steele. I don't think I could bear that."

Steele found her hand and clasped it tightly. "If you're not sure you can do this, tell me, Riley. I'll do it."

"No," said Riley. "I'm OK. Come on."

They crawled cautiously over to the motionless mound, which lay alongside the bars where the two dark figures had dropped it. They leaned close to the sack and listened for signs of movement or breathing, but they detected nothing except a faint buzzing sound and a strong metallic smell seeping from the rough, fibrous burlap.

"Blood," said Riley. "My God, Steele! What if it's a dead body?"

Fighting down his rising panic, Steele dug inside his sock and pulled out his pocket knife, a twin to the one Dirk had stolen from Mac.

Riley eyed the knife wistfully. "I wish I'd taken mine out of my backpack." She patted her jacket pockets. "I can't believe it," she murmured, excited. "I think I changed it to my pocket." Her hand disappeared into a pocket and reappeared a moment later gripping her knife.

At the edge of Steele's vision, something moved in the darkness at the back of the cell. It was Travis, awake and moving closer. Steele opened the blade on his knife and ran his fingers over the layers of cord that had been wound tightly around the top of the sack, searching for the knot. Finding it, he sliced through the knot, careful not to cut through other layers of rope. Then he unwound the rope, pleased that he now had a sizable length of cord that might prove useful. He slid it to Riley, who wound it into a ball and gave it to Travis.

Then Steele cautiously sliced along the sack from top to bottom. When he was finished, he and Riley peeled back the burlap, brushing away several fat flies that buzzed angrily out of the sack and stuck to their hair and faces. They found themselves staring into a single glazed, unblinking eye in a face that was bruised black and purple and cut so badly it barely looked human. The reason they could see only one eye, they realized, was that the other had been cut out of its socket.

At the sight, Travis covered his mouth with his hand and turned away, Riley started crying, and Steele swallowed repeatedly, his stomach churning.

"It's a boy," Steele said, between swallows.

They peeled more of the sack away, exposing deep slashes to the boy's chest and abdomen. Then Steele leaned over and put his ear near the boy's mouth. But he neither felt nor heard any signs of life. He felt for a pulse, but again found nothing. Gently, he covered the boy's face with the sack and looked from Riley to Travis, knowing his face was an anguished mask.

"They wanted us to see him," sobbed Riley, tears streaming unchecked down her face.

Travis nodded. "It's a message. They want us to know what they're going to do to us."

Shadow and Wraith

We believed that the shadow commanded the minds of our prisoners, and the wraith creatures were its creations. From the orchestrated actions of the Tsilihin, we surmised that they had been motivated by promises that fulfilled their need to burn—living things to rend with their bone-melting claws, and cities to devour with frenzied fire and deadly smoke.

We searched for the shadow-being, but it eluded us, snaking under rocks in our minds. We pondered over its identity and its origins, but we learned nothing.

Still, we were troubled by a sensation of familiarity.

—**Excerpt from** *The Wardens' Logs*

Chapter Ten

Summoning Magic

"Dirk and the others did that to him!" Riley had cried for a long time, but now her voice was angry. "And they left him to die." She walked to the back of the cell and sank to the floor.

"We've got to get out of here," Travis said in Steele's ear. The ball of cord had come undone and he was nervously twisting it about his hands. "We've got to call the police."

"What police?" Steele asked. "The city's deserted. Remember?"

Steele decided that now was a good time to tell his friends that he had only pretended to be electrocuted, and to outline his plan for their escape. But before he could speak, a low groan startled them. At first Steele thought it was Riley, but when he looked about and saw her huddled in the corner at the back of the cell, retreated into herself, he realized that the sound hadn't come from that direction. It had come from the body in the sack.

"Steele!" hissed Travis, his voice high with excitement or fear, or both. "Did you hear that? He's alive."

Quickly Steele lifted a corner of the sack and peered at the body in disbelief. The single eye in the boy's ruined face blinked once and then tried to focus on Steele.

"What are we going to do?" said Riley, appearing by his side.

Steele bent close to the boy. "Can you hear me?" he asked, stifling the urge to gag at the sight and smell of him.

The boy's eye found Steele. He tried to speak, but managed only a gurgling sound through his torn mouth. He blinked. Steele blinked too, to stop from breaking down completely. He cleared his throat.

"You're hurt," he said gently. "Badly hurt. Do you understand?"

The boy gurgled again and blinked.

"We have to get you to a hospital," Steele continued, but he was afraid that no hospital on Earth could save the boy. It was a miracle that he was still alive. "I won't lie to you. The people who hurt you . . ." He had to turn away then and bury his face in his arms.

Frowning, Riley shook her head. "Don't tell him stuff like that," she scolded Steele, taking his place beside the boy.

"My name's Riley." Her voice was surprisingly calm and soothing. "You're going to be OK. We're going to get you out of here. I promise. You must hang on."

Riley continued talking softly to the boy long after his eye closed and he slipped into unconsciousness. Travis was busy using Steele's knife to cut along the bottom of the sack. Then he and Steele peeled the burlap away and used their jackets to cushion the boy's head and to keep him warm.

"We should take turns watching him," said Travis, when he and Steele had done all they could. "If you want to sleep, I'll take first watch, Riley."

Riley shook her head. "I'll stay with him."

Steele moved back against the far wall, needing the darkness to shield him, needing to be alone with his grief. For some reason, the darkness comforted him. He felt invisible.

He closed his eyes, but sleep wouldn't come. The dying boy's face was imprinted on his eyelids. After a while he got up and crept over to the bars.

I've got to do it now, he thought. But he stood there for a moment longer, listening to the silence and stretching the stiffness from his limbs. Then he turned away. Crouching next to Riley, he put his hand on her shoulder and motioned for her to come with him into the darkness away from the boy.

Riley followed him. They dropped beside Travis, who seemed totally absorbed in winding the length of cord into a ball, unwinding it, and then starting all over again. Steele noticed that his face was streaked with tears, but he said nothing.

"What?" Travis unwound the cord and looked at them.

"He's going to die if we don't get him out of here," said Steele, motioning with his head toward the boy. "I'm going to try something. I don't know if it'll work, but . . ."

"You've got a plan?" Travis sounded doubtful.

"Listen," continued Steele. "Remember when I grabbed the bars and Dirk thought I got electrocuted?"

His companions stared at him questioningly.

Steele cleared his throat. This wasn't going to be easy. "I was only pretending . . ."

"What? That you were electrocuted?" Riley was scornful. "Steele, don't lie. We saw you."

"I know," said Steele sheepishly. "But I'm telling you I faked it."

Travis dropped the rope. "Why? I mean, what was the point in pretending to get shocked?"

"Stop it," said Riley. "I remember looking at Dirk. He wasn't surprised. He knew about the bars."

"You're right, Riley," said Steele impatiently. "There was a current running through the bars, but it wasn't an electrical current. It had to be magic. And Dirk knew it. Did you notice that he never touched them, and once when he went to punch you, he backed away awfully fast?"

"I remember now. I remember thinking he was acting weird."

Steele explained to them. "There was enough current running through those bars to kill a horse. I know because I could feel it. But it didn't hurt. I had to act as though I was being shocked so Dirk wouldn't get suspicious."

His friends stared at him incredulously.

"You're good," said Travis, impressed. "I really believed that you were being electrocuted." He picked up the cord and gave it to Riley.

Riley made a ball of the cord and shoved it into her jacket pocket. Then she turned to Steele. In the pulsing blue light he could see the puzzled frown on her face.

"I'm glad that you weren't electrocuted, but I don't know why you're telling us this now. How is that going to help us get out of here?"

"If you'll let me finish, I'll tell you," Steele said, but not unkindly. "It's got nothing to do with the magic current, which I think Dirk activated somehow, and those creatures turned off when they dumped the boy in our cell and turned on again when they left. But don't ask me how. I'm talking about something else, something that happened when I touched the bars. It's hard to explain, but it felt like I was turning into iron, or like the iron was turning into me." He stopped, wondering if what he had said made sense.

"And then what?" prompted Travis.

Steele sighed. "I don't know, exactly. I just had this feeling that I could bend the bars apart. I know it sounds crazy, but that's what happened."

"You're going to try to bend the bars so we can escape." Riley grabbed Steele's arm and pulled herself to her feet. "Oh, Steele, I know you can do it."

Steele looked from one to the other. "Do you think it's safe to move the boy?"

"No!" said Riley vehemently.

"Riley's right," said Travis. "His wounds are still open. You saw them, Steele. They haven't even begun to close over." He shook his head sadly. "He'd never make it."

Steele didn't like the idea of leaving the boy alone in the cell. It was as if they were abandoning him. "Come on! There's got to be something we can do. Can't we carry him or use our coats to pull him along?"

The others shook their heads.

Travis clapped Steele on the shoulder. "I don't want to leave him behind either, but I think he's better off here. If we try to carry him, we could make him worse. Besides, we can move a lot faster without him."

Riley took a deep breath and blew it out. "I'll stay," she said. "We can't take him with us and we can't leave him here by himself. If he died all alone I don't think I could live with myself."

"That's a bad idea, Riley. If those creatures come back while we're gone . . . well . . . you saw what they did to him . . ." The thought that someone would hurt Riley the way they had hurt the boy made Steele weak.

But Riley's mind was made up. "The sooner you bust through those bars, the sooner you'll be back with help. So take Travis and get out of here." She pressed something into Travis's hand. "You might need it."

Travis looked at the pocket knife resting in his palm. "Keep it, Riley. Steele's got his." He passed her the knife.

"If someone comes, play dumb," Steele advised her. "Pretend you were sleeping. Say you don't know what happened to us."

"I've got a better idea," said Travis. "Look surprised, and then tell them someone already came and took us away. That should confuse them for a while."

Steele looked at him and grinned. "That's brilliant."

"Don't worry about me," Riley said, her voice tight, dropping the knife into her pocket. "Just go, and hurry back."

Steele walked over to the bars. He took a deep breath and let it out slowly.

You need Ees!

You're going to fail!

Loser!

Shut up! Steele commanded the doubts that were springing up like thistles in his mind, choking his resolve. He wrapped his hands about the bars, feeling the hair on his arms stand on end as the magic current surged through him. Convinced that his own magic would keep him alive as it had before, he ignored the current. He closed his eyes, forced himself to relax, and concentrated on the feel of the cold metal against his sweating palms. He didn't know how long he stood there without moving, but it seemed like ages. After a while the doubts began to creep back and pick at his mind.

It won't work without Ees!

That's not true, he rebutted. *If the magic comes from Ees, I couldn't have got into Riley's mind. And I wouldn't have been able to touch the bars without feeling pain. So there!*

Steele re-focused on the bars, the iron now warmed by the heat from his hands. He stubbornly refused to admit that he didn't know what he was doing. He knew only one thing; he had to try to save the boy. If he could do that, then he'd think about finding Mac and Pyrus. Once the boy was safe, he'd hunt Dirk down and rip his mother's medallion from the bully's neck, snatch his sword, and punch Dirk's lights out.

He quickly chased such thoughts away and went absolutely still, trying to isolate his mind from the world about him. But it took a little longer before the image of Dirk the Jerk faded into nothing. After a while, time lost all meaning.

And then it happened. Steele gasped as his hands melded onto the iron. Within seconds he could no longer distinguish between the part that was him and the part that was iron. Flesh and bone and metal became as one. It was the strangest sensation he had ever experienced, almost as if he were being consumed or assimilated into the element. But it wasn't a scary or unpleasant feeling. As the sensation spread into his wrists and forearms, warmth and contentment washed over him. In that safe, comfortable state, Steele began to forget the reason he had taken hold of the bars in the first place.

Steele!

The sound of his name brought him back with a start. He didn't know who had called to him . . . it could have been Riley . . . or Travis . . . but he realized that whoever it was had probably saved his life. He was losing himself in the iron.

It took all of his resolve to reject the soporific sensation emanating from the living metal and pry himself free. Part of him ached to lose the struggle, to surrender completely. But the greater part, the part that made him who he was, took over and drove the iron out of his arms and back into the bars. He almost cried out at the aching void left inside him as the metal gradually retreated.

Reluctantly, Steele spread his hands out to either side. The iron, now as pliable as warm, wet clay, came with them. Judging that he had stretched the bars just far enough apart that he and Travis could squeeze between them, he let go of them and slipped into the passageway. Then he stared at the bent and twisted iron and staggered back, stunned by the immensity of the magic he had performed.

He wasn't aware that Travis had joined him outside the cell until he felt a touch on his arm. He turned. His friend was staring at him, mouth hanging open in disbelief. Steele shook his head. "Don't ask how I did that because I don't know." He reached for the bars to bend them back into place, but stopped abruptly when he realized that he'd have to merge with the metal again to get back into the cell when they returned. Just thinking about it made him break out in a cold sweat. He decided to leave them as they were, reasoning that the gap between them might not be noticed.

Travis quashed his decision. "You can't leave them like that. If Dirk or one of the others comes back, Riley's got to make them believe that someone already came and took us away. You've got to put them back the way they were."

He was right, Steele realized. The story Travis had concocted for Riley wouldn't hold water if their captors saw the bars twisted out of shape. Quickly, as though it hurt him to touch the metal, he gripped the bars, bracing himself to fight off the iron as it invaded his hands and wrists. But to his surprise, the metal was still pliable, and he bent the bars back in place effortlessly. Then he snatched his hands away as if they were burning, and stared into the cell.

Riley was sitting cross-legged on the floor, her head bowed over the dying boy. "Be careful," she said, without looking up. "Hurry back."

She looked so small and forlorn that Steele felt as if he was letting her down, just like Maddie Fey had let them down. He wondered what Riley was thinking about, but he was so horrified of finding himself in her head again that he quickly turned away. "We'll be back for you, Riley."

Steele thought he heard her say, "Please hurry."

He looked along the corridor in both directions. To his right, the passage seemed to go on forever, stretching away into darkness. But in the opposite direction it extended only a short distance and then seemed to take a sharp left turn. He glanced at Travis and raised his eyebrows questioningly.

"Let's go left, at least to the corner so we can see what's around that turn," Travis suggested.

Steele agreed. Without a backwards glance, they moved silently along the passage, sticking to the shadows close to the wall, their eyes on the spot where the corridor turned left. Steele noticed that it was brighter here than in their cell—the pulsing blue glow seemed to be coming from somewhere high above. He looked up, but all he could see was an iron catwalk, blue light filtering through the openings. He wondered if there were other levels above and below with more cells. He didn't want to think about who or what else, aside from themselves, might be locked up in this dismal place.

He glanced from his own hands to Travis's face. "You look dead."

"Thanks," Travis replied sarcastically. "Speak for yourself. Your skin is sort of blue."

At the end of the corridor, Steele stopped abruptly and peered cautiously around the corner. Ahead was a narrower corridor ending at a flight of stairs that widened dramatically as it climbed to another level. The ghostly blue lighting also pulsed from somewhere above. The passage was deserted and as silent as if no one had ever passed along its length. But Steele noticed shadowed areas along the walls that could be doorways.

They moved into the corridor and advanced toward the steps. Steele saw that the shadowed areas weren't doors, but openings that, he guessed, led to other areas of the prison. He paused outside one of the openings and peered in. The passage was so black that without a light, they couldn't see more than a foot in front of them, so they hurried past. When they reached the stairs, they crept cautiously up. At the top they were forced to stop; the way forward was blocked by two walls of thick metal bars, approximately twenty feet apart.

And just beyond the second wall, its broad back facing the bars, stood a creature whose bleached skeletal head stood out sharply in the pulsing blue light. It didn't matter that only the back of its head was visible; Steele would have recognized it anywhere.

The Disciplinarian.

As fear paralyzed him, Steele understood why the Maladroids gave way before this creature. They were terrified of it, and he didn't blame them. He knew intuitively that its methods of discipline would be cruel and swift, and delivered with cold-blooded precision. There'd be no begging for mercy from the Disciplinarian. Not that he would, Steele told himself, but if he ever dared to look inside this creature's mind, he'd probably lose his own.

A wave of cold hit him in the face like a fist. The Disciplinarian's head whipped about and faced where he and Travis stood motionless at the top of the steps. At the last moment, Steele threw himself onto his stomach and slithered backwards down the stairs until he was out of sight. A beat later he heard Travis stifle a gasp and hit the steps beside him. They stayed like that, facedown, stretched uncomfortably over the steps, until Steele thought he'd go out of his mind if he didn't soon move.

They were afraid to remain where they were, but even more afraid to flee. Steele strained to fix the Disciplinarian's location. Had it seen them? A moment later his heart sank as he heard the *clang* of the farthest gate opening, followed by heavy footsteps coming closer.

Steele twisted his head to the side and gauged the distance to the nearest dark opening in the wall directly opposite the base of the steps. Could he make it there before the Disciplinarian reached the next barrier? *Don't think about it, just do it,* he told himself. He shook Travis's arm and pointed at the opening. Travis stared at him through round, wild eyes. Hoping his companion understood, Steele took a quick breath, slid off the steps, and rolled toward the side. Bumping to a stop against the wall, he wriggled into the mouth of the dark passage. Then he sprang to his feet and flattened himself against the wall to make room for Travis. He was shaking.

But Travis didn't join him, Steele saw in disbelief. Travis was still there, spread as flat as a rug on the floor at the bottom of the stairs. His face, turned toward Steele, wore an expression of such desperation that Steele longed to go to him. Too late, Travis started to follow, but Steele could see that he'd never make it to the opening before the Disciplinarian reached the second barrier. Steele shook his head vigorously; at the same time signalling his companion to stay put. If he made a dash for the opening, he'd be spotted at once. But if he remained where he was, and didn't move a muscle or even breathe, perhaps the creature wouldn't notice him.

How can I stop it from reaching the gate? How?

The question replayed in Steele's mind. He was still shaking, but he ignored his physical stress as he wrestled with the problem of how to stop the Disciplinarian from spotting Travis. Could he use magic here? He thought of the times he had used his magic since he became aware of it. Twice he had trapped a Fire Demon inside an airtight dome and sucked the remaining air into his lungs to create a vacuum and suffocate it. But he couldn't do that here. Because the Disciplinarian wasn't a Fire Demon, it might be able to outlast Steele inside the vacuum.

A quarter of an hour ago, he had used magic to bend the bars of their cell. Perhaps he could work some magic on the gate so that the creature would be wary of touching it— make it sizzle or something. Focusing on the gate, he tried to imagine the cool feel of metal in his hands. But he wasn't physically touching them, and his mind was buzzing and his thoughts were racing in too many directions. When nothing happened, he stopped trying.

Steele rebelled against the magic. What good was it if it wouldn't work when he needed it? *I never asked for it. I don't want it.* Trembling with frustration, he wanted to turn his face to the wall and cry. But then he thought of Travis and wiped at his eyes, and just then he caught the flash of something shiny in the Disciplinarian's hand. He inched his head forward and strained to see what had caught his eye. Even in the pale pulsing light, Steele noticed the long claws protruding from the end of its sleeve. Had those claws slashed out at the dying boy, leaving the deep gashes Steele had noticed on his face and chest?

Just before it reached the second gate, the creature paused and stared through the bars, its bluish-white head slightly cocked as if it were listening intently.

It knows we're here, Steele thought. *Somehow it knows.*

Steele heard its slow, measured breathing, and held his own breath. As he watched the creature, an idea began to grow and take shape in his mind—an idea so horrible, so danger-ous, that his first instinct was to yell and chase the thought out of his head.

But the idea wouldn't leave. And the more he considered it, the more he felt tempted by it, despite the fact that a moment ago he was convinced that he'd never do such a thing. But what if he could get into the Disciplinarian's mind and read its thoughts? What if he could root through the dark, hidden corners there and see the place where Mac was being held? What if he could find Pyrus? What if he could find a way out of here? What if . . . ?

What if I fail? With Riley, it had simply happened; Steele hadn't consciously tried to read her thoughts. The very idea sickened him. But this creature wasn't a friend; it was an enemy, and if it ever caught him, it would rip his throat out with those sharp claws as easily as it might swat a fly, and with as much feeling.

What if I could save us?

No! It's too dangerous! said the voice in his head. *It could be a trap. It could be waiting for you—waiting to snare you. What would happen then? What if you go into its mind and can't get out . . . ever?*

Steele moved deeper into the shadows and pressed his back against the wall. He wrung his hands, which were trembling uncontrollably. He forced himself to breathe slowly. If they were here, Mac and Riley would tell him he was out of his mind to even consider the possibility of probing this creature's mind. A pang of loneliness struck his heart. He missed Mac. He needed to talk with him now, tell him what he was thinking. He shook his head angrily.

"Mac's not here. And Riley's back in the cell with a boy who's dying, who will die for sure if I do this thing and get caught."

But what if I could save us?

He edged forward. One glance at Travis told him his friend was struggling to keep still. Steele's heart went out to him. He knew how he'd feel if their positions were reversed—if he could not see what was happening. He smiled encouragingly and patted the air with his hand, signalling Travis to remain where he was. Travis grimaced and lowered his head until his forehead touched the floor.

Steele turned back to the Disciplinarian. Slowing his breathing, he concentrated on the creature's head and sent his thoughts pushing against its bony white skull. When nothing happened, Steele was almost relieved. By failing to break into the creature's mind, he wasn't running the risk of getting caught and he couldn't be blamed for making things worse. He was just about to look away when the creature's head jerked toward the opening where he was hiding . . . and the floor gave way beneath his feet . . . and he was falling into utter blackness, his head filled with a horrible buzzing.

Oh God! Where am I? Help me!

At first Steele thought he had actually fallen through the

floor into an enormous hornets' nest, but then he realized that he was inside the Disciplinarian's mind and the buzzing was the sound of lunacy—rampant and obsessive. The creature's thoughts spun about him, bumping against him and pushing at him. They reeked like rotting meat, and Steele was aware that his body was silently gagging, back where he had left it in the shadows.

Something warned him not to linger or he would be lost. He moved among the maelstrom that was the creature's mind, probing the thoughts that brushed against him, crying out, and cringing in horror.

Hurry! a voice whispered in his mind.

Help me! I don't know where to look!

Steele looked about wildly. The creature's buzzing thoughts were scattered as far as he could see. He latched on to a single thought and followed it. It was difficult at first, like trying to track a single snowflake in a blizzard. It swirled around and bumped into other thoughts, sometimes swallowing them whole and bulging into a larger, louder mass of twisting, writhing images, in a seemingly random motion. But then Steele noticed something peculiar. Its motion wasn't as random as he had supposed. It was gravitating, being drawn like iron to a magnet, toward a thick, tangled knot of blackness far beneath him. He started to drift downward.

Don't go there! the voice warned.

He pulled himself up sharply, staring at the tangled black knot.

It will consume you!

"What is it?" He thought he had spoken aloud.

It is the force that drives it! You must not go there.

Steele gazed up through the swirling maelstrom. If the

creature's thoughts were going down into that black thing, where were they coming from? It took a while before his eyes finally discovered a pattern in the chaotic movement of thoughts. They seemed to be coming from somewhere above. Had he found what he was looking for—the source of the Disciplinarian's thoughts?

Excited, Steele abandoned caution and moved swiftly now, almost desperately. He pictured the creature staring through the bars, and wondered if it felt the intrusion. *Don't think about that.* Up through the creature's madness he flew, smashing at evil thoughts, scattering them like dead leaves in the wind. And then, without warning, he was catapulted into the newly formed thoughts of the creature.

Steele followed the Disciplinarian's thoughts as they led him down a dark passageway, a secret passage, to the cell where Riley sat on the floor, the dying boy's head cradled on her lap. In the creature's thoughts, Steele saw her start at the sound of a panel sliding open in the wall outside the cell, and then her face registering terror as the Disciplinarian flew out of the wall. Its claws gripped the barred door and ripped the bars from their fittings. Grinning horribly, the Disciplinarian stepped into the cell. In its thoughts, Riley didn't make a dash for the opening in the bars; she steadfastly refused to abandon the dying boy. Trapped inside the creature's mind, Steele could only watch in horror as the monster dispatched the poor, doomed boy with one vicious slash to his chest and then turned its deadly claws on Riley and tore the life from her, tossing her broken body into the darkest corner of the cell.

Steele struggled to escape from the Disciplinarian's mind, but not before blackness closed in on him like a net.

Time

Hundreds of years passed and still we learned nothing of the shadow-being. That did not stop us. We looked in every dark corner, every underground passage. We listened to the elements as they spoke of a coming darkness, but darkness left no prints behind for us to follow.

The Tsilihin escaped more frequently, and burned indiscriminately, and learned more about us with each passing day.

And then, while we searched for it, the shadow took one of us.

—**Excerpt from** *The Wardens' Logs*

Chapter Eleven

Fire and Ice

"Steele?" The boy's voice was a blend of desperation and fear. "Answer me, Steele? Can you hear me?"

The sound of his name brought Steele's mind racing back into his own head. He blinked stupidly. For a moment he didn't know where he was; he didn't even recognize the boy holding him tightly in his arms, alternately squeezing and shaking him. He gulped, shuddering involuntarily from shock and cold. His clothes were drenched in sweat and his flesh felt numb and icy.

"Here. Put this on," said Travis, pulling his outer shirt over his head and handing it to Steele. "I don't need it."

They had covered the dying boy with their jackets before they had set out, and Steele noticed that Travis was trying hard not to shiver in his thin T-shirt.

"Keep it. I'm OK," he said. He struggled to stand, but his legs buckled under him and he collapsed again. "Help me up. We're going back for Riley and the boy."

"What happened?" asked Travis, gripping Steele's hand and helping him to his feet.

Steele put one hand against the wall to steady himself while he stretched his leg muscles. He glanced sideways at Travis but didn't see him. Instead, he was seeing Riley's terror-stricken face as the clawed monster went for her.

"Talk to me, Steele. Correct me if I'm wrong, but I thought we agreed that Riley would stay with the boy while we went to get help."

"Don't you understand?" Steele groaned. "It's going to kill her."

"Who's going to kill her?" The frustration in Travis's voice was palpable. "Steele, tell me what happened. Why didn't that creature suddenly tear out of here?"

Exasperated, Steele sighed. "I read its mind."

Travis stared at him in disbelief. "You what?"

"I read its mind, OK? It was thinking of killing Riley and the boy. We've got to go back."

Travis looked sick. "What else did you see?"

"Nothing."

"Weren't we there?"

"No. Just Riley and the dying boy. It knows we're gone, Travis."

Travis shook his head vigorously. "Come on, then. If you can't walk, I'll help you."

Steele took a tentative step back from the wall and stumbled. "I'm OK," he said quickly. But he didn't feel OK, not at all. He felt weak and uncoordinated, as if something inside were tightening and twisting, wrestling control of his body away from him. Then he thought of Riley and felt energy returning to his limbs.

"Let's go."

They sprinted along the narrow, empty corridor, back toward the broader passageway and the cell that had been their prison. A wild fear burned in Steele's chest. He had a sudden, overpowering urge to talk to his silent grandmother, to hear the soft clicking of her knitting needles, to be comforted. It didn't matter that she never replied in words; somehow just going to her and telling her his troubles made him feel better. For the first time, he realized that GM's silence had helped him work out his own problems. "Help me now, GM," he said under his breath.

He stumbled, and would have fallen if Travis hadn't caught his arm and dragged him forward. They had turned into the long, wide passageway that ran past their cell, and had covered half the distance when they heard a faint swishing noise up ahead. Heart racing, Steele stopped and clutched Travis's arm, pulling the boy into the shadows against the wall.

"We're too late."

Ahead, the Disciplinarian seemed to materialize out of nowhere. In the unearthly blue light it appeared even larger and more dangerous than before.

Travis gasped. "Did you see that? It walked right through the concrete wall."

"No, it didn't," said Steele. "It came through a secret passageway."

Travis stared at him. "You actually saw the passageway in that thing's mind?"

Steele nodded, grim-faced. "I'm scared, Travis."

"Yeah, me too." Travis put his hands on Steele's shoulders. "It's OK to be scared . . . I guess."

Steele removed Travis's hold on his shoulders and moved away, distancing himself, building the mental wall that would be his shield. Travis seemed to understand his need to be alone; he didn't follow.

As he prepared himself to face the Disciplinarian, Steele remembered the first time he had seen Riley. It was the start of junior kindergarten. They must have been only four years old. It was shortly after he and his father had gone to live with GM in the old, rambling house at number six Wychwood Park. Riley had plopped into the little chair next to him at the round table in their classroom, and said, "Everybody thinks your grandmother is crazy. But I don't. So if it's OK with you, I'd like to come to your house and show her my dolls sometime." They'd been best friends ever since. Steele couldn't imagine his life without Riley in it.

Now Riley was in danger because of him. If she and Mac hadn't followed him the night he found the mysterious note telling him to show up at a midnight meeting, she wouldn't even be here. Steele had to stop the Disciplinarian from killing her. And there was only one way to do that. Magic. Steele had to use magic. Not the kind he had used to break into the creature's mind, but a vicious, unfeeling, fireball magic that would blast it into a million pieces so that it could never hurt anyone again.

"If you think you're going to hurt Riley, you'd better think again," Steele said through clenched teeth, warmed by the surge of anger within, despite his damp, sweaty clothes and the wintry chill inside the prison.

"Wait here," he told Travis.

"What are you going to do?"

Steele shrugged. "Something . . . I really don't know."

Then he turned and moved swiftly down the hall. He stopped when he was only a dozen steps from the Disciplinarian, whose horrible clawed hands were fastened on the iron bars. Steele forced himself not to turn and bolt as his eyes locked on the creature's claws, each as long as his index finger.

"They're gone," he heard Riley say, sticking to the story Travis had devised for her. "Somebody already came and took them away."

"Stop!" Steele managed to shout, relieved that his voice sounded strong and fearless.

The Disciplinarian didn't even bother to look his way. It hissed impatiently, as if Steele were no more than a pest, a mosquito to be swatted. Then it tore the iron bars apart and stepped through the gaping ruin into the cell.

Steele faltered, stunned at the creature's display of super-human strength. His mind screamed at him to run. But he didn't. He called his magic.

"Stop!" He was certain he could feel the magic coursing through his body, waiting for him to unleash it. He moved closer until he was standing just outside the opening in the bars.

Riley screamed. The Disciplinarian's massive form blocked her from Steele's sight, but Steele could picture her shielding the boy with her body. The monster swung its arm, and Steele saw Riley fly across the cell and hit the wall. His heart stopped. But Riley was back on her feet in a flash, hands raised, fingers curled to scratch the creature's eyes out.

"I said, STOP!" thundered Steele.

In the act of swiping at the dying boy, the creature suddenly went still. Steele tensed, holding his breath as he waited for it to wheel about and lunge at him. But to his surprise, it remained poised over the boy as if it had been turned to stone.

Something's wrong, thought Steele, moving along the bars so that he could see around the creature to what was happening inside the cell. At first he thought his eyes were playing tricks on him. He blinked and pressed closer to the bars, gripping them in stunned disbelief.

An invisible force flung his jacket off the boy's chest. It joined Travis's on the stone floor. Thin fingers of smoke began curling and rising from the lacerations on the boy's body. And where they went deepest, Steele could see a brilliant white spark ignite in the exposed bone. The boy was literally burning up. The smoke stung Steele's eyes while the unforgettable smell of burning flesh stuck in his throat, choking him and sending him into a paroxysm of coughing.

Had the Maladroid poisoned the boy? Had it poured some sort of acid on his flesh? Was it so twisted that it needed to administer this final insult, to make him suffer unspeakable pain before it finished him off? At that moment, Steele had only one thought: to make this creature pay for what it had done, to inflict indescribable pain upon it, to watch it writhing in agony, and hear it screaming its black heart out for mercy. He felt such hatred and loathing for the creature that his vision blurred. Exhilaration flowed through him and he welcomed it.

He raised his arms toward the creature, intending to slam his magic into it, to hurt it a thousand times worse than it had hurt the boy. But the creature's odd behaviour held him back. It staggered, hissing and spitting like a great albino cat.

The white flame grew in volume and luminosity, spreading from the boy's chest, where his open wounds sizzled and steamed, along his arms and lower limbs. It flowed up his neck and over his face, consuming him like a ravenous, fiery beast. It burned with such ferocious brilliance that the Disciplinarian cringed and threw up its arms to shield its face.

Then the flame flared brighter and brighter, engulfing the boy until Steele could no longer see him. He felt the whiteness sear his eyeballs and penetrate into his brain, like a knife stab. Momentarily blinded, he squeezed his eyes shut and hid his face behind his arms. When he could see again, he shifted his arms to make a small space through which he could squint into the cell.

The figure that walked out of the white fire, silver neck shining like diamonds, took his breath away.

Compared to the Disciplinarian, Maddie Fey was small and slight. But despite her size, standing there, backlit by the brilliant flame, she dwarfed the other, making it appear puny and insignificant. Maddie Fey ignored Steele and Riley. Her silver-white eyes were riveted on the creature that her fire had driven back against the bars.

The Disciplinarian dropped its arms. It hesitated a moment, as if it were taking the measure of this girl opponent, gauging the potency of her magic. Then its gaze shifted from Maddie Fey to the brilliant fire flaring about her. In that instant, Steele realized what the creature was thinking. *The fire gives off brilliance, but not heat. It's just an illusion.*

Emboldened by its certainty, the creature swiped at the flame, laughing harshly when its clawed hand passed through unscathed. It thrust its hand near Maddie Fey's face, dismissing her as a threat. But then a sharp cracking sound came from its hand, and it started. Before it even realized what was happening, its limb was gone, shattered into a dozen pieces, the bits of fingers twitching spasmodically on the floor.

"Whoa!" breathed a voice near Steele's ear. "The thing's hand turned to glass."

Steele glanced at Travis. "I don't think so. I think it froze solid. Look at the puddles on the floor. Look at the fingers moving. I think the fire is cold, like ice." He frowned. "I told you to wait for me," he scolded, but there was no trace of anger in his voice.

"You were just standing around doing nothing," said

Travis. "I couldn't bear the suspense." He pointed at Maddie Fey. "Is that who I think it is?"

Steele nodded. "Riley and I were wrong, Travis. We should have known she'd never abandon us."

But Travis wasn't listening; he was staring at Maddie Fey as if she were an angel.

She *does* look like an angel, thought Steele, a cold angel with wings of white ice-fire.

The Disciplinarian was also staring, but not at Maddie Fey. It was staring at the bloody stump on the end of its arm where, until a moment ago, its clawed hand had been. The bluish-white head turned slowly toward Maddie Fey. A howl of pain and fury erupted from its open mouth and then, swifter than Steele could have believed possible, the creature lunged at her.

But it wasn't swift enough. Maddie Fey's arms were already up, fingers spread, palms facing the creature. White lines of fire danced between her fingers, pulsing with power. Abruptly, the fire surged from her hands and slammed into the creature, flowing like quicksilver over its massive form. As the whiteness coated it, the creature struggled to plow forward, but its movements slowed and it finally stopped in mid-stride less than a yard from Maddie Fey.

An expectant hush fell over the group as Steele and his companions stared at the frozen mass.

Crack!

A hairline fracture spread up and down along the creature's length, branching off into hundreds of minute veins. When the creature exploded, Steele shouted, gripping Travis's arm so tightly that it took all of the other boy's strength to wrest it free. Then Maddie Fey walked calmly through the shattered bits of the creature and slipped through the bars, Riley following on her heels like her shadow, hugging the boys' jackets tightly to her chest.

"Come," Maddie Fey said, turning her silver eyes on Steele. "We must be away from here before they come for us."

Frail Immortality

We are immortal beings—older than the wind. We will live forever unless our lives are taken through an intentional act of murder. But such an unspeakable act can only be committed by dousing our fire and then opening our hearts and cutting out the spark that ignites our flame.

Since we had no memory of such a thing ever having happened, we speculated on how a creature with murder on its mind would douse our fire.

Water? We shook our heads. While we prefer the thick fiery liquid, we have coursed the oceans and chased the creatures of the deep, our fire burning with cool radiance.

—**Excerpt from** *The Wardens' Log*

Chapter Twelve

An Absence of Light

Steele and Riley stared at Maddie Fey as if she were an apparition, while Travis looked on in awe. From the moment Steele had left Travis farther back in the corridor, events had happened so quickly that his mind was still grappling with them. In addition, his head was churning with at least a dozen questions.

"How did you get here?" he asked finally.

Maddie Fey turned and peered down the long corridor. "I let them find me."

"You were the dying boy," said Travis in a hushed voice. "The wounds, your eye, they were nothing but illusions."

The Mage turned to Travis, studying him for a moment before she answered. "Travis," she said. "Yes, I remember. You used your jacket to cushion the boy's head."

Travis nodded. "It was nothing,"

Maddie Fey smiled. "I am pleased to meet you, Travis. I am glad Steele and Riley found you."

Travis beamed with pleasure. "Your injuries," he said quietly. "Were they illusions?"

Maddie Fey sighed and her eyes clouded over. "I shed my true form to become the boy you saw. His injuries were real."

Riley burst into tears. "But you were him! I can't bear to think of how you must have suffered."

Maddie Fey smiled sadly. "Don't cry for me, Riley. The boy is gone. He is no longer in pain." She took Riley's hand and held it. "He knew you were there. He knew you tried to protect him with your life."

Riley sniffled and wiped fresh tears from her eyes.

For a reason Steele couldn't explain, listening to Maddie Fey calmly relating her near-death experience infuriated him.

"Why did you do it?" he demanded. "You didn't have to become that boy. You didn't have to let them hurt you. Your magic is so powerful you could have blasted this place apart and got us out of here as easily as blowing out a candle. I can't believe you let them take us here in the first place."

Maddie Fey turned on him angrily. "This is not about *you*."

Her words stung. Steele's face burned as if she had slapped him. He lowered his eyes, confused by his own angry outburst. Maddie Fey laid her cool hand on his arm. When she spoke again her words were kinder.

"Do I have to remind you that it's about stopping the Fire Demons before they devour your world? It's about finding the wardens before they are lost forever. And along the way, it's about finding Mac and the other missing children, and restoring the memories of those whose memories were stolen to fuel the Fire Demons." She took a slow, calming breath. "Do I really have to say these things to you?"

"You don't have to remind me of what we're doing," Steele snapped. "I know, even better than you, what it's about."

Maddie Fey gave him a long appraising look. Steele wondered if she was reading his mind. Then she nodded.

"Yes. Perhaps you do." She smiled suddenly, and for some strange reason, Steele found himself smiling with her. He noticed that Riley and Travis wore equally happy expressions.

"You're angry because you were afraid for the boy," Maddie Fey said. "But believe me, Steele, there was no other way. I had to get inside this prison without being detected. Before I changed to become the boy, it was essential that the boy know nothing. There must be nothing to suggest to his captors that he was more or less than he appeared. I hid who I was from him. I shed my powers. I hid everything that was me in a spark no bigger than a speck of dust. The spark would transform me only if the boy's death was imminent." She paused, searching Steele's face with her blue eyes.

But Steele shook his head at her. "I don't understand why you had to do it like that. We thought you were dying. We felt responsible."

"I'm sorry, Steele. But there was no other way." She paused and appeared to be listening. "We must go on now. When I used my powers, I was detected. The one who controls this place and those in it is now aware that a powerful alien magic is loose inside his barred kingdom."

"They already knew," cried Travis. "Steele used magic before, on the bars."

Maddie Fey laughed. "Don't worry, Travis. And please don't be offended, Steele, but your magic was too weak to be detected."

"You call bending iron bars weak!" exclaimed Travis.

"When Steele accepts the truth about himself," Maddie Fey replied, "then you will see true magic."

Steele felt himself turn red, but in the blue light his face appeared more bruised than flushed. His friends turned away, pretending they didn't notice.

"Let us go now." Maddie Fey glanced at each of her companions in turn. "I will go ahead. I must release faint magic to search for human life. Check the cells as we pass, but do it quickly and quietly." Without another word, she brushed past Steele and moved along the passage in the opposite direction from that previously taken by Steele and Travis. The others followed in single file. Steele slipped his arms gratefully into his jacket, and brought up the rear.

"It's not fair," complained Riley, keeping her voice down so that only Travis and Steele could hear. "I've got a billion questions. Like, why did the limo disappear? And where are Fidus and Wish?"

"Don't forget the giant talking rat you told me about," said Travis. "I can't wait to meet him."

"Be careful when you meet Nilats," cautioned Riley. "He's not exactly what you'd call nice."

"That's putting it mildly," said Steele. "It's disgusting. You should have seen him in that alley when he killed those worm creatures and then ate them."

His friends expressed their disgust by making various rude sounds. Then they pressed on in silence. Steele looked along the seemingly endless corridor. On one side there was nothing but a dark wall, barely visible in the shadows, but on the opposite side were more barred cells, the ghostly blue light making the iron glow eerily. Steele stopped at each cell and peered into the farthest reaches, calling Mac's name softly. No one answered. Once or twice, he thought he detected movement, no more than faint stirrings in the shadows, or heard the soft rustle of cloth brushing against cloth, but when he pressed his face against the bars and called softly, "Who's there?" all he got for an answer was silence.

He worked his way toward the end of the long corridor, doggedly searching for his friend in chamber after chamber until finally Travis came back and urged him to keep up.

"There are too many," said Travis. "You can't stop at each cell, Steele. If Maddie Fey's right and they know about us, we've got to get out of here."

Steele didn't say anything. He knew Travis was right. Either Mac was imprisoned in another part of the building, or he no longer remembered who he was and so had cowered in the shadows in one of the cells Steele had already passed, remaining mute when he heard his name. As desperate as he was to find Mac, their search for him would have to wait. Getting away before they were caught was their first priority. He nodded grimly and followed Travis down the corridor, but he couldn't help gazing into the cells as he hurried past and repeating Mac's name over and over again.

They met no one. Unless, as Steele suspected from the faint rustlings he had heard, the cells they passed harboured kids who were either too traumatized to reveal their presence or didn't know or care because they couldn't remember anything else, the prison appeared to be deserted. He thought of trying to invoke his heightened hearing, but he still felt weak from having used magic to breach the Disciplinarian's mind. But he remained wary and tried to prepare himself for the unexpected.

When they reached the end of the corridor where Maddie Fey and Riley were waiting, Riley pulled Steele aside. "I meant to tell you before but things got sort of crazy back there. I'm glad you came back," she said. "Just seeing you through the bars gave me strength." Then she looked at him, puzzled. "But what made you come back when you did?"

Steele swallowed and took a step away, anticipating her reaction when he confessed to having read the creature's mind. But he needn't have worried. Omitting any mention of the creature killing Riley, he told her how he had discovered its intent to go to the cell and take him and Travis. When he finished, he waited to see if she bought the lie. Riley studied his face. Then she nodded.

"I'd have done the same." She thought for a second and then asked, "Did you find out anything about Mac, or a way out of here?"

"No."

"Oh, well," she sighed. "It's too late now. The creature's dead."

Realizing that Maddie Fey and Travis were somewhere ahead, they turned into another corridor and ran to catch up. Steele was relieved to discover that the passageway hadn't come to a dead end. In the cold blue light they could just make out a dark rectangular opening at the far end. There was no sign of the others. They turned left and then right into other corridors. After a while Steele lost count. Their route was straightforward and tedious; they reached the end of one corridor only to enter another. So far they hadn't encountered multiple passageways.

As long as the corridors continued, they stood a chance of finding an exit. The thought of getting lost or having to go back was too depressing to contemplate. *No*, thought Steele, clinging to the faint thread of hope. *We'll find a way out.*

Travis was waiting for them in the next passageway. "It's definitely an old prison, but I've never read anything or heard anyone talk about it."

"It's enormous," Steele replied. "If it's completely underground, it must be under a park, or an old historic site. Think, Travis. Where's the most likely park?"

But Travis laughed. "Are you serious? There are dozens of parks in Chicago. It could be any one of them."

"What if we eliminate old historic buildings that have underground parking? Does that help?"

Travis shook his head. "Chicago's a big city . . . over nine million people. It could be anywhere. Besides, we don't even know what part of the city we're in."

"Where's Maddie Fey?" asked Riley.

Travis shrugged. "Ahead somewhere. She said she was going to send her magic to search for human life."

Depressed, they moved along another corridor. And always they were accompanied by the dismal blue lighting. They were not surprised to discover more cells along both sides of many of the passageways. Aware that they still hadn't found a place to hide out and were running a serious risk of getting trapped, Steele tried to hurry, moving silently, checking the cells on one side of the corridor while Riley and Travis checked those on the other side. But it was slow, discouraging work, and more than once he almost gave up.

"Mac, is that you?" He stopped outside a cell halfway along the hall, his skin prickling. Moving closer, he stared inside. There was something . . . a shadow in the far corner. "Who's there?"

Nothing.

"Talk to me," Steele pleaded. "I know about the missing kids. I've rescued some of them. I can help you."

Silence.

The hair on the back of Steele's neck bristled. He hurried

on, pulling Riley and Travis with him. "There's something in there," he said.

"What?" Riley stared into the nearest cell.

"I don't know," said Steele, "but . . ."

Travis gripped Steele's arm. "What if the cells are filled with kids whose memories were stolen? What if the reason they're not answering is that they can't—they don't remember how to talk?"

Riley joined in. "That makes sense. And what if they don't even know their memories are gone because they don't remember?"

"I thought of that," said Steele, shivering. "But I don't think the kids are here. I got a really bad feeling when I looked into that cell."

Riley suddenly tensed. A look of horror appeared on her face. "Maddie Fey is searching for humans. She would have told us if she had found any. Oh my God, do you know what that means?"

Steele gulped and glanced nervously over his shoulder. Then he looked at Riley and nodded. "Yeah, it means that whatever's in there isn't human."

The companions looked at each other. Then, with one voice, they yelled and took off for the end of the corridor, not daring to look over their shoulders. They skidded around a corner, through an arched tunnel, and came to an abrupt stop, holding their sides and gasping for air. The way was blocked by a sturdy door warded by an enormous black lock.

"No, no!" Steele groaned in frustration.

"We've got to go back," said Travis, "past that cell."

"Well, we can stare at that door all we want, but it's not going to open," said Steele irritably. "Let's go."

He turned and started to retrace their steps, forcing himself not to think of what was lurking in the shadowed cell they had passed on the way.

"Listen," hissed Travis, suddenly going still. "Hear that?"

Steele heard it, and recognized it immediately. It was the same sound he had heard the night the two Maladroids came to the cell dragging the dying boy, the sound of a cell door clanging open. The sound was magnified now because not one, but many cell doors had just clanged open. Steele tried to swallow, but his mouth was too dry. He looked from Travis to Riley. Should he tell them that whatever had been lurking in the shadowed cells were now loose?

"What do you think that was all about?" asked Travis quietly.

Steele opened his mouth to tell them that something had been set free, but Riley's excited cry stopped the words on his tongue. He turned from Travis and saw her staring intently at the door.

"It's not locked; it only looks that way," she said, rushing over to the door, twisting the locking bar, and lifting the lock free. She held it up triumphantly.

"We didn't pass her, so Maddie Fey must have left it unlocked for us."

Travis's expression went from disappointed to hopeful as he and Riley pulled on the heavy door. Steele joined them, feeling sick with relief. Sweat ran freely down his face and neck. The thought of being cornered by whatever was now following their scent or searching for them was too horrible to contemplate.

"Put the lock back," he cautioned Riley. "If anyone comes looking for us, they'll think the door is still locked."

"Too bad we couldn't lock it from the inside," said Travis, not really expecting an answer.

The door scraped open and they passed through in single file. Stopping just inside, they stared wide-eyed at what lay before them. It was immediately obvious that they had entered a different section of the prison. The strange blue lighting didn't reach here. Glancing up, Steele noticed that what lighting there was came from directly above—a single bare light bulb screwed into a socket at the end of a twisted wire dangling from the high ceiling. The weak light shone a large circle on the dark stone floor, but beyond the circle, rising to the ceiling like a great wall, everything was as black as the inside of a buried coffin.

"Where's Maddie Fey?" Riley looked about. "There weren't any other tunnels. She *had* to come this way."

"She did," said Steele. "Or at least someone's been here. Look!" He pointed at the floor where the light revealed years, perhaps centuries, of dust lying undisturbed except for a single set of footprints disappearing into the blackness.

They held a hurried conference to decide what to do.

"If you guys want to wait here, I'll go check out what's in there," Travis volunteered.

"I'm coming with you," said Steele. "All we have to do is follow Maddie Fey's footprints." He glanced into the gloom. "If we can see them." Then he added silently. *And let's hope they really are Maddie Fey's footprints.*

"If you think I'm staying here all by myself, you're wrong." Riley was emphatic. "Let's all go."

But they lingered a while longer, staring into the blackness as if they feared that it might devour them. As they stared, they moved closer together.

"Is it me, or does that black look *really* black?" asked Travis.

"It's not you," said Riley. "The footprints disappear." She spoke to Steele. "I don't like this. It's like emptiness—as if nothing's there."

"Sort of like a black hole," added Travis, extending his arm slowly toward the void.

The others watched as Travis stuck out his finger and cautiously touched the blackness. His finger vanished as if it had been abruptly severed. But when he snatched his hand back in shock, his finger was intact. He backed away, staring at his finger as if he couldn't believe it was still attached to his hand.

"If that isn't the freakiest thing," he said.

Steele grilled him. "What did it feel like? Did it hurt you? Did you touch anything?"

Travis shrugged. "It just felt creepy, sort of like if you were blindfolded and stuck your finger into honey. It didn't hurt a bit."

Steele felt strangely exposed under the light. While his eyes couldn't penetrate the black wall, he couldn't shake the feeling that something was lurking in the dark place, watching him. He heard Riley say, "I'm scared."

"Listen!" he said. "I know it looks scary, but those are Maddie Fey's footprints. The footprints lead into that black wall. If she went in there it must be OK. But stick close. This place gives me the creeps."

"That's because it is not a good place," agreed a voice nearby. Maddie Fey appeared like a wraith out of the blackness.

The Mage's sudden appearance startled Steele. One look at

his friends told him their hearts were also racing. They gathered about Maddie Fey, firing questions like bullets.

"Did you find Mac?"

"What about other humans?"

"Is there a way out of here?

"When we were going along the last corridor, we heard something in one of the cells, and it's *not* human," said Riley, making a statement while looking at Maddie Fey questioningly.

Travis was back to staring at the blackness. He appeared fascinated. "What *is* that black stuff?"

Maddie Fey's eyes were midnight blue as they travelled over the companions to finally settle on Steele. "Your friend is here . . . alive . . ."

"Mac's alive. Thank goodness!" exclaimed Riley, crying. Then she was hugging Steele so tightly he could scarcely breathe. "I was so afraid he . . ."

"No," said Steele, feeling a strange mixture of relief and angst. "I think we'd know. I mean, I don't think Mac could die without us knowing." When Riley released him, he turned to Maddie Fey. "Where is he? Did you see him?"

"Not in person," she replied. "I sent my powers to search for living humans. Where the darkness ends, there is nothing but a solid stone wall. It appears to be a dead end, but there is something behind that wall. I sent my powers through the stone, and Mac and others are there, somewhere. I could not search for an opening or hidden doorway because I had to find my way back to you."

"These powers you sent," said Steele, "would they know if Mac's memories were stolen?"

Maddie Fey shook her head. "I used very little power, mere tendrils that couldn't be detected."

"Then we've got to rescue him before that happens," said Steele, and before the others could stop him he turned away and stepped out of the circle of light and into the blackness.

The shock was instantaneous. Steele felt as if he had plunged into an ocean of thick black paint and he fought to breathe. A hand grabbed his jacket and yanked him back into the light. He dropped to his knees, shuddering as he gasped for air.

Maddie Fey frowned at him. "If I had not reached you, you would have been lost." She paused, her eyes staring at something that Steele could not see.

Watching her, Steele wondered if her knowledge came from experience. Had she been wandering lost in the blackness until they came through the door? He wanted to ask, but she looked so preoccupied that he remained silent.

"What is it?" asked Riley.

Maddie Fey shook her head. "I don't know what it is but I know that it was created by magic, a particularly dark magic."

"What are we going to do?" asked Riley.

"I can guide you to the end," answered Maddie Fey. "But you must do exactly what I tell you." She looked at each of them in turn. "You must obey me without question. Do you understand?" She waited until Steele and the others nodded before continuing. "I can keep you safe as long as you don't give in to your fear."

Travis brushed his hand over his rust-coloured hair. "I won't be scared as long as I know what to expect when we go in there."

"I would gladly tell what you will see in there if I could," said Maddie Fey. "But I cannot remember. Come now. Hold on to one another and do not let go, no matter what."

"We can tie ourselves together," suggested Riley, producing the ball of cord from her pocket and holding it up.

"Excellent," Travis praised her, taking the rope and tying it about Steele's wrist, then Riley's, and his own. But when he offered it to Maddie Fey, she shook her head.

"I do not need to be bound," she said. "I will hold your arm, Travis, and I will not let go."

Without another word, she stepped into the blackness, and they followed.

Searching

We searched for our lost brother for three hundred years, but we found no trace, not a single clue that might lead us to him. But three hundred years is but a single heartbeat in the span of our lives. We will not abandon the search until we find him or exact revenge upon his murderer.

The Tsilihins' attempts to escape from their molten prison grew in frequency and violence. They tore at Earth from the inside, ripping great jagged openings on the surface that swallowed islands and cities along with their inhabitants.

We recognized the shadowy hand that directed them from its dark place.

—**Excerpt from** *The Wardens' Logs*

Chapter Thirteen

A Light in the Darkness

It was like a living thing, a penetrating blackness that played with their minds and filled them with doubt and despair. It wrapped itself about them and clung to their clothes with invisible gripping fingers that threatened to pull them down. It found its way into their mouths and slipped down their throats. Steele blinked repeatedly to force his eyes to adjust, but when he raised his hand in front of his face, he saw nothing.

Riley's grip on his arm tightened and she screamed, drowning out the sound of Travis sobbing. Then Steele was screaming too, because the Prince of Darkness was in his house in Wychwood Park driving a long, pointed steel knitting needle into GM's heart, the fleshless lips in the creature's horrible scabby face leering. And when at last GM was still, the figure turned slowly, blood dripping from the tip of the knitting needle it held in its clawed hand. It opened its mouth, white fangs gleaming, and hissed, *"I'm watching you."* Then it lunged at Steele.

Steele screamed, struggling to free his wrist from the rope that bound him to the others, but Travis's knot held tight and he couldn't break away.

"Steele! It's all right," said Maddie Fey.

Steele realized that his eyes were closed tightly. He opened them, relieved to find that he could see again. In front of him, a massive stone wall extended about one hundred feet on either side. Overhead, a single light bulb emitted a pale, ghostly glow. The wall rose beyond the reach of the light. Steele looked at Maddie Fey in horror.

"I've got to go home," he said. But when he searched his mind for an answer to his friends' questioning looks, he couldn't remember why he had felt such a sudden, urgent need to get back to Wychwood Park.

"The dark reflected our worst fears," said Maddie Fey, "and twisted and magnified them in our minds."

"What did you see?" Steele asked her.

Maddie Fey smiled sadly. "It will not help you to know what the darkness held for me, Steele. It is enough if I tell you that everything I have worked so long and so hard to accomplish crumbled to dust in those moments, but I cannot recall any details."

Steele wanted her to say more, but the sound of the heavy door grating open at the other side of the blackness brought the discussion to an abrupt end.

Steele pulled Maddie Fey aside. "Just before we came into this place all the cell doors opened at the same time. There was something alive in at least one of the cells we passed. I think it and probably others are tracking us."

"And when were you going to tell *us?*" demanded Riley, sounding more indignant than Steele had ever heard her. She and Travis had come up behind him and had heard every word.

Steele felt himself turn guilt-red as he faced them. "I'm sorry," he said, appealing to Travis. "You heard the sound first, Travis. We were just outside the door. Remember?"

Travis nodded doubtfully.

Steele turned to Riley. "I recognized the sound because I had heard it before . . . the night they left the dying boy . . . I mean . . . the night they left Maddie Fey in our cell. They had to open the bars to drop her inside. You must have heard it too, Riley. It woke you up. It was the same sound Travis heard. I meant to tell you, but then you discovered that the door wasn't locked, and other stuff happened, and I guess I just forgot about it."

Riley glowered at him but said nothing.

"Knock it off, you two," said Travis. "We've got enough seriously bad creatures after us that there's no need to fight among ourselves."

Steele reached for Riley's arm. "I'm sorry, Riley. Honestly, I didn't do it on purpose,"

"I know," sighed Riley. "But it bothers me that you didn't tell me about the cell doors. I'm not a Mage, Steele. I can't read your mind."

She stomped over to Maddie Fey, who was studying the stone wall, looking for a way through. Travis joined Maddie Fey and Riley, and Steele followed reluctantly, arriving in time to hear Travis ask innocently, "Can't you just blast the wall apart with magic?"

"I could," answered Maddie Fey shortly, "if I wished to announce our whereabouts to whatever is on the other side of this wall." She placed her hands on the stone. "There is no magic in the stones; therefore the opening must be cleverly disguised." She stepped back and let her eyes travel slowly from one end of the wall to the other, studying the placement of the stones and searching for irregularities in the pattern.

Steele walked up to the wall and began tracing the outlines of the stones.

Maddie Fey encouraged him. "That's good. Look for indentations, or deep crevices, or any loose stones. Help him, Riley."

Steele noticed Travis moving toward the far end, pushing against the wall with his shoulder. Riley suddenly turned and stared into the blackness. "I heard something," she said, pointing. "In there."

Steele turned to face the same way. The longer he stared at the blackness, the more it seemed to twist and writhe into menacing shapes. He listened but heard nothing. Perhaps Riley had imagined the sound. He knew he should be helping Travis search for the opening in the wall. The thought of having to walk back through the dark place made him weak.

Then Steele heard it—a single low growl. He caught Riley's arm and backed up until he bumped into the wall, his eyes pinned to the black. The growl suddenly erupted into screams and snarls. Keeping a firm grip on Riley's arm, Steele hurried over to Maddie Fey. She was staring into the blackness, too, the expression on her oval face unreadable. Steele focused on the spot where she was looking. It seemed to be rippling, as if something had disturbed it. Steele narrowed his eyes. The ripples spread outward. Abruptly the screams and snarls died away, and a menacing silence filled the space. But the ripples continued to spread. Whatever was in there was coming closer.

Steele remembered the knife that was resting just inside the top of his boot. As he reached for it, he opened his mouth to warn the others, but at that moment two things happened simultaneously.

Something huge and dark leaped out of the blackness straight at his throat, and at the edge of his vision he saw Travis fall into the stone wall and disappear. And then the creature was upon him, snarling and frothing. It knocked Steele backwards. Pain erupted as his head connected with stone and he slid to the floor, the beast on top of him crushing his chest and forcing the air from his lungs.

It was over as quickly as it had begun. The creature bounded off his chest and Steele could breathe again. Dazed and hurting, he struggled to his feet, arms flailing. He looked about wildly, and found himself staring into the weird silver eyes of his attacker—Wish, Maddie Fey's silver hound.

Maddie Fey knelt beside Wish, stroking the Great Hound's neck. She looked up at Steele and smiled apologetically. "It wasn't intentional. Wish was following us, guarding our backs. The creatures that were let loose to hunt us down attacked him in the blackness. He fought, but there were too many. He barely escaped with his life."

For the first time, Steele noticed the matted wet fur on Wish's side and the spattering of bright red spots on the floor. He looked at his own hands, suddenly realizing that they were red and sticky with the hound's blood. He moved closer, but not too close. "He's hurt."

"But he's going to be all right, isn't he?" asked Riley. She crouched on the floor beside Maddie Fey and slowly reached out to touch Wish's head. "Poor Wish."

"The gashes are deep, but they will heal," said Maddie Fey. "I must stop the bleeding."

She reached into her coat and produced a miniature silver vial. Removing the stopper, she gently daubed a thick brown substance on the hound's injuries. "Aval, it's like your mud," she explained as she worked. "It will stem the bleeding and cleanse the wounds, neutralizing any poison that may have entered his system."

Riley paled. "Poison? You think . . ."

"There is confusion in Wish's mind that was not present before the creature raked his side."

"How do you know?" asked Steele. "And don't tell me he told you."

"He told me," said Maddie Fey, as if conversing with a hound was as ordinary as buttering toast. "He told me that there are hundreds of them and they are coming for us."

The words had barely left her mouth when Wish's hackles bristled and a low growl came from deep in his throat. The hound's head rotated toward the darkness. Steele looked about. Maddie Fey was facing the black space, her slim body poised to react quickly when the first creature broke through. Wish was in his usual spot by her side, body tense and trembling with some emotion. Riley was standing on Wish's other side, her fingers nervously making trails in the raised silver hair on his neck and back. . . .

"Where's Travis?" Steele shouted. Then he took off for the far end of the wall where he had seen Travis disappear into the stones. "Travis!"

Travis's head popped out of the wall. "What?" The rest of his body materialized.

Steele skidded to a stop, staring at his new friend in disbelief. "You found the hidden door!" He looked over his shoulder and shouted to Maddie Fey and Riley. "Over here! Hurry!"

Travis grinned proudly. "I tried to make it to the end, but I finally came back. I thought you might be freaking out wondering what happened to me."

His eyes widened and he pointed at Wish. "What *is* that?"

Steele told him, and then added, "The creatures from the cells were chasing him. They almost caught him, too. He leaped out of the blackness right on top of me."

Riley came up to them, breathless. She walked over to the wall and felt about with her hands until she found the opening. "Good work, Travis." Then, without taking her eyes from the wall, she took several steps back and stared at the spot that marked the opening. "It's amazingly clever. I know the opening's there, but I can't see it."

"Come on. Let's go," said Steele, desperate to get away before the creatures broke through. "Travis, you know the way, so you go first."

"Wait!" cried Riley. "We can't go without Maddie Fey."

They looked back the way they had come. Maddie Fey and Wish hadn't moved.

Steele sighed, exasperated. "Go ahead. I'll get her."

He ran along the wall until he reached the spot where Maddie Fey stood, silver eyes focused on the black space.

"Forget it, Maddie Fey. We've got to get out of here."

Maddie Fey glanced at him, her eyes shifting from blue to silver. "Remember what I said about passing through the blackness without giving in to your fears?"

Steele nodded.

"It changed you . . . made you stronger," she said. "Well, I too came through it unscathed. I am stronger, more powerful than you could ever imagine. I cannot leave this evil place standing. I must destroy it." She opened her right fist, her hand cupped to shield the white spark that winked in the middle of her snow-white palm. Bending her head, she gently blew the spark out of her hand. It shot into the darkness, and was gone.

"What was that?" asked Steele.

Maddie Fey smiled. "A light. I sent a light into the darkness."

Steele sighed heavily. "What good will it do?" he asked. "That black stuff extinguished it. I saw it disappear."

"No," said Maddie Fey. "Darkness is nothing, an absence of light. It cannot destroy light. The spark will grow and drive away the blackness."

"What about those creatures?"

With Wish at her side, Maddie Fey turned and began to walk toward Riley and Travis. "They are a type of Maladroid. I do not know what will happen to them, but if they are creatures of darkness . . . I mean if darkness is what binds them . . . then the light will reveal them to one another."

"And . . . ?"

"I suspect they will turn their hatred and rage upon their own kind," said Maddie Fey so softly that Steele had to strain to catch the words.

"And that makes you sad?" asked Steele, mystified. "Those creatures aren't like us. They don't think. They don't reason. They feel nothing. They would have killed Wish, and you know they'll kill us if they get out of there."

Maddie Fey glanced at him. "What you say is true. But I don't know how they were altered from their former state. I have never seen such creatures. I sent my power through the blackness and it lingered on them as if they were human. It returned to me uncertain. I believe that they, or at least a part of them, were once human. These creatures were altered, remade to track and kill. I do not know if they chose evil knowingly. But if they were caught and this was done to them, then it is their creator, not they, who is truly evil."

"I still don't feel sorry for them," said Steele.

They joined the others, and Travis reddened, beaming with pride, when Maddie Fey praised him for finding the opening and taking the initiative to check it out.

"It's tricky," he explained. "It's a series of walls built close together, and in such a way that the wall immediately behind the opening is the same pattern as the wall in front. It looks solid."

"Like an optical illusion," suggested Riley.

"Exactly," said Travis. "The second wall is made of glass or mirrors or some metal that's painted like rocks, or it's more sophisticated and the rocks are projected onto the wall." He shook his head. "It beats me how they did it, but I've got the bumps to prove it's hard to find the openings." He pushed the hair from his forehead to reveal several nasty-looking lumps, already darkening. "Before we go in there, I have to warn you to keep in single file, or you'll end up with a broken nose or a serious headache. I got through seven walls. I think I can find the openings again."

The others nodded and followed Travis through the opening. Maddie Fey and Wish went first, with Riley on their heels. Steele brought up the rear. Just as he stepped inside the opening, behind him in the blackness he heard the screams. He paused and looked back. Maddie Fey's spark was already doing its work. Everything was brighter. He could just make out another light bulb dangling from the ceiling, where seconds ago everything had been as black as tar. Maddie Fey was right. The creatures were turning on one another. He had said that he didn't feel sorry for them, but now he wished he could take those words back. The ripping, snarling, shrieking, dying sounds filled him with despair. He turned and fled blindly through the wall.

Their flight through the openings in the walls triggered an old memory in Steele's mind. On his fifth birthday, his father had taken him to the Canadian National Exhibition. It was in September. They had stopped outside the House of Glass and watched people bump into the glass as they tried to navigate the maze. Steele had giggled in delight and begged his father to let him go inside. Because the interior of the structure was visible from the outside, his father had capitulated.

Inside, Steele had found himself trapped in a nightmare. He couldn't distinguish the openings from the glass partitions and kept smashing into the walls. Panicked, he started to cry, running wildly about, bashing his face into the glass. His father watched from outside in horror as Steele screamed for help, blood streaming from his nose. Finally, his father raced inside, but couldn't make his way to Steele.

Just thinking about it brought sweat out on Steele's forehead. For him, the scariest part was seeing his father but being unable to reach him. If it hadn't been for an Exhibition worker who came to their rescue and led them out of the glass maze, Steele sometimes believed, in his darker moments, that he'd still be trapped somewhere in the House of Glass.

Now he followed Riley, counting off the openings as he passed through them. He appreciated the ordeal Travis had gone through as he had carefully, not to mention painfully, searched out each opening. They reached the seventh wall, and then managed to find and make their way through another seven before they reached the end.

Before them was a massive door, framed by an archway cut out of solid rock. Over the arch was a cracked and worn stone shield bearing heraldic symbols that were no longer identifiable. Much of the stone had broken away. Carved into the stone, directly under the shield, Steele could just make out a strange symbol, then a lot of letters, or marks that could be letters, followed by a different symbol.

"What does it say?" asked Riley, squinting at the letters.

"I can't make it out, but I don't think it's English." He thought of asking Maddie Fey to use her powers to create light, but when he looked her way, she was staring at the engraved symbols and markings with such intensity that he decided against it.

"Here, Riley," said Travis. "If you can balance on my shoulders, you should be high enough to read what it says."

"There is no need for that," said Maddie Fey quietly. "I know what it says."

The others looked at her, waiting.

"In your language it says: ABANDON ALL HOPE, YE WHO ENTER HERE."

Steele gulped. What did it mean, exactly? The expression sounded familiar. Where had he heard it before? He tried to match letters to words. "It doesn't even look like English letters."

"That is because the engraver did not use English," said Maddie Fey. "The one who carved those words into the stone used a language known only to the Mages of my planet."

Death

Time and again we saved the peoples of this world from extinction. There were times when we longed for the world we had left billions of years ago with such a fierce, wild longing that it left us disconsolate and trembling. There was no peace here. The Tsilihin, whom our Mages had deemed would die in Earth's fiery heart, or remain forever locked within the pods that had contained them, waged wanton war upon the planet. They burned and killed. That was what they did; that was all that they did.

At one time or another, they set every city that had been built ablaze; they spewed fire from the mountains and rained fire from the sky. They tore at Earth's tectonic plates, causing quakes that leveled great cities, and tidal waves that washed away all that was in their paths.

And when the Fire Demons weren't killing and burning, human arms were raised against humans.

—Excerpt from *The Wardens' Logs*

Chapter Fourteen

The Other Side of the Door

Steele whistled. "So a Mage engraved these words?"

"No. That is not possible," said Maddie Fey.

"Then who?" asked Travis.

Maddie Fey shrugged, seemingly as bewildered as the rest of them. "I don't know. I don't understand." She looked at Steele. "Except for me and Fidus, your mother and grandmother were the only Mages from my planet ever to visit Earth."

"If you're insinuating that they carved those words," Steele said defensively, "you're wrong."

"I have not accused your relations," said Maddie Fey sharply. "In fact, I know that they could not have engraved those words. The words were here long before your grandmother arrived."

"How do you know?" asked Riley.

Maddie Fey raised her arm toward the carved phrase. "Look at the engraving, at the cracks in the stone and the worn edges of the letters. This was done hundreds, maybe thousands of years ago. Steele's grandmother came to Earth much later."

"I know that expression," Travis announced. "It's from *The Divine Comedy,* a poem written by an Italian, Dante something, in the fourteenth century." He grinned sheepishly.

"I haven't exactly read it. It's just that it's used all the time in crossword puzzles and my dad's a puzzle maniac."

Maddie Fey smiled. "You have not considered the possibility that Dante may have learned of that expression from an earlier source."

The others looked at her, waiting for her to elaborate. But she would say no more.

"What are we going to do now?" asked Riley.

"We have only two choices," answered Maddie Fey. "Go back, or—"

"Open the door and go through," finished Travis.

"We can't go back," complained Riley. "Not after we've come this far."

Maddie Fey looked at Steele. "What do you say?"

"We go on," said Steele.

"Onward and upward," said Travis.

Maddie Fey reached for the handle and pulled on the door. It creaked open and they stepped across the threshold.

The sight that awaited them stole Steele's breath away.

Below, a vast, desolate valley stretched to left and right as far as he could see. On the valley floor was an oily black lake, its surface slick and smooth as glass. On the far side of the lake, set back against what appeared to be mountains, rose a colossal structure with four sloping triangular sides. It was as black as the bats on Maddie Fey's ears.

A black pyramid, thought Steele, feeling something cold touch his back. His mind replayed the words he had heard coming from the ground in Wychwood Park over a week ago. *Come here, little boy! Down into my dark place.*

"We can't stay here," he said, his voice scratchy with fear.

The others looked at him sharply.

"What are you talking about?" said Riley. "We've got to find Mac."

Steele shook his head repeatedly. "You don't understand." He waved his arm to indicate the valley. "This is the dark place. The Prince of Darkness . . . all of this . . . it's his. He's here."

No one spoke for a long time. Whatever they had expected to discover upon reaching the other side of the wall, it was clear from their expressions that it wasn't the scene below them. There were no signs of life in this terrible place. Nothing grew here; nothing moved on the valley floor. Everything was as still as the oily surface of the lake. Overhead, a thick, red haze replaced the sky. Steele's eyes came back to rest on the monstrous Black Pyramid. It was hideous and obscene, and he wanted to smash it into dust and scatter the particles to the ends of the Earth so that they could never come together again.

He glanced at Riley, wondering what she was thinking now. Was she worrying about Mac, in the clutches of the Prince of Darkness? She was gazing into the valley, her thin arms wrapped protectively about her chest. She looked so small and wretched that Steele went to her. He wished that he could think of something to say that would erase the despair he had seen in her mind.

"Is it ever going to end, Steele?" she asked, without turning.

Steele stared at the Black Pyramid, noticing for the first time the absence of windows. "Yes," he said. "It's going to end. But I don't know how or when."

Riley sighed. "I don't know if this makes sense or not. But it seems that whenever we set out to do something that sounds pretty straightforward, something happens. And instead of getting on with what we're supposed to do, we end up having to do other things first."

"I know," agreed Steele. "We set out to find the other missing kids, then Mac goes missing, and we have to find him first. Then we get captured by the Maladroids." He laughed bitterly. "If it wasn't so frustrating, it'd be funny."

Riley almost smiled. "I'm not sorry I came, Steele. Not for one second. But things seem so big, so beyond our control, that I keep wondering what we're doing here. Do you seriously think that we can do what the police in Toronto, New York, and Chicago couldn't do?" She sighed wearily. "Sometimes I feel that I'm disappearing, shrinking like GM. I've been scared to death so often, I'm starting to feel numb inside."

Steele put his arm about her shoulders. "I know the feeling, Riley. Sometimes I want to chuck everything—just turn my back on Maddie Fey, and Fidus, and all of this—and walk away. Sometimes I want to go home so badly I feel I'm going to die."

"But we can't," said Riley, "much as we want to. We'd never forgive ourselves, would we?"

Steele shook his head.

As Maddie Fey joined them, Steele looked about for Travis and spotted him gazing at the Black Pyramid in awe. Drawing Steele aside, Maddie Fey said, "There is a great evil in this place. Do you feel it?"

Steele nodded. "I felt it the moment we entered this place."

"We need to get inside," said Maddie Fey, pointing toward the Black Pyramid. "But for now, we should move farther along the ledge and find a protected place. Then, while you and the others rest, I will send small fingers of magic to probe the outer walls for a way in."

Steele, who had been operating for hours on nervous energy, felt a deep weariness creep through his body. His legs felt like blocks of concrete as he forced himself to stumble after his companions in search of a resting place. At that moment, his fear of the Prince of Darkness was driven from his mind by the more immediate need for sleep, water, and food.

After some searching they found a niche in a crevice that cut deep into the stone cliff. It was easily big enough to conceal them. No one spoke as they sank onto the hard rock floor. Wish positioned himself across the opening, head resting on his paws, and watched them. Steele leaned against the wall and tried to work out how many hours had passed since they stepped out of Maddie Fey's limo onto the bridge. At least twelve, he decided, but it felt more like a week. He pulled back his sleeve to check the time, only to realize that his watch was missing.

"Dirk!" he muttered, disgusted.

Steele tried to picture his father listening to the message he had left, but it made him feel sad and he quickly turned his mind to his present situation.

Through half-closed lids, he let his gaze wander from one companion to another. Maddie Fey was sitting just outside the niche on a footstool-sized boulder. She was staring down into the valley. Wish got up and padded to her. He dropped on the ledge beside her and also looked down, ears raised as if he were hearing sounds that were outside the range of human ears. But then Steele heard the sound of Travis's pen scratching across his notebook and wondered if that was the sound that had made Wish's ears twitch. Steele grinned at the sight of Travis scribbling furiously, his lips moving silently as he wrote about their adventures.

Riley was staring intently at the Mage. Steele sensed that she was seeing the limousine disappear from the bridge, and still hurting.

Then Riley took a deep breath and said, "When the Maladroids were after us on the bridge, why didn't you help us? Why did the limo disappear? We thought you had left us there all alone."

Maddie Fey resettled herself on the rock so that she was facing her companions, her eyes cloudy and thoughtful. "Your questions are intelligent and direct, Riley. They deserve straight answers. The second question is easy. The limousine didn't disappear. It just seemed that way."

"But how . . . ?" Riley started. Then she nodded. "Magic! You used magic to hide it."

"Yes," answered Maddie Fey.

"So it was there the whole time?" Steele asked, amazed.

Maddie Fey nodded. "You asked why I did not come to your aid when those creatures appeared on the bridge. The answer is more complicated than the question, but I will do my best." She looked down at her hands resting on her knees for a moment. Then she raised her eyes to Riley and continued. "Until Steele heard the voice of the Prince of Darkness calling to him in the passageways under Grand Central Terminal, neither I nor Fidus had heard that name. Later, Steele actually saw the creature in the shadowed hall as we drew closer to the missing children. At that time, we became aware of a new enemy, a powerful enemy who possessed magic that we had not encountered before."

She stopped and waited until she seemed satisfied that Riley was following her. "Just as we learned of the Prince of Darkness, he learned of us. He is now aware that there is more to Steele than he had believed. It must have come as a severe blow when he realized that the boy he sought was not a mere schoolboy, ignorant of his power to destroy the Fire Demons—"

"But how did he find out about you and Fidus?" asked Steele.

Instead of answering, Maddie Fey asked, "What was Fidus doing when you sensed that the Prince of Darkness was watching us?"

Steele racked his brain for the memory of their passage along the corridor with the darkened arches. Then he remembered that they were being pursued. "You're right. Fidus had one of the attackers trapped and he was trying to break into its mind."

"I asked you why you didn't help us fight the Maladroids," said Riley. "What does that have to do with what happened in New York?"

Maddie Fey smiled at Riley. "Be patient, Riley. What I am telling you forms part of the answer. Now then, when Nilats realized that Mac was gone, he came for me at once."

"Ha!" Steele exclaimed rudely, but Maddie Fey continued as if she hadn't heard him. "I could have acted rashly, but that is not my way. I asked myself what would be the effect if I used magic to fight the Maladroids. If they were simply carrying out their master's orders—capturing human boys and girls for their memories—there was a good chance that they knew nothing about Steele. If that were the case, by coming to your aid with magic I would have caused them to become suspicious, and they may have run off with you before I could stop all of them. Do you understand, Riley?"

"I guess," said Riley.

"On the other hand," continued Maddie Fey, "if the Maladroids were sent to kill the one who had the power to destroy the Fire Demons, I could not take the chance that they wouldn't kill Steele before I could act." She laughed. "Actually, I did not know what I was going to do until I got close enough to hear their thoughts, and that's when I learned that they had been ordered to capture you and bring you to the cells under the Water Tower—"

"What!" Travis wasn't taking notes now. He was staring at Maddie Fey, astonished. "Did you say we're under the Water Tower?"

Maddie Fey nodded. "But we've travelled a long way from the cells, Travis. We've gone deeper underground and farther."

"It doesn't matter," cried Travis. "I know where we are . . . I mean . . . I know where the Water Tower is . . . everyone in Chicago knows that . . . but . . . Look, it'll be easier if I draw a map and show you." Travis bent over the notebook and worked quickly, a frown of concentration on his face.

While he worked on his map, Riley pressed Maddie Fey for the rest of the answer to her question.

"As I was saying," continued Maddie Fey. "When I learned that the Maladroids' orders were to capture you, Fidus and I decided to let them capture me as well. That way, I could still protect you. I don't think the Maladroids knew that you were the one the Fire Demons have been seeking. Dirk certainly didn't know why they wanted you."

"That's true," said Steele. "He said as much when he came to the cell."

"He sounded almost jealous of Steele," added Riley. "But where did *you* see Dirk?"

"Dirk was there watching when they tortured the boy. I learned much about Steele's old enemy. Young Dirk is very worried. He took something from Steele and kept the theft a secret from the Prince of Darkness."

"He took all of our stuff," Riley complained bitterly.

"I am talking about Ees," said Maddie Fey. "Since Dirk did not mention the medallion to his master, he cannot suddenly claim that he forgot to turn it in."

"How does the POD even know about Steele's medallion?" asked Travis, looking up from his notebook.

"When Steele became aware of his presence in the shadows in New York, the POD watched Steele remove it from beneath his shirt."

"Talk about stupid," Steele said in disgust.

"It wasn't stupid, Steele. You reached for Ees instinctively, for comfort or protection."

"If you think about it, Dirk may have done us a favour by stealing Ees," said Riley. "The Prince . . . the POD knows that Steele has a curious medallion; since no medallion was found on Mac or Steele or Travis, he might think that they're not the one he's searching for, and instead of killing them, he'll treat them like all the other kids . . . take their memories."

"Very good, Riley," said Maddie Fey warmly. "There was another reason for allowing them to capture me. I had no knowledge of these Maladroids. I smelled the strong odour of dark magic in their flesh, but they do not possess magic. Their extraordinary ability to climb walls and leap from great heights is the result of altering. They were altered so as to be agile.

"I had to know who created them. The Fire Demons can shape-change, or animate the dead body of an animate being or inanimate object, but they do not possess the magic to effect a permanent change. They could not have created the Maladroids. Now that we are inside the realm of the Prince of Darkness, I must discover what sort of creature he is, how he came by his magic, and the nature of his alliance with the Fire Demons." She raised her eyebrows at Riley. "Have I answered your question?"

Riley sighed. "I think so. But didn't you take a risk in getting captured? What if they had put you in another part of the prison, or taken you to the place where they're holding Mac?"

"That was the easiest part," answered Maddie Fey. "I planted a command in the Maladroids' minds. They were to put me in the cell with you to frighten you, to show you what was in store for you."

Riley shivered. "It worked. We were terrified."

"I've got a question," said Steele. "When we got out of the limo on the bridge, we knew at once that we were not in New York. Riley and Mac knocked on the limo windows but no one came. Why didn't you open the door for us?"

His question seemed to surprise Maddie Fey. She stood, her face ashen. "You are mistaken," she said.

"It's true," said Riley. "Mac and I pounded on the windows."

"I do not understand," said Maddie Fey, sinking slowly onto the boulder. "Nilats was waiting outside the limousine. He would have seen you. So you see, what you are saying simply couldn't have happened . . . unless . . ." She stopped and seemed to collect her thoughts. "Unless there was another limousine on the bridge."

"Two limos," cried Riley. "That doesn't make sense."

"Yes, it does," said Steele. "It makes perfect sense." He locked eyes with Maddie Fey. "You're right. There had to be two limos. The one Mac and Riley knocked on was an illusion, a trick to prevent us from going back to the real limo."

"It wasn't an illusion," said Riley. "It was real."

"Why didn't Nilats see the other limo?" asked Travis, chewing on the end of his pen.

"For the same reason we didn't see Nilats or Maddie Fey's limo."

Maddie Fey got up and joined them inside the niche. "I'm beginning to understand the way magic was used to deceive us. There were two parallel realities on the bridge. You saw one; Nilats saw the other. I must ask Nilats what you were doing in his reality. You couldn't have been alarmed or he would have come for me."

Steele whistled under his breath. He was astounded by the complexity of the differing realities. Someone, probably the Prince of Darkness, had gone to a lot of trouble to ensure that Steele and his friends remained in Chicago.

"OK," said Travis, getting up and waving his notepad. "Take a look at this."

Maddie Fey indicated that Travis should use the flat surface of the boulder. He moved out onto the ledge and knelt on the ground, waiting until the others had joined him. Then, with the others huddled about, he laid the crude map he had drawn on the stone. They studied it in silence for several minutes. Steele noticed that it even showed directions.

"Here's where we met," said Travis, using his pen to point out what he'd marked as Trib Tower. Then he moved the pen ten blocks or more along North Michigan Avenue in a northerly direction, stopping at a castle-like structure with an arched entry and a slew of crenellated battlements, capped by a central domed tower.

Steele and Riley glanced at each other.

"The Water Tower," said Riley. "We saw it in the snowglobe."

"I saw it once before, when I looked in Ees," said Steele. "GM knitted it. But in the knitting Mac was in the tower, and I think it was on fire. I could hear him screaming."

"Are you saying they're going to destroy the Water Tower?" asked Travis, horrified.

"I don't know," admitted Steele. "Maybe Mac *is* there; maybe we should go back." He looked at Maddie Fey.

"I cannot interpret the symbols in your vision, Steele. They belong to you. But I can tell you that you will not find Mac in the Water Tower." She turned and pointed at the Black Pyramid. "I told you before that he is somewhere in there."

"What *is* the Water Tower?" Riley asked Travis.

"Originally it was a water tower, but now it's a tourist information centre," Travis replied. "It's a famous landmark, one of the few buildings that escaped the Great Fire of 1871. I'll tell you all about the fire later. Let's get back to our location." He returned his attention to the map. "Assuming our information is correct, the cell we were in is under the Water Tower." He marked an X on the Water Tower. "After we left the cell, we had no way of knowing whether we were going north, south, east, or west, but we weren't going in a straight line, because the passages twisted and turned a lot. I figure we must have walked a good two hours. And we stopped a lot. So I drew a circle around the Water Tower that represents how far we could have gone. I think we're somewhere underground near the perimeter of the circle." He sat back on his heels and looked at his companions.

"Where's our most likely location?" asked Steele.

"We could be anywhere," said Travis. "But my best guess is that we're probably somewhere around here, close to Lake Michigan, otherwise this place would have been discovered ages ago by construction crews digging underground parking garages."

He stuck the pen into the paper. The others peered at the hole in Lake Shore Park. "We would have been going east, under the Museum of Contemporary Art, between East Pearson and East Chicago Avenue."

"It makes sense that we're under a park," said Steele. "Look how close it is to Lake Michigan. This entire place could be beneath the lake." He looked about for Maddie Fey, but she had left them and was staring out over the valley. In her long black coat, she looked like a witch. He rose and went over to her.

"What are you thinking about?" he asked.

"I am thinking about magic," she replied without looking at him. "About the magic in this place. It is different from any I have ever encountered." She turned to Steele, a thin smile on her lips. "Do not misunderstand me, Steele. I am not afraid of the Prince of Darkness or his magic."

They stood together on the ledge and talked for a long time. Steele no longer felt exhausted; instead he felt wired and restless. At Maddie Fey's urging, he related all that had happened to him and his friends. When he reached the end, Maddie Fey surprised him.

"I was there for some of the time. I was there when the Maladroids captured you in the alley."

"But . . ." His eyes opened wide. "The sack the Maladroid was carrying over its shoulder. Sorry, I should have remembered."

"We will not speak of that," said Maddie Fey.

Steele noticed the tremor that ran through her body.

"Where's Fidus? What happened to the rat . . . I mean, Nilats?"

"I know that you have no love for my friend Nilats," she answered. "Nor he for you. But he and Fidus are searching for us as we speak. And they will keep searching until they find us."

"That's because of you," said Steele. "Not me."

"No," said Maddie Fey. "It's because of what we came here to do. Our mission will fail if we are lost in the dark kingdom. The Fire Demons will destroy your world."

"When Nilats let us out of the limo, we had no idea where we were. Why didn't he tell us that we were in Chicago?"

"Because he probably didn't know," said Maddie Fey.

"Did you know?"

Maddie Fey shook her head. "Sometimes, Steele, the doors take us where we should be, not where we want to be."

Steele didn't understand. A few minutes later, he left her and rejoined Riley and Travis. He saw that Riley was already asleep, and Travis was trying to find a comfortable spot on the stone ledge, his notebook and pen clutched tightly in his hand. He looked up as Steele entered the niche, and then grinned mischievously.

"Do you mind answering one more question?" he called to Maddie Fey, pen poised over the open notepad.

Maddie Fey turned. "What would you like to know, Travis?"

Travis suddenly seemed embarrassed. He took a moment to phrase his question correctly. "Uh . . . I hope you don't mind . . . it's sort of personal."

"I do not mind, Travis."

"Promise you won't get mad, or turn me into something nasty."

"Travis!" exclaimed Steele. "Just ask her."

"OK. If you're sure you don't mind, er, here goes. What does your alien form look like?"

For a moment, Maddie Fey stared at Travis so intently that Steele had a wild thought that she might actually possess another form and change into it. But then she bit her bottom lip as if struggling to control some inner emotion.

"I think you will sleep sounder if you believe that I am as I am," she said, turning away quickly.

Even in the dim light, Steele was positive that he could see her shoulders shaking, but whether she was soundlessly weeping or laughing, he couldn't tell. And then his eyes closed.

From his Dark Chamber in the Black Pyramid, the Prince of Darkness watched the companions as they tossed restlessly and called out in their sleep. Then he laughed silently, and with a long clawed finger, beckoned to Steele's image in the dull black globe on the stone table before him.

Regression

From AD 300 to 800, our prisoners wreaked such havoc upon the planet that civilizations were plunged into an age of darkness. Humankind regressed into being creatures of instinct, their intellects buried and forgotten. Mortals who claimed links to deities ruled others by terror. Those who professed differing opinions were denounced and silenced, tortured and burned alive. Intolerance and ignorance prevailed. Great works of literature and learning and art went up in flames, and in dark rooms by candlelight, the history of mankind was being fabricated in flowing script.

—Excerpt from *The Wardens' Logs*

Chapter Fifteen

Maladroids

It seemed to Steele that he had just fallen asleep when Travis shook him awake. "Go away!" he mumbled, rolling onto his stomach.

"Get up, lazybones," said Travis, "before we eat all the pancakes."

Steele was on his feet instantly, looking about ravenously as Travis and Riley snickered. "That's cruel," he said, his stomach protesting with a loud growl.

"Sorry," Travis grinned. "But nothing else seemed to work. You were out cold, man." He eyed Maddie Fey's hound. "We've been up for hours. I haven't had a bite since my last school lunch, and that must have been at least twenty-four hours ago. I'm so famished, even Wish is starting to look good enough to eat."

"That's horrible," cried Riley. She walked over to where Wish was stretched across the mouth of the niche and knelt down beside the big hound, covering his ears gently with the palms of her hands. "Don't listen to the bad carnivores, Wish." She examined his wounds and felt his soft nose. The Great Hound stared at her, but didn't seem to mind when she touched him. "Good boy! Are you feeling better?"

Steele thought that Maddie Fey's hound looked much better.

His peculiar eyes were brighter and he seemed to be more alert than the day before. Expecting to find Maddie Fey nearby, Steele looked about, but she was nowhere to be seen.

"Where's Maddie Fey?" He thought it strange that Wish was not in his usual place at his mistress's side.

"I am not far," said Maddie Fey, from somewhere outside the recess. "I haven't abandoned you, Steele."

Steele left the others and joined Maddie Fey at the edge of the cliff. He looked across the distance to the Black Pyramid. As he stared at it, a squiggly red line of fire crackled from its peak and danced about the top of the pyramid. The sight of the structure both thrilled and appalled him.

"What's causing those power flares?"

"Magic," answered Maddie Fey.

"Did you find a way in?"

Maddie Fey nodded slowly. "While you slept, I searched for a way in. There are several entrances, but they are heavily guarded and must be avoided. But I may have found another way."

She called the others to her. "I know you are hungry, and thirsty for fresh water. I cannot conjure up a hot breakfast from solid rock, but I can find a water source if one exists in this place. I will show you when we reach the valley, on our way to the Black Pyramid."

They set out then. Maddie Fey and Wish led the way to a narrow set of crude steps carved into the solid rock of the cliff face. Maddie Fey told them that she had discovered the trail while Steele and the others slept, but that she had not followed it. Steele could tell from the thick layer of dirt that no one had used the trail in years. The going was slow and hard. The trail zigzagged precariously; each step had to be tested before they could put their weight on it. Many of the steps were gone, eroded over the ages, leaving behind loose layers of shale that made the descent hazardous. Others looked solid, but had crumbled inside, and they dissolved into rubble when Maddie Fey tested them.

Once, Riley slipped and would have plunged hundreds of feet to her death if Steele and Travis hadn't caught her arms and pulled her to safety.

"It's like stepping on marbles," Riley observed, wincing as she smeared Maddie Fey's aval on her scraped knees and hands. When she was finished, she handed the silver vial back to Maddie Fey, who dropped it into a pocket of her long coat.

After Riley's mishap, Travis suggested that they link themselves with the rope, but the others vetoed the suggestion on the grounds that if one of them fell, that person's weight might drag the others off the cliff.

Stopping frequently to catch their breath and rest their stiff, aching limbs, they closed the distance to the valley floor, the Black Pyramid appearing larger and more menacing as they neared. Steele tried not to look at it, but his eyes returned to it again and again, almost as if they had a will of their own. The sight of the bleak, impenetrable structure made him feel lonely and forlorn.

"Do you get the feeling we're being watched?" he asked Riley, having dropped down beside her during one of their frequent rest stops.

Riley frowned. "I don't know about being watched," she said. "I feel something, though . . . small . . . I feel small . . . and sort of drained."

Steele noticed that her eyes had the same haunted look

he'd seen in his father's eyes when he was investigating a particularly heinous crime. He wondered if Riley saw the same look when she peered into his eyes. It occurred to him to ask her, but the moment passed, and then Riley was staring down into the valley.

"What are those?" she asked, pointing at the bumps dotting the ground below.

Steele shrugged. "I don't know. Rocks?"

"They don't look like any rocks I've ever seen," said Riley, getting up and setting out again.

They finally made it to the bottom of the steep trail. Bone-weary, Steele slumped against one of the large pod-like rocks. Riley collapsed beside him on the hard ground. Steele noticed that neither Travis nor Maddie Fey showed any signs of fatigue. Maddie Fey had removed a small silver case from a pocket inside her long coat. Opening the case, she withdrew two coils of thin wire, which she passed to Travis.

Travis looked at the wire coils for a second, and then he grinned and began straightening the wire. "They're divining rods. My grandfather could find water with two old metal coat hangers."

"It's the same principle," said Maddie Fey. She bent the ends of the wire. "You can be our dowser. Hold the bent ends lightly with your thumbs and place the rods over the backs of your hands."

Travis did as she said and then stared at the rod stupidly. "Uh, what do I do now?"

"You just said your grandfather—" said Steele.

Travis stopped him. "I said my grandfather dowsed; I didn't say *I* did."

Maddie Fey said, "Point the rods toward the earth. That's all you have to do. When they pass over water, you will feel the rods draw closer together until they cross."

Realizing that he hadn't seen Wish since they entered the valley, Steele looked about for the hound. He spotted him a short distance away, prowling about and sniffing one of the strange rocky protrusions that seemed to have sprouted from the valley floor like elongated black mushrooms. It was clear from the hound's deep growls that the stones were alien to him and made him edgy. From the top of the cliff, they had appeared as small nodes, but as Steele descended, he noticed that they were all of equal height, about seven feet tall.

He glanced at Travis, whose face was a study in concentration as he examined the long divining rods resting lightly in his hands. He moved slowly along the ground. Thinking he'd die if he didn't taste water soon, Steele ran his tongue over his parched lips; they felt like sandpaper.

As it had from the top of the cliff, the Black Pyramid dominated the valley. It didn't matter where Steele looked, it was always there, a gigantic brooding presence. Even when he closed his eyes, it loomed in his mind. What awaited them inside the pyramid? Maddie Fey's powers had detected human life somewhere in its vastness. Mac? The other missing kids? If Travis was right, over twenty-four hours had passed since Mac's abduction. What if they were already too late? Steele pushed the thought out of his mind. He had to believe that Mac was still alive, his memories intact. He had to keep believing. *Besides,* he thought. *There are as many questions as there are minutes in a day, and no one, not even Maddie Fey with all her alien powers, has all the answers.*

Riley touched his arm, bringing him back to earth with

a jolt. "What are you thinking?" She pressed her back against the black stone, but moved forward almost immediately. "Ugh! These things give me the creeps. They're all rubbery."

"What am I thinking? Oh, just the usual stuff," Steele answered sardonically. "You know . . . rescuing Mac and the rest of the missing kids, finding their memories, stopping the Prince of Darkness, destroying the Fire Demons . . . oh . . . and don't forget finding the wardens."

"Don't say it like that. You make it sound impossible," sighed Riley.

"Sorry," said Steele. "But sometimes, like now, it *seems* impossible."

Riley nodded. "Steele, remember Maddie Fey telling us that she travelled around the world searching for the wardens?"

"Yeah, she said there were no signs of them."

"That's right," said Riley, her hand tightening on his arm. "But I've been thinking. What if they're *here?*"

Her words echoed in Steele's mind. *What if they are* here?

As if she thought Steele didn't understand, Riley began to explain. "I mean, if they were imprisoned underground, there wouldn't be any signs on the surface."

"What made you think of the wardens?" Steele asked curiously.

"It's this place," said Riley. "It's so humongous and spooky. You could hide a city down here and no one would ever suspect."

"Yeah," agreed Steele. "Can you imagine having to live here? It's the most depressing place I've ever seen."

"I'd go insane," said Riley, "never feeling the sun on my face or seeing the stars in the night sky."

They fell silent then, comfortable in each other's company. After a while Steele asked if she thought they'd find the wardens alive.

"I want so badly for them to be alive, because Maddie Fey is really worried about them," said Riley. "But if I were the Prince of Darkness or the Fire Demons, I'd want them dead."

"I saw them once," said Steele.

Riley dug her short nails into his arm. "No kidding! Where?"

"Ouch!" Steele pried her fingers free. "They weren't real. The night I went to meet Maddie Fey, I ended up in her foyer, and there were these statues of gigantic things with wings. They looked like dragons. But the next time we went up the stairs in the foyer, they were gone—"

They were interrupted by Travis's excited cry. "Come quick! It worked. I found water!"

Using a sharp pick attached to their knives, Steele and Riley chipped away at the rocky ground until they had formed a small shallow basin. Travis kept up a running commentary on how he had felt the divining rods tremble and how they crossed at the spot where they were digging. Steele cleared away the loose debris and jabbed the pick repeatedly into the rock until he struck water and the liquid bubbled into and filled the shallow basin. Using his hands, Steele sloshed the water about to clean the rock and then brushed the basin clean until the water bubbled clear.

"Do you think it's safe to drink?" he asked.

Wish answered his question by sniffing the water and then lapping thirstily until Steele could have sworn the hound's sides were about to burst. Water dripping from his muzzle,

Wish looked at Maddie Fey as if to assure her that the water was pure.

Steele waited until the others had slaked their thirst before taking his turn at the basin. He drank deeply. Then he scooped up water in his cupped hands and doused Riley, sparking an enthusiastic water fight that made them forget their troubles for a few moments, and left him and Travis and Riley sopping wet. When Maddie Fey announced that it was time to go, Steele found that he was no longer weary. He felt refreshed and energized, as if he had awakened from a long, peaceful sleep. Eager to reach the Black Pyramid, they set out again.

Wish avoided the black stones and growled almost continuously. At first the hound's curious behaviour made Steele nervous, but after a while he grew used to it and by the time they had reached the halfway point, Wish's growls no longer registered in his mind. He gazed at the Black Pyramid. It didn't look that far now, but neither had the distance from the top of the cliff to the valley floor, and it had taken them several hours to descend the stepped trail.

Despite the cover provided by the black stones, Steele grew increasingly worried about the mysterious lack of security. He shared his concerns with Travis. "You'd think this place would be crawling with Maladroids."

"Yeah," said Travis. "Kind of makes you wonder if we're walking straight into a trap."

"I thought of that," admitted Steele. "But it doesn't make sense. The door we came through hasn't been used in years, maybe *hundreds* of years. If Maddie Fey hadn't guided us through the blackness, we'd still be back there trying to find our way out. The Maladroids couldn't know that we'd come that way, Travis. They have to think it's the one entry they don't have to watch because no one could make it through the blackness."

"You're assuming too much, Steele. They know about Maddie Fey, or at least they know that you've got a powerful friend. Why wouldn't the Maladroids and the Prince of Darkness suspect we'd come through the blackness? You know what I think? I think the Prince of Darkness has such strong magic that he doesn't need guards. I think he knows exactly where we are."

Steele blew air. "I was afraid you'd say that. Ever since Maddie Fey said there were two limos on the bridge, I've had the feeling that while we think we're making decisions, we're actually following a course that was already set."

Travis rubbed his arms as if to ward off a chill. "Do you think we'll find Dirk here, along with all the stuff he stole from you?"

"I hope he's here," answered Steele. "I don't care about the backpack, but I've got to get Ees and my sword back." He gripped Travis's arm. "And I swear, Travis, if he's so much as laid a finger on Pyrus, he's going to be very sorry."

Travis frowned at the sudden vehemence in Steele's voice. "I wouldn't want to be in his shoes when you catch up with him," he said. He changed the subject. "What are we going to do when we get there? Does Maddie Fey have a plan?"

"She found a way in," Steele answered. "She'll probably tell us when we get there."

Realizing that they had fallen behind the others, they hurried to catch up. They had been walking for several more hours when the stone forest gave way to a broad clearing. Ahead, the still surface of the lake reflected the haze above and glistened red, like a pool of thick blood. Steele shuddered as his eyes were drawn across the slick pool to the brooding Black Pyramid in time to see a jagged ribbon of red lightning burst from the peak, crackling and hissing. He looked back at the lake, scanning the flat edge, alert for Maladroids. But he saw nothing. As they drew nearer, the pyramid's size and might overwhelmed Steele, sapping his energy until he could barely stand. It sat there like a mountain, solitary and inviolate, and a terrible blackness seemed to gather about its walls and beat against it like a soul in distress.

The hideous, scarred face he and Riley had seen through the grate in Wychwood Park filled his mind so completely that he caught his breath at its nearness, cringing at the memory of the long, sharp, white fangs inches from his face and throat. Then panic took over, welling up inside like a geyser, shutting off his mind to everything except the overpowering need to run away.

"Aiii!" he cried, wheeling about.

"What is it?" exclaimed Riley, grabbing one of his arms while Travis lunged for the other.

Then Steele was twisting and struggling to break the hold Travis and Riley had on him.

"Steele!"

Maddie Fey's voice was sharp and commanding. It penetrated the wall of panic that had built up inside him. He stopped struggling and took several deep breaths.

"What's wrong?" Riley was still gripping his arm tightly.

"It's OK. I'm OK." He shook free and looked at Maddie Fey, embarrassed. "I'm sorry. I saw his face. I had to get away before he . . ." He left the sentence dangling.

"The Prince of Darkness," breathed Riley.

Maddie Fey studied him for a moment, her eyes boring into him. Squirming under her stern gaze, Steele looked down at his feet, ashamed. He couldn't help feeling that somehow he hadn't lived up to her expectations. The fact that she continued to look at him without speaking made him feel worse. But finally she turned to the others.

"There are four visible means of access into the pyramid from here," she said. "Using my powers sparingly, I probed them gently and was not surprised to discover that they are warded by magic. As I told Steele earlier, there is another way. At the back, where the base of the pyramid rests against the mountain, there is a narrow entry concealed as an air vent and covered with an iron grate. That is our destination." Taking their silence for acceptance, she continued.

"The black stones helped conceal us as we made our way to this spot, but they are behind us now. There is nothing between us and the pyramid. I cannot use my magic to cloak us, because by doing so I run the risk of giving away our location. We must move swiftly now. Do you understand?"

As Steele nodded grimly, he heard a sound from behind. It reminded him of the sound of leather rubbing against leather. He glanced over his shoulder. There was nothing there— nothing, that is, but the strange black stone forest. He was just about to turn back when he saw a ripple run down the length of one of the stones.

"Uh, guys," he cried urgently. "Something's happening."

"What is it?" Travis and the others wheeled about.

"Oh my God!" exclaimed Riley, staring at the stone forest in horror. "They're coming alive."

Maddie Fey spoke to Steele. "Take your friends and go. I will do what has to be done here. Find the entry, remove the grate, and crawl inside the vent. Wait for me there." She leaned closer so that the others couldn't hear. "Be careful, Steele. Now go. Quickly!"

Steele hesitated, his eyes moving from one rippling pod to another. Looking at them now, he found it impossible to believe that he and his companions had mistaken them for stones. He should have paid more attention to the reaction of Wish, who was crouched low, snarling as the first pod burst and a Maladroid stood in its place, its leathery cloak billowing behind it like a black sail.

Maddie Fey pointed at the Black Pyramid. "Go!" she cried to the companions. "You can do nothing here."

Her command spurred Travis and Riley into action. They ran, their long legs fairly flying across the clearing. But Steele still hesitated, his eyes glued to one of the creatures. His spine tingled at the thought of actually having rested with his back propped against one of these things. He stared at their black forms, at their black clawed feet, at the void where their faces should be, and felt his own blackness stirring inside his brain. These creatures, or ones very like them, had taken Mac. They were evil, just like the Prince of Darkness, who owned them, body and soul. Maddie Fey could feel sorry for them if she wanted to, but he hated them.

"They should die," he said through clenched teeth.

Maddie Fey reached for his arm, her eyes the colour of tarnished silver and filled with sorrow . . . for him or for the Maladroids, Steele neither knew nor cared.

"No, Steele!" she cried. "No!"

Steele wrenched his arm from her grasp and pushed her away. She staggered backwards, colliding with one of the Maladroids. Snarling viciously, Wish lunged at Steele. Steele opened his mouth to warn them to get out of the way, but it was too late. Something he couldn't control had taken hold of him, and instead of words of warning, black fire spewed from his open mouth. It slammed into the Maladroids. And it swept them up like dead leaves in a hurricane, incinerating them and anything else that stood before him . . . including Maddie Fey and her Great Hound.

The Dark Ages

Barbarian hordes, driven by the Tsilihin, invaded other countries, sacking and torching cities large and small. We feared that evolution would interfere and reverse the gains humans had worked so hard to achieve from the moment they became aware that they possessed intellect, and then sought to distinguish themselves from the lower animals.

Concealed within the darkness of those terrible times, the shadow rode his black carriage across the blood-soaked earth, manipulating humans with false promises and inciting them to commit unconscionable acts in the name of goodness.

And then, we lost another to the darkness.

—Excerpt from *The Wardens' Logs*

Chapter Sixteen

The Black Pyramid

Steele roared, elated, as his magic flames tore across the valley and licked at the base of the cliff.

Stop! screamed a voice in his mind, an instant before he lost himself in the blackness. *Stop!*

Frantically, Steele shut his mouth, but the flames found their way through spaces where his lips were not tightly compressed. He clamped his hands tightly over his mouth, his eyes fixed in terror on the devastated, smoking landscape.

"What have I done?" he sobbed, falling forward onto the hard ground. "What have I done?" Then he buried his face in his arms and howled like a child, lost.

Steele didn't know if minutes, hours, or days had passed as he lay there prone. He had let his rage control him, and now Maddie Fey and her hound were dead. The fact that he hadn't meant to hurt them was no consolation; it wouldn't bring them back. He raised his head and forced himself to face what he had done. The sight of the charred ground sickened him; the ash-infested air choked him. Coughing violently, he pushed himself up and wiped his face dry on his dirty sleeve.

"I'm sorry," he sobbed, a part of him clinging to the faint hope that the Mage would rise out of the ashes and tell him that everything was all right.

He waited for a long time, but Maddie Fey did not appear. He called her name over and over, and then he spoke to her as though she had returned from the dead, trying to explain what had taken hold of him. He told her about the blackness he had felt inside after he had broken into the Maladroid's mind and read its evil thoughts, and how, afterwards, he had felt contaminated.

"It's still here," he said, pressing his hand against his heart. "And it's spreading, Maddie Fey. I can't control it."

He said he was sorry again and then again before he turned away. Numb with shock and grief, he moved like a ghost across the clearing, struggling to find the words to tell Riley and Travis of the terrible thing he had done.

Contrary to Maddie Fey's instructions that they wait inside the vent, Riley and Travis were huddled behind the Black Pyramid. Steele went to them and told them everything.

A long grim silence followed. Riley cried soundlessly, while Travis gazed into space, a look of horror on his lean face. Steele waited for them to absorb fully what he had told them, and to realize the implications of his rash use of his power. When they finally accepted that Maddie Fey was gone, despair would set in. Without her, they were lost, their quest impossible. Steele stared at his clenched hands, dreading the moment when his friends would look at him with loathing in their eyes.

Surprisingly, Travis broke the silence by coming over to Steele and placing his hand on his shoulder. "We should be going now," he said gently. "We don't want to get caught out in the open."

"There's nothing left to catch us," Steele said, avoiding Travis's eyes. "I destroyed them, all of them." He sighed and began to move back the way they had come.

Riley stepped in front of him, blocking his way. "Where are you going?" she demanded.

Steele looked at her, bewildered. "I thought—"

"You thought we'd give up," said Riley. "We're not quitters, Steele. We've got to go on and find Mac and the others. Isn't that what Maddie Fey would have wanted us to do?"

"Riley's right," said Travis. "We can't quit now."

Steele shook his head. "Weren't you listening? Didn't you hear me tell you that I killed her?"

"We heard you," said Travis.

"Aren't you angry with me? Don't you blame me for ruining everything?"

"We weren't there," said Riley. "We didn't see what happened. But I've known you my whole life, Steele, and I know you couldn't kill a mouse." She flushed and added hurriedly, "Except for those horrible worms and the Fire Demons." She stopped and shook her head impatiently. "Oh! You know what I mean. You didn't mean to kill Maddie Fey. The magic that you couldn't control killed her. So whatever happened back there wasn't your fault."

Steele laughed bitterly. "Tell that to Maddie Fey."

Riley grabbed his shoulders and shook him. "Listen! You didn't even know you had magic powers until Maddie Fey came looking for you. She had to know those powers were dangerous and unpredictable, because you never got the chance to learn how to use them. She must have known this danger existed. So stop feeling responsible."

"I haven't known you very long," said Travis. "But I learned a lot about you over the past couple of days. One thing I learned is that you care about people. Look how you fought to save the dying boy. That was epic, man. Because of that, I'd trust you with my life."

Steele pressed his fists into his stinging eyes, doubting that he was worthy of friends like these. He cleared his throat. "Thanks. I don't know what to say." He took Riley's hand. "I don't know if I could have stopped the magic. I think I tried to warn her, but everything happened so fast I can't be sure. All I could think about was destroying those creatures. I saw black. Nothing else. Just black, everywhere. I wish I could undo everything, but I can't." He paused and said again, "I'm sorry about Maddie Fey . . . and Wish."

Riley squeezed his hand. "I know."

Travis coughed meaningfully. "I don't mean to sound heartless, but Maddie Fey is gone. We'll be sad for a long time and, Steele, you'll be sorry for the rest of your life. But if we're going to carry on and do what she set out to do, we've got to get inside that vent *now*. Listen!"

The sound of shuffling footsteps bombarded them from all directions. Steele realized that he had been wallowing so deeply in self-pity and grief that he hadn't even considered the possibility that he *hadn't* killed all the Maladroids. He grabbed his friends' arms. "The black stones. It just hit me. That's how the Maladroids are created or altered. It wasn't a forest at all, but a field—a field of Maladroids. What I destroyed was just the latest crop."

Riley and Travis stared at him incredulously.

"It's like they're cocooned, or planted," said Riley. "It's gross."

"Come on!" urged Travis. "Get out your knives. We've got to open the grate at the bottom."

Steele turned his attention to the vent. Rectangular in shape, it measured approximately four feet high by two feet wide. The opening led into a shaft and was enclosed by a black iron grille, the metal bars twisted into the shapes of grotesque creatures engaged in dispatching their unfortunate victims. An identical demon's face occupied each of the four corners. The eye sockets were hollow, to accommodate the thumb-sized screws that secured the grille to a metal frame set into the stone.

Under Travis's direction, Steele and Riley attacked the screws on the bottom corners using screwdrivers they found among the tools on their knives. But the large screws had rusted and seized up over the ages, and despite applying all of their strength, they couldn't get them to budge.

"What's this?" asked Riley, opening another tool on her knife and holding it up for the others to see.

Travis took the knife and examined the tool. "It's obviously a screwdriver," he said, placing the end into the groove in the head of the screw and trying to turn it.

"Why would there be two identical screwdrivers on the knife?" asked Riley, thinking out loud. "They must be there for a reason."

"Hey!" exclaimed Travis. "You're right." He spoke to Steele. "Change screwdrivers," he said. "And push in on it, like this."

Travis pushed on the knife and the screw began to turn. Within seconds, it dropped into his cupped hand. "It's powered by something," he said, staring at the miniature screwdriver in wonder.

"It's probably magic," said Riley.

When Steele removed the last screw, they pried the bottom of the grate out far enough for them to slip inside.

"I'll go first," said Travis, "and hold it open with my legs."

"What about the screws?" asked Riley. "If they look at the grate they'll see that the screws are missing. They'll know we came this way."

"We'll have to chance it," said Steele, dropping the screws into his pocket. "Besides, we can't screw them in once we're inside. But I'll keep them in case we have to escape this way. If we're followed, we can get out and screw them back in with our knives."

Travis slid his head under the grate, sucked in his gut, and slithered on his stomach into the narrow shaft. Riley went next, wriggling past Travis to make room for Steele. They had barely pulled the grating back into place when a shadow blotted out the reddish light seeping into the shaft through the openings in the twisted bars. They went still, holding their breath, their eyes fixed on the visible area on the other side of the grille. Steele's heart was beating so loudly that he was sure the Dark Prince himself could hear it.

Go away! Don't look in the grate! Steele pleaded silently, wishing he could use his powers the way Maddie Fey had used hers and plant a suggestion in the mind of whatever was lurking outside. *I've got to try,* he thought, forcing himself to relax, waiting for his heart rate to drop. Then, as suddenly as it had appeared, the shadow was gone. Steele and his companions waited for a good minute before releasing their collective breath in one long sigh of relief.

With Travis leading the way, they crawled deeper into the pyramid. They had gone several hundred feet when the bottom sloped downward, enlarging the canal until they found they could stand upright. Suddenly they heard a triumphant screech that came from behind, followed almost immediately by the clang of metal against metal.

"They're at the grate!" hissed Travis.

"Move faster," urged Steele.

"We're moving as fast as we can," objected Riley. "It's dark in here, in case you haven't noticed."

Steele bit back a sharp retort. "I know it's dark, Riley. But so far the shaft is clear. There's nothing to trip over. Would you rather take the chance of bumping into something or getting caught by whatever's back there?"

"Sorry," mumbled Riley.

They ran. Travis extended his arms out in front of his body to take the brunt of the impact with a wall should the shaft take a sudden sharp turn. When he stopped abruptly, Riley plowed into his back and Steele into hers.

"Why did you stop?" snapped Riley.

"I should have warned you," Travis explained, excitedly, "but my hands just touched something. I think it's an opening."

Steele and Riley crowded about Travis, examining his discovery with their hands. It was another pierced grate, only this time they couldn't see through the openings because a solid sheet of metal had been fastened to it from the opposite side. Their fingers felt along the edges of the grate for fastenings or screws. They couldn't feel anything but the rough iron.

"Argh!" Frustrated, Travis planted his fingers in the pierced openings, gripped the grate as best he could, and shook it furiously.

"It moved," said Steele. "It's a sliding panel. Quick! Pull!"

Travis repositioned his fingers and pulled on the panel until it began to slide sideways. Steele and Riley tried to help but only succeeded in getting in Travis's way. They backed off, eyes focused on the expanding shaft of pale light coming from beyond the panel as it inched slowly open. Back in the shaft, the sound of footsteps grew steadily louder.

"Hurry!" Riley's voice was desperate.

"There," said Travis, when the panel wouldn't slide any farther.

Steele let out a long breath and edged past Travis, closer to the square opening. Then he poked his head through and peered cautiously in both directions along a huge, dimly lit hall. He looked down, gauging the distance to the floor.

"We're at one end of a hallway," he informed his companions. "It's clear, but it's a good ten feet to the floor. I'll go first. If either of you decides you don't want to drop all the way to the floor, I'll stand under you and you can use my shoulders. OK?"

"Don't stand under me," said Travis. "I'm going to drop."

Not to be outdone by the boys, Riley declared that she too intended to drop.

Without hesitating, Steele climbed through the opening, his hands gripping the bottom edge of the track that allowed the panel to slide back and forth. When his body was fully extended, he released his grip and dropped, bending his knees to land lightly on the floor. His friends soon joined him and then all three gazed about, overawed by the immensity of the abode of the Prince of Darkness.

The vast hall was as wide as a football field and stretched away before them like a boulevard. Along the walls on both sides of the hall, flaming torches rested in black iron brackets affixed to gigantic columns. Between the columns, pairs of slender pillars framed arcades where human-sized stone gargoyles crouched, as if poised to spring from their stone perches. They looked so lifelike that, after stifling their gasps, Steele and the others quickly scurried into the middle of the hall.

Steele stared at the massive columns, placed at eight-foot intervals along both walls. Focusing on one that was close by, his eyes climbed it, over a hundred feet up to where the flat top helped support the arched ceiling. Jagged iron stalactite masses ornamented black beams that criss-crossed the ceiling.

"It smells," said Riley, wrinkling her nose in disgust. "Like mildew or something."

"Like the Mala-dees," Travis said.

Steele listened for the sound of their pursuers, but he heard nothing. Perhaps they had passed the sliding panel without noticing it, or had turned back. They couldn't be certain that Steele and his friends had entered the shaft, could they? The screws could have worked loose years ago. Still, he reminded himself that they had to continue with caution.

There were no windows in the Black Pyramid; no natural light shone here. The walls, the floor, the ceiling, the gargoyles . . . all were as black as ink. The only colour came from a symbol emblazoned upon dozens of banners suspended from thick black chains fastened to the ceiling beams. Steele stared at the symbol. It was in the shape of a shield. The background was bright red with a wide yellow band running across the centre. Two green frogs with splayed limbs were displayed on the upper, wider part of the shield; a third, larger green frog occupied the lower portion.

"It's not exactly how I pictured the coat of arms of the Prince of Darkness," said Riley. "It's not even scary."

Steele looked at her suspiciously. "Are you trying to tell me that you actually thought about this?"

Riley grinned sheepishly. "Not really. What I meant to say was if I had thought about it, I wouldn't have imagined it looking like this."

"Yeah, it is sort of lame," Steele said.

"Don't make fun of it," said Travis. "I sort of dabble in heraldry . . . as a hobby. I've come across this symbol before. It's ancient. In heraldry it's called the Devil's Arms."

Steele gulped. "Is that just a name or are you saying it really *is* the Devil's coat of arms?"

"I mean it's the arms attributed to the Devil."

Riley and Steele exchanged shocked glances.

"Do you know what this means?" said Riley, going white.

Steele nodded. "But he can't be the real Devil, Riley. He probably just calls himself the Prince of Darkness and uses the Devil's emblem to scare people. It's how he controls them."

"Rule by fear," said Travis.

Riley slapped his arm. "You'll make a good reporter, Travis. That's a great headline."

Travis smiled. "My dad says I'm certainly cynical enough to be a reporter. But Steele's right about the Prince of Darkness, Riley. He uses symbols and gargoyles, names and fear, to achieve the same result—control."

"It's always about control and power, isn't it?" said Riley, making a face.

They spoke in hushed tones as they crept along the hall, their shadows writhing before them like restless spirits. They scoured the walls for a door or stairway that would get them down to where Maddie Fey had detected human life. Steele and Riley tried to avoid the hostile eyes of the gargoyles following their every move, but Travis glared back at the creatures, undaunted. Halfway along the hall, a particularly ferocious-looking statue loomed at the edge of Steele's vision. He turned sharply and, to his surprise, noticed a crack in the black stone wall directly behind the figure.

Rushing over, but maintaining a safe distance between him and the gargoyle, he stared at the crack. "Look! You can barely see it, but it goes all the way up and across the top and down again. It's got to be a door!" He traced the crack along one side with his fingers.

"There's probably a hidden catch," said Travis, studying the wall, "and I know where I'd put it if I were the POD."

"Be careful, he probably stuck it in the gargoyle's mouth."

"Precisely, Watson." Travis grinned. Unfazed, he climbed onto the base of the statue and tried to peer into the gargoyle's cavernous mouth. "I have to get higher."

Using the creature's stone legs as steps, Travis scaled the gargoyle and pulled himself onto its hunched back. Then he winked at Riley, reached forward, and slowly edged his right hand into the gaping, fang-filled mouth.

"Be careful, Travis," cautioned Riley. "It might be a trap."

"Chill, Riley. I'm just going to feel around. I'd hate to meet this creature in the flesh. Look at the size of these fangs. Ouch! They're sharp, too. They feel as if they could bite through stone." Travis's hand reached deeper in the gargoyle's mouth. "What do we have here? This feels different."

Just then, Steele and Riley heard the sound of stone grinding against stone as the wall behind the statue slid into a concealed recess.

Travis froze. "Oh! Oh!"

"What is it?" asked Steele, but one look at Travis's face told him his friend was terrified.

"I think I'm in trouble, man," said Travis, his voice trembling.

"What?" cried Riley, wringing her hands nervously. Her eyes darted from Travis to the open space in the black wall.

Travis swallowed several times before he managed to speak again. "One of the molars felt different from the others. As I pushed on it, I accidentally pushed on the one behind it."

"What are you saying?" Steele's voice echoed in the long, cavernous hall.

"I don't think I can take my fingers off the teeth. If I do, I've got a feeling that the gargoyle's jaws are going to snap shut."

A.D. 1181

Throughout the ages, whenever trouble erupted on the surface of the planet, humans inevitably spoke of a great shadow that they had seen crossing the sky against the wind.

When the Tsilihin attacked Japan, burning buildings and setting crops ablaze, many of those who survived the initial fires claimed that wraith-like creatures with flaming scythes had roamed the fields cutting down crops.

We drove Death from the charred and blackened fields, down into captivity. Then famine came and starved a hundred thousand men, women, and children.

—Excerpt from *The Wardens' Logs*

Chapter Seventeen

The Dungeon

"Don't move, Travis." Steele felt panic, his familiar enemy, rise again. *I have to do something,* he thought. *But what? What?* He caught Riley's arm. "Get him talking, Riley. Keep him calm. I need to think."

Conquering her fear of the grisly stone gargoyle, Riley moved closer. "Travis, Steele's thinking of a way to get your hand free. I need you to talk to me. Tell me about your parents, your brothers, sisters, anything. Just keep talking, OK?"

"I know what you're doing," said Travis. "You're trying to take my mind off the fact that my hand is about to be bitten off by a stone gargoyle."

Riley nodded. "Yes. But I'm not trying to trick you. If you talk, you won't be so scared. Can we try it?"

"It won't work, but I'll try. What do you want to know?"

"What's your mom like?"

Travis answered in a monotone, his eyes wide and riveted to the spot where his arm disappeared into the gargoyle's gaping mouth. "I don't know. She's a mom—sometimes a pain, sometimes cool."

"Does she work?"

"She paints."

Riley sighed. This wasn't working. "You said you'd tell us about the Chicago Fire. I read somewhere that Mrs. O'Leary's cow kicked over a lantern and that was how it started."

"That's a myth," he blurted out. "The fire happened in 1871. It started in the O'Learys' barn but the cow didn't start it. A neighbour went in the barn to smoke a cigarette and accidentally dropped a lit match onto a haystack. A journalist made up the story about the cow, and people thought it was true. So the O'Leary family got blamed for the fire for over a hundred years. Now, everybody knows it wasn't their fault, or the cow's."

"Imagine how they must have felt," said Riley.

Travis nodded. "Yeah. It must have been pretty horrible living in Chicago and being blamed for a fire that killed hundreds of people and destroyed over fifteen thousand buildings, and all of the downtown, including the business district. The only building that survived was the Water Tower."

"Our Parliament Buildings burned down once," said Riley. "The only building that escaped the fire was the Library of Parliament. Mac has a theory that most of the big fires, like the Chicago Fire, were started by the Fire Demons."

"No kidding," said Travis. "I hope we find him, because I'd really like to talk to him about his theory—"

"Riley!" Steele broke in. "Give me your knife. I've got an idea."

Riley reached into her pocket and retrieved her knife. Then she dropped it into his hand alongside his own knife.

Clutching the knives tightly, Steele climbed onto the base of the statue and passed them to Travis. "You've handled them; they're stronger than they look," he said. "I can't reach the mouth, but without falling off the statue, can you use your free hand to wedge them between the upper and lower jaw?"

Travis nodded.

"You might have to move your fingers a bit to get one of the knives in place, but don't release the pressure. When you get my knife wedged securely, use Riley's on the other side of the mouth. But whatever you do, don't take your fingers completely off the teeth until the knives are in place and you're ready to yank your hand out of there."

Travis nodded again.

Steele held his breath as Travis worked methodically. Gripping one knife in his teeth, Travis used his free hand to lodge the other between the statue's upper and lower jaw. When he seemed satisfied that it was secured, he planted the other knife between the creature's jaws on the opposite side. Then he looked at Steele, sweat glistening on his face.

"Are you ready?" Steele asked, his body as rigid as an iron bar.

Travis gulped. "I guess."

"OK. Just do it . . . *fast.*"

Travis stared at the creature's mouth, his eyes widening as he prepared himself. "Aiiii!" He snatched his hand out of the gargoyle's mouth a split second before the gargoyle's jaws snapped shut. But the knives held firm, preventing the huge mouth from closing. Travis slid from the statue's back and tumbled off the base onto the floor, his legs trembling uncontrollably. As Steele and Riley rushed to help him up, there was a loud *crunch,* and splinters of Maddie Fey's crushed knives shot from the statue's clenched jaws. The wall began to slide back in place.

"That was too close," breathed Riley, shivering.

Travis stared at his hand. "No kidding!" He clapped Riley gently on the shoulder. "Thanks. Getting me talking was a good idea. It helped."

"Quickly! Through the opening," said Steele, pushing his companions toward the narrowing hole in the wall.

They were so preoccupied with Travis's narrow escape and getting through the opening before it closed that they didn't see the first Maladroid leap from the shaft at the end of the hall, its black cloak floating behind, or hear the *thud* of its feet landing on stone. But a heartbeat before Steele lunged through the hole in the wall, he felt the hairs on the back of his neck stirring, warning him of danger. He glanced over his shoulder in time to see the second black shadow drop swiftly to the floor.

When they were safely through the opening and the wall had closed with a dull thud, Steele told his companions about the pursuing figure.

"If we're lucky," said Travis, optimistically, "your knives broke the opening mechanism and they won't be able to get through the wall."

"If we're lucky," Riley repeated, emphasizing *If*.

Steps before them spiralled up and down to other levels of the pyramid. Steele pointed down. The others nodded their agreement. They descended in single file with Steele leading the way. No one spoke. A few torches high up on the wall beyond their reach provided meagre light, forcing them to pick their way cautiously down the steep, winding stairway. They met no one. They heard nothing. But that didn't ease Steele's growing feeling that unseen eyes were watching him. The words of an old saying suddenly played in his mind. *Come into my parlour, said the spider to the fly.*

The stairway ended at another door. Steele counted a dozen sliding bolt locks, but none that required keys or combinations. "They're not taking any chances on letting whatever's on the other side of that door escape," he observed, carefully studying the locks for booby traps.

"Do you think they put enough locks on there?" said Travis wryly, evoking a rude snicker from Riley.

Satisfied that the sliding bolts were nothing more than what they appeared to be, Steele reached out, grasped a knob on the topmost bolt, and slid it free. Riley and Travis pitched in and within seconds had released all twelve bolts. Steele seized the handle and pulled. The door opened, and they crossed the threshold into what seemed like another world after the monstrous grandeur of the great arched hall above.

Steele studied the low ceiling and the three narrow tunnels, each ending at a single door; he studied the filthy floor and the stained walls, his stomach churning. Here in the lower depths of the Black Pyramid, filth and decay were rampant. Garbage littered the ground. Bones, some as large as a dog's bones, others tiny and delicate, from mice or small birds, appeared white among darker bits of refuse. The sweet stench of dead or dying things mingled with the sharp, metallic scent of blood, and the rank, sweaty smell of human fear. There were other smells in the air, but Steele ignored them, and breathed through his mouth.

Cockroaches, bigger and plumper than a man's thumb, scuttled to the sides of the tunnel like receding waves. Fat, black rats scrabbled among stinking, decomposing matter, or picked at strings of gristle clinging to the bones of recent victims. One particularly large rodent reared up on its hind legs, bared its teeth, and squealed at the intruders, warning them away from its territory. Out of the corner of his eye Steele caught a glimpse of another rat waddling along the wall, its teeth clamped tightly on something white. He moved closer, curious. It was a white wing, all that remained of some unfortunate seagull or dove. The sight of the white feathers smeared with blood made him sad.

"We must be in the dungeon," he said, stating the obvious just for the sake of saying something to get his mind off the bloody wing. Despite his feelings of sadness and revulsion, he took perverse pleasure in the knowledge that the foundation of the Black Pyramid was rotten.

"Let's hurry and find Mac," urged Riley. "This place is freaking me out."

Thinking of Mac imprisoned in this filthy place made Steele queasy, but more than that, it made him furious. "Come on." He pointed to the corridor on his right. "We'll check them out one by one. We'll tear this place apart if we have to. If he's here, we'll find him."

They had almost reached the end of the first tunnel when they heard a key turn in the door about a dozen feet ahead. They stopped abruptly, and looked around for a hiding place. But the tunnel ran straight to its end, unbroken by side tunnels or dark corners that might have provided cover.

"Quick. Let's get behind the door," said Steele, praying that the door opened into the tunnel.

They all dashed toward the door and flattened themselves against the wall behind it. The door opened. Something flew through as if it had been kicked. It bounced on the filth-encrusted floor and rolled until the chain went taut, jerking it to a stop. Steele almost roared with rage when Pyrus rose unsteadily to his feet and looked about in alarm. He ached to scoop the salamander into his arms and comfort it, and at the same time he burned to smash the life out of whoever had kicked Pyrus.

Riley shot him a look that said, *Why aren't you doing something to help Pyrus?* She then pinched his arm and opened her mouth to speak, but Steele gripped her hand, raised a finger to his lips, and pointed at the door. Riley shut her mouth. They held their positions against the wall, and within seconds, Dirk breezed through the open doorway, the other end of the chain coiled about his hand.

"Get up, you smelly rodent," snarled Dirk, jerking the chain.

Pyrus struggled against the chain. Steele could see that he was confused and frightened. Until Dirk snatched the salamander, no one had ever hurt Pyrus.

Steele lost it.

"Get away from him!" he shouted, leaping forward.

Dirk started and spun about. A look of fear flitted across his face, disappearing almost in the same instant. "You!" he spluttered, shocked, then recovered. "I don't know how you got past the new Maladroid recruits, but you should never have come here."

So he doesn't know I destroyed the Maladroids. Steele took a step toward the bully. "Let Pyrus go, and give me back my medallion."

Quicker than thought, Dirk yanked on the chain that was attached to a choke collar around Pyrus's neck. The collar tightened about the pet's throat as Dirk lifted it by the chain and then grabbed it. He gripped the salamander's neck in both hands. "Take one more step and I'll snap its neck clean off."

Furious, Steele stopped in mid-stride. He considered charging at the bully, but he was afraid that Dirk would carry out his threat and break Pyrus's neck before he could reach it.

"I see you found your kingdom," taunted Riley, coming to stand beside Steele.

"Shut up, Puddlescum." Dirk's hands tightened on Pyrus's neck, but his eyes locked on Steele.

That didn't stop Riley. Her eyes swept slowly over the filthy tunnel. "So this is where you live, is it? This is your reward for capturing Steele. Wow! It's *so* you."

Steele glanced at Riley. But when she refused to look at him, he wondered what was going on. Was she trying to distract Dirk long enough for him to come up with a plan, or . . . ? Realizing that Travis hadn't uttered a word since Dirk kicked Pyrus through the doorway, Steele was just about to turn his head to look for him when it hit him. Riley was trying to keep Dirk's attention away from Travis. Steele didn't know what the pair was up to, but if he turned toward Travis now, Dirk would notice the other boy for sure.

Steele thought of what Riley had said a moment ago, about Dirk's reward for capturing him. At the time it had triggered a memory of something someone else had said about Dirk recently. What was it? He returned Dirk's hostile look with one of contempt. He couldn't help noticing the outline of Ees under the bully's shirt. As his eyes burned into the disk, the memory suddenly came to him and he could see the speaker as if she were standing before him. *Young Dirk is very worried. He took something from you and kept the theft a secret from the Prince of Darkness. Now, he cannot suddenly claim that he forgot to turn the medallion in.* As Maddie Fey's words echoed in his ears, a plan took shape in Steele's mind. *I've got you!* he thought triumphantly.

He spoke to Riley, but his words were meant for Dirk. "I don't think even Dirk would consider living down here a reward. No, Riley. If the Prince of Darkness thinks as highly of him as Dirk said he did, he'd give him a real reward." He locked eyes with Dirk, aware of the bully's fat hands squeezing Pyrus's neck. "Wouldn't he, Dirk? At the very least, he'd let you keep the stuff you took from the kids you caught for him."

Dirk shifted his weight from one leg to the other; his small dark eyes darted furtively about the narrow tunnel as if he was afraid the Prince of Darkness was listening.

"Shut up," he hissed. "Move back . . . through the door."

Steele and Riley remained where they were. Out of the corner of his eye, Steele caught sight of Travis creeping stealthily along the wall on Dirk's left, moving into a position where he could come at the bully from behind.

"What about it, Dirk? The medallion you stole from me . . . was that one of your rewards?" Steele was beginning to enjoying watching Dirk squirm.

Dirk seemed to realize that Steele was baiting him, but his puzzled expression told Steele he hadn't yet figured out why. Steele pressed on with his attack. It was time to turn the screws. He grinned, nodding knowingly at Dirk as if they were co-conspirators sharing a secret. "It must have made you laugh when your master let you keep the disk. If I were him and you showed it to me and told me about its powers, I'd keep it."

He stopped. Dirk was sweating now, his hands slipping on the salamander's neck.

"What are you talking about?"

Steele looked at something over Dirk's right shoulder, back where the three corridors converged. He raised his voice, wanting Dirk to think he was speaking for the benefit of someone listening in on their conversation. "Ah!" he said. "I get it. You didn't show him the disk. You didn't tell him it was magic."

"I'm warning you. Shut your face or . . ." Dirk glanced nervously over his right shoulder.

Steele dropped his voice. "Imagine what he'll do to you when he finds out that you kept something that he'd give his kingdom for."

"Bah!" spat Dirk. "What would he want with a piece of junk?"

"Why don't we ask him?" said Steele.

The blood drained from Dirk's face. "You're nobody, a nothing," he hissed. "He wouldn't listen to you. He's going to kill you."

Steele said with studied patience, "Think, Dirk! Why has he gone to so much trouble to kill a *nobody?*"

Dirk shrugged. Steele noticed that he kept glancing anxiously down at his hand, at one particular finger. It was the finger that sported the tattooed band and the black stone. The stone made Steele uneasy. What if it was magic? What if it allowed the Prince of Darkness to hear every word they said? But if that was its purpose, why had Dirk looked about so nervously a few seconds ago? Steele decided he had come too far to back off now.

"I'll save you the trouble of having to use your brain," Riley piped up. "The great Prince of Darkness is scared of Steele. That's why he wants him dead."

Dirk appeared to relax. Steele knew what he was thinking. *Steele couldn't scare anyone.*

Riley continued, weaving truth and fabrication. "Remember all those times you bullied Steele and beat him up? It was all an act. Steele let you do it to protect his real identity. Your master found out about Steele's magic powers and now he's got to kill Steele before Steele destroys him."

Even to Steele's ears, Riley's explanation sounded ludicrous. He waited for Dirk to break up. He didn't have to wait long. Dirk's initial expression of disbelief quickly turned to scorn, and he began laughing so hard he almost lost his grip on Pyrus. "You're pathetic, Puddlescum."

Steele knew he had to make good on Riley's bragging if he was going to rattle Dirk enough to get him to do what he wanted. He searched within for his magic. He had to find it and control it, make it do his bidding, just this once. When he found the magic, he reached out and felt it surge through him.

Dirk's laughter died in his throat and was replaced by a strangled cry as the chain about his hand slowly uncoiled, snaked up his chest, and began to wind about his neck. "What . . . ?" he croaked, releasing his hold on Pyrus's neck and grappling with the chain.

At that moment, Pyrus opened his mouth and snapped at the black stone on Dirk's right middle finger, his sharp teeth burying themselves in the bully's flesh. Dirk screeched and shook his hand, trying to dislodge Pyrus while trying to protect his neck from the chain. But Pyrus shook his head, biting and pulling, until he ripped the stone free.

The salamander streaked down Dirk and made a beeline for Steele.

Steele forgot all about the magic. He scooped Pyrus into his arms and pressed him against his chest. Gently, he loosened the choke collar, slipped it from Pyrus's neck, and let it fall to the floor. He could feel his pet's tiny heart fluttering wildly in his hands. Pyrus spat the black stone into Steele's palm.

"Steele! Stop! He's choking," cried Riley.

Steele looked at her sharply, almost irritably. And then he noticed Dirk writhing and convulsing as the chain tightened about his neck. Travis rushed in to help, but Steele could see that the chain was like a living thing. The end Steele had dropped whipped dangerously through the air, effectively preventing anyone from approaching Dirk, whose face was rapidly turning from light to deep blue.

Panicked over losing control of the magic as he had with the Maladroids, Steele stood glued to the floor. But when Dirk's purple tongue began to emerge from between his teeth, Steele's inner voice took over, prodding him into action. Forcing his panic down, he released Pyrus and stuffed the black stone in his pocket. The magic was waiting inside him, hungrily. He took a deep breath, seized it and approached Dirk.

"Go back!" warned Travis, his eyes following the end of the chain as it suddenly lashed out at Steele.

Steele was so absorbed in the magic that he didn't hear the warning. He didn't need to; this time he seemed to know what he was doing. In the tenth of a second before the end of the chain whipped his face, Steele's arm shot up and his hand closed over it. Instantly, the power that had animated it died; the chain clattered to the floor.

Steele didn't move when Riley and Travis ran to free Dirk from the end of the chain coiled about his throat. He stood motionless, feeling the power diminish inside him. "I did it," he said to himself. "I made it obey me." He didn't feel elated or astonished, just tired. He wished that Maddie Fey could have seen what he had done. But then, perhaps she wouldn't have been surprised; hadn't she always believed in him? Steele was the one who had doubted his own ability to control the magic.

Pyrus scrambled up his body and flicked its dry tongue against his face.

"I won't stuff you in my jacket just yet if you promise not to run off," he said, brushing Pyrus's head with a finger. Then he walked over to Dirk.

The bully was sitting on the floor, sobbing uncontrollably as he massaged the pressure welts on his neck with one hand and stared at the bloody hole in the middle finger on his other hand. Riley and Travis stood a short distance away, speaking quietly to each other and casting sharp glances Dirk's way. Steele looked down at the bully who had once used his size and strength to make his life miserable.

"Do you understand now why your master fears me?" he asked, his voice low and so cold that it sent chills up his own spine.

Dirk wouldn't meet his eyes. He wiped his runny nose on his arm.

"Give me the medallion and Mac's knife," Steele said firmly.

Sniffling and sobbing, Dirk groped at the neck of his shirt and removed the disk. Steele grabbed it from him, polished it against his jacket, and slipped the thin chain over his head. Ees felt warm against his chest; his chills disappeared. He took Mac's knife from Dirk's outstretched hand and released the sharpest blade. Then he pulled the black stone from his pocket and held it between his thumb and index finger.

"What is this?" he demanded.

"Nothing," whimpered Dirk, covering his bloody finger with his other hand. "Just a stone."

Steele dropped onto his heels and grabbed Dirk's hand. He turned it over, examining the tattooed gold band on the bully's middle finger. Then he stared at the hole in Dirk's finger, sickened by the realization that the stone had been implanted in his flesh.

"What does it do?" he asked.

"I told you. It's just a stone."

Moving away from Dirk, Steele ripped off a piece from his shirt and carefully wrapped it around the black stone, now sticky with Dirk's blood. He placed the package on the floor and raised Mac's knife above it.

"Stop!" cried Dirk.

Steele paused but didn't lower his arm. "What is it?" he repeated.

"He gave it to me. For being loyal, he said. It's just a stone, that's all it is."

Dirk might believe it's just a stone, thought Steele. *But it's much more than that.* He brought the end of the knife down hard, again and again, pretending to smash the stone to powder. Then he picked up the rag, squeezed the stone free, and tossed the rag to the floor. As he turned his back on Dirk, he slipped the stone into his pocket.

Riley took his arm and led him a short distance away.

"What was that all about?" she asked.

"I don't know," Steele admitted. "He had this weird gold band tattooed around his finger, with a black stone set into his skin. Something about it bothered me. Perhaps it was just a harmless black stone, but something tells me it's more than that."

"And you just destroyed it?" said Travis.

Steele grinned. "If you want to be a good reporter, don't believe everything you see, Travis." Opening Mac's knife again, he turned and moved back to Dirk.

"Now, where's Mac?"

A. D. 1099

Near the end of the eleventh century, shortly after the crusaders had captured the Holy City, word came of a great blackness that had fallen upon the city.

Anxious to discover a clue that would lead us to our lost brothers, we sent another one streaking across the sky to the Holy City. Those who saw his passing claimed that they saw a comet in the night sky more brilliant than previous sightings.

We guarded our prisoners—an endless cycle of driving them and their hatred back into the liquid flames, containing them for brief moments until they broke for the surface again. We guarded and waited anxiously for news.

But neither news nor our brother came back to us.

—Excerpt from *The Wardens' Logs*

Chapter Eighteen

The Paragon Game

Dirk took one look at the blade and opened his mouth. Words poured out in a steady stream.

"Please don't cut me. I'll tell you what you want to know. Mac was locked up with the others in the cell at the end of the first tunnel. But you're too late. Last night his name got picked, and they came for him this morning and took him." He rolled his eyes toward the ceiling. "He's in a room at the top of the pyramid. Don't hurt me and I'll take you there."

Steele stopped him. "What do you mean his name was picked?"

"It's a game. At least the new kids think it's a game," said Dirk woodenly. "They're scared when they're first brought in. My job is to convince them that everything's going to be OK, that nothing bad is going to happen to them."

"Why?"

Dirk appeared not to understand Steele's question, so Steele made it clear.

"Why do you have to convince them that everything's going to be OK?"

"So they'll stop being scared. You don't want them scared. When they go for the extraction, fear makes their good memories too faint to be of any use."

Steele nodded slowly, but his brain reeled with the information he was getting from Dirk. *So this is where it's done,* he thought. *This is where they steal the kids' memories.* "Go on. Tell me more about this game."

"He calls it the paragon game. I tell them that they've been chosen to come here because they're special, or gifted . . . whatever. I show them a bag of gold bars and tell them that when their names get picked they get to meet the Prince. Then they're taken to a place to be tested to make sure they're worthy of becoming paragons. Then I tell them that if they pass the test, they go to a big ceremony where they receive their titles, and a bag of gold to take home with them."

Steele was incredulous. "Are you trying to tell me that the kids actually believe you?"

"Why not? They want to believe. And they like it. You should see how excited they get when—"

Travis whistled. "You are one disgusting human be—uh, jerk," he said. "You don't deserve to be called human."

"It's not my fault," wailed Dirk. "I have to do it if I want to rule Neverland, and get my hands on more money than you could count in a hundred years." He appealed to Travis. "Who wouldn't?"

"I wouldn't," said Travis without hesitation. "Steele wouldn't. Neither would Riley or Mac. There are lots of people who wouldn't sell out." He stormed away, fists clenched at his sides.

Steele pressed Dirk for more information.

"What happens at the top? How are the memories extracted?"

Dirk shrank into himself. "I don't know. I've never been inside. Honest." He squinted at Steele as if waiting for the blow that must surely come. He seemed surprised when Steele didn't slug him. Instead, Steele hit him with another question.

"Who picks the names?"

"He does." Dirk's eyes momentarily darted toward the ceiling.

"Who? The Prince of Darkness?"

Dirk nodded. "He finds it amusing. They lose their memories to become paragons."

"How often does this happen?"

Dirk swallowed nervously. "Every night at midnight."

Steele left him and went to join Riley and Travis, who had been following the interrogation from a short distance away.

"We need to put our heads together and agree on what to do," he said. "We set out to rescue Mac, and now we know where he is."

"We can't trust Dirk again," said Travis.

Steele agreed. "But I'm sure he's telling part of the truth. We can trust him as long as I keep reminding him of my power, but he'll betray us the second he stops being afraid of me. The logical thing is to make sure the kids are being held in the first tunnel, and that they're not in immediate danger. Then we go after Mac. Once we get Mac, we'll search for the stolen memories. We'll free the kids and take them with us when we're done here."

Riley reached out and clutched Steele's arm. "We've got to find the memories. We've got to help all those kids in New York who don't remember one second of their lives, and Syd's brother is one of them."

Travis frowned. "What worries me is how we're going to know if we find the memories. I mean, what do they look like? Are they stored in bottles, or plastic containers, or on a computer chip? We have no idea what to look for."

"You're right," Steele admitted. "It's not going to be easy."

"So let's just get on with it," said Riley. "Your plan makes sense, Steele. We check out the kids, and then get Mac, the memories, and free the kids, in that order."

"And let's keep our eyes open for the wardens," added Steele.

"One more thing," said Travis. "We should also keep a lookout for any homeless people. Maybe they ended up here, like the kids."

Steele turned to Dirk. "Get up. You're coming with us while we check on the kids for ourselves. Then you're taking us to Mac. But first, you're going to return our backpacks and anything else you stole."

Dirk struggled to his feet, his finger wrapped in a rag he had torn from his shirt, which was now soaked with blood. As he drew abreast of Steele, Steele reached out, grabbed his jacket, and pulled him to a stop. "Remember how that chain felt around your neck? That was nothing compared with what I will do to you if you lie to me or lead us into a trap. If you force me, I will give your master a demonstration of the power of the medallion, and I'll make sure he knows that you kept it a secret from him."

Steele released his hold. Without a word, Dirk continued toward the door he had come through a short while ago, but Steele noticed that the bully's hands were shaking. *Good,* he thought. *But I can't let down my guard. I've got to keep him scared.*

Dirk led them through the door into another tunnel, as dank and dirty as the previous one, then through an opening into a dark square chamber with a large door in the middle of each wall. A single torch on the wall just inside the entry sputtered and smoked. Dirk crossed the floor to the door on the opposite wall.

"What's on the other side of those doors?" Steele asked.

Dirk hesitated.

"Don't even think of lying," hissed Riley.

But when Dirk looked squarely at Steele and told him that the doors opened into storage rooms, Steele didn't think he was lying.

"We believed him before and he betrayed us," said Riley. "I want to know what's in there." She pushed Dirk. "Open it."

Instead of listening to Riley, Dirk looked at Steele. Steele laughed. He knew what Dirk was up to; he was trying to create friction between him and Riley, play one against the other.

"If I were you, I'd do what she said."

Dirk's only response was to spit on the floor. He selected a key from a ring attached to a bungee cord on his leather belt and unlocked the door. Steele used his foot to open it.

"Oh my God!" Riley cried, and Steele caught her as she stumbled back.

Still holding her, Steele stood in the doorway and peered into the room. Behind him, Travis was breathing through his teeth.

It was a small room, much too small for the number of children staring at Steele with dull, lustreless eyes in their lean, pale faces. The room was damp; the floor was slippery. Steele noticed a bucket lying on its side near the door. The children looked to be about the same age as Steele, but some were younger. Their clothes were rags, their hair was tangled and dirty, and their bare arms, necks, and faces were marked with bruises, scratches, and even teeth marks. Near the door, a girl clutched and licked an empty plastic bag that had once contained bread. Steele could see that the bag had been licked clean of crumbs.

"We can't leave them here!" cried Riley.

Steele turned his face away from the children. "We've got to, Riley. We can't take them with us. Not yet. What would we do with them? I don't want to leave them either, but we've got to, at least until we finish what we came here to do."

"He's right, Riley," said Travis. "Besides, they'll be safer here."

Closing the door on the missing children was one of the hardest things Steele had ever done. Even after Dirk had locked the door, their haunted, frozen faces swam before Steele's eyes, and they all looked like Mac. He felt a deep shame burning inside.

The room and the state of the children also infuriated him. He ached to punch something or someone. Instead, he shoved Dirk roughly toward the opposite door and made him open it. They all peered inside, but it was empty. Then Dirk unlocked the last door and pushed it open. Steele and the others gathered in the doorway and stared into Dirk's room.

It was disgusting. Dirty clothes battled with food wrappers and soft drink cans for space on the floor. A bare mattress served as a bed. It was soiled and moth-eaten; broken springs protruded from holes in the fabric. Live cockroaches scuttled into cracks in the walls and floor, while others, the ones Dirk had killed, still remained on the walls, squashed into flat shapes and glued in place with their own insides. A baseball bat and something that looked like a riot stick rested against the wall in one corner, along with a number of sealed plastic bags.

Steele nudged Dirk inside, and waited for Travis and Riley to enter before closing the door. Dirk knelt on the floor and rolled the mattress back toward the wall, holding it in place with one hand. Then he pried one of the stones out of the floor, revealing a deep cavity. He fished about in the cavity and finally produced three backpacks. Steele recognized them as Riley's, Mac's, and his. Since Travis hadn't been wearing a pack, Steele handed him Mac's.

They shook their backpacks vigorously to get rid of any cockroaches that might be lurking inside, and then checked their belongings. Steele wasn't surprised that they found items missing. Riley accused Dirk of stealing her money, but Steele guessed that she'd seen the last of it.

"Where's my sword?" he demanded.

Dirk looked at him innocently. "What sword? I didn't see any sword."

Steele took a step toward Dirk and raised his arm, his finger pointing as if it were about to spurt fire. Dirk shrieked and scrambled over the mattress into the corner.

"Wait! Wait! I remember now. Just stay there. I'll get it." He crawled to the foot of the mattress, slipped his hand into a torn seam, and pulled out a dull black sword with a black horn hilt.

"Put it on the mattress, and then stand over there by the wall," Steele commanded.

Dirk stumbled against the wall, his eyes still on the sword.

"The first time I saw it, I wanted to hold it," said Travis. "Can I hold it now?"

"Go ahead," offered Steele.

Travis picked up the sword as carefully as if it were made of glass. "Whoa!" he breathed, testing its weight and balance. "It's awesome!"

"Yeah," said Steele, grinning proudly. "It's awesome all right."

Then he accepted the sword from Travis and held it for a moment, once again experiencing a strong sense of ownership. He had thought he'd never see it again and had deeply regretted its loss. He slid the blade carefully into the deep outer pocket on his backpack and was donning his pack when he noticed a small metal box on the floor near the door, partly hidden under a mound of dirty socks and underwear. He bent down and picked it up. It was about four inches square. Its burnished copper surface was badly dented. Inside, filling the box to the brim, were uniform squares of paper, folded in half. Holding the box in one hand, he reached in and unfolded one of the slips of paper. On it, printed in big letters, was the name, Matthew McCarthy.

"What is this?" he asked Dirk, holding up the box. "Why are all these names in here?"

"The paragon draw," muttered Dirk.

Steele gritted his teeth, sloughed off his backpack, and hastily stuffed the box and its contents inside. "There won't be a draw tonight," he muttered under his breath. Then he slung the straps over a shoulder, grabbed Dirk's shirt, and dragged him out the door.

But before them, blocking their access to the exit, stood the Maladroids. There were five of them and they were all dressed in long black cloaks, their faces invisible under baggy hoods. The flickering torchlight made their shadows perform grotesque dances on the walls and gleamed like diamonds on the blades of their long daggers. Steele glanced at the dagger in the raised hand of the Maladroid directly in front of him, saw the lifeless black stone embedded in its middle finger, and shuddered.

He grasped the hilt of his sword, freeing the weapon from his backpack in one easy motion. The backpack dropped to the floor. "How many Maladroids are there in this place?" he asked Dirk, twisting his arm.

"Hundreds," gasped Dirk.

He shoved Dirk toward Travis and Riley. "Don't let him get away," he said. "Lock him in his room. Stay with him. I'll knock once on the door when it's safe to come out." He opened his jacket and Pyrus scooted onto his shoulder.

"Riley, will you look after Pyrus?"

"We're not leaving you," said Riley.

"Please, Riley. There's no time to argue. I can look after myself. So please, just do what I say."

His companions obeyed reluctantly. Steele heard the door slam behind them. He tried to keep his sights on the Maladroids, but they suddenly split up and moved into position for a three-sided attack. Then they charged. It was clear to Steele that they intended to force him backwards against the wall, leaving him with nowhere to run. He mustn't let them trap him.

Steele waited until the Maladroid directly in front of him lifted his leg to take another step forward, then he opened his mouth, let out a blood-curdling howl, and lunged. Caught off guard, the creature tried to reverse direction, but its foot slipped on the black, stone floor; it lost its balance and stumbled backwards, arms flailing. The flat side of Steele's blade caught it on the side of its head and it crashed to the floor.

"Ahhh!" Brandishing a baseball bat, Riley flew out of Dirk's room toward one of the attackers on Steele's left. Without slowing her pace, she swung the bat at the creature's knees. It connected with a loud *crack*. The creature howled and tried to grab her, but she was already speeding toward her next victim.

"Take that, you creep!" she shouted, ramming the bat into the Maladroid's stomach.

Steele heard a low groan escape from the black hood as the creature doubled over, arms pressed tightly against its gut.

"Ahhh!" Travis had also found a weapon among the junk in Dirk's room. Armed with the riot stick, he ran in circles around one of the attackers, whacking its body at every opportunity.

Steele was overwhelmed by his friends' courage and loyalty. *Thank goodness they didn't listen to me.* He realized that Riley had been right. He couldn't have fought all five Maladroids at the same time, not without resorting to magic. And after what had happened to the Maladroids and Maddie Fey, the thought of using magic made him sick. As he watched his friends, stunned by their ferocity and the wild cries coming from their mouths, he forgot about the fifth Maladroid. He heard a *swish* and leaped aside less than a second before the blade slashed through the space where his neck had been.

"Look out! Steele!" Riley shouted at him, but Steele saw the Maladroid leaping through the air.

He was ready. As the creature landed, momentarily off balance, Steele threw himself at its chest, plowing into it and knocking it over onto its back. Steele's momentum carried him with the creature. He heard the sickening thud as the Maladroid's head hit the marble floor and split, killing it instantly. Quickly, Steele scrambled off the creature and spun about.

The fight was over. Their attackers lay motionless on the floor. Riley and Travis looked pale and exhausted, but seemed unhurt.

"And I thought *I* had to protect *you*," Steele said, as his friends made their way to him. "You were awesome. I couldn't have handled them without you."

Riley and Travis glanced at each other, eyes shining with pride. Steele retrieved his backpack from the floor and had just replaced his sword in its pocket when he sensed that one of the doors was opening. His head whipped about.

A Maladroid drifted from the darkness beyond the open door, its black cloak rustling on the floor. Others came behind. Steele grabbed his sword and edged slowly toward the exit, his eyes fixed on the creatures, his heart pounding so rapidly that he was certain it was beating ten years off his life. He felt Riley's hand on his arm, dry and cold as ice. He realized his own hands were hot and sticky.

"Riley," he said. "You and Travis . . . get Dirk and run. I'll meet you in the first tunnel."

"No."

"Last time was different. There were only five of them and I wouldn't use magic to fight them. Look. This time there are too many. We can't fight them *except* with magic."

"There are too many even for your magic," Riley said.

"No," said Steele, laughing bitterly as he felt the blackness course through his veins. "Remember? I've done this before."

Riley turned away. A moment later, Steele heard her speaking to Travis, somewhere behind him. When he saw them moving toward Dirk's room, he let the magic begin to simmer inside him. *Please don't let me lose control,* he prayed silently. *Let the magic be mine.* But he knew it was already too late for prayers . . . too late to smother the magic. He saw his companions break from Dirk's room, the bully between them, and race toward the exit. Riley was holding Pyrus in her cupped hands. He didn't want them to look back. The magic was boiling now.

The Maladroids came for him like a black flood. He pulled Ees from his neck, held it toward the ceiling, and unleashed the magic. The Maladroids seemed confused by his strange behaviour. Their hooded heads whipped back and they stared up in time to see white bars of fire shoot from above to lodge deep into the stone floor, erecting a cell of fire about them before they could react. Within seconds the creatures were trapped in a cage-like prison, the bars burning white.

Steele was as astonished by his magic as the Maladroids were. He had desperately wanted to control the power, make it do his bidding. And it had, but in a way he couldn't have imagined. Since he had lost control of his magic in the valley outside, incinerating hundreds of the creatures along with Maddie Fey and Wish, he hadn't been able to stomach it. Until now he had used it only once to convince Dirk that he was important to the Prince of Darkness. Perhaps his mother's medallion was helping him control it. Instead of blasting the Maladroids away, he had confined them in a place from which they couldn't escape, at least not until he and the others figured out what to do with them.

Thinking that he had used his magic in a good way, responsibly, Steele turned away from the caged creatures and hurried after the others. But when a howl erupted behind him, he spun about, startled. And then more creatures began howling in rage and twisting in agony as they tore at the burning bars. To Steele's horror, his magic scorched the flesh from their clawed hands and set their black cloaks ablaze.

"What are you doing?" shouted Steele, desperately. "Get back! Don't touch the bars!"

But the Maladroids were beyond listening. As one creature dropped to the floor, beating itself with its arms wildly to put out the fire, another took its place at the bars. Frantic, Steele tried to call up the magic and remove the bars, but he couldn't focus his mind on anything but the terrible scene before his eyes. As creature after creature disintegrated into ashes, Steele turned away helplessly and doubled over, vomiting onto the stone floor, then straightened and fled from the chamber.

In the chamber he had left behind, the white bars vanished as a low, satisfied breath filled the room. The black ashes swirled across the floor as if blown by a sudden draft. In his darkened suite, the Prince of Darkness smiled.

Searching

There are no words in any language in the universe to describe our sorrow over the loss of another of our companions. We had never given up hope of finding our first lost brother. Now we searched for three.

We circled Earth a thousand times, our great wings pounding, our huge hearts aching, but we found nothing. Our companions had disappeared without a trace, as if they had never existed.

Our hearts told us that they still lived, but our minds were filled with sorrow.

—**Excerpt from** *The Wardens' Logs*

Chapter Nineteen

At the Top of the Pyramid

Steele joined his companions at the mouth of the first tunnel. He barely noticed when Riley and Travis left to check on the kids whose memories were still intact. He stood there staring at Dirk without seeing him, oblivious to his discomfort. When the others returned, Riley reported that the kids were being held in two large rooms at the end of the tunnel.

"They look a lot healthier than the kids in that other room. They even seem happy."

Travis halted before Dirk, looked at him, and scowled. "They have to keep them happy, at least until they steal their memories. Then they throw them away."

"Travis, I told you, they feed them to the worms," said Riley.

Travis swallowed loudly.

When Steele remained silent, Riley touched his hand. "Are you all right?"

Steele moved his hand away and heard Riley sigh. He just wanted to be left alone. He felt something hurting inside his head, and realized that it was Riley who was causing the pain. She was talking to him again, her words hammering at his brain. He wanted to scream at her to stop, and struggled to find the words.

"What?" he asked her.

"You weren't listening," said Riley. "So I'll say it again. We're on our way to get Mac. We'll be there soon. I don't know what happened back there . . . with the Maladroids . . . but you can't quit on us now. We need you. Mac and the missing kids need you." When she paused, Steele knew she was trying not to cry. "Please, Steele. Don't shut yourself away from us."

"I can't do this," said Steele. "I can't take any more of this."

"You can and you will, because you've got to," said Travis, putting his arm about Steele's shoulders. "Without you and your magic, we'll fail."

"I don't want the magic. I don't want to hear about it. I don't want anything to do with it."

Travis's voice turned hard. "I was there when Maddie Fey said it's not about you. She was right. It's not about you, or me, or Riley. It's not about what we want or don't want. It's about saving Mac and a hundred other kids. It's about giving them back their memories. It's about doing what's right. So, you see. You haven't got a choice."

Steele tried to pull himself together. But everything was tilting, and his head and chest hurt terribly, and he saw Maddie Fey vanishing in flames, and the Maladroids gripping the white-hot bars and burning. *Oh, the burning!* Sinking onto the floor against the wall, he wrapped his arms about his knees, dropped his head, and began sobbing silently.

Pyrus wriggled onto Steele's shoulder and licked his neck. Steele looked up and into the salamander's moist, intelligent eyes and sniffled. Lowering his head, he wiped his eyes on his knees. "Oh, Pyrus," he whispered, gently running his hand along the salamander's side. Then he stood and looked solemnly at his friends. "I'm not a quitter."

They set out then, Dirk wheezing and groaning as they forced him to move faster and faster. He led them up several short flights of stairs and along so many passages that Steele lost count. Travis ran ahead, then back to urge the others to hurry, then ahead again. Finally they stopped at what appeared to be a solid wall. Dirk traced his fingers along a black seam, and the wall parted with a faint rattling sound. They passed through the opening in the wall and found themselves in another vast hall.

Steele recognized the massive columns that rose over a hundred feet to the arched ceiling; he recognized the human-sized stone gargoyles crouching on their stone perches in recessed arcades on both sides of the hall; and he recognized the shield-shaped arms of the Prince of Darkness—the three green frogs on a red ground with a wide yellow band crossing the middle of the shield—emblazoned upon dozens of banners suspended from thick black chains fastened to the ceiling beams.

As they hurried along the hall, Steele noticed that Travis's face was pale and he was staring straight ahead, avoiding the stone gargoyles on either side of him. Steele didn't blame him. If a gargoyle had almost bit his hand off he wouldn't want to look at them either. Travis only turned his head when they entered an enormous central square and Dirk stopped before a massive black stairway. They stopped for a brief rest. Dirk slumped forward, hands on his knees. His face was coated in sweat from exertion, and he was gasping for air.

Steele looked up the stairs and caught his breath.

"Whoa!" breathed Travis beside him.

It was the steepest, longest staircase Steele had ever seen. It sloped up and up until it disappeared into the shadows at the top of the Black Pyramid.

Breathing heavily, Dirk pointed at the stairs. "Mac's up there."

Riley groaned. "You're not serious! It'll take us a week to climb to the top."

Dirk smirked as he brushed past the others and climbed several steps. Steele heard the grinding sound seconds before the stairs began moving rapidly upward.

"It's an escalator," he shouted. "Quick! Get on."

They rode in silence, huddled together on one of the steps. There were no handrails, nothing to hold on to. Steele peered down and felt light-headed. One lurch would catapult him out into space, and it was a long, long drop to the black marble floor below.

"I'm scared," whimpered Riley, covering her face with her hands.

"Move up a step," said Steele. "Hold on to me and Travis."

But Riley was paralyzed beside him, so he and Travis slid cautiously onto the step below, using their backs to block Riley if she should pitch forward.

Steele felt overwhelmed by the Black Pyramid. Its vastness made him acutely aware of his own smallness. But more than that, it gave the Prince of Darkness substance in Steele's mind. From that evening when he had first heard the voice of the Prince of Darkness calling him down into its dark place, Steele had quailed at the mention of his name. But until now, that's all it had been—a scary voice, a hideously scarred face, and a shadow lurking somewhere on the fringe of Steele's existence, not quite real. But all of that changed now as he gazed about the Black Pyramid. This *was* the dark place. It was indistinguishable from its creator. Steele felt the presence of the Prince of Darkness in the massive stone walls, in the vast halls and dizzying heights. And as the great black escalator climbed higher and higher toward the pyramid's power-charged peak, Steele felt his confidence draining away. He struggled against a growing panic, knowing he was helpless before such immense power.

Riley squeezed his shoulder. "Think of Mac, only Mac."

When the escalator finally ground to a stop, Steele and the others scrambled off and quickly moved away. Directly ahead, an archway opened into a room. They entered, stopping just inside the opening, and looked about.

They were in a large room, its floor black marble, glossy and unworn, as if no one had ever walked on it. A dozen torches burned from brackets along the walls, providing enough light to see by. The four walls sloped inward, narrowing at the top where they met the ceiling. A wide, black metal table occupied the middle of the room with six black chairs placed haphazardly about it, and a desk and chair—with its back to the door—sat in the farthest corner. Three lower walls were lined with shelves. On two walls the shelves contained books, many of the volumes so massive that Steele doubted that he could lift them. The room smelled of mould, as if the books were rotting on their shelves. Glass doors enclosed the shelves on the third wall, which were crammed with clear vials and jars of all shapes and sizes containing coloured liquids, powders, and strange, misshapen specimens.

Steele walked over to the table and turned slowly, his eyes sweeping over the room. There was no sign of Mac.

"Come in," said a deep voice from somewhere in the shadows. "I've been expecting you."

Pandemonium erupted.

Riley screamed, Dirk shrieked and dashed for the door, only to find the way blocked by Travis. Travis grabbed his arm and dragged him over to where Steele stood motionless at the end of the table. Steele felt a heavy weight pressing on his chest, constricting his breathing. His eyes moved swiftly along the table and past the shelves to settle on the back of the large swivel chair. He didn't have to see into the chair to know what was sitting there like a great fat spider, a hideous smile on its scarred and scabby face.

They were alone with the Prince of Darkness.

Steele tried to turn and bolt to the escalator, but his legs buckled and he had to hold on to the table to keep from falling down. Minutes ago, he had faced a dozen Maladroids, but now fear paralyzed him as effectively as if he had stepped in cement. Horrified, he saw the large black chair begin swivelling slowly around. Beside him, Riley was mumbling incoherently.

The chair faced them now. At first Steele thought it was empty, but then blackness began to rise from the seat. It seemed to swirl about and coalesce until Steele could make out a tall figure completely concealed beneath black garments. As the figure moved toward them slowly, almost leisurely, Steele reached over his shoulder and slipped his sword from his backpack, relieved that he could still move his arms. His other hand clasped Ees.

Without warning, Pyrus shot down Steele's leg and streaked toward the towering black figure. Fear for his pet's safety overrode Steele's fear of the Prince of Darkness, freeing his limbs so that he could move again.

"No, Pyrus! Come back!" he shouted, dropping the sword to try to catch the salamander before the Prince of Darkness got him.

Steele was fast, but Pyrus was faster. The salamander hurled himself at the dark shape, and the Prince of Darkness raised his arms and caught him.

A hole seemed to open at Steele's feet; he felt himself slipping into it.

"Please let him go," he sobbed, struggling to keep from plunging down. "I'm the one you've been looking for."

The menacing figure held the salamander up before its face, studying it as if about to pop Pyrus in its mouth. Then it lowered its arms and looked at Steele, blackness swirling in the space under the loose hood.

"Yes," said the creature, reaching up and pushing the hood back and off its head. "I have been looking for you."

Time Passing

At times, we could not help but feel that the world we were trying to protect from our prisoners was doomed, like our lost brothers. At such times, we perched on mountain ledges and gazed at the stars with misty eyes and rending hearts, willing those we had left behind on Arjella to come to us from out of the immeasurable vastness.

And take us home.

But the only voices that answered were our own echoes.

—Excerpt from *The Wardens' Logs*

Chapter Twenty

Stolen Memories

"Fidus?" Steele exclaimed. "Is it really you? How did you get here? How did you know—?" A pang of sorrow struck his chest as he suddenly thought of Maddie Fey and wondered where he would find the courage and the words to tell Fidus that she and Wish were dead.

The old Mage handed the salamander back and then grasped Steele's hand and shook it vigorously. "It is good to see you, my friend." For a moment, his eyes rested thoughtfully on Pyrus.

Steele wondered what he was thinking, but remained silent. Then Fidus shook his head as if to clear his mind. He peered at Riley, his eyes twinkling like polished silver in the pale light.

"Come, Riley. Let me look at you."

Riley burst into tears and flew across the room. Steele thought she was going to collide with the old man, or hug him, or do something equally embarrassing, but she managed to stop at the last second. Fidus brushed her dirty, straggly hair off her forehead. Then his eyes lingered on her face, as if he were reading emotions that were hidden from the others.

"You cannot fight evil with kind words," he said. Then he leaned over and spoke in her ear.

Steele wondered what that was all about. He hoped Fidus would tell her something that would take away the despair he had seen in her mind. He wished someone would take away his own darkness.

"This is Travis," said Steele, taking the sword that Travis had retrieved. "He's from Chicago. He's helping us find Mac and the other missing kids."

Fidus greeted Travis warmly, and then noticed Dirk edging toward the escalator. "I would not do that, young man," he cautioned, his voice gruff. He spoke in an aside to Steele. "Is that Dirk?"

"Yes," Riley piped up. "That's Dirk the Jerk, sneaking off like the weasel he is. He told us Mac was here but, surprise surprise, he was lying."

"He may very well be a liar," said Fidus. "But he was not lying about Mac. Your friend *was* here."

Steele asked. "Did they . . . Is he still—?"

"He was very much alive when he left, or was taken from, this room. There are still faint traces of his aura here. But I could not release my power to follow him because the way is warded. I would have been detected at once."

"You're joking. Right?" Dirk laughed, disdainfully. "Have you looked in a mirror lately, old man? You're so old you're probably using all your power just to keep from falling down."

Fidus raised his arm so quickly, Steele thought he was going to fly across the room and incinerate Dirk. But then the Mage crooked a finger and beckoned the bully. "Come here."

Dirk swaggered toward Fidus and halted about ten feet away. He yawned, as if bored.

"Come closer."

"Who are you?" Dirk snarled.

"Never mind who I am," said Fidus. "Just answer my questions. Where have they taken Mac?"

Dirk muttered, "Stupid old fool."

Fidus's face turned as black as a thundercloud. "You *will* answer my questions. You will tell me where Mac has been taken. You will tell me if his memories have been extracted. And you will tell me what happens to the children whose memories are gone."

Dirk's eyes widened in shock as his mouth opened and answers poured out in a rush. "He's in a holding cell . . . through there . . ." He tried to cover his mouth with his hand, but the words just kept coming. "I don't know if they've extracted his memories yet. If they have, he'll be kept in the cell until tomorrow . . . then he'll be put with the other kids and shipped to New York. I don't know what happens to them after that." His mouth snapped shut.

"What are we waiting for?" Steele walked over to Dirk and pushed him. "Let's go."

Fidus raised his hand to stop them. "I know you are anxious to see your friend, Steele. But first, there are things we must discuss. Mac is not going anywhere for the moment."

He moved to the head of the long table and lowered his lanky frame into a chair. Then he picked up a knife and cut a slice from one of the crusty loaves of bread on the table before him, surrounded by other delicious-looking food.

"Am I dreaming?" said Travis breathlessly, staring at the table in surprise. "Where did that come from?"

Fidus smiled. "I thought you might appreciate a little something to restore your strength."

Steele's mouth watered as he stared at the feast spread out on polished boards on the table. There were cheeses, cold meats and pickles, crusty breads, buttery rolls, and a bunch of the plumpest, juiciest-looking green grapes Steele had ever seen. Near Fidus's right hand stood a glass ewer containing what looked like a rich red wine, and a large bottle of sparkling water.

No one moved. They stood there and stared at the table with half-hopeful, half-fearful expressions on their faces. It looked too good to be true. As he devoured the food with his eyes, Steele felt weak and dizzy. He couldn't remember the last time he and Riley had eaten. Then he recalled what he had to tell Fidus, and felt guilty. It didn't seem right to sit down and share the old man's feast and *then* tell him about Maddie Fey. He knew he should tell him now. But Fidus was calling them to the table, so he held his tongue.

"Sit down. Sit down," said Fidus. "There's enough for everyone."

They sat around the table and attacked the food like savages. Steele ate until his stomach felt round and full. Dirk ate nothing. He sat alone at the foot of the table, distanced from the others, his face dark and scowling. He thrummed his fingers on the metal until Fidus became so exasperated that he bellowed words that stuck Dirk's fingers to the table and sealed his mouth shut.

The smell of food drew Pyrus from under Steele's jacket, and all the companions laughed as the salamander crawled about the table, snapping up tasty morsels from their fingers with his tongue. When the last crumb was gone, and all that remained on the wooden platters was the woody grape stem picked clean of its fruit, Fidus planted his elbows on the table and made an announcement.

"One of the children has died."

Steele dropped his gaze from the old Mage's face and glanced quickly at Riley. She was staring at Fidus in shock. Steele looked back at Fidus.

"Who?" he asked.

Across the table Travis's face was a mask of sadness. Steele knew he was thinking of his school friend, David Draken.

"It was a girl," said Fidus sadly. "She was one of the first to go missing. She was from New York and her name was Megan."

Riley said to Steele, "Megan Traft. The girl your father told us about. Megan Traft is dead."

"There may be others," said Fidus. "And there will be others unless we—"

"Unless we find the stolen memories," Travis said.

The old Mage nodded slowly.

"How are we going to find the memories when we don't know what they look like?" asked Steele.

Fidus met Steele's eyes and smiled. "I have some ideas about those *stolen* memories."

Watching him, Steele realized that a smile could be more complicated than he would have imagined. Fidus's smile was rich and unfathomable. It was sad and kind and as hard as rock. It refreshed Steele like cool water from a deep well, and warmed him like a down-filled cover. Although Fidus was smiling at him, Steele sensed that his companions were also captivated by the smile and were reacting to it. He felt the tension that had evolved from sadness and despair over the death of Megan Traft lessen, and he heard with his mind the sound of their limbs relaxing.

"Now listen," Fidus said. "I am going to tell you something. I have given much thought to the problem of the stolen memories over the past days. At first I believed that they had been extracted by a powerful magic process unknown to me."

Travis grinned. "Hopefully, it would be more subtle than in the movies where the evil wizard places his hand on the victim's forehead and sucks out all the information in his brain. That's so lame."

"Yes, I was thinking of something more subtle than the movies," said Fidus dryly.

"Like what?" asked Steele.

"Exactly," Fidus exclaimed. "Like what? Magic cannot operate beyond its nature; it cannot do everything. I can use magic to enter your mind and read your thoughts and even memorize your memories. Using magic, I can make you believe that your memory is failing. But there is no known magic that would enable me to steal your memories, lift them out of your brain as if they had never existed there, and store them in some sort of magic container." He shook his head vehemently. "Once I accepted that it was impossible to use magic to steal memories in the manner I just described, I was free to move forward."

"You said that the Prince of Darkness used strong magic," said Riley. "Maybe it's a different kind of magic, one that you've never heard of. And if that's true, how do you know he can't steal memories?"

"Hmm." The old Mage reached for the wine ewer and refilled his glass, but he did not drink. "I have spent a life-time studying magic. But there are more powers in the universe than I could discover in a billion lifetimes. And yet, I have learned that, while the powers may differ greatly, there are certain laws, like in physics, that are common to all of the powers I have known. I believe that those same laws apply to all magic."

"I sort of understand, I guess," said Riley. "It's like you said before, 'it can't do everything.'"

"What was used? Some sort of virus?" asked Travis. "I heard on the news about a man who caught a viral infection that reduced his memory to seven seconds."

Riley was incredulous. "You mean he couldn't remember anything that happened more than seven seconds ago?"

"Right. If it happened eight seconds ago, it was gone."

Fidus rapped on the table and they fell silent. "That was a good suggestion," he said to Travis. "And you are absolutely right. Certain viruses can affect memory, but they cannot steal memories, leaving the mind blank. They destroy them. When the virus destroys a memory, we will not recover it."

"But if the memories weren't stolen by magic, then it must have been done by a machine," said Steele. "Nothing else makes sense. And that means the memories are stored digitally somewhere."

"You have not been listening," Fidus admonished them, but kindly. "I said that I did not know of a magic that would enable me to steal your memories. I did not say that the memories had been stolen."

"I'm confused," groaned Riley. "If that's so, then where are the memories?"

"Where they have always been," said Fidus, his sapphire-blue eyes settling briefly on each of the companions.

"I know," breathed Steele. "They're still in the kids' minds."

Fidus slapped his hands on the table. "Excellent! Now we come to the interesting part. Since the memories are in the children's minds, why can't the children remember them? The answer brings us back to magic. I believe that the Prince of Darkness used his magic to block memory."

"So all we've got to do is find a way to destroy the magic," said Riley.

"Exactly," beamed Fidus, pushing himself up. "Now then, let us go and find Mac."

"Aren't you going to tell us how to destroy the magic so the kids won't die?" asked Travis.

"Not yet," Fidus answered. "I have an idea, but first I must see Mac and determine his condition."

Steele gulped and squeezed Pyrus. "Uh, sir. There's something I have to tell you."

Fidus looked at him, his eyes kind. "What is it, Steele? Can it not wait until Mac is with us?"

I can't do this, thought Steele. "No, sir. It's very important. It can't wait."

"Then you must tell me now."

Steele swallowed again. "I'm sorry to tell you this," he said. "But Maddie Fey and Wish are dead. And I killed them."

No one moved or made the slightest sound.

Steele squirmed under Fidus's stern gaze and felt sweat trickle down his forehead and pool at the bridge of his nose. At last, the old Mage took a step back from the table and bowed his head. He stayed like that for a long time. Then his shoulders began to shake, slowly at first, and then uncontrollably.

Steele glanced at Riley, asking with his eyes what he should do. He had never seen a grown man cry before, and he felt helpless and guilty. Riley put a finger to her lips and waved him over.

"What can we do?" Steele asked.

"I think we should leave him alone," she said.

Then the strangest thing happened, and Steele squeezed his eyes shut and opened them several times before he could make himself believe it. The old Mage wasn't weeping, he was laughing.

Fidus tilted his head back and laughed and laughed.

Bewildered and frustrated, Steele cried, "Please stop! Didn't you hear me? I killed Maddie Fey."

"My dear boy." Fidus brushed away the tears from his laughter. "I am so sorry . . ." He turned away, covering his face with his arm while he struggled to contain himself.

"He's sure got a strange way of showing he's upset about a friend's death," Travis said.

"No, no!" protested Fidus, pressing his hands against his head. "I was not thinking of Maddie Fey. I was about to say how truly sorry I am that you have been carrying such a heavy burden. To think that you actually believed . . ." He paused as if searching for the right words. But then he dropped his hands and said with conviction, "You did not kill Maddie Fey. The very notion that you could do such a thing is ridiculous."

"But I was there. I saw the flames."

Riley asked quietly, "If she's not dead, where is she?"

"I do not know where Maddie Fey is. She does not answer to me." Fidus moved to Steele and laid his hand on his shoulder. "But believe me, my friend. Maddie Fey is very much alive."

Steele didn't believe him. As he followed Dirk and the others down the shadowy halls of the Black Pyramid, he recalled his last moments with Maddie Fey. He saw himself pushing her into one of the Maladroids, and Wish leaping at his throat, snarling. He saw his own mouth opening and black fire spewing out like vomit, incinerating the Maladroids and everything that stood between him and the base of the cliff in the distance, including Maddie Fey and Wish.

"He just doesn't want to believe she's dead," he said to Riley and Travis.

They walked in silence for a long time before Dirk stopped abruptly and pointed at a low door in the black stone just ahead.

"In there."

Steele moved alongside Fidus to get a closer look. He noticed a large iron key protruding from the door lock, and a bunch of smaller keys on a ring attached to it. He looked back in time to see Dirk trying to sneak away. "Get back here and open this door," he said threateningly.

Muttering to himself, Dirk stormed up to the door, turned the lock hard, and kicked the door inward.

Fidus turned to Riley and Travis. "Wait here and keep a sharp eye on Dirk. Steele will come with me."

He moved through the open doorway, stooping to clear the low overhead frame. Steele followed, feeling excited and anxious at the same time. Once they were inside, the ceiling was high enough for Fidus to stand erect. They paused inside the door and looked about. They were in a long, narrow room. Barred cells ran along its length on either side of a centre aisle. Steele grabbed the keys from the lock and they hurried down the aisle, peering into each cell. They were vacant. They had almost reached the end when Steele stopped suddenly and gasped.

"Fidus!" he exclaimed.

They stared into the second last cell on their right.

Except for the lone figure curled into a tight ball on the long, narrow, stone bench, shivering from the damp, chilly air, the cell was deserted. The figure on the bench was a boy. Steele couldn't see his face, but there was no mistaking the mop of white hair, despite the dirt and tangles.

Mac!

Steele tried to say Mac's name, but the word stuck in his throat. He felt hot tears spill from his eyes and roll down his face. Mac raised his head, his pale eyes moving from Steele to Fidus and back to Steele. His gaze was dull and lifeless, and his face registered nothing, neither interest nor recognition. Then his head dropped back onto his arm.

"They've already stolen his memories," Steele said. At that moment, he gladly would have given up every happy memory in his head to make Mac recognize him. He unlocked the cell door. Then he walked over to the bench and lowered himself onto his heels beside his friend.

"It's time to go home," he said, his voice breaking.

Between them, he and Fidus managed to lift Mac to his feet. Mac neither helped nor hindered them. He showed no reaction whatsoever. Steele talked to him softly. "Your name is Mac. We're not going to hurt you. We're your friends."

Suddenly, Mac snarled like a wild dog and lunged at Steele, kicking, punching, and biting. It happened so quickly, the attack caught Steele by surprise. At first the sight of Mac enraged was so funny, he almost laughed as he raised his arms to ward off the blows. But the boy who attacked him was not the Mac he knew. This was a vicious stranger, unrelenting in his assault. Steele was bigger and stronger and wasn't as worried about being hurt as he was about accidentally hurting Mac while defending himself.

Fidus came up behind Mac. "Stop!" His voice intruded on the punching and snarling like a clap of thunder. Then he wrapped his arms about Mac, pinning the boy's wild arms to his sides.

Mac stopped fighting as suddenly as he had begun, and his eyes went blank.

"We're not going to hurt you," Steele repeated. "Your name is Mac. You're my friend. I've been searching for you for a long time."

Mac looked right through him.

"Here," said Fidus. "Hold his arm tightly."

Together, they dragged Mac back along the aisle toward the anxious white faces of Riley and Travis framed in the doorway.

Riley burst into tears when she saw Mac's vacant expression. She looked despairingly at Steele, and he felt her eyes moving over the scratches on his face.

"It's nothing," he said. "He didn't know it was me. He didn't know what he was doing."

Riley sniffled. "It hurts so much worse when it's someone close to you. Now I know how Sydney felt when William didn't recognize her." She paused. "What happens now?"

"Ah," said Fidus, adjusting his hold on Mac's arm and leaning toward her and Steele. "We have come to the most difficult part of the problem—how to remove the magic that is blocking Mac's memory." His startling blue eyes bored into Steele. "This is where I must ask you to place your life in danger to save your friend."

"What must I do?" asked Steele, without hesitating.

Fidus looked at him for what felt like a long time. Then he said softly, "You must find your way into Mac's brain and destroy the magic that is slowly but surely killing him."

Time

We despaired over the preoccupation of humans with killing each other. We had watched over them and protected them for hundreds of thousands of years—from the moment they had emerged from the oceans. We had rejoiced at each step as they slowly inched their way up the evolutionary mountain toward its heights.

But perhaps the mountain appeared too high, the climb too difficult. They stopped and turned and began the rapid descent into war and chaos. They fought and killed one another over lands and riches. They waged wars in the names of their gods and countries and economies. They enslaved other humans, sold their own flesh and blood, and destroyed entire civilizations.

And then, just when it seemed that all hope was gone, a single human somewhere on the planet would do something so selfless, so splendid, that we could only shake our great heads in wonder.

—Excerpt from *The Wardens' Logs*

Chapter Twenty-one

Inside Mac's Head

Steele didn't know what he had expected Fidus to say, but it definitely wasn't that. He staggered backwards, dropping Mac's arm.

Fidus called Dirk and Travis to him. "Hold on to Mac. He is stronger than he looks, and might try to run. Do not let him go." Then he turned to Steele. "I know I am asking a lot of you . . ."

"What you're asking is too much. I can't do it," said Steele. "There has to be another way."

"There is no other way," said Fidus.

"It sounds sort of dangerous to me," said Travis. "I know Steele can get into people's minds, but this is different. You're asking him to get into Mac's brain and physically remove something. For him to do that, wouldn't you have to shrink him small enough to inject him into Mac's bloodstream?"

"I have no intention of shrinking Steele and injecting him into Mac's bloodstream," said Fidus shortly. "He will journey with his mind."

Travis didn't look convinced.

Dirk mumbled something unintelligible.

"I know you're not going to listen to me, but I don't want you to do this," said Riley. "What they did to Mac is bad enough, but if something happened to you, too, I couldn't bear to lose two friends."

Fidus ignored their protestations. His eyes remained fixed on Steele. Steele had the sensation that they were the only two people in the universe. Riley and Travis stared at them as the silence deepened and tension mounted.

"If I don't do this," said Steele after a while, "will Mac . . . die?"

"Memories are what sustain us; they keep us sane," replied Fidus. "Without memories Mac will not be able to think, or reason, or laugh. He will not be able to care for himself, or provide for his own needs. He will have no reference for the simplest activity. He will have to relearn how to stand every time he attempts it." He sighed deeply. "And then he will waste away to nothing. He *will* die, Steele, just like Megan Traft."

"It's so unfair," cried Riley. "We saved Syd's brother and all those other kids from the worms, and now they're going to die anyway."

"They will not die if we destroy the magic," said Fidus.

Steele nodded grimly. "Could I die . . . doing this, I mean?"

"Would my answer help you in making your decision?" Fidus asked him.

Steele shook his head. "I guess not. I said before that I'd give my life to help Mac." He felt his eyes begin to sting. "I'll do it. I have to."

Fidus nodded slowly. "He is fortunate to have a friend like you."

"Talk about stupid," muttered Dirk. "Why don't they let the moron die?"

When Riley flew at Dirk and slapped him across the face, Steele couldn't help cringing. "If you were always wetting yourself because you couldn't remember how to go to the bathroom, would you want us to let you stay like that until you died if there was a way to save you?"

Dirk's face was as red as Ees. "Shut your face, you little puke. You think you can save the world." He laughed harshly. "You don't get it, do you? It's too late. It can't be saved."

"You're wrong," Riley screamed at him. "The problem is creatures like you and your master who want to destroy it and make it an evil place where people are afraid to go out their front doors. You believe it's cool to be bad. You make fun of values and families and traditions that we started developing when we first discovered that we could think and reason. Now you and your kind are doing everything you can to turn us back into animals." She stopped and spun away. "What's the use!"

"Way to go, Riley!" Travis cheered.

Riley flushed and smiled through her tears.

"Puddlescum!"

She looked over her shoulder just as a gob of spit splattered against her face.

Back in the room where they had shared Fidus's magical feast, Steele stuck to Riley while the others struggled to lower Mac onto one of the black chairs. It had taken the combined strength of Steele and Fidus to pull Riley away from Dirk. Her anger had died as quickly as it had flared up.

"Are you OK?" Steele asked.

"Yeah. I sort of lost it back there," Riley answered.

"Don't feel bad. I'd have done the same."

"You are much too young to hear what I had in mind for Dirk," said Fidus, appearing before them. "Riley, you are a wonder."

Steele felt warm inside when Riley grinned impishly at the old Mage and said. "It did feel good when I punched him."

"I must take Steele from you now," said Fidus, taking Steele's arm. "It is time."

Fidus led Steele toward the table where Travis and Dirk were standing guard over Mac. They had managed to subdue him and he was slumped on the chair, his chin resting on his breast. A second chair had been placed so that it faced him.

"I heard Travis say that you could read minds," said Fidus. "Tell me what happened to make him say that."

Steele told him how he had accidentally found himself in Riley's mind. "But the next time, I made it happen," he explained. "The Maladroids were controlled by a creature called the Disciplinarian. Before Maddie Fey destroyed it, I used magic to break into its mind to find out where they had taken Mac. But I don't know if I can do it again."

Fidus's eyebrows rose. "A very foolish *and* an exceedingly brave deed, Steele. You could have become lost. You must have been frightened."

Steele nodded. "It was horrible. After, it made me sick."

The old man patted Steele's shoulder. "I should think so, my friend. Now listen carefully, and answer truthfully. Are you absolutely certain that you wish to do this thing? I would not have asked you to embark on this journey if there were another way. But there is no other way. My magic is too old and too alien. It would do more harm to your friend than good."

"I'm sure," answered Steele.

"When you reach Mac's mind, you must have a general knowledge of the brain and how memory works so that you will recognize the magic."

"I know about the brain," said Steele. "I know all about neurons and how they fire."

"Well then," said Fidus. "Let us begin. And remember, I will be here beside you. I will come for you if you lose yourself."

As Steele dropped onto the chair facing Mac, Mac became increasingly agitated. His eyes rolled back in his head and his body shook violently, and all the while, a horrible rasping scream came from his open mouth, flecking his face with spittle. Steele could see that Riley, Travis, and Dirk were using all of their strength just to hold onto him. Their faces were red and shiny with sweat.

And then the strangest thing happened. Pyrus suddenly appeared on Steele's knee. As the salamander stared at Mac, Mac's wild, rolling eyes focused on him and his body relaxed. Then, to Steele's surprise, Pyrus leaped across to Mac's chair and settled there, his head resting on Mac's leg as he turned the colours of a rainbow. No one moved or breathed as the shadow of a smile formed on Mac's lips.

Thank you, Pyrus, Steele said silently.

Steele looked at his friend's dear face. He took a long, slow breath and concentrated on shutting his mind off from the room and everything in it. He shut out Riley, and Travis, and the old Mage watching him, his eyes dark and anxious. He forced images of the Prince of Darkness, the Maladroids, and Dirk back into a compartment in his mind and locked them there. Then he went deep inside himself, calling out to the magic as he went. It came to him in a rush, filling him with raw power.

Steele gasped as he plunged into the bright red, fast-flowing river of blood. Confused and disoriented, he almost panicked when the swift current sucked him down and swept him away, carrying him through dark pulsing tunnels, his head throbbing in time with the steady ear-shattering beat of Mac's heart. He rode the blood-stream current into the eye of a violent lightning storm and gazed in wonder as electricity forked and snapped all about him.

He was in Mac's brain, but he saw at once that something was wrong.

Quickly, he reviewed the memory sequence in healthy brain cells. The neuron fires. An electrical impulse travels along the neuron to a terminal at the nerve ending. The neuron releases a neurotransmitter that flows across the synapse to a receptor site on the next neuron. Then that neuron fires, and the process is repeated, over and over again, until the sequence is completed.

But the cells in Mac's brain were not behaving like healthy cells. Steele could see dozens, perhaps hundreds of neurons firing, releasing lightning-like impulses that rippled along their lengths. But when the electrical impulses reached the nerve endings they couldn't enter the terminal and trigger the release of the neurotransmitters because the nerve endings were clogged by magic.

And across the synapse where the receptor sites awaited the arrival of the neurotransmitters, there was no activity at all. There again, magic blocked the receptor bays so that the memory sequence could not be received or transmitted.

Destroy the magic.

Fidus's words flashed in Steele's mind. He thought of Mac without a single memory to comfort him. Unlike Mac, Steele possessed all of his memories. They were all there, stored away inside his brain—every thought, word, blink, smile, sight, sound, smell, touch, of every second of every day of his life. He couldn't imagine not having any memories. What if they suddenly disappeared? He knew the answer. It was there in the silent, inactive cells that were turning as black as the magic that was choking them. Mac's brain was dying.

I've got to save Mac.

Steele knew he'd have to call up his own powers to destroy the magic clogging Mac's memory, but he had no idea how to go about it, since he was already using his powers just to stay in Mac's mind. Could he use his powers to do two or even three things at once? He had to try.

Once, he had extinguished a Fire Demon by cutting off the oxygen that fuelled it. Could he do that here? The brain needed oxygen. The magic blocking Mac's memory had been conjured up to block nerve cells, so it must be aware of the cells' properties. One of those properties was the need for oxygen. What would happen if Mac's nerve cells were deprived of oxygen? Would the black magic sense that it was not where it should be, and disintegrate? Steele didn't know, but the more he thought about it, the more he was convinced that creating a vacuum was the only solution. He had to get closer.

He focused on a tiny fragment of his mind, and let his thoughts linger there until nothing else existed and he and the fragment were one. Then he slowly severed the fragment from the rest of his mind and released it, steering it toward the black magic. When he was beside it, he slowed and eased closer. Then he touched it—a tentative probe—as lightly as a bubble bouncing off flesh. The magic responded instantly, shimmering and trembling with power.

And then, so swiftly that it left Steele breathless, something dark and twisting rose up, seemingly out of nowhere, and lunged at Steele. Deciding that it was some sort of snake, Steele pushed off from the magic and sped back, joining with his larger mind. As he passed over a coiling section of black, he realized that the thing pursuing him wasn't a snake after all. It was like a thick black vine and he had seen it spreading through Mac's brain like ivy claiming an old brick building.

Unsure of what oxygen deprivation might do to Mac, but knowing that he had to destroy the magic, Steele called on his powers. Working quickly but carefully, he built a perfect dome about Mac's brain. And then he began to draw the oxygen into his lungs, not his spirit lungs, but his very large physical lungs in the chest of the body back in the chair. Then he concealed his spirit form with magic and waited.

The black vine shuddered in response to the weakening brain cells. Tendrils, hundreds of them, shot out of the vine and whipped about the neurons, searching. They shattered the magic Steele had used to hide his spirit form and wound about him, squeezing his life away.

Fidus!

Steele felt gentle hands on his shoulders. The familiar face of the old Mage swam before his eyes. He looked about, disoriented. He felt he should be somewhere else. Then he remembered and realized that he was back with his friends in the Black Pyramid. His eyes took in Mac, sitting opposite him, staring fascinated as Pyrus turned from yellow to vivid green. Riley was sitting cross-legged on the floor, and Travis was stretched out beside her on his stomach, rusty head bent over his notebook. Steele noticed Dirk the Jerk was slumped in a chair, his expression alternating between bored and disgusted. But his eyes were sharp and alert, and kept darting about the room as if he were waiting for something.

"You're safe now," said Fidus, his face haggard.

Steele brushed his hand over his face. He felt old and weak, but he managed to turn his chair so that he was facing the old Mage. "The magic was killing Mac. I tried to destroy it, but it found me." He looked into Fidus's eyes. "I failed Mac again. I failed all of those kids like him."

Fidus raised an eyebrow. "You must have a very high opinion of yourself if you believe that you are responsible for what happened to your friend and the other children who have no memories."

Steele opened his mouth to protest, but Fidus shook his head sharply. "No! If we are to move ahead, you must hear me out. I know that you blame yourself for what happened to Mac. You believe that you should not have allowed yourself to be distracted by what you saw in the window on North Michigan Avenue. Can you look me in the eye and declare with all honesty that you were in control of the situation and *allowed* yourself to be distracted, while Riley was not in control and therefore couldn't help but be distracted?"

"That's not what I think," protested Steele vehemently.

"Then tell me why you blame yourself, and not Riley, for what happened to Mac."

"It wasn't her fault," said Steele. "She couldn't have done anything to prevent it."

"And you could?" asked Fidus.

"No. I—" Steele paused. "I've never thought about it like that," he admitted.

Fidus patted Steele's shoulder. "Short of keeping Mac

under lock and key, there was nothing you could have done to prevent his disappearance."

"Fidus is right," said Riley. "It wasn't your fault, so stop beating yourself up."

Steele looked at her thoughtfully, but said nothing.

"There is one more thing," said Fidus. "I believe that I speak for everyone in this room when I say that no one blames you for trying and failing to destroy the magic in Mac's mind. What matters is what was in your heart at the time. You risked everything to help a friend."

"You make it sound so simple," said Steele. "But when it's actually happening to you, it's not like that at all."

The old man laughed. "And sometimes, my friend, we make things more complicated than they are."

The sound of a chair toppling brought Steele to his feet. His head whipped around just as Pyrus streaked up his leg and disappeared beneath his jacket. He saw Mac standing by the fallen chair, his face dark with a mixture of anger and fear.

"Just who the hell are you? And what am I doing here?"

A. D. 1200–1600

Wars raged across the planet. In Europe, the Roman pontiff authorized the Inquisition. Church states arrested and expelled those who held different beliefs. Torquemada presided over the Spanish Inquisition with an iron fist, and ordered suspected witches and heretics to be burned at the stake. Neighbour spied on neighbour. Sons spied on fathers. Lies killed. In France, a peasant girl who led an army was betrayed by those she served—she was murdered, her body reduced to ashes. The empires of the Aztecs and Incas were destroyed, never to rise again.

–Excerpt from *The Wardens' Logs*

Chapter Twenty-two
Making Plans

"You did it, Steele. You destroyed the magic," said Riley, crying. She rushed over to Mac. "Mac, it's me, Riley. And Steele."

Mac backed away. "I don't know who you are, but if you lay a finger on me, you'll be sorry."

Steele turned back to Fidus. "There's something wrong. Why doesn't he know who we are?"

"Give him time," said Fidus. "Mac seems to be aware of the present so you obviously destroyed some of the magic. You cannot attempt another excursion into his mind so soon after your last effort. Let us wait and see what happens." He gave Steele's shoulder a reassuring pat and turned to Mac.

"No one is going to hurt you, Mac," said Fidus. "These are your friends. They have been searching for you, and they found you in this place."

For a second, Steele thought that Mac was going to bolt for the escalator, but then he seemed to relax.

"You said 'Mac.' Why did you call me that?"

"Because that is your name," answered Fidus.

Mac gripped his head in his hands. "I don't know that name . . . but I can't think. . . ."

"Come," said Fidus. "Let us sit, and we will tell you everything you wish to know."

As they moved over to the table, Steele heard Dirk muttering angrily under his breath, and saw him aim a vicious kick at the chair Mac had occupied a moment ago. At the angry sound, Pyrus crawled out of the neck of Steele's shirt, turned a pale pink colour, and shot back inside. Steele grinned and joined the others.

This time it was Mac who sat alone at the foot of the table, away from the others. When Dirk got there, the chairs had all been taken, and he had to go back and retrieve the one he had kicked out of his way. Instead of carrying it to the table, he moved the chair farther away and sat with his back to the rest of them.

"What a jerk," said Travis.

Brow furrowed in concentration, Mac looked from one face to another, as if he were memorizing them. Then he said, "If you're my friends, how come I don't know you?"

Fidus answered. "The reason you do not know your name or recognize your friends is that your memories began less than five minutes ago."

Despite frequent interruptions by Steele and the others, Fidus told Mac all that had occurred since Mac's disappearance. When he was finished, he folded his hands on the table and seemed to stare at something beyond the solid walls of the Black Pyramid. At that moment, the old man reminded Steele of his grandmother, whom he frequently caught gazing into a far-off place that only she could see.

Thinking of GM caused a sudden ache in Steele's heart. *Don't go there,* he told himself, dropping his eyes from Fidus's face and gently nudging thoughts of his grandmother from his mind.

For the next half-hour Mac fired questions at Steele, Riley, and Travis so relentlessly that Steele's head started spinning. Finally, Mac seemed to run out of things to ask, and he fell silent, his eyes flicking from Riley to Steele and back again.

When he finally spoke again, he asked, "Are my memories lost for good?"

"Your memories are still in your mind," Fidus quickly reassured him. "But they are blocked by magic. Steele destroyed some of the magic or you would be unable to speak with us now. Perhaps the remaining magic will disintegrate now that part of it is gone. And perhaps the binding spells will also disintegrate. If your memories do not return, we will find a way to free them, Mac."

Travis said, "I'm especially anxious for your memories to come back, Mac, because I'm dying to talk to you about the Great Chicago Fire and hear your theory."

"Huh?"

"Never mind," said Travis. "It can wait."

"You won't know that we're really your friends until you get your memories back, Mac," said Riley. "So you'll just have to trust us until then."

Mac didn't look happy, but then he sighed and directed a question to Steele. "And you actually went into my brain and destroyed some of the magic that the Prince of Darkness put there to block my memories?"

Steele nodded.

"Thanks." Mac smiled. "I think you saved my life."

Steele laughed. "I *totally* saved your life."

Then Fidus pressed Steele to tell them how he had destroyed the black magic. Steele related what he had seen and done inside Mac's brain.

"At least the other kids have a chance now," said Travis.

"Even if you destroy only some of the magic, they can have new memories. They won't die."

Steele looked doubtful. "Mac was just one person. There are hundreds of other kids whose memories are gone. I wouldn't be able to use my power on more than one or two kids in a day. It's too draining." He turned to Fidus. "And it's going to take too long. Some of the kids might die before I can get to them."

Fidus patted Steele's hand. "You are not alone, Steele." He winked meaningfully. Then he became serious and raised his voice to include the others at the table. "It took courage and daring to enter the realm of the Prince of Darkness. Yet you did just that. You found Mac. You discovered where the missing children are being held. And Steele learned to use his power against the black magic blocking their memories." He stopped, tilted his head, and looked thoughtful. "But we are not yet finished here."

Steele and Riley shared a quick questioning glance.

Fidus turned to Dirk. "Tell me what goes on in the chamber directly overhead."

Dirk spun about on the chair. "There's nothing up there."

Fidus spoke sternly. "Do not lie to me again. The chamber exists. It must be important or you would not have bothered to lie."

Steele looked up, and shivered as his eyes moved slowly over the ceiling. He went still and listened for the sound of movement in the chamber overhead. Nothing. Wishing that he understood more about his magic and how to use it, he pressed his hand against Ees, squeezed his eyes shut, and strained to project his hearing. A sudden tumultuous pounding in his ears almost jolted him out of his chair.

Steele sifted through the sounds, identifying and eliminating those around him first—Pyrus's heartbeat, Dirk's muttering, his companions' steady breathing. Then he shut out the sounds of other living things—the barely perceptible rustle of a spider spinning its web in a corner of the room, the slightest skittering of insects in the ceiling, the scratching and scrabbling of rats behind the stone walls. Finally, he shut out the groaning and grinding of the great Black Pyramid as its massive weight shifted and settled. When he had eliminated all of the identifiable sounds, he sent his hearing through the ceiling and into the chamber above.

He heard nothing. There were no sounds of movement or breathing or swallowing. There were no sounds at all . . . except . . . It was so faint that he almost dismissed it. What was it? Steele strained and strained. And then he heard it again, and this time he recognized it—laughter no louder than a hand brushing through air.

"There *is* a chamber overhead," he said. "And he's there."

"Who?" cried Riley, Mac, and Travis in unison. Dirk paled.

"The Prince of Darkness," said Steele. "He was laughing." He looked at Fidus. "You said that we're not finished with this place, and you're right. Before Maddie Fey di—I mean, one of the last things Maddie Fey and I talked about was how important it was to discover whether the Prince of Darkness is human, or something else. She told me she intended to find out how he got his magic, and how he's involved with the Fire Demons." He looked at his friends. "I'm going to find a way into that chamber. You guys don't have to stay. You can't help me, so it might be better if you got the missing kids out of here."

"No way!" Mac exploded. "The Prince of Darkness stole my memories. I don't even know who I am. I want revenge."

"I'm staying," said Travis, waving his notebook. "I can't run away and miss the ending."

When Riley sided with Mac and Travis, Steele looked at Fidus and sighed in resignation.

"Do you have a plan?" Fidus asked him.

Without a word, Steele found his backpack and removed the metal box he had taken from Dirk's room. He placed it on the table. He couldn't believe what he was thinking. Everyone, including Dirk, gathered round and stared at the box.

"What's that?" asked Mac.

"It might be our key into the chamber of horrors upstairs," said Steele quietly.

Dirk spat on the black marble floor. "You're a fool, Squeal. No one enters the Dark Chamber. There is no way in or out."

Steele lifted the lid of the box. The others pressed closer and Mac reached in, spreading out one of the sheets to read the name printed on it.

"It's the names of all the kids imprisoned here. The ones who still have their memories," Steele explained, spilling the contents of the box onto the table. "Can you spare some paper, Travis?"

Travis tore several sheets of papers from his notebook and put them on the table along with a couple of pens.

"Tear it into the same sized squares as the ones I emptied out," Steele said. He turned to Fidus. "Dirk told us that every night at midnight he takes the box to his master, who draws a name. Dirk then brings that kid to meet the Prince of Darkness before he blocks the memory. We're going to replace all of the names in the box with one name, Jane Doe. When it's time for Dirk to bring the box to his master for the draw, I'm going to sneak in with him and take a look around."

"Are you deaf, or what?" Dirk sneered. "Nothing *sneaks* into his chamber. Nothing. Not even a fly."

While Steele and Riley quickly wrote *Jane Doe* on the squares of paper and dropped them into the box, Steele walked over to Dirk. "How do *you* get into the Dark Chamber?"

"With my ring." He held up his right hand, the bloody rag still tied about his middle finger. "Before that disgusting reptile almost tore my finger off and took the orb." He stared at Pyrus with loathing. "I should have killed that stupid lizard when I had the chance."

"You wouldn't have killed Pyrus," said Steele coldly. "You were having too much fun hurting him."

Fidus came closer, his eyebrows raised. "What was that about an orb?"

Steele explained. "I've never heard Dirk call it an orb until now. Before, he called it a stone. When we found him in the alley, I noticed it on his finger. After we escaped from the prison, Pyrus bit it out of his skin and I smashed—" He stopped abruptly and searched his pocket. "I *was* going to smash it, but I didn't. I kept it." Aware of Dirk's eyes burning into the stone, Steele held it out to Fidus.

The old Mage took the orb and walked over to the wall, where he held it up to the torchlight, turning it about and studying it from many angles.

"Do you know what it is?" asked Steele.

Fidus looked thoughtful. "I know what it is, but I do not

know what it does. It's an exact miniature of the ancient black orb in the possession of the Mages of Arjella."

Too shocked to speak, Steele stared at the tiny black object resting in the old man's palm.

"The Mages again," said Riley, laying her pen on the table and looking up. "It's like the expression carved over the archway into the valley. It can't be a coincidence." She repeated the expression to Fidus. "But it wasn't in English. Maddie Fey said it was a language known only to the Mages."

Steele caught the worried expression that briefly clouded Fidus's face before vanishing. "What is it?" he asked.

"It's preposterous. It's totally impossible," the old Mage replied. "But it appears that the Prince of Darkness has knowledge of Arjella and my fellow Mages."

"All this talk about Mages," said Mac impatiently. "We're wasting time. Come on. Can't you use magic to stick the stone back in Dirk's finger long enough to get us into the Dark Chamber?"

Travis stopped writing on the squares of paper and called to Steele. "Here's what I think we should do. Steele will sneak into the Dark Chamber with Dirk. After the POD picks the name from the box, Dirk will be sent away to get the kid whose name was picked, and Steele will slip out then, bring Dirk back here and tell us what's in there. When it's time for Dirk to return with the kid, we can all follow him into the chamber."

Fidus shook his head slowly as he returned the black stone to Steele. "I do not like the idea of you going in there alone, Steele. Something is troubling me." He tapped his fingers on the table. "It has been too easy. I feel like a fly about to land on a dung heap unaware of a hidden spider's web."

"I know what you mean," said Steele. "I keep thinking someone is watching me. I first felt it when we left the limo on the bridge. It's like we're being pulled somewhere. I heard the Prince of Darkness laughing. I thing he was laughing at me."

"Then you must be on your guard, Steele," Fidus cautioned him. "Do not take anything for granted." He bent over until his face was close to Steele's ear and said, "And whatever you do, do not trust that boy."

"I'll remember," said Steele. Then he spoke to his companions. "It's a good plan. And if Dirk's telling the truth about the black stone, it just might work. We can't stay here forever. We've got to do something."

"I think we've got to find a way to destroy the Prince of Darkness and his horrible Black Pyramid," said Riley. "I don't think we can walk away knowing that this place is still here."

"She's right," said Mac. "As long as the Black Pyramid is standing, kids will disappear. We've got to destroy it."

"And to do that," added Travis, "someone's got to get into the Dark Chamber and check it out."

"I am not disagreeing with you," said Fidus. "I, even more than you, am aware of what has to be done here." He paused and studied each of them in turn. Then he said, "Very well, Steele. But once you are inside the Dark Chamber you will be at your most vulnerable."

When Steele nodded, the old man gripped his arm and lowered his voice, adding, "One more thing. Don't let Dirk keep the stone. I want it back."

Steele nodded again. Then he picked up the metal box and removed his sword from his backpack. "Come on, Dirk," he said, moving toward the doorway. Dirk rushed past him.

Just as Steele reached the door, he stopped and looked back at Fidus. The old man had turned away and was staring up at the ceiling as if he were trying to peer into the Dark Chamber and learn its secrets.

"Be careful, Steele," said Riley.

"I will," said Steele, turning away.

Dirk was already moving swiftly ahead, nervously chewing his fingernails as he went. Steele easily kept up with him, his eyes scanning the shadows, searching for signs of danger. As they crossed in front of the escalator, Steele suddenly slowed. He felt an overpowering urge to peer down; it was the same sensation he experienced whenever he watched a volcano erupt or a twister hit down on TV, both horror and fascination.

He reached for Ees and fought to keep his eyes on Dirk, who was ahead, moving fast. And then the escalator was behind them and he had to run to catch Dirk.

As they hurried toward the Dark Chamber, Steele kept glancing at Dirk. He knew it didn't make sense to feel sorry for the bully after all that Dirk had done to his friends and to others, but nevertheless he did.

"What happened the night you disappeared?" Steele asked, not really expecting an answer.

But Dirk seemed willing, almost anxious, to talk. "It doesn't matter if you know, so I'll tell you. Nothing happened. I wasn't abducted. I walked out of the house and went to him."

Steele let the silence build, waiting for Dirk to say more. He wasn't disappointed.

Dirk laughed contemptuously. "You want to know how I found him. It was that night in the park when you said you heard voices coming from the ground. I went back later and called to the voice. He spoke to me and told me how to find him."

"Why did you do it, though? I mean, who'd want to be part of this?" Steele waved his arm in a wide arc.

"You're just jealous," said Dirk. "I'm going to be rich, and you've got nothing."

Steele told himself not to argue. "So how did you get to Chicago in the first place?"

"None of your business," snapped Dirk.

Steele decided not to press him, though he burned to know if Dirk had followed the Prince of Darkness through a portal that opened in the Black Pyramid. He felt his hand tighten on the hilt of his sword. They continued their journey in silence.

Dirk finally stopped outside a door that was so inconspicuous that Steele would have walked past without giving it a second glance. Dirk turned to Steele and held out his hand.

"If we're going in, I need the stone."

Reluctantly, Steele dug it from his pocked and dropped it onto Dirk's palm. Dirk faced the door and held the stone up.

Soundlessly the door slid open. They passed through a large room whose walls were illuminated by burning torches wedged into brackets high on the walls. An enormous archway dominated the far wall, and through it Steele could see the lower portion of a great winding staircase. He looked over his shoulder in time to see the door closing silently. It was too late to turn back.

As the realization that he was about to enter the private chamber of the Prince of Darkness hit him, Steele felt panic, his old nemesis, rise up, choking him. If the door had been open, he would have bolted back to the lab where he might not find safety, but at least he wouldn't be alone.

"Come on!" Dirk hissed.

Steele swallowed his panic and forced himself to hurry. But Fidus's words sounded a warning in his mind. *It has been too easy.* It's true, he thought. Except for their run-in with the Maladroids, they hadn't encountered any resistance within the Black Pyramid. They passed under the arch and moved swiftly toward the enormous staircase that, Steele noticed, was carved from solid black marble or some other black stone. The room, like the one they had just passed through, was deserted and smelled musty. Like the inside of a tomb, Steele thought. He followed Dirk up the stairs, creeping like a ghost, listening intently for voices, footsteps, or other sounds that could mean a trap. But he heard nothing except Dirk's heavy boots on the stone steps and his own ragged breathing.

Reaching the top of the stairs, Dirk pointed, unnecessarily, toward the only door in sight. Steele handed him the box.

"When we get inside, you can hide behind the pillars," Dirk said in a low voice, as if he had experienced a change of heart and now wished to help, but Steele wasn't fooled. Dirk hadn't been quick enough to hide the sly smile that had momentarily played at the corners of his mouth.

Steele hardened his features to make himself look cruel. Raising his sword, he thrust it at Dirk until the point of the blade touched the spot on Dirk's chest where his heart rested behind his rib cage. "If this is a trap," he said in a flat harsh voice. "I will make you wish you were dead."

Dirk's Adam's apple bobbed up and down as he gulped repeatedly and backed slowly away from Steele's sword.

"You don't have to threaten me," he said, rubbing his neck where the chain had left it raw and bruised.

Steele lowered the blade and watched as Dirk held the stone before the door. The door swung inward with a high-pitched scraping sound that made Steele want to scream. It was so dark inside the chamber that Steele could scarcely see, but he was also relieved: the darkness made it harder for him to be spotted. Dirk stepped into the Dark Chamber and waited just inside the door for Steele to join him. He pointed off to the side, indicating where Steele should plant himself. Then, clutching the box in his arms, Dirk walked purposefully along the centre aisle toward the far end of the chamber. Steele moved stealthily away from the door, his eyes fixed on Dirk's back.

The door had just begun to swing shut when the scraping sound was drowned out by another noise from behind. Steele spun around. As the sheet of black steel dropped over the door, he heard the metal box slip from Dirk's hands and clatter to the floor. Steele looked and saw carefully folded squares of paper spilling onto the marble.

"You have something for me, my loyal paragon?" said a deadly quiet voice from the end of the chamber where the darkness seemed to be pulsing.

Steele knew what was coming; he had known all along that he couldn't trust Dirk. Still, he watched, horror-stricken, as Dirk stopped about halfway down the aisle and bowed deeply to the darkness.

"Yes, Master," he said, his voice devoid of expression. "Over there."

Then he turned and pointed at Steele.

Hope

Yet, during those turbulent times, humans also found time to advance their knowledge of the world about them. Books were written that would influence people for hundreds of years. Dante published La Divina Commedia. Explorers set sail across the Atlantic Ocean to search for new lands. The first globe was produced. Great works of art adorned human holy places. And a man known as Copernicus proposed the heretical theory that the earth revolved around the sun.

—Excerpt from *The Wardens' Logs*

Chapter Twenty-three

The Dark Chamber

Sweat ran down Steele's neck and back. He was weak and shaking, and the room was spinning around him so fast that he could hardly stand. His sword began to slip out of his hand, but he tightened his grasp. Inside his shirt he could feel Pyrus trembling.

"Uh, Master?"

Steele heard Dirk's wheedling voice, but he couldn't pick him out; the room was whirling into a blur. He closed his eyes and willed himself to calm down. He had to think about what had just happened, what it might mean.

"*Speak,*" came the low, menacing voice.

"There's a medallion around his neck," said Dirk. "If you've got no use for it . . . I mean . . . if it was just going to be thrown away after . . ."

"*Take the medallion from his neck and bring it to me.*"

A faint tremor rippled along Pyrus's body and Steele felt the salamander climb up his back and settle between his shoulder blades. At the same time, he was surprised to find that his head was clearing and he was no longer shaking.

As Dirk moved swiftly toward him, Steele remembered how afraid he had been of the bully, and took a step back. He tried to convince himself that things were different now—he was different. But Dirk was bigger and stronger, and Steele knew he'd have to use magic if he hoped to keep his mother's medallion. Yet he hesitated, knowing how he was going to feel if he used his powers against Dirk. If they were going to fight . . . and they *were* going to fight, Steele had to defeat the bully fairly . . . without magic. He took another step back and stood his sword against a pillar.

Dirk stopped a short distance from Steele and demanded, "You know what I want, so hand it over."

"If you want it, you're going to have to take it," Steele said, clenching his fists.

Dirk struck, moving in fast, and punched Steele on the side of his face. Steele stumbled sideways, but before he could regain his balance, Dirk was all over him, fingers clawing at his neck, and Steele felt a sharp stinging sensation as the chain holding Ees cut into his flesh and snapped apart. Dirk pushed Steele backwards, but he managed to stay on his feet. Pyrus pushed his head out of Steele's jacket and bared his teeth at Dirk, spitting angrily. Steele hurtled at Dirk, lashing out blindly, but Dirk sidestepped, grinning, and dangled the medallion before Steele's eyes.

"Loser," Dirk spat. "You fell for my paragon story. There was no game, you stupid turd."

Cruel laughter filled Steele's head, and he glanced quickly toward the back of the chamber.

Steele's mind raced. He felt that he was on the brink of understanding Dirk's role in all that had occurred from the moment they had found him in the alley. He had to keep the bully talking, but he was also very much aware of the darkness at the end of the chamber. There wasn't a lot of time. He decided to attack.

"You were never very smart, Dirk. That's why it was so easy to fool you. If you think we believed a word you said, you're an even bigger idiot. I was laughing behind your back when you bragged about how you weren't abducted, how you found your Master, how much he values you. I knew all the time that you had been abducted. They took you just like they took all the other kids—only they couldn't extract your memories, could they. You don't *have* any happy memories. So they were going to feed you to the worms, weren't they. And then you thought of a way to save your own neck. You offered them me. Because I'm the one your master wants, Dirk. Not you. He never wanted you."

As he talked, he watched Dirk's expression go from smug to incredulous, and he knew that he had finally hit upon the truth.

"We saw you smirking as you watched us making our plans to get into the Dark Chamber when it was part of your plan all along. Well, I'm sorry to disappoint you, but we knew and we played along. I had to get into this room, and thanks to you, I'm here. Now give me back my medallion."

Dirk's eyes darted from Steele to the blackness at the end of the room. He opened his mouth but shut it almost immediately. Then he wheeled about and ran.

Springing at him, Steele crashed into Dirk and sent him sprawling face down on the floor. Dirk grunted as the air burst from his lungs. Steele saw Ees fly from Dirk's hand, hit the smooth black marble floor, and slide. Dirk pushed himself up and lunged for the medallion, but Steele leaped onto his back. Wrapping one arm around Dirk's neck, he grabbed a handful of hair and yanked it as hard as he could. Dirk howled in pain. But Steele held on to his hair, wrenching and wrenching until he had pulled clumps of it from his head.

Use your magic, little boy. Kill him.

Steele was so stunned by the voice of the Prince of Darkness urging him to kill Dirk that he let go of Dirk's hair. At that moment, Dirk crouched as if he were going to do a forward somersault, flipping Steele over his shoulders. Just before he landed hard on his back, Steele felt Pyrus slither to safety. Then Steele slammed onto the floor, cracking his head on the stone. Ignoring the pain, he quickly rolled to the side as Dirk's foot stomped on the spot where his head had struck the floor. He was back on his feet instantly, and threw himself at Dirk, who lost his balance and toppled sideways. As he crashed to the floor, Steele heard the loud crack of bone breaking, and in the instant before Dirk screamed, he heard the tinkle of something bouncing on the marble. He peered down. At first he saw nothing, and then he saw the dull black spot on the shiny black marble, and reached down for the tiny orb that had slipped out of Dirk's grasp. Then Steele snatched Ees and turned back to Dirk.

But Dirk was already limping toward the end of the Dark Chamber, his right shoulder hanging lower than his left. When he reached the blackness, he turned and pointed a finger at Steele. Steele was too far away to see his eyes or read the expression on his face, but he felt Dirk's intense hatred tear into him. Then Dirk disappeared into the blackness.

Steele looked about and found his sword. Things had happened so swiftly, he couldn't remember dropping it. He looked at the darkness and shivered. It seemed to be watching him. He moved cautiously toward the side wall, searching for a way out of the Dark Chamber while casting nervous glances at the thick, black shadow. As he looked about, Steele realized that Dirk had been right about one thing; there were enough pillars for an army to hide behind. He ducked behind one now and took a moment to study his surroundings.

Now that his eyes had adjusted to the darkness, he could see that the Chamber was a vast square. A broad centre aisle, flanked by enormous pillars, ran from the door to the opposite wall where steps led up to the shadowed area that concealed the Prince of Darkness. At regular intervals about the perimeter of the room larger columns rose to support the pyramidal peaked ceiling. Banners, emblazoned with the familiar three frogs, hung from the walls and from supports suspended from the ceiling.

Steele poked his head around the pillar and peered along the aisle. Dirk hadn't reappeared, but Steele thought he detected movement at the very edge of the blackness.

I've got to get closer, he told himself, aware that he was crazy to be thinking of moving toward the Prince of Darkness when he should be running away. But he had to know what was there.

Dropping into a crouch, he sprinted toward the pillar just ahead.

You disappoint me, Steele. You should have killed my paragon and taken his place beside me.

There was no sound. But Steele felt the voice vibrating through his body like the throbbing of a giant sub-woofer at a rock concert. He flattened his back against the pillar, despising the way fear crippled his mind and body, morphing him into a creature as helpless as a paper tiger in a fire.

Get a grip, he thought angrily. *Don't let him do this to you. He knows you're afraid. He's counting on it. He's just another bully, like Dirk, only bigger. Don't let him beat you with fear.*

Steele felt his face harden. He knew he should keep moving, but he hesitated a moment longer, his thoughts taking him into wild, dangerous place where he knew he shouldn't go. The Prince of Darkness was evil. He abducted children and fed their minds to the Fire Demons and their bodies to the worms. He was no good to anyone—a monster who destroyed everything he touched. But what sort of monster was he? Was he human? What was the source of his magic? *Could my magic destroy him?*

Could it?

Steele breathed in and out slowly. It seemed to him that he had only two choices. He could hide behind a pillar, hoping that Fidus would eventually grow worried and come looking for him before the Prince of Darkness grew weary of waiting. Or he could strike now.

What should I do? He wished that GM were here; he could ask her anything. Not that she ever answered him directly, but somehow, mysteriously, in her silence he always found an answer to his problems.

Steele edged around the pillar and stared at the shadowed area at the top of the steps. So near the darkness that they seemed to be part of it, several small figures were sitting cross-legged on the floor. They looked like children, but he quickly dismissed the notion. What would children be doing here? He glanced around; the fact that Dirk hadn't come back made him uneasy. Then he moved swiftly to the next pillar, looked again at the figures on the steps, and gasped.

They *were* children! Steele stared in disbelief. He counted them. They numbered nine, and from where Steele stood they appeared to be several years younger than he. They were engrossed in playing with, or perhaps eating, something on the floor before them. Their heads were bowed and still, but their small hands were busy snatching bits of whatever was on the floor and raising their hands to their faces or mouths. Steele was still too far away to see exactly what they were doing, but the sight of them in this place sickened and infuriated him.

"He can't let him live, you know," said one of the children, carrying on with what he was doing as if Steele weren't there.

"He's a very bad little boy," said another. "He came here to hurt us, to kill us."

"That's why he has to die," added a third child.

Steele stepped from behind the pillar and opened his mouth to tell them they were wrong, but they looked so pathetic that he said nothing.

Instead he pointed his sword at the blackness. "You're a coward," he shouted. "You hide behind children."

Silent laughter exploded from the darkness and vibrated through Steele. He felt as if he were being pounded to pieces from the inside.

The children were so absorbed in their game that they didn't even look his way. But it was their lack of emotion and their unnatural silence while playing that set the warning bells pealing in Steele's head. *It's all wrong,* he thought. *Little kids are supposed to be noisy and rambunctious. Aren't they? Unless . . .* "Unless the monster stole their memories," he said softly.

Steele moved slowly toward the children. He had to get them off the steps and away from the darkness. The chamber was enormous, but except for the dozens of pillars, there was nowhere to hide. The only thing he could do was shepherd the children back toward the door and try to get them to remain there until he returned for them. He couldn't risk using his magic against the Prince of Darkness until the kids were safely out of the way.

"He's coming," said one of the children.

"To kill us," said another.

"Don't be afraid." Steele spoke to the children the way he spoke to Pyrus, keeping his voice calm as he climbed the steps. "I'm not going to hurt you. I'm going to take you someplace safe."

The children reacted as if they had been caught doing something forbidden. They snatched at whatever was on the floor with both hands and quickly crammed it into their mouths. Then they raised their heads and turned their dull, lifeless gazes on Steele, their expressions blank. Steele looked down at the floor to see what they had been eating, but all that remained were a few large crumbs.

"Come on," he said, reaching for the nearest child's hand. "You can't stay here."

But the child shied away from him and pushed itself backwards with its feet until it had joined its companions at the mouth of the dark shadow. At the same time, Steele saw one of the crumbs wriggling on the floor below. He blinked and leaned over to see what it was. Had the children been living on live insects? Dropping onto one knee, he reached down to pick up the moving crumb. It was a dog—a miniature thing, no bigger than a wad of gum. As he tried to pick it up, his fingers passed through it and it vanished.

Baffled, Steele stared at the remaining crumbs, identifying the upper torso of a man with a missing arm, the broken limb of a tree with a tiny bird flapping its wings on one of the branches, and bits of a house and pieces of furniture. It came to him slowly—the realization that he was looking at crumbs of a memory. The children had been picking at an animated, perhaps holographic, depiction of a memory that had once been stored in another child's mind. A chill swept through Steele's body. He knew the creatures that feasted on memories, and he knew what he'd find even before he raised his eyes to the children.

Pushing himself up, Steele turned to the darkness and backed slowly down the steps as the child-creatures shed their youthful forms and morphed into massive shapes of living fire. Before his eyes, the blackness began to swirl and pulsate violently, and then it vanished as if it had never been. Steele gasped, confused. He couldn't pull his eyes from the area where the blackness had been. There was nothing there. It was now just part of the vast chamber.

Where was the Prince of Darkness? Had he actually been in the chamber, or had it all been an illusion? And where had Dirk disappeared to?

Steele gulped. He didn't understand what had happened, but he knew one thing. The Fire Demons had cornered him at last, and this time there were nine of them against one.

A. D. 1347

The Tsilihin struck again and again during those years, inducing paranoia across the planet. Fear of the black-clad wraiths that had been spotted wherever fire broke out compelled cities to lock their gates against innocent strangers or tradespeople.

In one year alone, our prisoners ravaged the forests of the Crimea and drove flea-infested rats into vastly populated areas. The fleas jumped from the rats to humans. Plague struck, killing tens of thousands of Tartars, peoples native to the area. Ignorant of the cause of the plague, the Tartars blamed the European merchants whose ships crowded Caffa, a port on the Black Sea. They attacked the walled city, catapulting the plague-riddled corpses of their dead soldiers over the city walls. The streets were littered with rotting, diseased bodies. The Europeans fled back to Genoa, unaware that fleas, rats, and Black Death were stowaways on their ships.

—Excerpt from *The Wardens' Logs*

Chapter Twenty-four

Fighting with Fire

The roar of the Fire Demons shook the Dark Chamber and set the pyramid shuddering from its peak all the way down to its rotten foundation. Steele could feel the intense heat scorching his clothes and hair and flesh, but when he looked down, his clothes were steaming but not burning, and flesh still covered his hands. He glanced at his sword, knowing that it was useless against the nine creatures spreading out to either side to hem him in.

"What am I going to do?" Steele desperately scoured his mind for a way to use his magic on all nine creatures simultaneously. He couldn't destroy them one by one. There wasn't enough time. While he was finishing off one creature, the others would be busy finishing him off.

Water destroys fire. Lack of oxygen destroys fire. Steele couldn't think of anything else. In fact, the creatures' intense heat mingled with his fear made thinking of even the simplest thing difficult. When one of the creatures swiped at him with long arms and sharp, fiery claws, it took Steele a moment to react. Then a single desperate cry filled his head. *Run!* Nothing else mattered. All of the things he and his companions had set out to accomplish vanished from his mind. *Run!*

And that's what Steele did. He dropped his sword and fled toward the sealed doorway, not thinking of what would happen when he got there, knowing only that he had to reach it. He was halfway there when he realized he'd never make it. Several creatures were already moving in, flowing across the room like lava, to close the gap between him and the door. But he kept running.

"Please, God! Oh, please, Maddie Fey, Fidus, someone, help me! Don't let me die."

"Steele!"

The voice was clear and cold and it came from behind, where the darkness had swirled and dissipated moments ago.

Steele skidded to a stop on the stone floor and turned abruptly. A figure was striding down the aisle, its long black coat flapping in its wake. Then he noticed that the figure wasn't alone; another, smaller figure loped at its side. Shadows seemed to cling to them. Steele's heart stopped. The Prince of Darkness hadn't disappeared after all. He and Dirk had been somewhere in the chamber the whole time. As they swiftly approached, Steele searched desperately for a way through the Fire Demons. The creatures had formed a wide circle around him and were now closing in.

Steele raised his arm and looked back at the two figures, only to realize that he was no longer clutching his sword. In his panic, he had dropped it. Now he saw that the taller figure carried something that looked like a sword in one of its hands.

Oh, God! Oh, God! My sword!

Locking his eyes on the figures, Steele ran his tongue over his dry lips, took a deep breath, and summoned his magic. He felt it stirring within him.

"Stop!" he shouted.

Heedless of Steele's command, the figures continued toward him. Suddenly, they seemed to emerge from the shadows and Steele could see them clearly. He stepped back, as if buffeted by invisible blows. The magic died inside him.

"What are you . . . ? How did . . . ?"

Maddie Fey stopped about ten feet away, Steele's sword in her hand. Her startling silver eyes stole Steele's breath away. Wish eyed him quizzically.

As he continued to back away, Steele was reliving that night in Maddie Fey's house when a Fire Demon, hiding in the body of the boy, Wood, came to his room to destroy him.

"I am not what you think," said Maddie Fey. "Look."

She raised Steele's sword and lightly touched the sharp blade with the tip of her finger. Then she pointed her finger at Steele and he saw a drop of blood fall from her finger and splash on the floor.

"Fire Demons don't bleed, Steele" she said, holding out his sword.

As if he were in a dream, Steele walked over and took it from her. "I thought I killed you."

With heart-rending gentleness, Maddie Fey reached out and took Steele's hand. "You did not kill me. But your magic did transport me far away. And it has taken me a long time to find my way back to you."

Steele nodded, not trusting himself to speak.

Maddie Fey released his hand and looked about at the Fire Demons gliding closer. "I see I have arrived just in time."

"I don't understand," said Steele, his voice breaking. "How could my magic send you away?"

"I'll try to explain later," she answered. "At the moment, we should think about how we are going to get out of here alive."

"The Prince of Darkness was here," said Steele. "Back there, where you and Wish came from. He disappeared. Dirk, too. I thought you and Wish were them."

"He is not here," said Maddie Fey. "But I can still detect traces of his power in the air."

She turned to the nearest creature and raised her hands. Steele felt a wild rush of excitement as he watched the glowing white dots burst from her palms and shoot hungrily toward the Fire Demon. He knew that he should be helping, but he continued to stare at Maddie Fey, afraid that she might disappear if he looked away.

The Fire Demon roared as the white flakes ate into it, creating twisting black tunnels as they burrowed deep into the creature. Even before that demon disintegrated in an explosion of ash, Maddie Fey's raised hands were already moving to another creature.

"Look out behind you," she shouted, and her voice whipped Steele to action.

As Steele turned to confront the Fire Demon coming at him from behind like a flaming tree, he suddenly knew what he must do. He must take their fire—absorb it into himself, just as he had seen himself do in the magic scarf GM had knitted in Ees. In the image, he had confronted hundreds of Fire Demons before fire began licking at his clothes. But had the images been real? Were the things he had seen predestined? What if he had missed something? Steele shook his head. *I can do it*, he thought. There were only eight creatures now. If he could take the fire from two or even three, it would give him and Maddie Fey the advantage. But he must control his magic.

He glanced down at his feet and saw steam or smoke rising from the black marble floor. His was sweating all over. He felt Pyrus lose his grip on his slippery shoulder and slide down his back. Steele ignored the heat and the sweat—and called his magic. It had been waiting just inside him like a wild thing, and now it surged through him, infusing him with raw power. Steele wrestled for control, using physical and mental strength that he hadn't realized he possessed.

Then Steele aimed his magic at the creature, willing it to collect the flaming liquid—glug it down like a glass of milk and feed it back to him. The power tore out of him like a cyclone. But instead of drawing the Fire Demon's fire into Steele, it encircled the approaching creature, sucked it up and spat it out. The gigantic fireball shot through the air and splattered against the wall near the door, showering the air with sparks and scattering smaller blobs of flaming magma in every direction.

Steele's magic homed in on another Fire Demon. But the first one was already reforming itself, snatching the flaming bits that had broken away and gathering them into its mass. Other, smaller blobs of fire raced down the wall or flowed across the floor, drawn to it.

The second fireball shot toward the peaked ceiling. Steele thought he could see the Fire Demon twisting and writhing in an effort to hold itself together. Roaring with the fury of a volcano, it slammed into the peak, spreading out and coating the black stone masonry, and set it ablaze as if it were dry timber soaked in oil. A moment later, fire began to rain from the ceiling.

"Run!" Steele shouted at Maddie Fey, and he raced toward the nearest pillar, dodging huge drops of flame that plunged from the ceiling and sizzled on the floor where he had been standing. He flattened himself against the pillar, his chest heaving. Overhead, three dwarf-sized stone gargoyles perched on a narrow decorative ledge that wrapped about the pillar and protruded just far enough to protect him from the fire storm. Maddie Fey joined him and pressed her back against the pillar next to him. Wish pushed his way between them.

"We've got to get out of here," Steele said, coughing and trying to wipe his stinging eyes with his fingers.

He glanced at Maddie Fey, noticing that *she* wasn't coughing and that *her* eyes were as clear and as blue as a cloudless winter sky.

"What have you done?" she demanded, her eyes flashing angrily.

Steele had no idea. "I tried to absorb their fire."

"You did *what?*" Maddie Fey clutched his arm, her slim fingers squeezing tightly.

"I couldn't smother all of them at once," Steele explained, lifting her hand from his arm. "So I tried to take away their fire by drawing it into myself."

"That is the most ridiculous, most reckless, most dangerous use of magic that I have ever heard of," snapped Maddie Fey. "No wonder your magic turned wild."

Steele blinked, surprised and hurt. He tried to think of something to say, but her anger was like a wedge between them. Just then, a Fire Demon hurtled across the room and slammed into a nearby pillar, disintegrating into thousands of smaller fires that curled and sprang and slithered in serpentine shapes to meld with one another into one enormous form. Maddie

Fey had destroyed three. His magic had slowed the advance of another three, but they had almost completely reformed themselves. That meant there were still six Fire Demons. He looked about, accounting for the six creatures. They were closing in.

He shook his head and looked at Maddie Fey. "I lost control of the magic, OK. I'm sorry. But considering I didn't even know I had magic until a week ago, I don't think I did such a bad job of slowing down the Fire Demons."

"I'm not angry because you tried to use magic to stop the Fire Demons and lost control. I'm angry that you would try to use magic to do something that cannot be done."

"Like what?"

"Like thinking you could draw their fire into yourself and live. You abused your powers." She stopped and turned away, her hands extended toward one of the creatures.

Steele was shaking, not from fear of the Fire Demons but from anger of his own. "I did not intentionally abuse my powers," he shouted at Maddie Fey's back. "I did what I had to do, and no thanks to you."

He stomped away from the pillar, trying to push Maddie Fey out of his mind. He searched inside himself for his runaway magic, but it was quiet now. He wasn't sure what that meant. Since he hadn't felt it fade inside him, he worried that it was still out there somewhere.

Feeling intense heat near his foot, he looked down in time to see a wriggling blob of fire leap onto his leg and cling there like a leech. He yelled, frantically scraping the fire onto the floor with the blade of his sword. Then he stamped on it until the fire was extinguished and all that remained was a scattering of smoking black ashes.

He tried to find the pillar he had just left, but the smoke

had thickened and he could barely even see the sword in his hand. And then he felt pain as claws grabbed his arm and yanked it almost out of its socket. The voice that rasped in his ear was just as nasty as he remembered it.

"Get moving! Before I tear your arm off."

Steele squinted through the smoke and saw the red hairy hand with its cruel claws digging into his flesh. Then he looked up and into a pair of gleaming yellow eyes.

"Nilats?"

The giant red rat sank its claws deeper into Steele's arm. "Go!" he shrieked, pointing. Then he spun Steele around like a top and shoved him toward . . . the great, black limousine barely visible in the smoke-filled chamber.

"I hate that rat," Steele muttered as he streaked toward Maddie Fey's limo and the passenger door at the front, which stood open like a welcoming smile.

"Get in!" ordered the rat, scuttling past and motioning for Steele to hurry.

But when he reached the vehicle, Steele stopped abruptly and wheeled toward the Fire Demons. He saw that one of the demons had moved between Maddie Fey and the limo, cutting her off. But the creature was already twisting violently as her magic began to consume it.

"Nilats, open the other door! Now!"

Steele could barely hear her above the roar of the fire. He looked back at the limo and let his eyes travel down its length to rest on the second-to-last door, the eleventh, on the passenger side. It was the door he had been about to open in New York when Maddie Fey had suddenly stepped between him and the limo. *Not that door,* she had said, without offering an explanation.

Was she now telling Nilats to open that one?

Steele stared at the door, remembering how he and Mac had speculated about what was on the other side. They had even convinced themselves and each other that it was a portal to another world. They had been watching for an opportunity to open it a crack and peer inside, but the opportunity hadn't come along. Until now!

"Nilats! Open it! Now!" shouted Maddie Fey.

Steele raced toward the rear of the limousine. Too late, Nilats lunged at him. When he reached the eleventh door, Steele didn't hesitate; he gripped the handle and pulled. The door opened, and for one heart-stopping second Steele found himself teetering on the brink of space—vast and immutable. There was nothing on the other side of the door except darkness, and pinpoints of white light in the distance, winking below and above and as far as he could see. As if they were aware that a stranger had intruded on their world, the lights abruptly ceased winking and began to grow in luminosity and size—and to speed like coments toward Steele.

Steele leaned over the brink, mesmerized by the kaleidoscopic movement of millions of lights rushing toward him. An overpowering longing seized him. He ached to go to the lights. He had to reach them or his life would be empty and unbearable for as long as he lived. Unable to resist the lure, Steele stepped off the brink. If Nilats hadn't grabbed his arm and roughly dragged him back and away from the door, he knew he would have been lost.

Fire Demons roared past him, shrieking with rage and struggling to break free of the lights that were pulling them inexorably toward the eleventh door and whatever fate awaited them on the other side.

"Stupid!" Nilats spat at Steele, his whiskers bristling with contempt and fury. "I should have let you fall."

Steele was too drained to respond. He slumped against the limousine, his arms wrapped tightly about his abdomen. He felt that if he let go, he wouldn't be able to hold himself together; his body would break apart and float away into the white lights. His teeth chattered, despite the sweat streaming down his face and chest from the intense heat of the Fire Demons surging past him and through the portal.

In moments it was over. When the last creature was gone, the rat slammed the door shut, waddled on all four legs to the front of the limousine, and leaped through the open door. Steele was vaguely aware of Maddie Fey and Wish emerging from the smoke and walking toward the limousine. When she reached his side, she lightly touched his arm, and then she too disappeared inside.

Steele followed slowly, his arms tight across his chest, his mind still dazzled by the memory of those white pinpoints of light.

A. D. 1346–1352

The Black Death claimed twenty-five million lives. We watched helplessly, seething with rage, as the plague flooded the earth, decimating the populations of city upon city. We watched as stacks of blackened corpses were rolled into trenches and covered with soil.

People died on the streets, or alone in darkness. Children died in their dead mothers' arms, their pets dead at their feet. The plague struck with impunity, killing humans and animals alike.

Inspiration came to us unbidden. We turned our heat on the Black Death and the bacteria shrivelled and died, ending the plague's long siege.

—Excerpt from *The Wardens' Logs*

Chapter Twenty-five

Back into the Darkness

Seconds, or minutes, later—Steele lost track of time—the winking white dots in his head vanished in the glow from hundreds of flickering candles in the giant chandelier in Maddie Fey's foyer. The soft light shone down on the heads of the others in the room. Mac was there, sitting next to Travis on the steps of the massive sweeping staircase. His white head seemed to cast its own light as he gazed about in wonder, filling his head with memories. Riley was there, too, the strain of the past days evident in her faded eyes and on her pale pinched face. Steele noticed his backpack on her knee. Travis's unblinking eyes were pinned on the rat. His notebook slid off his knees onto the step, but Travis didn't seem to notice. Stretched across the bottom step was Wish, the Great Hound's penetrating silver eyes fixed on his mistress.

Steele looked at Maddie Fey. She was huddled with Fidus and the rat a short distance from the others. When she moved, the candlelight turned her silver neck to gold. They were speaking quietly.

They were talking about me, and the magic, Steele thought, experiencing the sudden sinking feeling he got whenever he did something wrong. Riley called it the *oh, oh!* feeling. And because he didn't think Maddie Fey was being fair when she

318

accused him of trying to make his magic do the impossible, especially when she didn't know what he had seen in GM's magic scarf, he felt a surge of anger and defiance. As if he sensed his friend's turmoil, Pyrus slithered out of Steele's jacket, crawled along his arm, and blinked at him.

Fidus hurried over to him. "What happened? When you didn't come back—"

Steele cut him off. "Why are you asking me? I bet Maddie Fey couldn't wait to tell you how stupid and irresponsible I am."

Fidus stopped as abruptly as if he had walked into a wall. His eyebrows rose. "What is wrong?"

Maddie Fey took a step forward. "We were not discussing you, Steele. We arrived only minutes ahead of you." Her eyes seemed to be burning with a cold, silver flame.

Steele didn't believe her. And besides, he felt so rebellious that he didn't care if she was telling the truth. He glared at her. "Who gave you the right to tell me how to use my magic? Where were you when I needed someone to help me understand it?" He glanced at Fidus. "Did you ever once try to explain things, or offer to teach me how to control it? I don't think so." He looked back to Maddie Fey. "You said that it was impossible to do what I tried to do in the Dark Chamber. Well, you're wrong. I know differently. So don't tell me about my magic and what I can and can't do with it."

Steele found he was shaking again. Everyone was looking at him in open-mouthed shock. He had to get away—away from this room. The *oh, oh!* feeling was making his stomach churn. But his friends were blocking the stairs; there was nowhere to go. He turned his back on his companions.

Before him, in alcoves about the room, stood eight silver-necked stone figures—the Mages. Steele stared at them, aware, despite his anger, of their quiet power. They stared back at him through empty eyes. Steele's eyes came to rest on the young woman in the eighth alcove, who had so intrigued him the first time he had seen her. This time he recognized her, not with his sight, but with his heart.

"Steele's right," cried Riley to Maggie Fey. "You just told him he was magic and then you left him to deal with it on his own. You don't know how hard it's been for him."

Mac jumped in. "Yeah. That doesn't sound fair to me . . . although I don't really remember anything about Steele and magic . . ." His voice trailed off.

"You should have helped him," said Travis. "We're just kids, in case you haven't noticed."

Steele knew he had to turn around and face Fidus and Maddie Fey. He had to say something, perhaps even apologize, but he couldn't, not yet. Realizing that he was still clutching his sword, he carefully stood it against the wall, then walked, almost casually, over to the alcove and gazed at the statue of his mother. He wanted to memorize her oval face and the faint crinkles about her eyes. He wanted to memorize the slight tilt of her head. Her unsmiling mouth smiled in his mind and told him everything was going to be OK. Against his chest, Ees seemed to hum.

Riley, Mac, and Travis gathered about him, and Steele was grateful. They didn't know it, but they were his shields; as long as they were there, he couldn't feel Maddie Fey's cold disapproval coating his back.

"Your mother?" said Riley.

Steele swallowed and nodded.

"She's beautiful." Riley looked from the statue to Steele. "You sort of look like her."

"What's going on, Steele? Why would Maddie Fey call you stupid and irresponsible?" asked Travis.

"Whatever grievances Steele feels he has against Maddie Fey, and me for that matter, will have to wait," said Fidus impatiently. "We are not finished with—"

Maddie Fey interrupted. "Please. I need a moment alone with Steele."

Steele's friends moved back toward the stairs, dragging their feet.

"I was wrong," she said, her eyes on the salamander clinging to Steele's wrist. "Instead of lashing out at you, I should have made an effort to understand what you were trying to do. I'm sorry. I had no right to criticize you."

Steele took a deep breath. His anger was gone as suddenly as it had appeared; he felt emptiness inside where it had been. He tried to remember how he had felt when he destroyed the Mac thing in the alley, and the Maladroids, and to tell her—tell her about the exhilaration, the fear, the blackness. He wanted to explain to her about the Fire Demons in GM's magic scarf and how he had seen a vision of his drawing the fire away and into himself. Perhaps if she knew, she wouldn't think he had been reckless.

"It's OK," he said instead, staring at the tiny black bat clinging upside down to her right ear. "You were right, partly. I couldn't control the magic. But you were wrong about absorbing fire. I know that it's possible."

Maddie Fey touched his arm. "Steele, you can't know that." Steele shook his head. "I . . . I can't talk about it. But believe me, I know."

Maddie Fey ran her finger along Pyrus's side. "Does it have a name?"

"His name is Pyrus."

"I cannot tell you about your magic, Steele," Maddie Fey said, dropping her hand to her side. "But when we return, I will tell you about mine. Perhaps it will help you understand your own power and how to control it."

"Where are we going?" Steele asked, moving to fetch his sword.

"Back into the Black Pyramid," answered Fidus. "We must get the children and discover what we can about this creature that calls itself the Prince of Darkness."

Just before they stepped out of the limo into the Dark Chamber, Fidus drew Steele aside and said, "Did I ever tell you about the time Maddie Fey lost control of her magic and made the entire population of Arjella stutter?" He laughed. "It was most embarrassing, not only for Maddie Fey, but for me and my fellow Mages. The counter-spell had to be spoken. We were stuttering so badly, we could not speak the words to counter the magic. It took seven months for the effect to wear off." He laughed again, and patted Steele's shoulder. "She doesn't like to be reminded of it, so we'll let this be our little secret, hmm?"

Steele grinned. "I won't tell. And about the magic, I'm sorry if I yelled at you. It's just—"

"No need to apologize, my friend. We have expected a lot, perhaps too much, from you." The old man smiled at Steele and turned away, and Steele followed him out the door.

The Dark Chamber looked like a battlefield. Massive columns lay broken and crushed on the marble floor. Most of the ceiling was gone, along with a large section of the peak.

Through a gaping hole, Steele could see the red haze that hung over the Black Pyramid like an alien sky, and for an instant he ached to be outdoors under the true sky, feeling the sun on his face or gazing up at Mars growing smaller as its orbit took it farther and farther away. He felt the weight of the great city overhead pressing down on him, and he hated the damp, smelly, underground world.

Dropping his eyes, Steele noticed that the intense heat generated by the Fire Demons had actually melted stones in the walls, which were now hardening into grotesque shapes. The metal barrier that had dropped to seal the chamber was twisted and broken. The marble floor was cracked and pitted and felt like gum under Steele's feet. The arms of the Prince of Darkness, bearing the splayed frogs, hung in blackened tatters, or lay smouldering on the floor.

"He was over there," said Steele, pointing toward the back of the chamber and the raised dais where the voice of the Prince of Darkness had vibrated from the writhing shadows.

"What happened here?" gasped Travis, wide-eyed.

Steele turned to his companions and told them the short version of how Dirk had tricked him. From his new perch on Steele's shoulder, Pyrus seemed to be listening as spellbound as the others.

When he reached the end, Riley said, "You mean Dirk the Jerk actually made up all that stuff about the paragon game?"

"I'm afraid so," Steele answered. "As soon as he dropped the box of names on the floor, I knew I'd walked into a trap. But it was too late to turn back. A hidden barrier had come down and sealed off the exit."

"If I ever get my hands on that creep," muttered Travis, "he'll—"

"I fought him," said Steele. "I fought him without magic and he ran."

"All right!" cried Riley. "I only wish I'd been there to watch."

Mac sighed. "Not having memories really sucks."

Steele caught a glimpse of red over by the limousine and turned quickly. But it was just the rat, poking and picking among the rubble. Disgusted, Steele looked away. Wish coursed ahead, his black nose inches from the floor, and the companions followed the Great Hound. Mac, Riley, and Travis stuck to Steele like shadows, as if they were afraid to let him out of their sight. Steele didn't know if they were afraid for him or for themselves. He didn't care; he was just glad they were there.

He reached into his pocket and found Ees. Pulling the medallion free, he wrapped his hand about it and continued toward the raised area at the back of the room.

"Do you think the POD is still around here someplace?" asked Travis, peering anxiously over his shoulder.

Steele shrugged. "I honestly don't know if he was ever really here. I saw a shadowed area just over there." He tilted his head toward the right rear section of the dais. "And I heard him speak to Dirk, and then his voice was in my mind. Dirk ran into the shadows and I didn't see him again. When the kids morphed into Fire Demons, the darkness vanished."

They reached the top of the steps. Steele peered down, half expecting to see crumbs of memories wriggling about at his feet like cut-up worms. But the floor was barely visible under debris that had fallen from above.

Maddie Fey took Riley, Mac, and Travis aside. "There is nothing you can do here. Fidus, Steele, and I must use our powers to search for traces of magic that might lead us to a portal, and other signs that could help us identify the Prince of Darkness."

"And just what are we supposed to do?" asked Travis.

"I must ask you to do something equally important. Go with Nilats and take the missing children back to the limousine. And hurry." She looked about the vast chamber. "Hurry," she repeated.

"I can't go," cried Riley. "Nothing could make me get back on that escalator."

"I'll go," Mac volunteered. "If it weren't for all of you, I'd probably be locked up with the kids whose memories are gone. So I'll go. I'll bring them back."

"Then you'll need me," said Travis. "Since I know where they're being held and you don't."

"Get moving, then," snuffled the rat. "If you know what's good for you."

Travis leaned close to Steele. "I see what you mean about Nilats. He isn't exactly friendly, but he is sort of awesome."

"Hah!" Steele snorted, and then watched as the rat hustled Mac and Travis toward the limousine. Then he caught Riley's arm. "You could have gone. Look. They're not taking the escalator."

"They don't need me to help with the missing kids. I don't think I could bear seeing that horrible room again. I can help here. While you and the others are using magic, I'll use my eyes."

Steele smiled at her. He stood in the spot where the shadow had disappeared and looked about. The marble floor was cracked and covered with chunks of stone that had broken away from the ceiling, obliterating footprints or other signs that might have indicated that someone or something had been here earlier. Nearby, Maddie Fey was staring into space, her eyes glowing silver. Fidus was tracing his long fingers over the stone behind the raised area, mumbling to himself. Steele felt sweat break out on his face and neck again as he clenched his teeth and concentrated on hearing sounds that couldn't normally be heard. He strained until his body trembled and his ears roared.

"You are trying too hard," said Maddie Fey, suddenly appearing beside him. "Instead of releasing your hearing, you are blocking it. If you want to control it, relax. Imagine that your hearing is reaching out from your mind, stretching farther and farther."

Steele took a deep breath and tried it. He loosened his grip on Ees and forced himself to relax. Then he shut out the sounds about him and focused on letting his hearing flow toward the wall ahead, like a stream. He felt something at once—a difference in his power, as if, for the first time, he wasn't struggling to control it or hang on to it. He was directing it.

He stretched his hearing farther, through a crack in the wall and into the stone. Then he stretched it farther still, down to the room where they had gathered with Fidus, down the massive escalator, along darkened halls and hidden passageways and into the squalid chambers of the lowest levels of the pyramid. And all the time he listened for sounds of life aside from him and his companions and the missing children. But he heard nothing. Nothing else breathed, nothing more stirred within the Black Pyramid. Quickly, Steele drew his hearing back.

"If the Prince of Darkness was here, he's long gone. Dirk, too." The silence he had met at every level of the Black Pyramid made him uneasy. He glanced up at the ruined ceiling and roof.

"What?" asked Riley, also looking up.

"It's probably nothing, but I think we should get out of here," Steele answered. He shifted Ees to his other hand.

"The chain is broken," said Riley.

"Dirk tore it off my neck. He actually asked the Prince of Darkness if he could keep it. But I took it back." Steele looked at the disk, but when he tried to look away, he couldn't. His eyes were drawn to the pea-sized cloud in its centre, and then he heard himself screaming as he felt something pulling at his body, dragging him down and down directly into the path of a raging wall of fire. It happened so swiftly, Steele lost his breath. He thought he heard Wish barking, but then the sound was gone. He had no time to brace himself for the shock, no time to prepare for the pain, no time to even think about trying to absorb the fire when it slammed into him.

Nothing! The fire had roared through him, and he had felt nothing. Giddy with relief, Steele looked about. The fire was behind him; he was in a cold, shadowy world, devoid of colour and substance—just patches of grey and darker areas that reminded him of the mouths of giant caves. A heavy, unnatural silence hung over everything.

As his eyes adjusted to the varied shades of grey and black, Steele could make out dozens of stone structures dotting the gloomy landscape in a circular pattern at the bottom of a small rise. They looked like mausoleums, or entrances to underground crypts.

"It feels like a graveyard," he said to Pyrus, who had turned as blue as a glacier and was shivering on his shoulder.

Steele looked from the mausoleums to a darker area in the middle of the circle and others around the perimeter and realized that they were not shadows but motionless groups of Maladroids. He felt them watching him intently. Even as his hand tightened on the shaft of his sword, Steele dismissed them. He knew, without knowing how, that they couldn't harm him. His eyes returned to the dark area in the middle of the circle of mausoleums. Thinking that it was just another group of Maladroids, he almost dismissed it as well. But it held his attention, and as he stared at it, it suddenly materialized into a mausoleum, larger and blacker than those surrounding it. None of the Maladroids were near it. It stood alone, silent and forbidding, an island of darkness. An icon! Steele's heart raced.

"He's here," he said, and the silent answering laughter vibrated through him like a shock wave, knocking him backwards.

He was back on his feet in an instant. A tiny fragment of his mind registered movement among the Maladroids. They were advancing. But the greater part of his mind was focused on the largest mausoleum. He raised his hand, holding Ees before him, and moved toward it. Ahead, the Maladroids pressed together to block him, but Steele didn't falter. In his raised hand, Ees was a blood-red glowing circle. A gentle breeze lifted his hair from his forehead, and then a windstorm broke from the disk and pounded the Maladroids, tossing the seven-foot creatures aside as if they were made of fluff.

Within seconds, they and the wind were gone and Ees was no longer glowing. Nothing stood between Steele and the top of the rise. Reaching it, he paused and looked back. The slope was littered with the twisted bodies of Maladroids, their black cloaks covering them like body bags. Looking at them, Steele felt sad; he had to remind himself that they belonged to the Prince of Darkness, their creator. He walked over to one of the motionless creatures and used his foot to roll it onto its back. Then he carefully eased the point of his sword beneath its loose hood and lifted the fabric off its head.

"Ahh, no!" Steele covered his mouth with his hand and took a step back, recoiling from the staring eyes in the human face beneath the hood.

The Maladroids were human! Suddenly Steele saw everything with such perfect clarity, and heard himself gasp . . . the homeless people who had disappeared from Chicago . . . the Maladroids. They were the same. The Prince of Darkness had snatched the homeless and altered them somehow. Were the mushroom-like pods parts of the altering process, the pupal stages in the development of the Maladroids? Just thinking about the rubbery black pods made Steele's skin clammy.

He didn't believe that the homeless had freely chosen to follow the Prince of Darkness. Their minds and lives had been shattered by poverty, drugs and alcohol, or mental illness; they could not have made the choice consciously. No! Steele believed that the Prince of Darkness had stolen them from the streets, as surely as he had stolen the kids, and then he had used them up.

"He's just a bigger Dirk," muttered Steele, turning back to the black mausoleum where he suspected the Prince of Darkness was waiting for him. "We've got to stop him, Pyrus. We've got to end it here."

He called his magic and it surged forth, wrapping itself about him like a mother's arms. Then he moved quickly down the hill toward the circle of mausoleums and the lone black structure in their midst. When he reached the nearest mausoleum, he laid his sword on the ground, caught Pyrus in his hand, and slipped his arms out of his jacket. Despite the cold, he was hot and sweating. Then he placed Pyrus on his shoulder, grasped his sword, and surveyed the open ground between him and the black tomb. He would be at his most vulnerable crossing the clearing. There were no trees or boulders to hide behind, no shadows to conceal him. He would have to move swiftly. His eyes rested on the window- less structure. He studied it, noting that the only access from where he stood was a single arched door.

Steele set out in a crouch and sped across the clearing. When he reached the black tomb, he stopped and pressed his back flat against the outer wall. Winded, he waited, motion- less, until his breathing sounded less harsh in his ears. Then he slipped around the corner of the structure and stepped up to the arched stone door. There was no handle, just a large iron ring attached to an animal mask mount that appeared to be bolted into or through the stone. Steele grasped the ring and pulled. The door grated open wide and he peered cautiously inside.

The interior of the tomb was darker than outside, but only slightly. Holding his sword before him, Steele took a step inside, keeping one foot on the threshold to stop the door from closing. He turned back and examined the inside of the door and around the doorway, looking for a trip-lock or a mechanism that would prevent the door from opening from inside the tomb. Finding nothing amiss, he took another step into the chamber. As the door shut behind him, Pyrus scur- ried inside his shirt.

Steele searched the chamber with his eyes, staring longest into the dark corners before moving on. Despite the high ceiling, the chamber had the claustrophobic feel of a cellar. It even smelled like a cellar, dank and musty. The temperature was cold, almost freezing. Steele regretted having left his jacket outside. Teeth chattering, he moved deeper into the chamber. The room was bare. Well, not quite bare. There was something, a large chest or wardrobe—*or was it a coffin?*—barely visible in the shadows against the back wall.

A coffin! Steele froze and stared at it, forcing his eyes not to blink in case he missed the soundless opening of the lid. He couldn't have said how long he stood there, but it felt like hours. When nothing happened, he inched closer.

Steele's legs trembled with relief when he realized that it wasn't a coffin at all. It was the door of a huge vault built into the stone. In the middle of the door, about halfway along its length, was a large iron wheel.

He wondered what it was, thinking that he may have been wrong about the building. "Maybe it's where the Prince of Darkness keeps his valuables."

Perhaps the surrounding buildings also contained vaults filled with gold and precious gems and other stuff. Dirk had told the stolen kids that they'd receive gold to take home with them after the paragon ceremony. Steele knew it was a lie, but what if Dirk had introduced the notion of the bag of gold into his game after he had been here and seen such riches with his own eyes?

And hadn't the bully said something else down in the dungeon, when Steele had almost strangled him with his magic . . . ? Hadn't he said he had to do what he did to gain a kingdom and get his hands on more money than Steele could count in a hundred years? He walked up to the vault and stopped, searching the door for traps. There seemed to be nothing on the shiny surface except the large wheel. Just as he was about to reach for it, the wheel began to turn.

Steele felt the temperature in the room plunge to below freezing. He stumbled backwards, realizing that he hadn't sensed his magic swirling about him since he had entered the stone chamber. He called it now, but nothing happened. Desperate, he searched for it deep within. It was there, but he couldn't reach it. Whenever he got close, it slipped like water through his fingers.

"Please don't do this to me now," he moaned, trembling from fear and frustration.

The handle stopped turning. There was a moment of complete silence, and then the heavy vault door shrieked open. Steele backed away from the figure filling up the doorway, his eyes locked on the red lidless eyes in the scarred and tattooed face that he and Riley had seen in the grate in Wychwood Park that Saturday afternoon—the face that had driven them screaming back to Steele's house.

Steele wanted to run or throw up. Cold beads of sweat formed on his head and face, and his heart pulsed in his ears. Unlike the face of the dead Maladroid, this one before him was not even remotely human. With lips drawn back exposing fangs as long as Steele's little finger, the visage belonged in a nightmare, not in the sober, wide-awake, rational world.

The figure raised an arm and a clawed finger emerged from the loose black sleeve, beckoning Steele closer. At the same time, words vibrated through Steele.

I knew that you would come, Steele. I have been waiting for you since you took your first breath!

Steele tried to scream, but his vocal cords were twisted into knots. He tried to retreat toward the door, only to find that his legs wouldn't budge. He felt something in his head, something alien, twisting, and poking among his treasured memories and his most private thoughts.

"No!" Steele realized how Riley must have felt when he accidentally trespassed into her mind. He felt helpless and exposed, as if someone were watching through a peephole while he bathed. It was a shameful, degrading feeling, one that he didn't want to experience ever again.

You do not realize it, but you have been waiting for me. There have been others before you who gave their lives so that I might live. But there has never been one like you, never one with a heart of blackness. Do not fight me, Steele. Your powers will live in me and you will know immortality.

Obediently, as if they were acting independently, Steele's legs began to carry him toward the vault and the creature waiting there. Steele fought hard to regain control of his limbs and his voice, but he was powerless. What a fool he'd been to believe that he could destroy the Prince of Darkness. He couldn't even find his magic; it was hiding, cowering somewhere inside him as if it realized that it was a trifling thing compared to the power wielded by the creature in the doorway.

Pyrus pushed from the neck of Steele's shirt and hissed a warning at the Prince of Darkness. The sound, faint as the salamander's heartbeat, gave Steele strength, which he used to take back control of his limbs. He stopped and focused on Ees, straining to make his mind go blank.

The Prince of Darkness flinched as Steele's mind suddenly shut down. A sigh, like a mournful wind, issued from his mouth as it glided out of the vault into the chamber. Steele looked up and noticed something flash gold at the creature's neck. It was a chain, and hanging from it was a medallion the same size and shape as Ees. But it was dull and black . . . dead, like the smaller stone Pyrus had bitten from Dirk's finger. Without thinking, Steele opened his hand. Ees rested there like a pool of blood. He extended his arm toward the Prince of Darkness, as if offering him the medallion.

Ahhh!

The sigh throbbed in Steele's body. The Prince of Darkness stared at the red stone, transfixed, and then reached for it. In a single movement, Steele snatched his hand back, raised his sword, and lunged at the creature, thrusting the blade clean through its long, black garments. But as he drove the blade home, the empty clothes crumpled to the floor, followed by the hideous head that bounced several times like a soccer ball before coming to rest on top of the pile of clothing.

"Ahhh!"

The sound came from the severed head, like air escaping from a balloon.

Steele stared at the head in horror. Its open lips lay slack against the sharp fangs; its tongue protruded from one side of its mouth and seemed to be stuck to the floor. He shoved Ees into his pocked, raised his sword, and brought it down, splitting the head in two. Then he hacked at it until it was a ruined, unrecognizable thing in his mind and on the floor of the tomb.

Breathing raggedly, Steele stepped back. His sword slipped from his hand and fell, clanging as it hit the stone floor. As he stared at the grisly pulp and felt sick, Steele's own head swam with questions. What had happened here? Had there been anything at all inside the black robes? How had the head remained on the empty garments? Had the Prince of Darkness been in the tomb and if so, where was he now?

The answer came in the cold, clammy, spirit hand that gripped Steele's throat and lifted him off the floor.

Frail human brat! In your naive mortal heart did you hope to harm me with your paltry magic?

Pain erupted in Steele's head as something icy cold battered at the barriers he had erected to keep the creature out of his mind. He summoned his remaining strength and fought as he had never fought before. He twisted and struggled, kicking, punching, and scratching at something he couldn't see. The coldness tightened on his throat until he felt his eyes bulging and his tongue swelling, filling his mouth. As his arms fell to his sides, his right hand knocked against something in the pocket of his jeans.

Mac's knife!

It is not a weapon . . . but it may help you out of a tight spot.

The words spoken by Maddie Fey the night she gave Steele, Riley, and Mac their knives echoed in Steele's head. He tried to raise his hand to his pocket, but he couldn't feel his hands, and then he couldn't remember if he had ever had hands, and besides, he didn't care anymore.

The barriers collapsed in his mind; the coldness hurt his head as it flowed into his consciousness. Through a haze, he saw his arm float past his face and a part of his brain registered the fact that he was gripping Mac's knife and that the knife was slashing at the spirit hand about his throat.

A. D. 1600–1700

One of the things that had always puzzled us was how the humans of this planet flourished. Despite constant warring among nations, and civil wars and revolutions that claimed millions of lives; despite the sixty million additional deaths as a result of fires, earthquakes, tsunamis, hurricanes, volcanic eruptions, floods, epidemics, and famine—some natural disasters, some caused by the Tsilihin—the population of the planet continued to increase.

And as populations grew, imperialist fever swept the globe. Driven by greed, nations rushed to extend their rule over other territories. The Dutch sailed for Africa. The British set their sights on India, South Africa, and America. France and Britain fought for control of India. British and Dutch warred over Africa. French armies entered Egypt. The Turks invaded Italy. And still the human population grew.

But our numbers decreased. Early one morning, mid-way through the eighteenth century, two of our fellow wardens flew through the rivers of fire and did not return.

We were now seven in number.

—Excerpt from *The Wardens' Logs*

Chapter Twenty-six
Pondering the Mystery

"What's wrong with him?" Riley was crying. "Why are his eyes bulging like that?"

"He went into the medallion again," said Maddie Fey. "But I do not know what has happened there."

"Can't you do something? Look at his face. It's turning blue." Travis's voice trembled.

"Is Steele going to die," asked Mac, "before I even get to know him again?"

Steele hated when they talked about him as if he wasn't there. He tried to sit up, but the Prince of Darkness was throttling him, pinning him to the floor, and he seemed to have lost Mac's knife, and everything was foggy.

"Fidus, look at Pyrus," said Maddie Fey. "He is spitting at Steele's neck. Do you think he is trying to bring him back?"

"No," answered Fidus, after a long silence. "Pyrus is spitting at whatever is slowly but surely choking Steele to death."

"What is it?" cried Riley. "There's nothing there."

"We cannot see it, but it is there, Riley. I must find it and remove it."

Steele felt warmth on his neck. He heard Fidus's startled shout as the old Mage's hands came in contact with the cold thing and attempted to grasp it. As Fidus struggled to wrench it off, the cold grip loosened and Steele swallowed air. Despite the fog before his eyes, he could just make out the figures of Riley, Maddie Fey, Fidus, and others, and he realized that he was back in the Dark Chamber.

"Arrr!" Steele heard an animal sound break from his throat as he pushed Fidus' hands away and tore frantically at the cold, unearthly thing. Finally he broke its hold, and he clawed and brushed at the area about his neck to get the thing off him.

Riley screamed. "Something touched my arm. What was that?"

Steele saw her jumping and brushing frantically at her clothes. Wish growled as Fidus and Maddie Fey began to stomp on the floor, trying to crush the spirit hand. Mac and Travis knelt by Steele, their faces streaked with tears.

"You've got to stop weirding out," Travis said, helping Steele sit up. "You're giving me a heart attack."

Steele tried to speak, but his throat was sore and raw and his tongue was so fat that it wouldn't let the words out. He gently gathered Pyrus in his hands and held him against his heart. His shoulders heaved as he cried soundlessly, and Mac and Travis cried with him and patted his back and tried to comfort him.

"Come, Steele," said Maddie Fey quietly, reaching for Steele's hand and helping him to his feet. "We are finished here."

Steele stood and, thinking that there was something he had forgotten, looked around. He saw Riley sitting on her heels, staring at something on the floor. Then she reached out and picked up a round black object.

"Drop it, Riley!" He meant to shout, but his voice sounded like the croaking of a large bullfrog.

It was enough. Riley reacted as if she had been slapped; the dull black medallion flew out of her hand. Fidus glanced at Steele, then quickly snatched the medallion and dropped it in a pocket inside his long cloak.

"We will not speak of this until we are away from here," he said.

Steele couldn't imagine how the black medallion had ended up in the Dark Chamber. He tried to recall if he had seen it among the empty garments on the floor of the tomb, but the only images he remembered were the pile of clothes and the ruined head. He looked about, the feeling that he had forgotten something gnawing at him again.

He saw the missing kids at once. They were in two groups, with maybe a hundred or more in each group. It was obvious from their blank eyes and sullen expressions which group had no memories. The kids in the other group were also quiet and subdued, but they were alert. They kept glancing nervously from the other group to the giant rat who was watching them like a hawk.

"They didn't want to come with us at first," said Travis. "They were excited about becoming paragons."

"We told them it was a lie, but they didn't believe us until they saw the kids whose memories had been stolen," said Mac. "I don't remember them, but luckily, some of them remembered me and a few of the other kids."

"Did you find David?" Steele asked Travis. His voice was still hoarse and his throat hurt terribly.

Travis's chin trembled as he shook his head.

"I'm sorry," said Steele. He said nothing to Travis, but he

knew that David Draken had disappeared around the end of November. Steele guessed that that was over two weeks ago. Since David wasn't among the Chicago missing kids, Steele feared that his memories had been extracted and he had already been shipped to New York. He couldn't bring himself to remind Travis that the worms might have eaten David Draken.

"Did you find anyone else?" he asked.

"If you mean the homeless," said Travis, "No. We searched but they weren't there." He found a tissue in his pocket and blew his nose.

"The Prince of Darkness used them to create the Maladroids," Steele told him.

Travis bowed his head and turned away, sniffling harder. Steele noticed his notebook lying forgotten on the floor. He picked it up and went to return it to him, but he knew that Travis was crying and he decided the notebook could wait. As he stuffed it in his jacket pocket, he remembered that he had removed his jacket just before he entered the mausoleum. Now he was wearing it. Everything about Ees mystified him; he couldn't even begin to grasp how the spirit hand had followed him out of the Prince of Darkness' medallion while still attached to his throat, or attempt to explain how he was wearing the jacket he had left behind. He shook his head, thinking that he could go insane trying to understand his mother's medallion—though it now belonged to him.

"We must leave this place," said Maddie Fey, jolting Steele back to reality. "Listen."

Steele listened. He heard the low rumbling deep below in the Black Pyramid. "The Black Pyramid is coming down."

She nodded.

"Good riddance," said Riley.

The walls of the pyramid shuddered and the floor cracked beneath their feet.

"But . . . the Prince of Darkness . . . I couldn't destroy him in Ees. . . . He's still out there," said Steele.

"Yes, but he has abandoned this place," said Maddie Fey. "He will not return here." She turned to the group of children who hadn't lost their memories and spoke softly.

Steele leaned closer, but he couldn't make out what she was saying. "What are you doing?" he asked.

"It is a mild spell, an illusion. The children will see a tunnel instead of the limousine, and they will remember a man with a face like a rat."

Overhead, they heard a loud snapping sound. Wish looked up and barked a warning. But Steele and Maddie Fey were already racing toward the limousine, leaping over seams opening in the floor before them that were widening and spreading like cracks on a frozen lake. They dodged massive columns that split and shattered and crashed to the floor in an explosion of marble and dust. Steele wiped blood from his face where the flying shards of stone stung him, and kept one arm pressed against his chest to protect Pyrus.

Ahead, he saw the red rat pushing the missing kids through the open limo door, where they disappeared into the blackness. When he reached the door, Steele paused and looked back in time to see the gigantic peak of the pyramid break apart and plummet. Then the floor buckled and opened and swallowed it in one loud, reverberating gulp.

"Good riddance!" Steele murmured, echoing Riley's sentiments, and dived into the limo, just as the realm of the Prince of Darkness imploded all about him.

Back in Maddie Fey's house, Steele and Riley searched for
Ryan Massey, the Toronto boy who had disappeared on
November fifth. The kids whose memories were intact shook
their heads and said they'd never heard of him.

"The one who looks like a rat said he's going to take us to
the police so we can go home," said one of the kids, a girl
with watery eyes. "It's just that he seems awfully fierce. . . . I
mean . . . is it safe to go with him?"

"You'll be safe," said Riley. "I don't think Nilats means to
be fierce."

"Who are you?" asked a boy about Steele's age.

Steele and Riley shared a quick glance.

"The people who abducted you stole kids in other cities.
We're just trying to find them," said Steele.

"Were they really going to do that to us . . . you know . . .
what they did to the other kids?"

Steele nodded at the girl who had spoken.

"Why?" asked several children at once.

Steele felt torn; he didn't want to say too much, but he also
thought that the kids deserved to know why they had been
abducted. He said, "They were doing experiments on kids'
minds."

"But you don't have to worry about that anymore," said
Riley. "You're safe now and the place where they did the
experiments is gone, destroyed."

When Nilats came and took the children away, Steele
noticed that many of them were crying.

Steele and Riley wiped tears from their own eyes as they
unlocked a door and entered another room to search for Ryan
among the kids who had no memories. These kids looked old
and smelled sick. Their faces were grey and gaunt; their eyes

were dull and listless. They were so thin that Steele wondered if Dirk had bothered to feed them. He remembered the girl who had been licking the plastic bread bag and looked for her now, his heart heavy. But he didn't recognize her. As he and Riley walked among them, breathing through their mouths to avoid inhaling the stench, they spoke quietly

"We're not going to hurt you," or "You're going to be OK."

Not that it made any difference. The children's dull eyes followed them, their expressions either sullen or as blank as stone. Against Steele's back, Pyrus felt like a coiled spring.

"Ryan's not here," said Riley, "unless he looks a lot different from the pictures on TV."

Steele noticed that she was trying hard not to cry.

"Liars!" cried one of the kids, in a voice that tickled the hairs on Steele's neck.

"Riley, I think we should leave. Now!" Steele caught her arm and backed toward the door.

If they had hesitated another second, they wouldn't have made it. The children surged toward them, not as individuals but as a single mass of hostility, hands clutching and scratching, mouths open and jaws snapping.

"Get back!" Steele shouted, swinging his fists blindly.

"Quick!" cried Riley, opening the door a crack and slipping through.

Steele felt his fist connect with flesh as he backed through the doorway. He put his shoulder against the door and pushed with all of his strength. "Turn the key. Hurry, Riley." He didn't know how long he could hold the door shut.

Riley fumbled at the lock and Steele finally heard the key turn. Then he slumped against the door, breathing fast.

"Talk about scary," said Riley, pressing her hand against her heart.

"No kidding," said Steele. "Mac was like that when we found him. I forgot you weren't there. I should have warned you."

They went in search of the others and found them in Maddie Fey's library, where Mac was loudly protesting Fidus's suggestion that they shed their torn, smelly, bloodstained clothes and report back in an hour, freshly scrubbed.

"What about my memories?" Mac stormed. "I can't wait a whole hour. I want Steele to go into the other kids' heads now and maybe this time he'll be able to destroy the black magic all at once and I'll get my memories back. I can take a shower later. Besides, I don't smell nearly as bad as some of the Moles we met when Sydney took us down into the sewers under New York."

Everyone stared at him.

"Well, I don't," he said. "Do I?"

"Mac," cried Riley. "Forget about whether you stink or not. Do you know what you just said?"

"Duh, yeah," said Mac sarcastically. "I said—"

"Oh, Mac, just shut up," said Riley, laughing as she went and hugged him until his face turned red.

Steele laughed, too. Soon everyone had joined in, aside from Mac, who still hadn't realized that his memory was returning.

When they finally stopped laughing, Riley told Mac that he had remembered the Moles and Syd and New York's sewers. But when Mac seemed bent on dredging up and sharing with them every memory stored in his head, Steele was the first to flee.

And he left with Maddie Fey.

In the bathroom, Steele stripped and stepped into the shower. The hot water was like medicine for his bruised and aching body. It eased the stiffness from his shoulders and cleansed a score of cuts and scrapes on his arms and torso. He felt it washing away layers of dried blood and grime. He stood there for a long time, eyes closed. There were so many things he wanted to know, the present whereabouts of the Prince of Darkness uppermost among them. And Dirk. What had happened to Dirk? Was he on his way to Neverland? Thinking of Dirk depressed him. He hated the bully, now more than ever, but he no longer wished him dead. *It's probably because I'm not afraid of him anymore,* he thought.

When he emerged, refreshed from the shower, he saw that someone had laid out clean clothing on the bed. He dressed quickly. He had just stuffed Ees and Travis's notebook into his pocket when Nilats scratched at the door.

Scuttling on all four limbs, the rat led him along several corridors and down a short flight of stairs. At the bottom of the stairs was an open area before a dark wooden door, which opened soundlessly as they approached. Through the open door Steele saw Maddie Fey and Fidus and his friends, poised motionless, staring at something that wasn't visible from where he was standing. He brushed past the rat and then halted, gaping in wonder at what appeared to be a long pane of glass, suspended in the air several inches off the floor in the middle of the room. As he stared at it, he realized that it wasn't glass at all, but something animated, undulating like a rectangular bubble. It was emitting faint green light and shimmering like a heat vision.

"What is it?" Steele breathed.

Maddie Fey turned her head toward him; the light reflected

green in her silver eyes. She said, "It's a window for the children, a memory window."

Steele slowly circled the memory window, overwhelmed by the power of the Mages to create something so extraordinary. He felt that his own powers were inadequate, almost childish by comparison. Perhaps the Prince of Darkness had been right when he called Steele's powers paltry. Sighing, he looked about. Except for the memory window, the room was bare.

"How does it work?" he asked Fidus.

Fidus smiled at him. "You were worried that most of the children would die before you could destroy the black magic in each one's mind, and I told you that when the time came, you would not be alone. Do you remember?"

"Yes, Sir."

"Well, my friend, the time has come. What you see before you is a simple device that will link all of the children, eliminating the necessity of having to enter each child's mind."

Travis said, "So if Steele gets into one mind and destroys the magic, he'll cause a chain reaction in the other kids. That's so awesome."

"It's brilliant," Riley agreed.

"Exactly," Fidus said.

"I understand what you're trying to do," said Steele. "But I don't understand how the memory window links the kids."

"Ah, yes," said Fidus. "Let me explain about the window. Neither Maddie Fey nor I dare use our powers to enter the children's minds. Our powers are too potent, or alien if you prefer, and such an excursion could cause irreparable harm. But we have used our combined magic to create the memory window that will link the children's minds to one another.

"Sweet," said Mac. "I wish I had magic."

"Well you don't," retorted Riley. "So shut up."

"Has anybody seen my notebook?" asked Travis, patting his pockets frantically, and then looking about as despondently as if someone had told him his faithful dog had died.

Steele pulled the notebook out of his back pocket. "Here," he said, holding it out. "You dropped it in the Dark Chamber. I picked it up and forgot all about it."

Travis brightened. "Whew! Thank goodness. My notes . . . everything that happened . . ." He took the notebook. "I thought it was gone. Thanks, Steele. You don't know what this means to me." Morphing into a reporter hot on the heels of a story, Travis opened the notebook, turned to Fidus, and asked, "What sort of magic did you and Maddie Fey use to create the memory window?"

"Do not trouble yourself over that," said Fidus, his eyes twinkling with amusement. "It is like asking the stars to reveal their names." He walked over to Steele, who was circling the window, studying it.

"Are you ready to do this, Steele? Shall we bring in the children?"

Steele licked his lips, which had suddenly gone dry. At the same time, he felt an overpowering urge to sink onto the floor in a corner of the room and close his eyes. He dreaded the thought of struggling with the dark magic. But for the time being, he had to forget about himself and think of the children. He had to forget that his throat was still hurting terribly, as if the hand of the Prince of Darkness had crushed something inside. He had to forget about his fight with Dirk that had left his body bruised and aching all over. He had to think of the children, and nothing else.

"I'm ready," he said.

Fidus placed both hands on his shoulders. "I can only imagine what you have endured already today. I would not ask more of you if it were not absolutely necessary."

Steele looked into the old man's dark, sympathetic eyes and nodded. "I know," he said. "I'm OK."

A moment later, Nilats appeared in the doorway with the children.

Fidus nodded at the rat, then turned and spoke to the companions. "On my command, Nilats will move the children toward the window. Riley. Mac. Place yourselves on either side of the window and help each child through. You may have to take their arms and lift them. Travis, the children are unpredictable; they may panic and try to force their way into the window as a group. You must be ready to step in front of the window to ensure that only one enters it at a time. Do you think you can do what I am asking of you?"

"Yes," they answered.

"Good. Maddie Fey and I will be concentrating on holding the window together until the children have passed through it and Steele has returned to us. Once all of the children are on the other side, Steele's life will depend upon his ability to concentrate. You must remain absolutely still and not speak until the window vanishes. Do you understand?"

Steele's friends nodded solemnly.

Steele dug Ees out of his pocket. A tingle shot up his arm as Maddie Fey clasped his hand. She was so close that Steele could feel power radiating from her. He wondered how she could pay attention to him and maintain her hold on the memory window at the same time. He glanced down at her hand in his, and for a moment, felt a sense of detachment, as if that large, rough, bruised and scraped paw gripping the perfect, slim white hand didn't belong to him. But she didn't appear to notice, and if she did, she didn't seem to mind the state of his hands.

Maddie Fey smiled, "Good luck, Steele."

Steele swallowed. "Thanks."

"Begin," said Fidus.

Steele watched as Nilats and the others ushered the kids through the memory window. It took much longer than he had thought it would. But finally all of the children were on the other side. It was now up to Steele.

The magic was easy to find, as easy as when he had been pulled into the medallion. It answered his call in an exhilarating rush. The air about him crackled and hissed with forces as wild and as powerful as the wind, and he fought to control them. He knew his magic was responding, in part, to the combined powers of the Mages—powers that were far older and far greater than his. From a great distance, he thought he heard someone gasp, "Look! His eyes! They're silver!"

This time Steele focused on a girl, one of the last to have passed through the window. The reason he chose her was because she was the smallest and thinnest child among the others and she had a racking cough that made Steele cringe. He worried that she was sick, or even dying, and his heart went out to her. No longer pressed for time as he had been when he had entered Mac's mind in the Black Pyramid, Steele went slowly. He didn't want to end up in the girl's bloodstream, so he concentrated on her head, letting his thoughts flow from his mind into hers.

Still, when he suddenly found himself plummeting downward in her brain, the shock was like a physical blow. As he fell, he saw the mass of magic below, contracting and expanding like a black heart. He tried to slow his descent, but tendrils were sprouting from the mass and stretching up toward him. They coiled about his legs and arms and pulled him down into the black, vine-like mass. Steele thought he was shouting, thought he was struggling to break free from the tangled tendrils, but the power was spinning about him, confusing him.

Foolish boy! You cannot hide from me. Look into the blackness that you feel growing within and you will find me there. I know you. I have always known everything about you. Look into your own blackness and you will know what lies ahead. You and your feeble Mages will fail. It is your destiny.

The flat, emotionless voice of the Prince of Darkness came to him from the blackness and broke into his mind in a blinding flash. Steele felt something pecking at his thoughts like a crow pecking at carrion on the side of the road. As his strength began to fail, Steele wondered if he was being torn apart, or if he had been in an accident and his life was gushing out into a pool of red on the street—or was it Ees, glowing and spreading before his eyes. Then he felt strong arms lifting him up and he thought he was a little kid again and his father was carrying him upstairs to bed.

Knowledge

We soared to our lofty mountain perches, and there we seven remaining wardens turned our faces to the Heavens, toward Arjella—suspended in space near the centre of the Galaxy too far distant for our keen sight to identify. We opened our great mouths and roared our frustration and grief at the twinkling stars.

Help us!

The answer, when it came, shook the mountain with its force.

We are not alone!

—Excerpt from *The Wardens' Logs*

Epilogue

Steele woke up in bed, disoriented and short of breath. Groaning, he sat up and removed Pyrus from around his neck. Realizing that he was bare-chested, he looked under the covers and noticed that he wasn't wearing any clothes. Quickly, he pulled the covers around him and looked about. It took a moment before he realized that he was in his room in Maddie Fey's house. Riley and Travis were there, perched on the edges of chairs on either side of the fireplace. Mac was there, too, sitting on the arm of Riley's chair. They were conversing quietly and looked up when they noticed Steele.

"It's not fair," said Mac, eying Steele with disgust. "You're not the one who had his mind invaded and his memories stolen. You're just the one who gets to sleep all day. Get up." He grinned wickedly. "Or perhaps I should call Nilats."

But Steele was only vaguely aware of him; he was thinking of the girl with the hacking cough and hearing the Prince of Darkness speaking to him from the black magic in the girl's mind as the crushing tendrils pulled and tore at him.

"What's wrong?"

Steele shivered and shook his head, chasing the Prince of Darkness away. He looked at his friends, who were now crowded about his bed wearing worried frowns.

Dreading the answer, Steele asked, "What happened to the kids?"

"They're OK," Riley answered. "You destroyed the magic in one girl. Maddie Fey said that she was sick and so malnourished that she couldn't have survived much longer."

Mac hopped onto the foot of Steele's bed. "Now we're waiting to see if you started the chain reaction that will destroy the black magic in the other kids."

Steele tried to get out of bed, but sank back into the pillows, his forehead beaded with perspiration. His body ached all over; his limbs and muscles felt as if he had just walked all the way from Toronto to Chicago. But the tears that leaked from his eyes were tears of gladness for the girl.

"It wasn't like with you, Mac," he said. "The minute I broke into the girl's mind, the magic was waiting for me . . . *he* was waiting for me."

"You mean—?"

Steele nodded. "The Prince of Darkness. The magic grabbed me and started pulling on me, stretching my arms and legs until I thought I was being torn apart. It was torture. And all the while I could hear his voice and he was telling me that I'd never be able to escape from him."

"Steele, you've got to tell Maddie Fey and Fidus about the POD," said Travis. "In fact, they sent us to get you, but you were so out of it that we decided it would be cruel to wake you up."

"What happened to my clothes?"

"Don't look at me," said Riley quickly. "I certainly didn't take them."

Mac explained that he, Travis, and Fidus were responsible. "When you came back from the girl's mind, you were covered in black and your clothes were horribly grungy and smelly. We held our noses, and Fidus said some seriously unpronounceable words, and your clothes just sort of vanished. Then we stood you under the shower. Most of the black came off, but no way were we about to bathe you, so you might want to use soap next time."

"Where are my old clothes?" said Steele, worried that he might have put Ees in one of his pockets."

"I suspect they're floating about in some sort of parallel universe," said Travis. "But your stuff is safe. We put everything in the bureau, top drawer."

Mac flashed Riley a conspiratorial grin. "Too bad Steele didn't disappear with the clothes."

"Too bad you remembered how to be a pain in the butt," Riley retorted, slapping him on the head as she passed behind him on her way to the door.

"Ow!" cried Mac, rubbing the back of his head. "You're dangerous, Riley. Dangerous and twisted."

"Aw! Are you going to cry?" teased Riley.

"Cut it out," growled Steele, his head beginning to pound. "And *get* out while I get dressed."

"We'll meet you in the dining room," said Mac.

Riley pointed at a large wardrobe standing against the wall near the door. "There are clothes in there."

After they had gone, Steele hobbled to the wardrobe and dressed in the shirt and jeans and shoes he found there, which were just his size. Then he took Ees and Dirk's tiny black stone from the bureau drawer, dropped them in his pocket, and headed for the door, wondering again what had happened to the bully. Pyrus dashed out from under Steele's pillow, leaped onto his leg and stuck like glue.

"Stupid salamander," Steele said fondly, and left to join the others.

They were all there, seated about the long, dark, wooden table. Maddie Fey was in her usual place at the head, the candlelight reflected off her silver choker. Steele had seen it dozens of times but he still hadn't got used to the way it made her neck look scaly. Wish was stretched out on the hearth behind her, the flames from the burning log making his silver fur appear to be on fire. He lifted his head as Steele entered the room, and to Steele's surprise, his long tail thumped a greeting. Pyrus hissed and scurried up Steele's leg and into his shirt pocket.

Fidus sat in the high-backed chair on Maddie Fey's right, his long hands folded on the table, his bright eyes fixed on the black medallion resting there like the shadow of the red disk hanging from his neck. From the chair next to Fidus, Riley smiled at Steele.

"Hey!" she said.

Across from her, Mac and Travis looked up at Steele. Travis's notebook was spread open between them on the table. "Hey!" they said.

Steele greeted the others and dropped into the chair at the foot of the table. He looked about for the rat, and felt some relief when he couldn't spot the rodent in the room. He reached for the bejeweled goblet on the table before him and drank from it thirstily. It was thick and tasted like apricots and bananas and something else that Steele couldn't identify. It was good, but Steele had a sudden craving for chocolate milk. Pyrus slipped out of his pocket and climbed onto the top of the chair.

Maddie Fey tapped a long silver spoon against her goblet. "We have a lot to discuss, and Travis must be anxious to go home, so let us begin."

Steele thought that Travis looked as if he'd be quite content to remain with them forever. Besides, even if he wanted to go home, he couldn't, not until they discovered what the Prince of Darkness had done with all of the people in Chicago. He said as much to Maddie Fey.

"There were never any people in Chicago," she answered.

"What!" Steele and the others were incredulous.

"The Chicago that you entered upon leaving the limousine does not exist, not in your reality. It was an alternate reality meant to lead Steele to the Prince of Darkness."

Travis asked, "How did I end up there?"

"Somewhere between your school and the building where you met the others, you entered the alternate Chicago," said Maddie Fey.

Travis combed his hair back with his fingers. "I am so confused."

"No kidding," Riley agreed.

Maddie Fey continued. "Nilats has already placed the missing children whose memories had not been extracted in the custody of the Chicago Police—authorities in the real Chicago. If they have not already been united with their families, they will be soon. The others will be leaving here as soon as we determine that their memories are returning, and according to Nilats that is already happening. Most of the children are now fully aware and out of danger. The girl in whose mind Steele destroyed the magic is recovering rapidly." She smiled at Steele. "I'm glad that you chose her. She was mere hours away from death. Thanks to you and to Fidus's healing magic, she has been saved."

"The way she was coughing, I thought she might be sick," Steele said.

There was a single sharp rap on the door behind Steele. He looked around as it opened. The giant rat entered the room and stepped aside to avoid being trampled as a hundred ragged children spilled past him.

"Oh, Steele, look. It's working," said Riley, without crying.

Nilats pointed at Steele. "They wanted to see him."

Steele stood, aware that tears were flooding *his* eyes as he looked at the children whose memories he had helped bring back. He noticed that they were also smiling and crying. He found it hard to imagine that the last time he had been among these very same children, he had been terrified of them.

A pretty but filthy girl with long, wavy, auburn hair and clear blue eyes stepped forward dragging a small, thin girl with her. Steele recognized the smaller girl. He knew he'd never forget her, for she was the one he had picked, the one in whose head he had heard the voice of the Prince of Darkness.

"My name is Lara Mahoney," said the girl with the auburn hair. "This is my best friend, Kathy Lee O'Shea. We want to thank you for finding us and . . ." She sniffled, and Steele heard Riley answer with a sniffle of her own. "And for not giving up . . . and for giving back our memories."

The Libertyville girls who went missing on Halloween!

Steele was too choked-up to speak.

"We were trick-or-treating with my dad," Lara continued. "And the next thing we knew we were in this big room with lots of other kids . . . and this boy named Dirk told us that he had picked us of all the kids in Chicago to become paragons . . . He said when it was time to go home we'd be so rich our parents would never have to work—"

Kathy Lee broke in, smiling at Steele shyly. "He said our parents knew about the game and didn't tell us because it was a surprise. But he's a liar. He liked hurting the younger kids. I saw him."

"Do you remember a boy named David Draken?" asked Travis. The girls nodded.

"His name got picked," said Lara.

"Dirk took him away," said Kathy Lee, starting to cry again.

The children thanked Steele and the others again and then they left with Nilats. As soon as the door closed behind them, Travis said in a quiet voice, "He's dead, isn't he? David's dead."

No one answered. They looked at Travis sadly.

At last Maddie Fey spoke. "If he is alive, we will find him."

Travis looked at her, but Steele noticed that his eyes were dull. He believed his friend was dead.

"Will the other kids be OK now that they've got their memories back?" asked Riley. "I mean . . . what about long-term effects?"

"You mean are we going to drop dead or something a year from now?" asked Mac, looking extremely worried.

Maddie Fey smiled. "You may very well drop dead *or something* at any time, Mac. But not as a result of losing your memories and getting them back."

Everyone heard Mac's loud sigh of relief.

"I tried to imagine what it would be like to have no memories, but I couldn't," said Steele. "Whenever I tried not to think of something, I automatically thought of it."

"Yes," said Fidus. "Without memories, life would be unbearable."

"What if you had only rotten memories?" asked Riley. "Life would be even more unbearable."

"There are people like that," said Travis sagely. "Your pal Dirk, for one."

"Don't call him our pal," said Mac fiercely. "And he'd better stay away from me, or—"

"Or what?" laughed Riley. "You'll run away."

At Maddie Fey's urging, Steele related everything that had happened from the moment they stepped out of the limo onto the deserted bridge until he fought the Prince of Darkness in the dark mausoleum. The other companions were encouraged to fill in the gaps in Steele's narrative and they did so enthusiastically.

Mac was outraged when Steele described how he had destroyed the Mac-thing in the alley.

"The nerve of that Fire Demon," he said, and then he looked at Steele suspiciously. "What if it really had been me?"

Steele laughed. "I knew it wasn't you."

But Mac didn't seem convinced. "That's easy to say, but how did you know?"

"Just drop it, Mac," snapped Riley. "Let Steele finish."

Mac clammed up, but not for long. As soon as he heard how Travis had wedged Steele's and Riley's knives in the jaws of the gargoyle to prevent the statue's jaws from snapping Travis's hand off, he remembered that Dirk had stolen his knife. He railed at Dirk non-stop until Steele produced the knife and slid it along the table. Mac was suddenly speechless.

When Steele had finished, no one spoke for a long time. The only sounds in the huge room were the logs crackling

and spitting in the fireplace, Travis's pen scribbling frantically in his notebook, and snapping sounds as Mac opened
and shut all of the parts of his knife.

After a while, Travis said, "I still don't understand how
Steele could run straight into that Fire Demon and not get
burned."

Steele took Ees out of his pocket and peered into it for a
moment. "I think it has something to do with my medallion.
I think it protected me."

Fidus shook his head. "Steele, I do not think that Ees pro-
tects you from fire."

Steele didn't believe him, but he said nothing. When Wood
had morphed into a Fire Demon, Steele had never heard of
Ees. The fire had scorched his clothes and raised blisters on
his face and hands. Sometime later, Maddie Fey gave him
the medallion. He was wearing it about his neck when they
faced the four Fire Demons that erupted from beneath Park
Avenue. Then, despite the fact that heat from the fiery creatures melted the pavement at his feet, he felt nothing. The
medallion *had* protected him.

"There are some things I don't understand," he said, changing the subject. "When I bent the bars of the cell, I almost
lost control of the magic. I almost turned into metal, but I
forced the metal back into the bars. It did what I wanted.
But sometimes it does the exact opposite of what I want,
and it scares me." He turned to Maddie Fey. "What would
have happened if I hadn't been able to drive the metal out
of my arms?"

"Magic is scary, Steele. You are right to fear it. Remember,
though, that it was your magic that spoke to the metal
bars and transformed them. They bent to your will. When

you felt threatened, you forced the metal back where it belonged." She paused for a moment before continuing. "I believe our strong sense of self-preservation instinctively acts when we are in danger. It also prevents us from using magic unrestrainedly."

Mac burst out laughing. "In plain-speak, she doesn't think you'd have turned yourself into Metal Man."

"Very funny," said Steele. He turned back to Maddie Fey. "I think I know what you mean. When the metal started to take over, something called me back."

"Yes," said Maddie Fey. "Your consciousness was aware of the danger."

"When you tried to stop me from using magic on the Maladroids, I wasn't even planning to use it. I was thinking about how evil they were and that they should be destroyed. I didn't call the magic. It just came, and I couldn't stop it. I thought I had killed you."

"You should have seen him," said Riley loyally. "He felt terrible."

Maddie Fey laughed. "Steele's power cannot kill me, Riley. At least not yet." She turned back to Steele. "I know that you did not consciously summon your magic. But your anger may have triggered it."

"You said my magic sent you away," Steele said. "Where?"

"I did not know the place," she said. "But it was not in this world."

"Remember, Steele," Fidus added. "Your magic is young. You and it are growing together."

"It's so confusing," Steele sighed. "Sometimes the magic really freaks me. It's unpredictable. Like the time it broke into Riley's mind without any warning. Or when it wouldn't come when I needed it to fight the Prince of Darkness."

Fidus shrugged. "With Riley, your magic may have sensed that you were worried about her. But with the Prince of Darkness, it is another matter altogether. You were within the medallion, Steele. You couldn't use magic because you were experiencing a vision."

Steele shook his head. "It couldn't have been a vision. When I was in the medallion I hacked off the Prince's hand. But when I came back from the disk, the hand was still around my neck. How do you explain that?"

Fidus and Maddie Fey glanced at each other and then at Steele.

"See," said Steele. "You can't explain it."

"You are right," said Maddie Fey. "I told you before that, except for you, I have never heard of anyone physically experiencing the visions shown in the medallions."

"Another thing," said Steele. "I called my magic in the vision. It came. I could feel it all around me. But when I went into the tomb, it disappeared."

"Perhaps your fear prevented you from using it against the Prince of Darkness," said Maddie Fey.

At some point, Steele noticed Nilats feeding an enormous log into the fireplace. He hadn't heard the rat return and seeing him sparked a memory.

"When I opened the eleventh door of the limo, what were those lights?" Steele asked Maddie Fey, feeling the rat's eyes on him.

"It was a reckless thing to do," Maddie Fey said, but there was no anger in her voice. "If Nilats had not been there you would have been lost."

Steele avoided the rat's sharp yellow eyes. The notion that he owed his life to that creature made him squirm. "You haven't answered my question," he said.

"It is enough if I tell you that it is another dimension from which there is no returning," answered Maddie Fey.

"That's so lame," said Mac, indignant. "You should tell us more. What if I had opened that door by mistake? Are you saying I would have got sucked in there forever?"

Fidus laughed. "Do not worry, Mac. That particular door would not have opened for you."

"And why not?" demanded Mac. "Steele opened it. What's so special about him?" He glared at Steele as if Steele's head had suddenly sprouted horns. "Oh, I get it. Steele's a Mage."

Steele felt as if Mac had slapped him. "I didn't ask to be a Mage."

"He saved your life, Mac, so why don't you shut up," said Riley.

Mac's face reddened. "Sorry," he mumbled at Steele. "It came out all wrong."

Steele didn't say anything, but he was thinking that being a Mage might turn his friends against him. The thought filled him with sadness.

"Maybe Mac meant to ask why the door is there," said Travis, chewing thoughtfully on his pen. "I mean what's the purpose of a door that leads to a place like that?"

"That's the same as asking what's the purpose of a planet," said Riley.

"No, it's not," Travis argued. "A planet is different. There might not be a purpose for it. But doors were made for a purpose."

Steele changed the subject. "What about the Maladroids? I couldn't detect any sign of them when I sent my hearing through the Black Pyramid."

"The Maladroids are gone," said Maddie Fey, "and you must not think of them as poor homeless people who were lured or stolen from the streets of Chicago. There was nothing human about them after the Prince of Darkness altered them." She paused and looked from one face to another. "No. Do not waste your tears on the Maladroids."

"Unfortunately, the homeless will not be missed," said Fidus. "Their places on the street will be filled by new homeless." He shook his head slowly. "The way your race mistreats its own kind is incomprehensible to me."

From its spot near the fireplace, the rat snuffled and glared at Steele as if he were to blame for the way humans treated other humans. Steele looked away.

"I wonder if they were Maladroids from the real Chicago," said Travis.

"They were certainly real enough," said Maddie Fey. "But I do not know where they came from." She paused a moment and then continued. "Because of each of you, we found and rescued over two hundred children, we found a way to eliminate the black magic, and we destroyed the stronghold of the Prince of Darkness. None of the things we accomplished could have been done by any one person. It took all of us, working together." She smiled at Travis. "You have been a true friend to Riley and Steele when they dearly needed one. And if you had not found a passage through the wall, Mac and the others might still be trapped inside the Black Pyramid."

Next she turned to Riley. "You said that you would use

your eyes while we used magic in the Dark Chamber. We found nothing with our magic, but with your eyes you found the black medallion. You also gave immeasurable comfort to a dying boy."

Riley's green eyes sparkled with pleasure.

"Except for getting myself kidnapped I didn't do anything," said Mac, fidgeting with his knife.

"That's not true," said Maddie Fey. "Your contribution was the most powerful magic of all, Mac—the magic of friendship. It was so powerful that your friends risked their lives to find you."

Mac blinked at Steele and Riley. "I am sort of loveable, aren't I?"

Maddie Fey and Fidus laughed. And Steele, Riley, and Travis groaned and shouted. "Shut up!"

"That's just my way of saying thanks," mumbled Mac, suddenly turning serious. "I know I can be a pain, but what you did for me makes me feel sort of exuberant. If you know what I mean."

Steele felt Maddie Fey's eyes settle on him.

"We have come a long way and accomplished a great many things in just nine days, Steele."

Steele nodded. He was thinking, *Nine whole days since I saw Dad and GM.*

"I will not recount the things you have done," said Maddie Fey. "Since all of us at my table know them only too well. I have been hard on you because I believe in you and in our goal. Both Fidus and I are grateful to have had you with us. Thank you."

"But it's not over," said Steele. "The Prince of Darkness told me that we're going to fail. He said it was my destiny."

"Nonsense!" said Fidus. "Destiny is a malicious lie. The Prince of Darkness uses such words to justify unspeakable acts. There is no destiny."

"I have a question for Fidus," said Riley, reaching out and touching the old man's arm.

Fidus covered Riley's slim hand with his own. "What is it, Riley?"

Riley pointed at the black medallion on the table. "I noticed that it's exactly like Ees . . . except for the colour. What is it?"

Fidus picked up the medallion, careful to touch only its gold chain. "It may be a clue to the identity of the Prince of Darkness, but I must study it," he said, clasping his own medallion and holding it next to the black one to compare the two. "I suspect, though, that it is the opposite of our Mage symbols."

"It's the same kind of stone as this," said Steele, removing from his pocket the small black stone Pyrus had bitten from Dirk's finger. He slid it along the table.

Everyone stared at the small black stone. Then Fidus looked at Steele. "I will keep this for a while." He placed the large black medallion on the table, then scooped up the small stone and put it in a pocket inside his garments.

"What now?" asked Mac.

Nilats scuttled over to a delicate tripod serving table where four silver-wrapped boxes rested on a silver salver. The boxes were identical and approximately three inches square. He carried the salver to the table, placed it before Maddie Fey and went back to his spot near the hearth.

"I have a small gift for each of you," she said. "Think of it as a memory restored." She passed the salver to Travis, who took the one with his name engraved on a round, silver disk and passed the salver on.

As Steele and his companions eagerly opened their gifts, Maddie Fey said. "Words are not enough for what you have gone through, Steele. Therefore I will let my gift speak for me."

Steele had already opened his. On top of silver tissue paper lay a silver-coloured chain. Steele picked it up and read the card attached to it. *For Ees.*

"Thank you," he said, producing Ees from his pocket and feeding the chain through a loop on the edge of the medallion. Then he slipped the chain over his head. Ees hummed against his chest. "I think Ees likes it, too," he said.

"This chain cannot be broken," said Maddie Fey. "It was made in Arjella of *marflow.*"

"Be careful," chided Mac. "Next time someone tries to steal Ees, your head will probably come off."

Steele opened the tissue paper. Inside was a round silver disk about the size and thickness of a quarter. His first thought was that Maddie Fey had given him a coin from her world, but the moment he picked it up he knew that it was something else entirely. Abruptly images flashed through his mind. He saw himself with Mac and Riley on the bridge in the alternate Chicago. He saw Travis dart from the elevator in the Tribune Tower and streak toward the door. He saw it all, every moment of their adventure imprinted on his mind as if he were watching it on television.

From his friends' excited exclamations, he knew that they, too, were reliving the events of the past days.

"This is awesome!" he said.

Fidus laughed. "The memories are not on the disk. The disk stimulates your brain to replay the memories in a chronological sequence. When you reach my age and memories begin to fade, the disk will help you remember."

"Thank you," cried Riley, wiping tears from her eyes.

"It's like having a permanent record of everything we did," said Travis.

"People have to believe us now," said Mac, holding up his disk. "Here's the proof."

"No, no," said Fidus. "The memories belong to you and your friends. No one else has experienced those memories so no one else can see them. Because Steele has told you all that befell him and Riley and Travis in their search for you, you will be able to see those memories."

Mac dropped his disk in his pocket. "So, what happens now?"

"It's not over yet," said Steele. "We found most of the kids, or so we hope. But there's still Ryan Massey and David Draken, and probably others."

"Right," said Riley. "And we've got to restore Syd's brother's memories and the memories of all the New York kids. And there are the lost wardens . . . and Steele still has to figure out how to stop the Fire Demons."

Travis looked from Fidus to Maddie Fey. "I wish I could stay and help."

"You have done enough," said Maddie Fey kindly. "It is time for you to return to the real Chicago, and to your family."

"I know," said Travis. "My parents are going to kill me as it is. But there's one more thing you've got to add to your to-do list."

"What?" asked Steele.

"Find Dirk and stop him from going to Neverland, or he'll get eaten by the cannibals."

"I hope he does," said Riley.

"It'd serve him right," growled Mac.

"Don't wish more evil on him," said Maddie Fey, rising to signal the end of discussions. "He has enough trouble avoiding it as it is." She moved toward the door. "Come, Travis. You have been gone four days and your parents will be worried sick."

As Steele rose from the table, he exchanged glances with Riley and Mac and knew that they, too, ached to go home.

They stepped out of the limousine that was parked in the shadows halfway along a narrow alley. Maddie Fey and Fidus said warm goodbyes to Travis, and Maddie Fey even asked Wish to see that the boy made it safely through the Chicago streets. In silence, Steele, Riley, and Mac walked Travis to the mouth of the alley. When they reached the street, they looked about in wonder at the great city, the real city, alive with sound, light, colour, and movement. Christmas trees and lights gave it a festive air. Cars, taxis, vans, and buses roared past. People skirted around them, their arms laden with brightly wrapped packages. Steele breathed in the frosty air, tilted his head back, and gazed up. The moon was white and cold, and not as full as it had been the night he, Riley, and Mac found themselves on the deserted bridge in that other Chicago. It felt good to be out in the open under a real sky after the underground gloom of the Black Pyramid. It felt good to be alive.

"Look!" cried Riley, pointing.

Steele looked across the street. In the moonlight the old water tower looked like a fairytale castle, its walls and main tower glowing as if they had been touched by a magic wand.

"I'm glad we got to see it," he said to Travis. "I wish we could see more of your city in daylight."

"Maybe you could all come and visit me sometime. It'd be fun showing you around. I'll even show you all the things from around the world that are embedded in TribTower, including a real moon rock, a chunk of stone from the Alamo, and a fragment of the Great Wall."

"That settles it then," laughed Steele. "We'll be back."

"I'm really going to miss you guys," said Travis. "Don't forget me." Then he turned away.

They stood in the mouth of the alley watching Travis sprint along the street trying to keep up with Wish. In the distance, Steele recognized the Tribune Tower where they had tackled Travis three nights ago.

But no, he thought. *That didn't happen here.*

When Travis was no longer visible, they turned back into the narrow alley and walked, shivering, toward Maddie Fey's limousine. It was waiting silently, its black exterior gleaming silver in the moonlight. Maddie Fey and Fidus were no longer there.

They heard one of the limo's doors click open and saw Nilats scrabble out of the door, his yellow eyes glowing fiercely.

"Get in," the rat hissed.

Steele and the others filed into the darkness of the vehicle.

"I really hate that rat," Steele said under his breath.

In Maddie Fey's deserted dining room, Pyrus leaped from Steele's chair onto the table and crawled along the surface toward the heat radiating from the massive fireplace. He paused and stared through bulbous eyes at the black object that Fidus had left on the table. And as Pyrus stared, his fiery-orange colour began to darken until he was as black as the image before him. Slowly the black salamander approached the black thing. He peered into it. The surface of the dark medallion wavered and seemed to stretch toward the salamander.

A moment later, both the medallion and Pyrus were gone.

Acknowledgements

Special thanks to Allyson Latta for her extraordinary editing skills and to Lynne Missen at HarperCollins for her insight, advice, and endless patience as this story unfolded. Thanks to both for their encouragement and enthusiasm.

Be sure to read The Serpent's Egg Trilogy by J. FitzGerald McCurdy.

Ottawa is under siege. Parliament Hill has fallen to the Demon. The fate of the entire world rests in the hands of Miranda and her Ottawa school friends. You won't be able to put these books down!

The Serpent's Egg
0-00-639333-0
$7.99 mm

The Burning Crown
0-00-639334-9
$7.99 mm

The Twisted Blade
0-00-639335-7
$13.99 tpb
Coming in September 2007